DOXY FOR THE TON

Misfits of the Ton
Book Seven

by
Emily Royal

ARE YOU SIGNED UP FOR DRAGONBLADE'S BLOG?

You'll get the latest news and information on exclusive giveaways, exclusive excerpts, coming releases, sales, free books, cover reveals and more.

Check out our complete list of authors, too!

No spam, no junk. That's a promise!

Sign Up Here

www.dragonbladepublishing.com

Dearest Reader;

Thank you for your support of a small press. At Dragonblade Publishing, we strive to bring you the highest quality Historical Romance from some of the best authors in the business. Without your support, there is no 'us', so we sincerely hope you adore these stories and find some new favorite authors along the way.

Happy Reading!

CEO, Dragonblade Publishing

Additional Dragonblade books by Author Emily Royal

Misfits of the Ton
Tomboy of the Ton (Book 1)
Ruined by the Ton (Book 2)
Thief of the Ton (Book 3)
Oddity of the Ton (Book 4)
Harpy of the Ton (Book 5)
Heartbreaker of the Ton (Book 6)
Doxy for the Ton (Book 7)
The Taming of the Duke (Novella)

Headstrong Harts
What the Hart Wants (Book 1)
Queen of my Hart (Book 2)
Hidden Hart (Book 3)
The Prizefighter's Hart (Book 4)
All I Want for Christmas is My Hart (Novella)
Haunted Hart (Novella)

London Libertines
Henry's Bride (Book 1)
Hawthorne's Wife (Book 2)
Roderick's Widow (Book 3)
A Libertine's Christmas Miracle (Novella)

The Lyon's Den Series
A Lyon's Pride
Lyon of the Highlands
Lyon of the Ton

CHAPTER ONE

Brighton, June 1813

THE CLOCK ON the mantelshelf issued a cascade of chimes, descending like a waterfall, until it settled on a single long note, ten times.

He's late.

Jemima's stomach fluttered with apprehension.

He was *never* late.

She always admired his promptness—and how he kept his promises.

Which made him unique among men.

She lifted her left hand and her gaze fell on the emerald ring—the mark of his promise. She could hardly bring herself to look at the ring—it was far too grand for her, a penniless orphan.

Of course, *he* would never permit her to voice such an opinion. So, she contented herself with gazing into the stone's depths, marveling at the hues of blue and green that pulsed in unison with her heartbeat, almost as if it were alive.

And it is *alive, my love. This stone embodies my heart, which beats for none but you.*

A pretty enough speech—one that, no doubt, was used by men over the years to coax women into bed. But he had no need to waste his breath on fine words for one such as her.

One such as I…

Mistress. Whore. Such words had long since ceased to wound her heart. The wounds had, over the years, hardened into scars with each insult, each cut direct, and each disapproving look.

How would the world react when forced to utter a different word altogether?

Wife.

Or rather—Lady Mayhew.

Lady Mayhew…

It was almost too perfect.

His acquaintances would disapprove. But the value they placed on titles and lineage would prevent them from insulting her openly. She smiled to herself at the notion of being introduced to Society, where she would outrank almost every snobbish creature she encountered.

And her children…

She placed a hand over her already thickening belly.

For any woman, the onset of a child signaled the ending of one chapter and the beginning of another. But for women in Jemima's position, a pregnancy usually required her to be hastily removed from her home—and either tucked away in obscurity, lest her disgrace taint her protector's reputation, or tossed out onto the street with a coin or two for her trouble. No man wanted to be saddled with his mistress's child.

Except Walter…

Jemima's heart swelled as she recalled the love in his eyes when she announced her condition—the joy at the prospect of a child, and his shame when he realized she'd expected him to abandon her.

She lifted her gaze to the dressing table mirror. The woman who smiled back looked contented, and filled with hope—the bloom on her cheeks that of a prospective wife and mother.

Her heart swelled as she heard the clatter of hooves on the road, and she approached the window, lifted the sash, and leaned out, inhaling the fresh, salty air. Seagulls circled overhead, screeching at each other in perpetual irritation. One stood on the ledge of the adjacent window, a single, baleful yellow eye staring at her.

"I've nothing for you," she said.

The bird continued to stare. Doubtless it, and its acquaintances, knew that the occupants of this house doled out bounty to the needy—both human and feathered.

A carriage came into view at the end of the street. The gull turned its head, then opened its wings and launched off the ledge, its ungainly body tumbling toward the ground. Then its wings caught the air and it soared upward, screeching in celebration of its freedom.

A freedom you'll never have.

Jemima flinched as her conscience whispered in her mind. Freedom—true freedom—was not the province of her sex. But the adoration of a man she loved as a dear friend, together with her status as his wife, was the next best thing. And it was the best she could hope for.

The carriage drew to a halt, and she caught sight of the Mayhew crest emblazoned on the side. The door opened and the carriage tilted to one side as its occupant climbed out. Jemima withdrew into her chamber, plucked a bottle of cologne from the dressing table, and placed a dab on her neck and the inside of each wrist. The scent was Walter's favorite, and it helped to stem the nausea that had been plaguing her.

She descended the stairs and entered the parlor. Shortly after, a footman appeared.

"You have a visitor, Miss King."

"So formal, Timothy?" Jemima said. "Please send Lord Mayhew in, then have Mrs. Riley bring tea."

The footman colored and lowered his gaze.

"Timothy, is anything amiss?"

"Miss, I…"

"Out of my way—you!" a voice interrupted.

The newcomer pushed the footman aside and strode into the room, tapping his silver-topped cane on the floor.

It wasn't Walter.

Swallowing the apprehension rising in her stomach, Jemima dipped into a curtsey and addressed her fiancé's son and heir—

Ralph Mayhew, Viscount Purley.

"Viscount Purley," she said, "to what do I owe the pleasure of—"

"Spare me the niceties, madam," he said. "We both know you take no pleasure from my company." He ran his fingertips along a table, then inspected them for dust, curling his lip into a sneer.

"You'll find it perfectly clean," Jemima said, allowing herself a moment's irritation at the man who, though a similar age to her, would soon be her stepson.

"So I see," he replied. "But then, considering the pater's generosity toward his whore, I'd be disappointed if your"—he cast another glance about the parlor, wrinkling his nose—"your *premises* lacked the necessary hygiene to enable you to carry out your business."

Jemima curled her hands into fists, tempering the rising indignation. But he was within his rights to be affronted at the news that she was to become his stepmother.

Give the boy time, Jemmy my love—he'll come round.

Dear Walter had such faith in others. He believed everyone was inherently good, even the profligate son he'd often despaired over while he lay in Jemima's arms, seeking the love he'd never found within his own family.

Mayhew turned to the footman. "Go. I'll not be wanting tea."

The footman bowed then exited the parlor.

"I understand your disapproval of me, Viscount Purley," Jemima said, "but I hope, for your father's sake, we can be civil to one another."

Mayhew fixed his pale-gray gaze on her and curled his lip into a smile, triumph glittering in his eyes.

"How wrong you are, Miss King," he said.

A ripple of nausea clawed at her as he flicked his tongue out and moistened his lips.

"Surely a little civility…" she began, but he raised his hand.

"I meant in your address," he said, "not your pathetic attempt at cordiality."

"Viscount Purley, I—"

"Viscount *no more*," he said, stepping toward her, his teeth gleaming in the sunlight, and Jemima's gut twisted with fear. "You address me as Earl Mayhew."

Earl Mayhew…

"B-but that means…"

Her voice trailed off as her corset grew overly tight. The world slipped out of focus, and her legs began to shake. She stepped back, reaching for the back of the sofa to steady herself.

"Wh-when…?"

He shrugged his shoulders. "Last week. The funeral was yesterday."

"Yesterday?" she cried. "You didn't think to—"

"To what?" he snarled. "Invite my father's whore to flaunt herself at his graveside? What sort of a fool do you think I am?"

A wave of nausea crashed through her body and she bent forward, drawing in a lungful of air. Her legs gave way and she crumpled to the floor, closing her eyes against the pain and loss. But the pain remained—filling her heart with blackness.

Then she opened her eyes to see Mayhew's booted feet on the rug, while he stood, looking down at her, a predatory smile on his lips.

Walter…

Hot tears threatened to spill, but she kept them at bay. Her tears were for Walter—not his profligate son.

Mayhew leaned forward and extended his hand. For a moment, Jemima stared at him, then she took the proffered hand and he hauled her to her feet.

"Th-thank you."

She tried to withdraw, but he pulled her close, and her nausea increased at the acrid stench of brandy and sour wine.

"Unhand me, sir," she said.

"Only if you address me properly."

Jemima swallowed her dislike. "Unhand me if you please, Lord Mayhew."

"There's a good girl."

He lowered his gaze to her décolletage and his eyes flared with lust. Jemima lifted her hand to cover her neckline, and he let out a huff of derision.

"Don't play the coquette with *me,*" he said. "You earned your keep spreading your legs for my father. You can hardly admonish me for wanting to inspect the goods, given the price he paid."

He reached forward and placed his hand on her throat. Then he curled his finger around her necklace and pain sliced through the back of her neck as he gave a sharp tug. Her necklace broke and pearls clattered onto the floor.

"Stop!" she cried. "That's my necklace."

"Bought and paid for with *my* money," he sneered. "Just like your body."

She shuddered as he dipped a finger below her neckline, brushing his fingertip across the top of her breasts. His eyes darkened with fury as his gaze fell on her left hand. He took her wrist, then grasped the ring on her third finger and pulled it off.

"Old fool!" he muttered. "Did he really think he could give my mother's ring to a slut? Do you have any idea how much it's worth?" He wrinkled his nose in disgust. *"Nobody's* that good at riding cock, surely?"

Jemima cringed at the hatred in his voice.

"Please," she said, "Ralph...I mean, Earl—"

"Spare me the mewling!" He gestured about the parlor. "This is *my* house. You took advantage of my father by parting those fat thighs of yours. But the day of reckoning has come, and it's time for you to go."

A sharp pain stabbed at Jemima's stomach and she caught her breath. "Please..."

"Now, now—no histrionics," he said. Then he arched an eyebrow, his gaze settling once more on her neckline. "Unless..."

A glimmer of hope swelled inside her. "Unless what?"

"Unless you'd like to continue to earn your keep. If you were willing to stiffen that old man's cock, you might relish the prospect of servicing mine."

Nausea swelled as another stab of pain ignited in her stomach. "How can you say such things?"

"Quite easily," he said. "It's how a slut earns her keep, is it not?"

She gestured to the ring. "Your father and I were—"

"My father was a fool if he thought his family would ever accept a whore!" he snarled. "To think—a grubby slut polluting Purley Manor!" He turned his head toward the door. "My man—come here!"

The door opened—a little too quickly—to reveal the red-faced footman.

"Ma'am, is everything—" he began, but Mayhew interrupted.

"Do not address her thus, unless you wish to be dismissed!" he barked. "You're under my employ."

"But sir…"

"Was anything I said unclear?"

The footman colored. "No, sir, but…"

"Timothy, it's all right," Jemima said. Her fate was already sealed—it would do no good to have Timothy share it.

"Remove this doxy from my house," Mayhew said. "Immediately."

"But my belongings," Jemima said, "they're—"

"They're *mine* now," he sneered. "Count yourself fortunate I'm letting you keep the clothes on your back."

"B-but—where will I go?"

"I care not, as long as I don't have to see your sniveling face," he replied. "Footman—must I ask a second time? Get rid of her!"

"Sorry about this, miss," the footman said as he took Jemima's wrist.

"The back entrance, if you please," Mayhew added. "I've a reputation to uphold. I don't want my neighbors thinking this a bawdy house."

As the footman led Jemima to the door, Mayhew called after them.

"Thomas, I've changed my mind."

Jemima turned to face him, a flicker of hope in her heart.

"I *will* take tea after all," he said. "Bring it after you've discarded the rubbish."

A sob swelled in Jemima's throat as Thomas pushed her out of the parlor.

"Ever so sorry, miss," he whispered. "But don't worry, I'll take you to the kitchen and have Mrs. Riley set you up before you go on your way."

"I can't…"

"Yes, you can," he said. "You've been good to us, looked after those in need hereabouts. Now it's our turn to look after you."

She clung to him as he led her to the stairs that descended toward the kitchen. Another wave of nausea gripped her and a sharp pain sliced through her stomach. She reached for the handrail, but slipped and somersaulted down the stairs. The stone floor at the bottom rushed toward her, then with an explosion of agony in her head, she plunged into oblivion.

CHAPTER TWO

London, December 1818

HOW IN THE *name of the devil's cock have I ended up in this godforsaken part of town?*

Alexander stumbled, wincing at the pain in his leg. The numbness brought about by the liquor had all but gone. In fact, it had transformed into the most almighty pain behind the eyes. Doubtless he'd wake up with a shocking megrim that his friends—his few remaining friends—would say was richly deserved.

He caught his foot on a paving slab, tripped forward, and slammed into a wall.

Fuck, that hurt.

He hurt all over. His leg, his head, and his right eye…

He grimaced at the memory of someone—Foxton, if he recalled, or was it Westbury?—planting a shiner on his face before marching him out of White's and tossing him onto the pavement.

Curse him—curse them all!

Alexander righted himself and glanced about, the familiar thirst tearing at his throat. Surely there must be a tavern nearby— wasn't every other building near the docks supposed to be an inn, or a gin parlor? Nothing but liquor would dull the agony brought about by guilt over what he'd done—the deaths he'd caused. He needed to render himself unconscious to silence the little devil in his mind that told him exactly how much of a bastard he was.

But there was nothing to see other than the squalid little houses in this dingy little street with the ditch running through the center, glistening with slime and clumps of mud.

At least, he hoped it was mud—the odor that churned his stomach spoke of something far less palatable.

Blurred figures moved ahead, and Alexander caught a murmur of voices—the drunken slur of a man, punctuated by the high-pitched, coaxing tones of a woman. A street whore, most likely, offering her wares to the sailors who wandered about the docks looking for a little companionship and a good, hard fuck.

He stumbled forward and collided with a figure, wrapped in a scarlet shawl.

"Mind how you go, sir."

The figure turned, and Alexander caught sight of a painted female face with bone-white-powdered skin and ruby-red lips, plump enough to wrap around a man's cock.

"Forgive me, madam," he slurred.

Her eyes widened and he let out a silent curse. In this part of town, his Society accent gave him away.

Her mouth curled at the corner—a smile or a sneer, he knew not—and he braced himself for the inevitable offer of her body for a shilling or two. Instead, she shook her head and frowned.

"You shouldn't be in this part of London, sir. Not if you value your life."

"My life is mine to do as I please with," he said, inhaling sharply at the wave of nausea.

The stench from the road thickened in the air. No wonder whores wore cheap perfume—not to be more alluring to their customers, but to cover the stench of shit.

"What about your coin?" she said, extending her hand. "Or that pretty fob watch I see—would you care to lose that? I'll wager a gentleman such as you has more to lose here than his life."

I'll wager?

What sort of talk was that for a street whore from the wrong side of London?

And her accent…

Perhaps she sought to ingratiate herself by imitating a lady's voice. Doubtless some men paid extra if a whore screamed their name in the accent of the *ton* as she climaxed.

He let out a snort, which finished in a hiccough as his body convulsed. "You speak fine words for a whore who makes a living spreading her legs for all comers."

"Better that than a lord who makes no living at all."

Her accent had shifted back to the harsh notes of the slums.

Alexander stepped away and grimaced at the pain in his leg.

"Sir, you're hurt." She reached for his arm, and he shoved her aside.

"Get away from me," he snarled. "I've come here to drink cheap liquor, not rut cheap sluts."

Hurt flickered across her expression, then she threw her head back and let out a harsh laugh. When she caught his gaze again, her expression was filled with loathing.

"Fine words for a pretty lord lost in the slums," she said. "I wish you joy of your evening, sir, and pray you get exactly what you deserve."

One day, Sawbridge, you'll get exactly what you deserve.

Unwittingly, she'd uttered the exact same words that his friends had said earlier that evening.

He deserved to be punished. After all, he'd caused the death of his best friend, Robert Staines—and not only Staines, but the finest doxy in England also. To kill a fellow wastrel required a few months of penitence, a pretty speech at a funeral, and several rounds of drinks at White's to atone. But to kill the woman who'd given countless nights of pleasure to almost every member of White's…

Some sins could never be forgiven.

Alexander opened his mouth to reply, but as he looked at the whore's painted face, he saw only Danielle—the finest doxy in town, whose eyes had haunted his dreams from the moment he kneeled beside her broken body and watched the life drain out of her.

He drew in a sharp breath, then regretted it as the stench of the street filled his nostrils. Then he turned from the whore and stumbled along the street.

Coarse laughter echoed ahead, and he caught sight of a sign swinging in the breeze. Fueled by the prospect of liquor and oblivion, he increased the pace. Then two thick-set silhouettes appeared before him.

"Well, well—what do we 'ave 'ere?"

"I'm looking for an inn," Alexander said, gesturing toward the building.

"An inn?" the man said, a mocking tone to his voice. "D'you hear that, Bill—an inn?" He approached, and the stench of waste mingled with another—stale sweat and equally stale ale. "What's a fancy-arsed gent like yourself doin' in a place like this?"

"Looking for a drink," Alexander said.

"Them fancy clubs not good enough for you? Thought you'd save yourself a penny or two and come onto our street?"

The first man drew something out of his coat. At first it looked like a stick, until the moonlight picked out the edge of a blade.

Alexander stepped back, his stomach twisting. "*Your* street?"

"Aye, that's right, Mr. High and Mighty. You may think you rule the world, but it's us that rule here. But we're disposed to be kind, ain't we, Bill?"

His companion nodded. "Aye—for the right price."

Alexander thrust his hand into his pocket and fished out two coins. "There you go," he said. "A sovereign each for your trouble."

"A sovereign, eh?" the second man said. "How about that?"

"I'll bet there's plenty more where that came from."

"Now, gentlemen," Alexander said, "I think a sovereign's quite enough…"

"Ha!" the first man cried. "Gentlemen! This nob thinks we're *gentlemen?*"

"Perhaps we would be, if we had the same fancy clothes."

The second man gestured toward Alexander. "That cloak must be worth a bit—it'd keep me warm all right."

"You've got your Wilma and her cunny to keep you warm, Jack. Let me have the cloak, and you take his boots."

Alexander drew out his fob watch. "Take this," he said. "It's a John Arnold."

"A—what?"

Alexander flipped open the back of the watch. "John Arnold—see the inscription?"

The man snatched the watch. "Pickings for all, this one has, Bill," he said. "What else has he got?"

"I've given you enough," Alexander said. "Let me pass."

"Hark at him! *Let me pass*, indeed!" The man held up the knife, the curved blade gleaming like a sinister smile. "It's finished when we *say* it's finished."

Alexander curled his hands into fists, then lunged at the first man, but he dodged to one side.

"Oh no you don't, fancy-man!" He rushed forward, and Alexander caught a blur of movement, then pain exploded in his face and he reeled back.

Pondering on what cursed bad luck it was to be struck twice in the same place on a single night, Alexander crumpled to the ground. The stench of waste intensified, but at least oblivion, when it came, would give him respite from the odor.

Then he let out a bitter laugh as the world slipped sideways. Perhaps his friends—and that street whore—would see their wishes fulfilled tonight. For if anyone deserved to be murdered in the gutter, it was him.

Two shapes advanced, then were joined by a third, and Alexander braced himself for the final blow.

But it never came. Instead, he heard a deep grunt, followed by a curse.

"Bleedin' hell, woman—keep yer nose out and bugger off."

"Bugger off yerself!"

He struggled to his feet, but another strike sent him reeling and he fell forward into the ditch. He reached out with his hand, grimacing at the notion of crawling about in the waste, then he felt a blow to the head and the world went black.

ALEXANDER OPENED HIS eyes to a blurred world, filled with softened shapes and a dull yellow light. He winced as pain sliced through his head, and closed his eyes again.

A sharp odor filled his nostrils, and the metallic taste of blood filled his mouth.

Then the memory thrust into his mind: the street near the docks, two men coming at him with a knife, beating him to the ground.

Forcing his eyes open, Alexander lifted his head, then yelped at the stab of pain in his neck. He blinked until his vision cleared, and focused on familiar items: the fireplace with the clock on the mantelshelf, the bureau, the washstand and basin—and the table by the sash window bearing a half-empty decanter and four beveled glasses, their facets twinkling in the candlelight.

He was in his bedchamber.

In fact, he was in his bed, and…

He lifted the bedsheet.

He was as naked as the day he was born.

Had the encounter by the docks been a dream?

No, the memory was too sharp—the painted face with the scarlet lips, the sign swinging in the breeze depicting a red-faced sailor, and the knife…

He shuddered at the fear that had gripped him at the curved blade, which matched the curved, gap-toothed smiles of his assailants. He'd been at their mercy. And then…

And then nothing.

In which case, how the blazes had he survived, let alone ended up in his bedchamber?

Devil's breeches—how much did I drink?

The door creaked open, and soft footsteps approached. Alexander's valet knew his constitution—at least after having drunk a skinful—well enough to avoid making sudden noises.

Alexander gestured toward the table. "Fetch me a brandy, would you?"

"Fetch it yourself," a voice—a *female* voice—replied.

He opened his eyes again, to see a painted face leaning over him, powder-white skin and scarlet lips, surrounded by a cascade of gaudy red curls.

"Who the devil are *you?*" he asked.

Her mouth curled into a grin. "A fine question to ask, considering the state you was in when I—"

She broke off as he grasped her wrist. "I take it you're a whore," he said through gritted teeth. "What are you doing in my house?"

Her eyes narrowed in pain, and he released her. She withdrew her wrist, and her smile broadened.

"Mimi La Fleur," she said.

"What kind of name is *that?*"

"A whore's name," she retorted, wrinkling her nose. "At least you don't stink no more."

"What are you talking about?"

She let out a chuckle. "You don't remember? Hardly surprising, given how drunk you were."

He sat up, his head throbbing, to get a better look at her.

Despite the gaudy wig and overly made-up face, she was comely enough. His gaze wandered over her body, taking in the flare of her hips, the dip at the waist, and the swell of her breasts. What pleasures could be found beneath the thin material of her gown?

She approached the fireplace, moving with the loose-hipped gait of a woman born for seduction, then tossed another log onto the fire. Alexander's cock stiffened at the sight of her derriere as she bent over to poke the fire.

"Did you remove my clothes?" he asked.

She turned, still holding the poker. "You didn't want your bed stinking of shit, did you?"

"That's a filthy mouth you've got there," he said.

"Not as filthy as your clothes. Only your necktie emerged unsoiled."

Then he recalled it—the stench of the ditch in the center of the road, the ditch that moved toward him at speed as he tumbled to the ground, reached out with his hands, and…

Bloody hell!

He lifted his hands, beset by the memory of his fingers covered in a thick layer of evil-smelling slime. But they were clean.

Tentatively, he lifted his fingers to his nose and sniffed.

She set the poker beside the fire. "Your butler's a weak-bellied one, ain't he?"

"What?"

She gestured to his hands. "He wouldn't touch you—ha! Wouldn't let me in at first, even when he saw you—but the stench of shit will always level folk who think they're too good for the likes of me."

Infuriating creature! Why did she talk in riddles?

"What *are* you talking about?" he demanded. "And how did you get here?"

"Same way as you, *Your Grace*," she said, a flicker of contempt in her voice. "In a hackney. The driver wouldn't take you at first, but your coin soon persuaded him—and you talk too much when you're drunk. Wasn't too difficult to get the direction out of you. Duke of Sawbridge, eh? What the bleedin' hell was a *duke* doin' in that part of town?"

"Minding my own business."

"It's *my* business now," she said. "Thought you'd soiled yourself, your butler did."

Dear Lord—Gillingham was stuffy enough at the best of times, always admonishing him over some transgression or other. Alexander only kept the old goat on because he'd served the Sawbridge family almost all his life.

"Never you worry, though," the doxy continued. "I set him straight. Offered to clean you up meself, seein' as nobody wanted to come near enough to even poke a stick at you."

She grinned, then a flash of recognition caught him—that same face, her brow wrinkled with concern, soft lips parting as she murmured words of comfort while she bathed his body and bandaged his leg…

"My leg." He shifted position on the bed and groaned as the pain in his left leg flared.

"I changed your bandage," she said. "Nasty wound. How did you come by it?"

"You wouldn't want to know."

"If I didn't want to know, I wouldn't have asked. You're a bigger fool than I took you for."

"Why's that?" he asked.

"That leg's in danger of goin' putrid. It's all the same to me if you lose the leg, but I imagine *you'd* miss it."

"I care not," he said, sinking back. "It's just a leg—there are worse things to lose."

Anger flared in her eyes. "Says one who's never known loss. Men like you are all the same."

It ought to have been laughable that she—a street whore— held him in contempt, but she spoke with a fierce conviction, and an undercurrent of deep loss.

"Only when you've lost something do you truly come to appreciate it," she said. "But then it's too late."

"What did you lose…Mimi?"

She flinched and looked away. "Nothin' *you'd* care for. And I don't mean to lose anything tonight. I'll want payin'."

"What for?" he asked.

"For bringing you home."

"That's not your business."

"For cleaning you up, then."

"That's not your business either."

"Then what?" she asked.

He shrugged, affecting nonchalance as his manhood surged with want. "I'm sure you'll think of some way to earn your coin."

"I could just take it," she said.

"Then why don't you?"

"Because I'm not a thief."

"No," he said, "you're a whore."

Her expression hardened. "That I am," she said. "But I'll want paying up front. I know what your sort are like."

He let out a laugh. "My sort? Since when does a whore lecture a duke on honor?"

"Honor!" she scoffed. "A word used by men of your rank to excuse petty vengeance on those they believe to have done them wrong. I'm talking about honesty, sir, not honor."

Her voice had changed again—the harsh tones of the street whore replaced by the clear notes of another creature altogether—almost as if she were a lady.

Then he shook his head. The liquor must have addled his wits.

"How much do you want?" he asked.

She cocked her head to one side and looked over his body, as if sizing him up. Then she lowered her gaze to his groin, where his stiffened cock was already lifting the bedsheet.

"That depends on what you're wantin' me to do."

The coarse accent had returned.

"What *do* you do?" he asked, his cock twitching in anticipation.

She reached for her gown and lifted it over her head with practiced ease. He suppressed a groan at the sight of her undergarments, the thin material leaving little to the imagination—the soft, shapely body, with the dark pink centers of her breasts, and the dark triangle between her thighs.

"I'll do anything if you pay the right price." she said.

"Now, *that's* what a man wants to hear."

He peeled back the bed sheet to reveal his naked form, then patted the bed.

"Well?" he said. "What are you waiting for?"

"Payment."

"You whores are all the same," he said. "You'll get it once I'm satisfied."

"A man like *you* is never satisfied."

"Satisfy me, woman, and I'll give you more money that you could hope to earn in a lifetime."

She tugged at the laces of her chemise and climbed onto the bed. He rolled toward her and winced.

She placed a hand on his leg, her skin pale save for a darkening bruise on her wrist.

"Does it pain you?" she asked.

"It's a little better."

"Good." She caressed the skin of his leg with her fingertips. "You broke it, yes? It was unwise of you to venture out. Why did you—and in such a place?"

She glanced up, and he caught a flicker of concern in her eyes.

Then he dismissed it. No doubt the doxy was playing on his pain to secure a higher price.

"Just get on with it," he growled. "I'm not paying you to *talk*."

She curled her lips into a smile of cold seduction. "As you wish."

She pulled off her chemise and tossed it across the room, then she crawled toward him. His mouth watered at the sight of her skin, milky white and gleaming in the firelight—and her breasts, soft and round, perfect to fit into his hands. He cupped a breast, drawing in a sharp breath as her nipple hardened against his palm. He squeezed, softly, and she froze. Yearning flickered in her eyes.

Then it was gone. The diamond-hard expression of the doxy returned and she clambered over his body and straddled him, her breasts pressed against his chest.

He leaned forward to capture her mouth, but she gripped his shoulders and pushed him back. Then she circled his cock with her hands. Desire surged through him and he jerked upward in an instinctive need to claim her. But she held him firm, running her hand up and down his length in unhurried strokes.

Pleasure surged, and he gritted his teeth.

Not yet…

Every man knew that the intensity of the pleasure increased with the length of the wait. If she brought him to pleasure too soon…

"No…" he groaned. "It's too…"

"Too what?" she asked, a smirk on her lips. "Too much?"

The tide of pleasure swelled and Alexander focused his mind on his breathing—long and slow—to divert his mind from her wicked ministrations.

She gave his sac a gentle squeeze, and a fizz of pleasure tore through him—tortuous pleasure…

"W-witch…"

She laughed. "I've been called worse, *Your Grace.*"

Then she removed her hands and he let out a groan of loss. He jerked upward and, with a swift, slick motion, she impaled herself on him.

"Fuck!" he cried out, as the burst of pleasure threatened to disintegrate him.

"Now who's got a filthy mouth?" she taunted him, but before he could respond, she withdrew, then thrust forward once more. He gripped his hands about her waist, then she tilted her hips. His cock surged as her body squeezed him, and he could swear he saw stars.

"*Sweet Lord*, woman—how did you learn to do *that?*"

She grinned. "Have I earned an extra sovereign?"

Must she remind him that she only sought to pleasure him for the sake of his coin?

Then he checked himself. Weren't those the terms by which he entered into any relationship with a woman? Why, then, did her actions make him feel less of a man, rather than more?

Perhaps it was because, unlike the other women he'd rutted, she took no pleasure from the act. In fact, unlike most doxies, she didn't even trouble to give the appearance of pleasure. She might as well have been his steward, working on a ledger.

"Mimi, I… Oh!" he cried out as she thrust against him once more, the glorious sensation almost too much to bear. "S-slow down, woman, for pity's sake!"

She paused, her eyes dark against her painted face. "Let me earn my coin," she said, and he winced at the hard edge to her voice, akin to anger.

He pulled her close and leaned forward to claim her mouth, but she jerked her head to one side.

"Kiss me, woman," he growled.

"No."

"Why not?"

"It's not what you're paying for."

"It is, if that's what I want."

She squeezed his cock with her body again. He was close, and judging by the triumph in her eyes, she knew it—curse her, she *knew* it.

"Tonight is about *your* pleasure, Your Grace," she said.

"And yours?" he replied. "I want to please you."

She grew still. "Why?"

"It's what I do—give women pleasure."

Longing flickered in her eyes, then she let out a harsh laugh.

"Would it stoke your pride if I showed pleasure, Your Grace?" she said. "Or perhaps screamed your name? For an extra coin I could promise to tell everyone I encounter that you took me like a bull."

Shame rose in his gut. "Don't say such things."

"Then don't be talking about my pleasure," she said. "My body may be for sale—but no man will have my pleasure."

"Do you want another sovereign?" he asked. "Every whore has a price."

"Not this whore," she snarled. She continued to ride him until the wave of pleasure threatened to break. "Some things are not for sale—the cost is too great."

He bit his lip to stem the surge in his body. He couldn't hold on much longer…

Then she reached down and ran her fingertips along the sensitive skin at the base of his cock. He jerked upward and his resolve shattered.

"Sweet heaven!" he cried.

Almost immediately she withdrew, then grasped his manhood as he exploded with pleasure. He threw his head back as his body disintegrated whilst she wrung every drop of pleasure from him until he lay back, utterly spent.

When he opened his eyes he saw her naked form striding across the bedchamber toward the washstand. She dipped a cloth into the basin and wiped it over her legs, then she returned to the bed and wiped the evidence of his pleasure off his body. His manhood twitched as she ran the cloth along his length, then she tossed the cloth onto the floor, wrinkling her nose as if in contempt.

His stomach churned in shame. Had she found the act so distasteful?

Or was it *him* she found distasteful?

"Did you have to do that?" he asked.

She shrugged. "It was no different to when I wiped the shit off you earlier."

"Don't say that," he said. "It's—"

"It's what?" she snapped, anger illuminating her eyes. "Sordid? Demeaning?" She made a dismissive gesture. "It's all the same to me—just business."

"So, I'm just another man to you."

"As I'm just another whore to *you*," she said. "If you don't like what you see, then you shouldn't have purchased the goods. I'm what men like you made me."

Gone were the harsh vowels of London's slums. Her accent—and her words—were not those of a street whore.

He opened his mouth to respond, then closed it again. What had she said that was not true? Perhaps his shame was because in looking at her—at a person who was a mere commodity, who had no worth in the world—he was looking in a mirror and seeing himself for the first time.

What was he other than a commodity—someone who had no worth? Worse, even—for he had been responsible for the loss of two innocent lives. At least a whore earned her keep giving pleasure to others.

He heard a rustle of clothing and looked up to see her slipping her chemise back on.

"Stop," he said.

"I've earned my coin," she replied, reaching for her gown.

"No."

She rolled her eyes. "You're all the same. More money than Croesus, yet the least willing to part with it."

"Croesus? Who's he?"

She stiffened, then averted her gaze. "Some rich nob who didn't like payin'."

"I'll pay you," he said. "I-I only meant that I don't want you to go. Stay—for the night, at least."

She closed her eyes and her chest rose and fell in a sigh, and Alexander suppressed the urge to take her into his arms. Then, after a pause, she opened her eyes.

He patted the bed. "Ten pounds."

A dark corner of his soul whispered of the desire to see her vulnerability again, to penetrate that hard shell.

"It's a good price," he said. "But you must earn it. I want to rut you again before breakfast."

Her jaw bulged as if she gritted her teeth.

"Guineas," she said. "Make it ten guineas and you have a deal. But I want to see the money first."

"You have my word as a gentleman."

She pulled her chemise off and climbed into the bed.

"You trust me, then?" he said, lying back.

She settled onto her side so she faced him. At close quarters, he could see the paint on her face creasing as she smiled.

"I'll get my money either way," she replied. "If I decide not to trust you, then you'll wake up in the morning with a knife in your heart."

"I have no heart," he said.

"Then, sir, we are equal."

He shook his head. "You and I are not equals."

Her eyes narrowed. "It'll cost you extra if you wish to talk all night."

"Then I'll stop talking." He rolled over, turning his back to her. After a moment, he heard a soft sigh, then her breathing steadied.

She'd misunderstood him. They may not be equals, but she assumed he'd meant that he was her superior. But he'd caught a glimpse of the expression in her eyes—a flicker of a human soul. She had a heart, though she hid it well.

She didn't have to bring him home tonight. She could have robbed him, left him for dead, and secured herself more money than she'd earn from pleasuring him.

No—he was not her superior.

She was his.

CHAPTER THREE

"N O!" A VOICE cried.

Mimi opened her eyes and sat upright. The room was dark, save for the orange glow from the fireplace.

Dawn hadn't broken yet.

Not that she minded. Darkness, rather than something to be feared, was her friend. It provided shelter from predators. And it was a great leveler. The darkness concealed the sneers of those who considered themselves superior.

And it concealed her soul.

The man lying next to her—the Duke of Sawbridge—twitched in his sleep.

He was typical of his breed, save for the self-loathing concealed behind his arrogance.

"No—you can't die!"

"Hush!" She poked him in the side. He stirred and rolled over, then his breathing steadied.

Doubtless whatever dreams plagued him were born of the liquor he'd imbibed. He stank of the stuff, even after she'd bathed the muck from his body.

His head would be sore in the morning.

As would her face, if she didn't clean it. Her face paint itched. If she left it, her skin would be red raw in the morning. Then where would she be? No customer would want her.

With a sigh, she slipped out of bed and padded across the

floor to the washbasin. She rinsed the cloth in the water, then pressed it against her face, relishing the coolness against her skin. Then she reached for the cake of soap and held it to her nose.

Her gut twisted at the rich scent of spices and the memory it evoked—a man, with kind eyes and a soft smile.

She bit her lip to distract her mind from the rising ache in her heart.

There's no use remembering him. He's long gone, and there'll never be another like him.

Mimi dried her face, then she removed her wig and ran her fingers through her hair, digging her nails into her scalp. She let out a small sigh of relief—that wig itched almost as much as the face paint. But men seemed to prefer red hair, and the extra coin was worth a little discomfort.

She set the wig aside, then approached the window and drew back the curtain. A thin sliver of gray stretched across the night sky. Dawn was approaching, and with it, her ten guineas. She yawned, lifted her arms toward the ceiling, and inhaled, drawing in a lungful of air as she stretched.

Heavens! She couldn't recall when she'd last been this tired. Clearly a night in a soft bed rendered her weak. She didn't want to soften and grow used to it.

Not again.

Succumbing to another yawn, she returned to the bed and slipped inside, allowing herself the luxury of leaning against the warm body of the man inside.

He let out a long, low groan, and the anguish in his voice threatened to claw away the defenses around her heart.

She placed her hand on his arm. "Hush," she whispered. "All is well."

"They're dead," he said. "I killed them."

"Killed who?"

He gripped her hand.

"Sir…"

"They're dead because of me!" he cried. "Do you understand

that? I'm going to hell because of what I did."

The bed moved as he shook.

"The devil awaits me, and I deserve his retribution."

He tossed his head to one side, then let out a howl of despair that shattered her soul.

"Be still!" she cried. "It's just a dream."

He sat upright, his profile silhouetted against diffused light from the glowing embers. "Are you a demon—come to take me to hell?"

"No." She drew him close. "I'm here to give you pleasure."

"And ease my pain?" he asked, his voice a hoarse plea.

"If you wish it."

He relaxed in her arms, and she sank back onto the pillows, pulling him on top of her.

He brushed his lips against her chin, and a flare of longing ignited in her heart as his lips moved toward her mouth.

A kiss…

The most intimate of gestures—there was a reason why it was called the doxy's downfall.

Surely one kiss wouldn't risk her soul? To her, he was a means to coin, and to him, she was merely a soft body to rut.

"That's it," he whispered, his breath warm against her lips. "Mimi…"

She stiffened and turned her head to one side, and his kiss fell on her cheek.

She tried to push him away, but he held her closer, the firmness of his grip speaking of desperation and pain.

But it was not a pain that she could ease. Not with a kiss, at least.

Time to earn my ten guineas.

She reached lower and found his manhood, already hard for her. He sighed as she parted her thighs and he slipped inside her. He began to thrust, weakly, sliding through her with slow, tender strokes. For a moment, she ignored the danger and allowed herself to feel. Warmth blossomed in her heart to match the desire in her body.

"Oh, Mimi..."

As he whispered her name, a ripple of pleasure threaded through her, and she bit her lip to stem the tide.

"No..."

"Yes," he murmured, his lips tracing a path along her throat. A fizz of need threaded through her breasts as his lips caressed her skin, and she gritted her teeth, steeling herself against the tide of longing...

Then, with a sigh, he relaxed and slid back into sleep until, finally, he was at peace, his breathing steady—the nightmares gone.

She ought to be relieved that she'd not come to pleasure at his touch, but instead, she was overcome by a sense of loss.

Think of the money, Mimi. Ten guineas is worth it.

Perhaps it was—but no sum was worth risking her soul.

CHAPTER FOUR

WHY DID THE world relish the dawn rather than dread it? Particularly the birds—opening their mouths to declare, sharpy and rudely, the beginning of a new day.

To most, the dawn heralded life, and love.

But not to me.

To Alexander, the dawn served as a reminder of his sins—and the prospect of eternity in hell for what he'd done.

Dawn was the precursor to death.

And yet, this morning, for the first time since that day in the park, the pain in his soul had lessened. A pair of warm arms enveloped him with tenderness and a soft voice shushed his cries and eased his pain.

Perhaps, in time, he'd be able to sleep through the night, unmolested by images of twisted bodies, broken bones, and the lifeless eyes of his best friend.

He sat up and stretched, wincing at the stab of pain in his leg. He glanced about the bedchamber and caught sight of a gaudy orange object beside the washbasin.

A wig.

Then he recalled a hard, painted face, fixing him with her dispassionate gaze as he came to pleasure at her touch.

He lowered his gaze to the bed and caught his breath.

She lay beside him, her back to him. Her body rose and fell with each breath. Soft, pale-brown hair spilled over the pillow in waves, not quite concealing the creamy-white skin of her shoulders. He lifted the bedsheet for a better look. She stirred and he withdrew, his cheeks warming with shame.

He wasn't some eager adolescent taking an illicit peek at a woman. He was a duke, and she was the doxy he'd bought and paid for—at least for the night.

She rolled onto her back and he caught his breath.

Gone was the harsh whiteness of powder, the gaudy red on her cheeks and lips. Before him lay a fresh-faced creature, her skin almost translucent. A gentle smile of contentment curved her lips, which were a soft pink. In the stillness of repose, she looked innocent—angelic.

In that moment, she was neither the painted whore he wished to bed, nor the brittle porcelain lady he was expected to wed. She was merely a young woman, in the tranquility of sleep, awaiting the joy of a new day.

He had never seen anything so lovely.

He placed his palm on her face, then caressed it with his thumb, tracing the outline of her mouth. Her lips parted and his skin tightened at the gentle warmth of her sigh against his fingertips.

Her eyes fluttered open. They were a light shade of brown—like rich honey—with small green flecks in the center that shimmered in the sunlight.

He hadn't noticed their color last night—overpowered as they were by the excess of powder and rouge, and that wig, the megrim-inducing shade of orange that hid her soft brown tresses.

"Mimi…" he breathed.

The name suited her—elfin and delicate.

She blinked, slowly, and he caught a flicker of vulnerability in her eyes. Then she stiffened and her expression shuttered. Clutching the bedsheet to her body, she sat up. Then she ran her hand through her hair and her eyes widened with a flicker of panic.

She glanced toward the washstand and slipped off the bed,

taking the bedsheet with her as she reached for the wig.

Alexander darted toward the washstand and snatched the wig.

"Give that to me," she said. "It's mine."

"No."

"A thief, are you?"

He held the wig up. "Why hide yourself beneath this—this *filth?*"

Pain glistened in her eyes. "You were willing to pay for that filth last night. You came to pleasure quick enough."

His gut twisted with shame and he tossed the wig toward her, but she remained still, clinging to the bedsheet as the wig fell to the floor.

"Forgive me," he said.

"For speaking the truth?" She blinked, then shook her head and stooped to retrieve the wig.

"Leave that," he said. "Please."

She stiffened. "That wig cost money."

"I'll pay you for it."

She smirked. "Fancy it yourself?"

"I intend to destroy it, so you never have to wear it again."

"It'll cost you."

He let out a bitter laugh. "You think I can't afford it?"

"You know nothing about having to pay the price for something you cannot afford."

"You think because I'm a duke I've not been faced with too high a price?" he said. "How about the loss of two lives—the loss of my respectability? My peers cannot bear to look at me—even those below me won't associate themselves with me. I cannot even find a respectable mistress. I…"

His voice trailed off as he realized the meaning of his words. But the damage had already been done.

"So you thought you'd settle for a filthy whore such as myself?" she said.

"Perhaps at first, I thought…" He gestured in the air between them. "But then you—you were not like I'd expected."

"What was I like?"

He stepped toward her and winced at the pain in his leg, which bore a fresh bandage from last night. She lowered her gaze to his leg, and he caught it again—the concern in her eyes.

Though she might not want to admit it, she *cared*.

"I never thanked you," he said.

"What for?"

"For last night—bringing me home. And those two men who accosted me. Did they—"

"They'll be waking with sorer heads than you this morning."

"They were big brutes," he said. "Do you mean to say you…?"

"I don't expect a pampered man such as yourself to understand."

"Understand what?"

"I've learned to defend myself," she said. "It's the finest education a doxy can have. I've no use for the skills taught by governesses. Your ladies concern themselves with whether their embroidery stitches are neat enough. I concern myself with warding off would-be violators."

"I didn't think a whore could be violated," he said.

It was a cruel riposte, and the pain in her eyes told him that his arrow had hit home.

"Women such as I are violated all the time," she said. "Men like you use our bodies for your own gratification before returning to your wives—men who cry with pleasure at our touch, then snub us in front of your more respectable friends while you spit on us like we're the dirt under your polished calfskin boots."

He caught her hand, and her eyes flared with surprise.

"Forgive me," he said. "I-I didn't mean to hurt you. In fact…"

In fact, I want nothing more than to see you smile—that beautiful smile you gifted me with in your sleep.

How could he say such a thing to her? Most likely she'd laugh at him.

But he could have the next best thing.

"I'd like to make you an offer," he said. "I want you to be my mistress."

He stepped back, waiting to see her smile. But instead, she gave a gasp and retreated. Rather than joy in her eyes, he saw fear.

CHAPTER FIVE

“**I** WANT YOU to be my mistress.”

Mimi’s gut twisted at his words. The need in her body warred with the rational part of her that reminded her of the consequences of the life of a mistress…

The life of a pampered peacock, growing soft, weak, dependent on a man—until she was tossed out on the street with nothing but the dress on her skin.

Never again.

Some prices were not worth paying. But this time, as she looked into his eyes and saw the soul hiding beneath the cold demeanor of the duke…this time, she knew that the stakes were far higher. Not only was her body at risk, but her heart. His cries at dawn had pierced her soul, for they spoke of a tenderness she had only ever seen once before in a man.

It was a tenderness that she had no wish to succumb to again.

Fighting the urge to throw herself into his arms and accept, she shook her head.

“No.”

He arched an eyebrow. “You’re refusing me?”

“Clearly you’ve not experienced refusal before,” she retorted.

“Oh, I have,” he said. “But to refuse me without discussing your price?”

“I won’t be beholden to any man, with an uncertain future.”

“There’s no uncertainty about it,” he said. “I’ll pay you an agreed sum to be my mistress until next summer."

"Next summer?"

"The start of the London Season," he replied. "At which point I'll have no more need of your services."

"Because you'll replace me with a more *respectable* mistress?" she sneered. "Or a wife?"

He snorted. "I've no need for a *wife*. The offer's there—take it or leave it."

"Why would I?"

"Because we can help each other."

She let out a laugh. "How can I help *you*?"

His eyes narrowed, and for a moment, she saw the pain in his eyes—pain brought about by grief, shame…

…and loneliness.

What would a duke—a man who could purchase anything on a whim—know about loneliness?

Then he blinked and the expression was gone. He was almost as accomplished at playing a part as she.

"Are you willing to consider my offer or not?" he asked. "If not, you should leave before my valet catches you in here."

"Not without my ten guineas," she replied. "And I doubt *your* valet would be surprised to find a whore in his master's bedchamber."

He flinched.

"I have yet to hear what I stand to gain," she continued. "So far, you've only told me what *you* want."

"A thousand pounds."

Her stomach fluttered and she fought to retain her composure.

Surely she'd not heard that right?

Then he sighed.

"Very well," he said. "Guineas. One thousand *guineas*."

Sweet heaven! It was more than she could dream of. Enough to set her up for life—and others who relied on her.

Enough to make a *difference*.

He stepped closer. "Well?"

The arrogant tilt of his chin needled at her. No doubt he'd make her earn every penny, having her at his beck and call. In which case…

She folded her arms, tilted her chin, and met his gaze.

"Two," she said.

A smile danced on his lips and his eyes twinkled with amusement. Then he extended his hand.

"Very well. Two thousand."

She reached toward him then paused. He lowered his gaze to her arm, which was covered in bruises.

"Guineas," he added. "And I'll meet your reasonable expenses during the term of our arrangement."

It was almost too good to be true.

"And—the payment?" she asked.

"You'll receive payment once you've fulfilled your part of the bargain," he said. "At the end of the term."

So it *was* too good to be true.

She lowered her hand, and his forehead creased into a frown.

"Don't you intend to fulfil your part of the bargain?" he asked.

"You question my honesty when I'm the one who bears the risk of our arrangement?" she said. "What's to stop you reneging and leaving me with nothing?"

"My word as a gentleman."

Mimi suppressed a snort. "From my experience, a gentleman's word is worth nothing—*less* than nothing."

"From your experience?"

Damn him! She'd almost revealed herself. "It's an expression, nothing more."

He stared at her, and her cheeks warmed under his scrutiny. "Can't you take me at my word, Mimi?"

"You can promise all you like, but what if something happens to—"

She broke off.

What if something happens to you?

His expression darkened.

"What a practical little creature you are," he said. "But I suppose if this is a business transaction, it makes sense that we allow for every contingency while negotiating the terms. Very well—if you agree, then tomorrow I'll place a deposit in your name with my banker, to be released to you either at the end of the term or if I should die beforehand. Does *that* meet with your satisfaction, madam?"

She flinched at the ice in his voice.

"Yes," she whispered.

"Good," he said. "Now, if I'm to pay such a sum, I expect a certain standard of behavior. I am, after all, seeking to improve my standing among the more...*fastidious* members of my acquaintance."

"By purchasing the services of a whore?"

"Beginning with your behavior and appearance," he continued, ignoring her. "If this is to be a success, you must give the appearance of respectability..." He lowered his gaze to her body, and she tightened her grip on the bedsheet as she fought to conquer the shame coursing through her at the contempt in his eyes.

"The *appearance?*"

"Yes," he said. "You can be a widow—lately returned from the Continent. Italy, perhaps..." He nodded. "Yes, Italy—so few of my acquaintances are familiar enough with Italy to be suspicious if you're unable to answer their questions."

"A *widow?*"

"Come now," he said. "You'll have played many different roles to satisfy the men who pay for your services. You only need to speak properly, look a little sad, and make a pathetic comment or two about how the man you loved left you to face the world alone. Are you capable of that?"

She fought to suppress the memory of the day she learned that the only man capable of loving her had been taken from her.

The tears she'd fought to conquer swelled in her eyes, and she turned away.

"Good," he said. "That's very good. A passable effort at the tearful widow. The whole world will believe you if you do that."

You bastard.

He chuckled. "That I am."

Heavens—she'd spoken aloud. But his cruelty made it easier to protect her heart. Let him spend his fortune on fancy clothes and jewels, and two thousand guineas at the end for good measure. She would smile when needed, part her thighs when required, then leave London and claim her freedom when their business was concluded.

She might even be able to persuade Mrs. Briggs and her charges to leave London also, for a better life—a life free of the men who believed they owned women like her.

Meeting his gaze, she thrust her hand forward.

"I believe we have a deal, sir."

He clasped her hand.

"Do you know something?" she said, curling her lip into a sneer.

"What?"

"Had you insisted, I'd have settled for one thousand."

He chuckled. "And I'd have willingly paid three. You've undersold yourself, my dear. It's a poor whore who cannot read her customer when negotiating the price for her body."

She withdrew her hand and wiped it on the bedsheet. "Then I congratulate you, Your Grace, on sealing yourself a fine bargain."

"Excellent," he said. "I'll make the arrangements. There's a house for rent across the square I can set you up in, and I'll give you details of a modiste I've patronized before."

"Or rather, your mistresses have patronized before."

"As you say," he said. "All that remains is to think of a name for you. Mimi La Fleur is hardly the name for a respectable widow. What's your real name?"

My real name.

Mimi hadn't heard that name for five years—and she had no intention of hearing it again, least of all on the lips of a gentleman.

"My name—shall be Mrs. Rex," she said.

"And your first name?"

"You call me Mimi. My real name—like my pleasure, and my heart—is not for sale. Not even for two thousand guineas."

She flinched as he placed his hand on her cheek. Then he caressed it, and she fought the urge to lean into his touch.

A smile danced in his eyes. "I'll take that as a challenge, sweet."

Her skin tightened with apprehension, as if she had just soul her soul to the devil.

CHAPTER SIX

As Alexander cupped her cheek, her eyes closed, and he caught the almost imperceptible gasp from her lips.

A very different creature lay beneath that hard exterior of hers—a soft heart encased within a steel cage.

Alexander withdrew his hand and regarded the woman he'd just purchased. Naked, save for the cotton bedsheet she'd wrapped around her frame, she resembled a queen, her head held high while she negotiated her price. Had she been born a man, he could imagine her leading others into battle—or running a ducal estate.

What a challenge it would be to penetrate her armor to discover the woman within! Few could look him straight in the eye. But she had met his gaze, boldly, almost contemptuously, as if she were his equal.

Only once had she shied away from him—when he suggested she masquerade as a widow.

His mouth watered at the prospect of parading her about town on his arm. If she had the power to command a room in nothing but a bedsheet, imagine her allure when bedecked in the finery of a Society lady! Plain Mrs. Rex was too insufficient a pseudonym for her.

"You shall be Lady Rex," he said, "for a little extra respectability."

"*Lady* Rex?" She shook her head. "N-no—I could never…"

"It's perfect," he said. "Your late husband can be an earl."

"No!" She jerked back.

There it was again—the fear.

"Why not?" he asked.

She turned away. "A-an earl might be difficult to verify if required. But a knight—there are many more knights than earls, yes?"

"A knight it is, then," he said. "Now—how about a name for your late husband?"

"I care not," she said, in a voice that conveyed anything but.

There it was again, the undercurrent of sorrow. Perhaps she was a widow fallen on hard times, who took to the streets to fend for herself. Or a mistress, whose protector had abandoned her, or…

Or had died, leaving her destitute.

Was that why she'd insisted on securing her payment in the event of his not surviving? A woman in her circumstances had every need to be practical, particularly if she had trusted in the past and been exploited because of it.

And I as good as accused her of being a grasping hussy.

"How about Sir John as a name?" he suggested.

She shrugged. "It's as good as any. The world must be awash with Sir Johns—one more won't arouse suspicion."

"Good," he said. "So that's settled, save one final question."

Fear flared in her eyes. "Which is?"

"Is there anyone in this part of London who might recognize you?"

Her throat bobbed as she swallowed. "I-it's unlikely."

"Unlikely—but not impossible. Has a gentleman paid for your services before?"

Her color deepened, but she maintained her gaze, her eyes bright. "Not as a whore, no."

"As something else?"

Her eyes shone with distress, and he cursed himself for being a cad. But if his scheme were to succeed…

"I've never been in this part of London before," she said, carefully, as if she considered each word. "That doesn't mean to say I won't encounter someone I recognize. I..." She hesitated, then blinked. "I spent a few months in Sussex and encountered a man of *your kind* who might be in Town." Her voice hardened as she uttered the final words. "But that was several years ago. I've changed much since then."

"Did you"—he gestured to her body—"with him?"

"Not with *him*!" she spat. "I have some standards."

"I'm flattered you consider me desirable enough to meet your exacting standards."

"Don't be," she retorted. "You have but one desirable quality. Or, should I say, two thousand."

He found himself admiring her resolve. She met his salvos with an equally fierce response.

"I see we understand each other," he said. "I'll not take you with me if I visit Brighton."

"Brighton?" Her voice tightened. "I-I said nothing about Brighton."

"It's in Sussex, yes?" he replied. "But I have no reason to visit the south coast. My estate's a day's ride north of London."

"O-of course," she said. "I presume you'll prefer it if I stayed in London for the duration of our arrangement."

Her air of nonchalance didn't fool him. But though he yearned to press her, to discover what distressed her, he refrained.

He wasn't a complete bastard, no matter what she believed.

The clock on the mantelshelf began to whir, then seven notes rang out. Like an echo, the clocks dotted about his townhouse responded, as if calling to each other.

She turned toward the mantel clock, a soft smile on her lips, as if reliving a memory, and Alexander was overwhelmed by the desire to take her in his arms and kiss her. Then she turned away.

"It's time I got dressed," he said. "Can you dress yourself, or should I send someone?"

She responded with a harsh laugh, and he withdrew, slipping through the adjoining door into his dressing room.

His valet wasn't due yet. Alexander had to distance himself from the alluring woman in the bedchamber.

He glanced about the room. He'd never dressed himself before—but it couldn't be that hard, could it?

A wicked thought crossed his mind. Perhaps he should instruct *her* to dress him—make her kneel before him while she rolled his stockings onto his legs, his cock at her eye level, before she pleasured him with that pretty mouth of hers…

Or would she laugh at him for not even knowing how to put his stockings on? He didn't even know where Larry kept his damned stockings.

He approached a chest of drawers. Larry kept his cravats in the top drawer and the shirts in the middle drawer. Logic would suggest the stockings were in the bottom.

On top of the chest was a neatly folded cravat. Alexander tutted under his breath. Larry was such a stickler for neatness— why the devil hadn't he tidied it away?

He picked it up, then lifted it to his face, inhaling the soft scent of wood and spices. Had it been clean, he'd have expected the faint undertone of vinegar that Larry insisted kept the moths at bay. So it must have been the cravat he'd worn last night.

Only your necktie managed to emerge unsoiled.

She'd said that. Perhaps she'd ventured in here after undressing him. In which case, where were the rest of his clothes?

A watch had been placed next to the cravat. He picked it up and flipped it open, reading the inscription.

John Arnold & Son, London.

It was his pocket watch—the one those ruffians had taken from him. She must have put it there. Which meant only one thing.

She was in league with them and had played him for a fool.

Swallowing his anger, Alexander strode into the bedroom.

She stood by the window, still holding the bedsheet around her body. As he entered, she turned to face him, her eyes glistening in the sunlight.

But he was no longer fooled by her pretense. He held out the watch.

"What the devil is *this*?"

"Your pocket watch," she said. "I put it in your dressing room."

"I can see that. I meant—how did you come by it? Which of your accomplices gave it to you?"

"Accomplices? You believe I was with the men who attacked you? Or, that I manipulated myself into your bed at the request of a pimper?" She let out a snort and turned to face the window.

"I should have left you to rot and kept the watch for my trouble."

"You mean…"

"I *mean*, I retrieved it before I brought you home."

He continued to stare at her.

"You're welcome, by the way," she added, her voice dripping with sarcasm.

"But—how?" he said. "Those men overpowered me."

"Therefore, *I* couldn't possibly have defeated them?"

"You must agree it's hard to believe."

"I retrieved your watch," she said. "Something I now regret. Whether you believe that is nothing to me."

"How?"

She smiled, her attention still focused on the world outside. "I learned a long time ago that the way to defeat your enemy was not to use your strengths against him, but to exploit his weaknesses. And all men have the same weakness."

"Which is?"

She turned to face him. "Your unwavering belief in your own superiority. The men who attacked you thought themselves more than a match for a lone man—and a whore. All I had to do was catch them off guard. When one of them took hold of me, I let him believe he was in control, until I could use his weight against him."

So that explained the bruises on her arm.

Sustained, perhaps, in the act of saving my life.

He held out his hand. "Thank you."

"I've already said, you're welcome," she said.

"But I would have you take my hand—as my savior."

She stared at his hand, then took it.

"My valet will have something for those," he said, nodding to her bruises.

"It's nothing. They'll heal in no time."

Such nonchalance over the ugly marks marring her skin! Were she a lady, she'd have had a fit of apoplexy if a gust of wind rendered a single hair out of place.

But Mimi—the woman before him, the tough little thing with the soulful eyes—she was worth more than all the ladies of the *ton* combined.

Devil's bones—from where had *that* notion come?

Alexander froze as footsteps approached. Shortly after, the door opened and Larry entered, stopping short as he caught sight of Mimi.

The valet wrinkled his nose. "Your Grace, it's time for you to dress. Will your...*guest* be staying?"

Mimi drew in a sharp breath and gave the valet a look of equal dislike.

"Larry, this is"—Alexander hesitated—"Lady Rex. She's lately returned from Italy and is looking for lodgings to rent. I believe there's a house on the square that's vacant. Would you speak to Gillingham so he can make the arrangements?"

Larry was no fool. The knowledge that Alexander lied thickened the air.

"In whose name will the lease be drawn up, sir?" Larry asked.

"Mine," Alexander said. "I've agreed to act as guarantor until Lady Rex's late husband's stipend is settled. And I require an account to be opened in her name at my bank."

"You *do?*"

"Yes, Larry, I do," Alexander said. "With all haste."

"The partners at Coutts are very particular about new account holders, sir."

"Then go to the Hart bank instead."

"Very good, sir," the valet replied. "The Hart bank caters to…a *wider variety of clientele.* Mr. Hart will take money from anyone."

The valet glanced about the bedchamber. "I cannot find your clothes from yesterday, sir," he said, "save your cravat. Where are they?"

Alexander glanced at Mimi.

"They're in the scullery," she said. "In a bucket. I put them there to soak."

The valet wrinkled his nose. "They're not rags—Mrs.…." He hesitated and cocked his head to one side.

"Lady Rex," Mimi said.

"*Lady* Rex, yes. They're not rags, *Lady Rex.* They were crafted by the finest tailors of Savile Row. They could be ruined. In future, leave me to tend to the master's clothes."

"Then the next time your master rolls about in a ditch, I'll leave *you* to scrub it off," Mimi said.

Larry arched an eyebrow.

"Though," she continued, "I suspect a prig such as yourself would faint at the stench of shit."

Alexander suppressed a smile as the valet blushed to the tips of his ears.

"Well, I-I suppose, just this time…" he stammered, then wrinkled his nose.

A cold smile curled on her lips as she stepped toward the valet.

"That's right, dearie," she said, her voice flattening to the accent of the slums. "Leave the shit scrubbing to the likes of me, and you can amuse yourself folding silk and wallowing in your superiority."

Oh hell—what was she about? A sense of anticipation threaded through Alexander, as if she were planning something.

Then she released the bedsheet, which fell to the floor, revealing her naked form.

Alexander's mouth watered at the sight—her glorious curves, despite her lean frame, the soft, pert breasts with their dark-pink nipples, and the thatch of curls. His cock surged with the need to be buried between those sweet thighs. And to think—she was his until next summer.

A low whimper made him look around. His valet stared open-mouthed, raw, base desire in his eyes.

Mimi let out a laugh. "Take a good look, Larry," she said. "I usually charge, but you get your first gawp for free."

"I-I…" The red-faced valet stepped back, his eyes flaring with shame.

"Larry, I'll see you in the dressing room," Alexander said.

The valet mumbled an apology, then slipped into the dressing room, closing the door behind him.

Mimi made no attempt to move. She met Alexander's gaze with a mixture of pride and hurt in her eyes. Suppressing the need to claim her luscious body, he stooped to pick up the bedsheet, ignoring the raging torrent in his groin. Then he placed the sheet around her shoulders, drawing it close around her body.

"Would you like something to eat?" he asked.

She nodded.

"Good. I'll return when you're dressed, then I'll escort you to breakfast. If there's anything you need in the interim, I can send my housekeeper."

"Anything like what?"

He gestured toward her gown—the gaudy, tattered garment draped over the back of a chair. "My housekeeper can lend you a gown should you need it, at least until you've visited Madame Deliet—the modiste I mentioned."

She nodded, but the smile he'd been hoping for didn't materialize.

"We'll have you settled into your house in a day or two," he added. "My housekeeper can oversee the hiring of your staff." He glanced toward the door through which Larry had gone. "Or you can direct her in the choice. It's for appearance's sake, of course, but that's no reason not to hire staff who'll tend to you properly—and with respect."

"Thank you," she said.

"You're welcome."

She smiled at that, and his heart soared at the beautiful expression in her eyes.

Resisting the urge to take her in his arms, he left the bedchamber and entered the dressing room, where a subdued Larry stood waiting to dress him.

CHAPTER SEVEN

*T*HIS IS NOT *like the last time.*

Mimi stood on the pavement and stared at the building before her. The white façade of number 16 Grosvenor Square gleamed in the sunlight, and she lifted her hands to shield her eyes from the glare.

A tier of steps led to the front door—dark wood with a polished brass handle, surrounded by an elaborate architrave and flanked by two white columns that reminded her of the Grecian temples she'd seen in books.

She tilted her head up, casting her gaze over three stories, the first two with huge bay windows that reflected the sunlight, the upper story with flat windows where the new housekeeper had already taken residence.

Or so *he* said, her…

Her what? What *was* the Duke of Sawbridge? Her lover, protector, employer?

No—he was her business partner.

A ripple of apprehension threaded through her as she continued to stare at the building.

This was not like before. Her situation with Sawbridge was a soulless business relationship—with a definitive termination date, and payment at the end. After which they'd part company.

Just as she wanted. No expectations, no hopes.

And definitely *no love.*

The building before her wasn't her home. It was merely a place to stay while she earned her two thousand guineas.

The door opened to reveal a smartly dressed man in black, with close-clipped gray hair, a weathered face, and deep-set dark brown eyes.

He gave a stiff bow. "Lady Rex," he said.

"And you are?"

"Wheeler," he said. "Welcome. If it would please you to come inside?"

His demeanor was stiff and formal, but at least it lacked the contempt she'd expected. He cast his gaze over her badly fitting gown and the threadbare valise in her hand, both courtesy of Sawbridge's housekeeper.

"Have you any other belongings with you, ma'am?" he asked.

"I'm afraid not."

"Perhaps they're at the duke's townhouse?"

Her cheeks flaming, she shook her head.

"Well, that can't be helped," he said. "Come inside, and I'll send for Mrs. Hodge. She'll know what to do with you."

He stepped aside, and Mimi entered the building.

The hallway was elegant in its simplicity. Light filled the space, refracting off the crystals from the chandelier, casting myriad colors on the polished marble floor. Tall plants flanked the walls, their frond-like leaves spread out like giant fans.

At the end was a wide staircase with a banister—intricate iron uprights, topped with a polished wooden handrail. The staircase ascended straight ahead, to a turn, guarded by another palm, then it curved to the left before ascending to the upper floor. A row of paintings, landscapes in clean, bright colors, adorned the wall, following the line of the stairs, drawing the eye upward.

Mimi approached the staircase, her footsteps echoing on the floor, and reached out to the banister, tracing the curved ironwork of the uprights with her fingertips, before placing her hand on the handrail.

"I trust you find it to your satisfaction," the butler said.

"Yes, thank you, Wheeler."

"I understand you've brought no maid with you."

Mimi felt her cheeks warm at the disdain in his tone. Sawbridge might have promised the staff would treat her with respect, but a woman such as her would be viewed with contempt by even the lowliest servant. Merely surviving in this house would prove to be a battle.

"I have no need of a personal maid," she said.

"Very good, ma'am. I'll have Charles escort you to your chamber. Then I suggest tea in the parlor at eleven o'clock."

His tone implied that refusal was not an option. He arched a brow, and she nodded. "Thank you."

He reached for a bell on the side table and rang it. Moments later, a thin-faced youth in blue livery arrived.

"Ah, Charles," the butler said. "Please escort"—he hesitated—"Lady Rex to her chamber. Then show her to the parlor at eleven." He glanced at Mimi's valise. "And help her with her…luggage."

Her cheeks flaming, Mimi handed the valise over, then she turned to the butler.

"I prefer to take tea at half past eleven," she said.

"But…"

"Mr. Wheeler, I trust I do not have to repeat myself."

"No, ma'am."

The butler issued a stiff bow, then Mimi followed the footman upstairs.

She had survived the opening salvo, but the battle had just begun.

As a clock struck half past the hour, Mimi followed the footman across the hallway floor. He pushed open a door, then gave a shy smile.

At least some of the household treated her with courtesy, though doubtless Charles's civility was due to his youth—red spots marked his forehead and cheeks, and his voice bore the hoarseness of a boy on the cusp of adulthood. He was too innocent to understand who and what she was.

The parlor was already occupied. A woman sat on a chaise longue by the window, her dark hair fashioned into a tidy style, and wearing a dark-blue gown trimmed with lace. She rose as Mimi entered.

"Lady Rex, I presume." She dipped into a curtsey.

So this was the housekeeper. She should have waited downstairs until summoned. If not even the staff could hide their contempt, how would Mimi survive among Sawbridge's acquaintance?

"You must be Mrs. Hodge," Mimi said, keeping her voice even, though she was aware of her cheeks heating. She glanced about the parlor—elegantly furnished in blue and yellow, with two chairs beside the fireplace that matched the chaise longue and a table in the center laden with a tea tray.

Mimi approached the table and lifted the teapot. "It was most kind of you to join me for tea, Mrs. Hodge."

"I thought it wise, given the circumstances."

Mimi's hand faltered as she poured tea into a cup, and a splash of brown liquid fell onto the table.

"Circumstances?" she said, aware of the tightness in her voice.

"I understand from the duke that you've not taken a house in London before," the housekeeper said. "I therefore thought it prudent to instruct you in any matters you might want assistance with."

Prettily put, but Mimi could hardly expect the woman to say outright that she didn't want a whore disrupting her establishment. Did she perhaps expect to find a row of lust-fueled men lining up outside her bedchamber each night?

Mimi continued to pour her tea, and followed it with a splash of milk, then she took a seat at one end of the chaise longue.

The housekeeper remained standing.

"Please continue, Mrs. Hodge."

"A house such as this requires a certain degree of order to run," the housekeeper said. "The staff each have their roles and know how to undertake them. Each occupant—both above and below stairs—must understand their role."

"Even those who reside above stairs but whom others believe are better suited to life below?"

The housekeeper's eyes widened.

"You may find it hard to believe, Mrs. Hodge," Mimi said, "but I've been mistress of a household before, albeit five years ago. Assuming the roles and traditions you speak of have not changed materially since then, I'm confident I'll do nothing to bring this household into disrepute."

To her credit, the housekeeper blushed. "Forgive me, Lady Rex—I meant no offense. I was merely—"

"You were merely offering your assistance in case I was unsure of my role in this household," Mimi said. "Rest assured, Mrs. Hodge, that I fully understand my position. I will carry out my duties—all of them—to the best of my ability."

Her voice wavered, and she lifted her teacup to her lips and took a sip.

A flicker of understanding shone in the other woman's eyes.

"Please, help yourself to tea, Mrs. Hodge," Mimi said. "We've much to discuss."

The housekeeper poured a cup, then glanced at the chaise longue. Mimi patted the seat.

"Sit with me if you please, Mrs. Hodge."

The housekeeper smiled and sat. "May I say, Lady Rex, you're not what I expected."

"That's kind of you to phrase it so politely," Mimi said, "but, like it or not, I'm mistress of his house."

The housekeeper placed a light hand on Mimi's arm.

"That you are, ma'am. And my duty is to help you, to make sure your life here is as comfortable as possible for as long as you require it."

"It's only for six months, Mrs. Hodge. We can both be thankful for *that*, at least."

The housekeeper smiled. "Life takes a turn for the unexpected sometimes. Nothing is certain."

"I know that better than most," Mimi replied. "The unexpected is often where life takes a turn for the worse."

"Perhaps, my dear, the unexpected may bring about an improvement in your life. Contentment can be found in the most unlikely of situations."

Mimi took another sip. "I'd gladly settle for contentment."

"And happiness?"

"Happiness is a dream," Mimi said. "And while I'd advocate indulging in dreams on occasion, it does no good to place any faith in their realization."

"It's a sorry creature who lacks faith, Lady Rex."

"A rational creature, also," Mimi said. "Faith can be very dangerous—more than hope, for at least hope carries with it an understanding of the risk of disappointment. We can recover from having our hopes dashed. But faith?" She shook her head. "Better to have no faith at all than to have lost it."

The housekeeper stared, and Mimi averted her gaze. What had possessed her to lower her defenses to a stranger merely because she showed a little kindness?

She reached toward the table to set her teacup down. The cup rattled against the saucer as her hand shook, then two hands clasped hers, and the rattling stopped.

"I can manage, Mrs. Hodge," Mimi said.

"I'm sure you can, my dear, but that shouldn't prevent me from helping you where I can." She plucked the teacup and saucer from Mimi's hand and placed it on the table. "We're here to make your life comfortable, Lady Rex." Mimi met her gaze, and the housekeeper smiled, her eyes crinkling at the edges. "Even Mr. Wheeler. He's a little fastidious, but he'll undertake his duties appropriately."

"And the rest of the staff, will they…"

Will they look down on me like everyone else?

"They'll give you the respect you command as their mistress, Lady Rex. Mr. Wheeler and I will see to that." Mrs. Hodge gave a soft smile of indulgence. "Young Charles is a little inexperienced, but he's a fast learner, though I say it myself—he's my nephew, you see. The duke was kind enough to let me engage him. Will you be wanting a lady's maid?"

Mimi shook her head.

"We can arrange for one later if you wish—there's no need to decide just now. And, of course, we have a cook, Mrs. Brennan. You must tell me your favorite dishes and I can have her cook them for you. If you wish to meet the staff yourself, I can arrange it."

"Perhaps later."

"Of course, my dear, I understand. You must be tired. Perhaps after luncheon I can take you to the kitchen and introduce you."

The housekeeper smiled and nodded, and Mimi caught the unspoken words in her eyes.

You have nothing to fear.

Perhaps not in this house. But out in Society, the realm of predators of a very different nature—Mimi had everything to fear.

As if Fate had read her thoughts, a knock came on the front door. Mimi startled and rose to her feet. The housekeeper placed a steadying hand on her arm.

"I'll see to it, Lady Rex."

Mrs. Hodge approached the door, which opened to reveal the young footman. She gave him a smile of affection.

"What is it, Charles?"

He held out a silver salver. "Message for the mistress."

"Take it over to her, then."

"Yes, Aunt…I mean, yes, Mrs. Hodge."

The boy colored, the spots on his face seeming to glow, as he approached Mimi, his hand trembling.

She gave him a smile and plucked the note from the salver.

"Thank you, Charles," she said. "You're very kind."

He glanced up at her and his blush deepened.

"Charles?" Mrs. Hodge said.

The young footman issued a bow, then scuttled out of the parlor.

Mimi tore open the note and read it.

Madame Deliet, 55a St. James.

Give my name as a friend of the late Sir John Rex, and she'll tend to you.

A.F.

"A.F." She handed the note to Mrs. Hodge. "Who's that?"

The housekeeper took it, a flicker of sympathy in her eyes. "That's the duke."

"I-I thought his name was Sawbridge."

"That's right. Alexander Ffortescue, fifth Duke of Sawbridge. And Madame Deliet is…"

"A modiste, I know," Mimi said.

The housekeeper let out a huff. "It's not my place, I know, but I confess I'm disappointed."

"That a woman like me should be going to a modiste?"

"Bless you, no! I'm disappointed in *him*, expecting you to go alone, and you unused to London! He usually accompanies all his other…" Her voice trailed off and she colored.

"You know him well?" Mimi asked.

"By reputation, though perhaps…" Mrs. Hodge glanced at the note again. "Perhaps he views you differently. Six months is a long time."

Perhaps too long.

Focus on the prize, Mimi—the pot of gold at the end with which you can purchase your freedom.

"I'll ask Wheeler to send the duke a message," the housekeeper said.

Mimi shook her head. "Please don't, Mrs. Hodge. The one lesson I've learned is the futility of asking a man to do anything he doesn't wish to. As you say, he views me differently to the other women he's…" She hesitated, her cheeks burning with shame.

"I know, my dear," the housekeeper said. "I was going to ask that he give you the use of his carriage if he cannot accompany you himself."

"I'd rather walk," Mimi said. "I've no wish to grow dependent on his…generosity. Besides"—she glanced toward the window through which the winter sun shone—"a walk will give me a chance to familiarize myself with the area."

The housekeeper nodded. "You're a sensible young woman, and clever, I'll warrant. Though we live in a world where intelligence in a female is to be criticized rather than applauded, I suspect it's enabled you to survive. But I wouldn't dream of your wandering about London unaccompanied. It's not the done thing for a respectable widow of a knight. The late Sir John Rex would turn in his grave if he were to know I let you wander the streets alone. Charles can accompany you. He knows the way, and can carry any purchases you make."

"Mrs. Hodge, I think we both know that Sir John was not…I mean, is not—"

"No sense in getting yourself upset, Lady Rex. I'm sure Sir John, wherever he may be in the world beyond, would want you taken care of, would he not?"

Mimi met her gaze, and her heart softened at the understanding in the older woman's eyes.

Then the housekeeper opened the door and called out, "Charles?"

After a heartbeat, the young footman appeared. "Yes, Mrs. Hodge?"

"Would you accompany your mistress to St. James? Here's the direction." She handed him the note, then glanced toward the window. "And fetch my cloak—the wind has a bite this time of year. That is, if you don't object, Lady Rex? I don't want your catching cold in that thin gown on your first day in London."

Blinking back tears at the housekeeper's kindness, Mimi nodded. "I'd be obliged, thank you."

"Well?" Mrs. Hodge demanded. "Don't stand there staring, lad—you don't want to keep the mistress waiting."

"No, ma'am," Charles mumbled, then scuttled off.

The housekeeper followed him with her gaze, an affectionate smile on her lips.

"He'll take care of you, Lady Rex," she said. "Now, I ought to be getting on—I've a host of young girls to interview about the remaining positions, if you'll excuse me?"

"Of course," Mimi said. "Thank you for your kindness, Mrs. Hodge. I didn't expect it."

"I'm sure you didn't my dear," the housekeeper said, taking her hand. "And I hope, with all my heart, that you'll be happy here."

She placed her hand on Mimi's cheek.

"Not just content," she said, "but *happy*."

"Here we are, ma'am."

Charles gestured to the white-fronted building with a paneled window that bowed outward, through which Mimi could see an elaborate display of flowers set against a backdrop of cream-colored silk.

"It looks like a florist's," she said. Then she glanced upward to the sign over the door, displaying the word *modiste* in large black letters, and to the side, in a cursive hand, the inscription *Mme. Deliet*.

Mimi approached the window, her stomach churning at the display—roses and orchids of every conceivable color. It exuded wealth and ostentation. Not a single petal was out of place, and each one looked as fresh as the day of first blooming.

By comparison, her gown and cloak—a housekeeper's hand-me-downs—looked shabby and worn.

How the devil could she even begin to belong here?

"Ma'am? Shall I accompany you inside?"

"Thank you, Charles," Mimi said, "that would be most kind."

He pushed open the door, a bell tinkling overhead, and Mimi followed.

The interior was even more ostentatious than the window display. Row upon row of silks lined one wall, and a display of ribbons, trays of buttons, beads, and jewels adorned another. The shop was larger than it appeared from the outside, stretching toward the back, where two ladies stood, deep in conversation. They turned to face Mimi as she entered.

The taller of the two, with a cascade of blonde curls and eyes the color of ice, drew in a sharp breath, while the other, with pale-red hair and acrid green eyes, wrinkled her nose.

"Tradesmen enter at the back," she said in a sharp, brittle voice.

"I'm here to see Madame Deliet," Mimi began.

"Well of course you are!" The blonde woman turned to her companion. "Do you hear that? She's here to see Madame Deliet!"

"Which of you is she?" Mimi asked.

"Sweet heaven—what sort of riffraff is Madame having to deal with these days?" the second exclaimed.

"Are *neither* of you Madame Deliet?"

The blonde woman rolled her eyes and let out a sharp huff. "Do we *look* like tradespeople? I'm the Honorable Sarah Francis."

"Now, Sarah," the redhead said, "you mustn't be too hard on this…" She cast her gaze over Mimi's form, the contempt in her eyes eliciting more shame in Mimi's heart than she'd felt when standing naked before Sawbridge's valet. "This—*person*," the redhead said, at length. "Given her apparel, one can hardly expect her to discern the difference between a modiste and a baron's daughter."

I am a baron's daughter.

"Perhaps, my dear," the Honorable Sarah said, "you had better return another time."

"Or not at all," her companion added.

"Now, Elizabeth, we mustn't be uncharitable. This poor creature lacks understanding, given that she brought a *footman* into the shop."

Blushing, Charles sidled toward the door.

"Stay where you are, Charles," Mimi said. "We're going nowhere. I'm here to see Madame Deliet, as a customer."

"Really? And you are?"

"Lady Rex."

"Lady Rex? And your husband is…?"

"*Was.* Sir John Rex."

"A knight, I presume, not a baronet."

Mimi nodded.

"Yes, I see," the redhead said. "The regent's a little more discerning when giving out baronetcies. But it seems that *anyone* is given a knighthood these days."

"Exactly, Elizabeth. Look at Sir Leonard Howard—parading about the place with his upstart daughters whom we must treat as our equals merely because they married above their station. I mean, that Eleanor is quite the dimwit, yet because she's a duchess now, we must treat her as our equal."

"I doubt this Eleanor—whomever she may be—could be considered *your* equal," Mimi couldn't help saying.

"Exactly." Both women nodded, and Mimi suppressed a smile as they missed her meaning.

"At least you appreciate *our* station, if not your own," Sarah said. "Madame is rather discerning when it comes to her clientele—and you wouldn't want any unpleasantness, would you? You should try elsewhere."

"But—"

"We're thinking of your best interests. I'm sure you'd much rather leave this establishment of your own accord."

"Well, I..." Mimi began, then the curtain at the back of the shop was swept back and a petite woman appeared, dressed in white, her hair an abundance of dark curls.

She held up an array of yellow ribbons.

"Here we are, *mes amis!*" she cried. "I 'ave found the perfect ribbons for your gowns. You'll be the belles of all the balls, no? In fact, I said to my niece, only yesterday, that—" She broke off as she spotted Mimi in the doorway. Then she dropped her gaze to Mimi's feet, and slowly raised it, taking in the thick boots with the scuffed toes, the frayed hem of her gown with the dusting of dirt, the creased skirt, the plain brown woolen cloak, and Mimi's neck, which lacked any adornment—unlike the other two ladies, whose jeweled necklaces twinkled in the sunlight.

"Who might *you* be?" the modiste said, her accent slipping, and Mimi detected an undercurrent of the flat vowels she'd grown used to during the past five years.

"This is Mrs...." Sarah began, then shook her head. "Do forgive me—this woman, apparently, is *Lady* Rex."

"Is she, now?"

"I understand you're expecting me?" Mimi said.

The modiste wrinkled her nose. "I've never heard of you."

"I'm here to purchase a gown," Mimi said.

"One doesn't purchase a gown in my establishment, Mademoiselle..."

"*Lady* Rex," Mimi said. "My late husband was a friend of—"

The modiste raised her hand. "Pay me the courtesy of letting me finish."

The redhead leaned toward her companion. "Such incivility to interrupt one's betters!"

"Quite so, Lady Elizabeth," the modiste said. "Now, Lady Rex, my clientele do not simply *purchase* their gowns." She gestured about the shop. "Do you see any gowns here?"

Mimi shook her head.

"No, *madame*, you don't. And do you know why? It's because the ladies who frequent my establishment purchase my expertise—my services. Each gown I make is created by hand, after establishing a relationship with the lady. And"—she curled her lip in a sneer—"each gown is—what do you English say?—très expensive."

"*Chaque robe est très cher,*" Mimi said.

Confusion clouded the modiste's expression. Then she shook her head.

Madame Deliet, you're a fraudster.

"I doubt you could afford anything in my establishment," she said. "I'd advise you to look elsewhere. There's plenty of establishments where you can purchase a gown."

"Charitable establishments," the blonde said.

Her companion let out a giggle. "Sarah, we mustn't be unkind, I'm sure my maid has donated some of her old gowns to such places—those she doesn't cut into rags and give to the butler to polish the silverware with."

Their laughter filled the air.

"I have money," Mimi said. "My late husband's friend, he—"

The modiste strode to the door. The bell overhead tinkled angrily as she yanked it open.

"Please leave," she said, her voice cold and hard, with no trace of a French accent. "Do not attempt to enter my establishment again."

She pushed Charles toward the exit and faced Mimi, contempt in her eyes. Then she called over her shoulder, "Evelina!"

"Yes, Madame?" a thin voice called in the distance.

"Bring my cologne—there's a nasty odor I must see to."

Mimi retreated through the door, and the modiste slammed it shut.

Mimi turned from the shop, blinking back the moisture in her eyes. She'd be damned if she'd give them the satisfaction of seeing her tears.

"Charles, take me home."

"Ma'am, it's raining."

Mimi stepped out from beneath the awning and tipped her

head toward the sky, letting droplets splash onto her face.

"I care not," she said. "I'd rather be out here in the rain than inside with those creatures—with *any* of their kind."

"So would I, ma'am," Charles said, then his color deepened. "Forgive me. My aunt's always sayin' I shouldn't speak out of turn. In fact, she says I shouldn't speak at all most times—certainly not in front of my betters."

"On the contrary," Mimi said. "You have shown me that you're a better person than those…" She gestured toward the shop.

"Ladies?" he asked.

"Oh, I think we can do better than that," she said.

He hesitated. "Nasty ladies?"

"How about vipers?"

He let out a nervous laugh. "What about cheesers?"

"*Cheesers?*" she asked. "As in lumps of cheese?"

He lowered his voice. "It means… It's when you…" He gestured to his behind and waved his hand to and fro. "When you do a particularly potent one. If it stinks, it's called a cheeser." Mimi bit her lip to suppress her laughter, and his eyes widened. "Beg pardon, ma'am, I didn't mean to offend!"

"And you didn't, Charles," she said. "In fact, I think my life will be the better for having you in it. You're a credit to your aunt, and I'll tell her as much when we return. Now, shall we?"

He nodded, then led the way as they retraced their steps to Grosvenor Square and the rain began to fall more steadily.

Perhaps she might survive six months in this hostile environment if she had allies—even if those allies were just a housekeeper and her adolescent nephew.

CHAPTER EIGHT

T HE CARRIAGE HIT a rut and jolted sideways. Alexander groaned as a spike of pain shot through his leg.

Fuck—that hurt.

A sharp sigh from the woman opposite told him he'd spoken aloud.

Shit. That was all he needed—yet more disapproval from his friend's wife, one of the few respectable women in London who tolerated his company, even if only for her husband's sake.

"Does it still trouble you?" she asked, gazing at him with her usual intense expression.

"What, Duchess—my leg, or the reason it was broken?"

"I was inquiring after the former," she replied. "The latter is a matter for your conscience."

"Eleanor, we discussed this." Her husband, the Duke of Whitcombe and perhaps Alexander's only friend, took her hand.

"That we did, Montague," she said, turning her attention on the world outside, through the raindrop-spattered carriage window.

"It's most obliging of you to take me home," Alexander said. "I could have sent for my own carriage."

"It's not out of our way. We've been taking tea with Lord and Lady Radham—and their new daughter."

"Had I known, I'd have asked you to give them my best wishes," Alexander said.

The duchess turned her gaze toward him, then opened her mouth to respond. She was never one to engage in the bland social niceties such as conveying meaningless *regards* to an acquaintance. Instead, she had a discomfiting habit of saying that which everyone else was thinking, but was too polite to voice.

Such as Alexander's many transgressions toward Lady Radham, the duchess's younger sister, who had once been the subject of salacious gossip—gossip that Alexander had, to his shame, relished.

But he'd learned his lesson. The pleasure in having indulged in sordid tales about others made the humiliation of being the subject of such tales himself all the more intense.

The carriage turned into Grosvenor Square and the duchess sighed, her breath misting against the window.

"Look at that poor woman caught in the rain," she said. "She'll be soaked without an umbrella."

Whitcombe leaned toward the window. "She has her footman with her, Eleanor. Doubtless he'll be in for a tongue lashing for forgetting to bring one."

"She looks more sad than angry."

"How can you tell at this distance, my love?"

"I can't see her expression, but there's something about the way she carries herself, as if she feels she doesn't belong."

Alexander laughed. "How can anyone know what another person is thinking merely by looking at their *stance*?"

The duchess focused her dark eyes on him, and he felt his cheeks warm under her scrutiny.

Whitcombe took her hand, and her expression softened as she shifted her gaze to her husband.

"I'm fortunate to have a clever wife, Sawbridge," he said, mirroring her smile.

Ugh. Perhaps getting soaked was preferable to being stuck in a carriage with a lovesick couple. Though Alexander couldn't deny the pang of longing at seeing two people so much in love—so different, and yet so perfect for each other. Opposites, yet equals.

She glanced outside again. "Thank heaven for that," she said. "That must be her home."

Alexander leaned toward the window in time to see two figures—a cloaked woman and a thin youth in blue livery—climbing the stairs toward the front door of a house…the house across the square from his own that had been vacant.

Until yesterday.

Her cloak clung to her form, and his manhood stirred in recognition—and in anticipation of being buried inside her. To think—in a matter of hours he could be parting those lovely thighs.

Mimi…

"Beg pardon?" Whitcombe asked. "Do you *know* her?"

"I…" Alexander's cheeks warmed as he felt the duchess's gaze fall upon him once more. "Sh-she's my…"

Devil take him! What ought he to call her? Mistress? Lover? Doxy?

The duchess let out a huff.

Damn. Of all the people to witness his discomfort, it had to be *her.*

"I think it's a disgrace," she said.

"Eleanor, my love, you know nothing of her," Whitcombe said.

"You think her unfit to live in Grosvenor Square, Duchess?" Alexander asked.

"No," she said. "I am disappointed that your…" She hesitated and lowered her gaze to the bulge in his breeches.

Go on, Duchess, say it. Call her my whore and be done with it. Show me what you're really *like beneath that pretense at kindness.*

"I'm disappointed that your *friend* must fend for herself in the rain while you luxuriate in our carriage," she said. "No wonder nobody respectable wants anything to do with you."

"Eleanor," Whitcombe said, "it's not Sawbridge's fault if his paramour takes a turn in the rain."

She let out a huff. "At the very least, he could have put his carriage at her disposal."

In that, the duchess was right. Mimi must have been to Madame Deliet's, and Alexander hadn't concerned himself with how she'd get there. It had been for her sake that he'd not offered to escort her personally. If their ruse of her being the respectable widow of a knight were to be believed, she was better off attending the modiste while *not* being on the arm of the man with the worst reputation in London.

At least she'd had the good sense to take a footman with her.

"She's not my paramour," Alexander said. "She's a respectable widow."

"But you and she are…" Whitcombe leaned forward, a smile of mischief on his lips.

Aware of the futility of lying before the sharply observant duchess, Alexander nodded.

"Then she's a brave woman—or perhaps a fool—for associating with you. Does she know of your reputation?"

"She's an old family friend—at least, her late husband was."

"And he was?"

"Sir John Rex."

Whitcombe frowned. "I've not heard of him. Rex, you say? There's Sir John Wrexham, though he must be at least sixty. He has an estate in Yorkshire. But I thought him still alive."

"Sir John and Lady Rex lived in Italy," Alexander said. "Now her period of mourning is over, she's come to London."

"And you've settled her in the house opposite," Whitcombe said, amusement in his tone. "Most magnanimous, I'm sure."

"I'm dealing with her solicitor," Alexander said. "Surely there's no harm in that?"

"Does she have any acquaintance in London?" the duchess asked.

"Not yet."

"I could introduce her to Lady Arabella," she said. "She spent some of her childhood in Italy."

Bugger.

"I don't think Lady Rex would want—"

"Shouldn't that be up to Lady Rex to decide? I'd have thought she'd welcome the opportunity to speak to someone who knows something of her former home."

"Eleanor, my love," Whitcombe said, "Sawbridge knows Lady Rex better than you."

"*Do* you know her well?" she asked, turning to Alexander.

He glanced at the house into which Mimi had entered, recalling the shuttered expression in her eyes, the coarseness which she had, at first, used as a shield, until her accent had lapsed into that of a lady. His heart twitched at the memory of her smile—the soft smile of contentment that he'd glimpsed as she slept. But he was yet to see that smile when she was awake, buried, as it was, beneath layers of steel.

No. He didn't know her well—in fact, he didn't know her at all.

"Perhaps I should pay her a call," the duchess said.

"Eleanor, why?" Whitcombe asked. "You dislike strangers."

"Montague, aren't you always encouraging me to speak to strangers in case I find them to my liking?"

"She may not welcome the intrusion," Alexander said.

"Shouldn't she be permitted to decide for herself whether to receive visitors?" the duchess said. "Or is she dependent on *you?*"

Alexander shook his head. "She has an independent income."

The knowledge that he'd lied clung to the air, but if the duchess recognized it, she gave no sign.

"And she chooses to spend her time with *you?*" she said. "She must be a remarkable woman. I look forward to knowing her better."

"Eleanor…"

"No, Montague. I'm determined."

There was no deterring her. Duchess Whitcombe was a contradiction. Most of the time she remained quiet, especially at parties. But when a subject interested her, she could be neither silenced, nor deterred.

Alexander knew enough of the tenacity of women—this woman in particular—that the very last thing he should do was warn her off. It would only pique her interest further.

But if Mimi were to enter Society, Alexander could think of none better to make her acquaintance. Duchess Whitcombe had the kindest soul in England. She wouldn't punish Mimi for her association with him.

He leaned back in his seat. "Duchess, I've no objection to your visiting Lady Rex. She may welcome the company."

She arched an eyebrow, then nodded. "That's settled. I'll call on her later this afternoon."

Damn. He'd wanted to visit Mimi today—but the last thing he needed was to be caught *in flagrante delicto* by Duchess Whitcombe.

After depositing Alexander outside his front door, the carriage circumnavigated the square, then disappeared onto the adjoining street. He glanced across at number sixteen. Perhaps, if he were quick, he could pay Mimi a visit, take his pleasure, and be gone before the duchess returned.

Then the door opened, and his butler appeared at the threshold.

"Ah, Your Grace," he said. "Your solicitor is here. I believe you're expecting him."

Mimi's bed would have to wait. But Alexander could console himself in the knowledge that the longer the wait, the sweeter the pleasure.

CHAPTER NINE

THE CARRIAGE THAT had followed Mimi and Charles into Grosvenor Square was enormous, bearing an ornate crest. Two men in red livery sat at the front holding the reins, seemingly oblivious to the rain, while another two clung to the back.

So many men, and horses, to convey a handful of people too idle to walk.

A woman's face appeared at the carriage window, blurred by the rain—another Society lady to look down on her.

Then a second face appeared—the Duke of Sawbridge.

Mimi turned her back and followed Charles up the steps, where the door opened to reveal the butler.

He stepped aside to admit her, looking over her soaked form, then his gaze settled on the water dripping onto the floor, already pooling at her feet.

"Charles and I were caught in the rain, Wheeler," she said.

"So I see."

Why did his face bear a permanent expression of disdain? Or was it merely when he looked at her?

"Charles!" he snapped. "Don't just stand there."

"Yes, Mr. Wheeler. Sorry, Mr. Wheeler." Trembling, the footman took Mimi's cloak.

"Ma'am, I suggest you change your gown," the butler said. "Do you have another?"

Mimi nodded, feeling like a wayward child admonished by a

schoolmaster.

"Good. Do you require assistance?"

"No."

"In which case, would you oblige me with an audience once you've changed? I'll await you in the study. Now, if you'll excuse me, I need a word with Charles." He bowed and began to retreat.

"Which room is the study?" Mimi asked.

He gestured to a door on the right. "In there, ma'am."

"Very good, Wheeler—you're dismissed."

He arched an eyebrow at her attempt at authority, then bowed and retreated, his footsteps clicking on the floor. Once he was out of sight, Mimi sprinted up the stairs to the sanctuary of her bedchamber.

AFTER CHANGING INTO another of Sawbridge's housekeeper's old gowns, Mimi made her way to the study, where she found the butler seated beside a squat dark wooden desk.

He rose and gestured toward the chair at the head of the desk, waiting until she'd taken it before resuming his seat.

"Why have you summoned me?" she asked.

He arched an eyebrow. "If I recall right, I merely *requested* an audience, Lady Rex."

"It didn't sound like a request."

"Perhaps not to one unused to how a Society townhouse is run."

"I see you're not sparing me your frankness," Mimi said.

"I merely feel obliged to warn you of the inappropriateness of your behavior today."

"*My* behavior? Is it your place to admonish me over my behavior, or for me to admonish you over yours?"

"It's my duty to ensure that propriety is observed at all times," he said, "both below stairs—and above."

"Very well, Wheeler," she said. "Let me bestow upon you equal frankness. We both know that I'm not who I appear to be."

He opened his mouth to reply, but she raised her hand.

"Permit me to finish. While you may have formed certain conclusions about me, you know nothing of my history. Neither does the Duke of Sawbridge. However, His Grace has instructed you to behave as if I am the mistress of this house—a respectable widow. You may lack respect for me—and believe me, I'm used to dealing with the contempt of others—but out of respect for your employer, I expect you to carry out your duties without complaint."

His eyebrow twitched—most likely the only expression of emotion he would display.

"All you, and anyone else, needs to know," Mimi continued, "is that I am *Lady Rex*."

"Then, ma'am, it behooves me to advise you to behave as Lady Rex ought."

She leaned back in the chair and sighed. "Wheeler, where is the fault in my behavior?"

"For one thing, walking in the rain without an umbrella," he said. "Though I hold Charles responsible, for which he has already been admonished."

"And?"

"And," he said, his nose wrinkling, "it's not done for a lady residing in Grosvenor Square to wander about Mayfair dressed like"—he gestured to her gown—"the housekeeper's grandmoth-er."

"This is the best gown I have!"

He frowned. "I understood His Grace was to take you to a modiste. At the very least you should refrain from venturing out of doors until properly attired. Living in Grosvenor Square is a privilege."

Anger burst within her at his pomposity, and she slammed her fist on the desk.

"It's a *punishment*, rather than a privilege to live here," she snarled. "For your information, I was at a modiste! With Charles—because nobody else cared to accompany me. Yet you punished him for it!"

"He wasn't punished for accompanying you, ma'am. But even he should recognize the impropriety of venturing outside, dressed as you are."

"How do you suggest I improve my state of dress, when they refused to serve me?"

"Who refused to serve you?"

"The modiste," she said. "That woman with the fake French accent—Deliet, she calls herself—who tossed me out of the street to the amusement of her customers, as if I were a pile of horseshit."

This time he raised both eyebrows, and she braced herself for a lecture on her vocabulary.

But it never came.

"She threw you out?"

"Yes!" Mimi cried. "And you know why? Because she's just like you—she judges by appearance and looks down her nose at anyone she considers beneath her."

"Ma'am, I'm not—"

"You *are*," Mimi interrupted. "Why else would you punish that poor boy merely for showing me kindness? Do you think I minded getting caught in the rain? No—I found it infinitely preferable to being stuck inside a stuffy townhouse with people like you. In fact, Mr. Wheeler, I'd rather roll in horseshit than suffer your company."

She heard a muffled cry and looked up to see Mrs. Hodge in the doorway.

The housekeeper placed her hands on her hips. "Well! I've never heard anything the like!" she said. "You ought to be ashamed. Why the duke thought you fit to be here, I'll never know."

"Let me remedy that at once, Mrs. Hodge," Mimi said, rising, but the housekeeper lifted her hand.

"I was speaking to *you*, Mr. Wheeler," she said. "What right have you to speak to the mistress with such disrespect? And to shepherd her into the study as if she were your subordinate without even offering her tea—what will the duke think of you?"

"Mrs. Hodge, even *you* must understand the need for propriety," the butler retorted.

"Yes, but there's no need further the cause with such a heavy hand." Mrs. Hodge turned to Mimi. "My nephew tells me your visit to the modiste was not a success."

"It seems as if I'm not the type of customer Madame Deliet wishes to serve," Mimi said.

"I feared as much. The duke ought to have accompanied you himself instead of gallivanting about town. Men! They know *nothing*." Mrs. Hodge glared at the butler, who remained stoic apart from a faint reddening of his cheeks. "Go and see to the wine cellar," she said.

Wheeler bowed and exited the study, and the housekeeper took the seat he'd vacated.

"What am I to do?" Mimi asked. "The duke insisted on my having new gowns."

"Then he should have accompanied you," the housekeeper said gently. "Would you like *me* to ask him?"

"And have him know that Madame Deliet doesn't think me good enough for her establishment? No, I couldn't bear that. He might not want to keep—"

Mimi broke off, the unfinished sentence hanging in the air.

He might not want to keep me.

A warm hand took hers. "He's gone to a lot of trouble to settle you here, my dear, and he'll want you looking your best. I might have a solution."

"I cannot go back there," Mimi said. "If he accompanies me, it'll only make it worse, for they'll know I'm his…"

"Do not speak it," Mrs. Hodge said. "We should never allow ourselves to be defined by what we're compelled to do for a living."

Mimi's cheeks heated under the housekeeper's scrutiny. "I-I know I must dress appropriately."

"Might I suggest a solution?"

"Please—anything."

"My cousin Peg's a seamstress—a dressmaker, really, though she has yet to have an establishment of her own. But she's so talented. See this?" Mrs. Hodge gestured to the lacework on her neckline. "Made with her own fingers, that was—I couldn't afford to buy lace this fine."

Mimi glanced at the lace tuck, the intricate floral pattern, and caught her breath at the memory of another lace tuck—a gift from a man from another period in her life, the finest lace from Flanders. A gift she had long since lost, along with everything else. She blinked and wiped away the tears that threatened to fall.

"Give Peg a chance, ma'am," Mrs. Hodge said.

"Would the duke approve?"

"He'd approve of the cost—my Peg would give you three gowns at half the price of one of Madame Deliet's. And she'll come to you. I could send Charles for her today, if you like."

"Wouldn't she object to making gowns for a…"

"For the widow of a knight?" Mrs. Hodge shook her head. "My Peg's not one to judge another by their rank. She judges a person by their deeds."

"Then," Mimi said, "if it's not too much trouble, perhaps you could send for her. I find myself in need of the company of those who do not think less of me for what I am."

The housekeeper rose and approached the door, then she turned and smiled.

"You'll be the prettiest widow in town," she said. "If he doesn't fall in love with you, then he's a fool. Now—how about that tea? I'll have it brought to the parlor."

Mimi nodded, and the housekeeper exited the study.

If he doesn't fall in love with you, then he's a fool.

She let out a bitter laugh.

"Mrs. Hodge, you're the biggest fool of all if you believe him capable of falling in love," she said to the empty room.

The question is—how much of a fool am I?

CHAPTER TEN

B Y THE TIME the seamstress had gone, armed with measure-
ments and a book full of sketches, the rain had ceased. The
sun had traversed the sky, plunging the parlor into shadow, and
Mimi moved to the drawing room at the back of the house,
which contained a square pianoforte and overlooked the
garden—if a stretch of ill-kept grass could be called a *garden*.

Perhaps she could ask Wheeler to hire a gardener to tidy it,
plant a few rosebushes to bring a splash of color.

Then she checked herself. By the time the roses bloomed,
she'd be gone.

But she would have the means to purchase her own house—
complete with rosebushes—rather than the house procured by
the man who now owned her.

The man who had not yet deigned to visit her.

Where is he?

As if in answer, she heard a knock on the front door. She
placed herself on the chaise longue by the window and lifted the
book of poetry she'd been reading over breakfast.

Footsteps approached, and to her shame, Mimi felt a pulse of
longing. She inhaled and counted to five, focusing on the book in
her hand. She let her gaze wander over the lines of verse without
reading them, then the footsteps paused outside the drawing
room door and her heart gave a jolt of anticipation.

The door opened and Charles appeared.

"You have a visitor, ma'am."

Mimi set the book aside and smoothed down the front of her dress. "Please send him in, Charles."

"Oh, b-but…" he said as he moved aside to reveal the newcomer.

A lady, dressed in pale lilac silk.

The cut of her gown lacked the ostentation of the women at the modiste's, but its simplicity reeked of elegance. She wore a plain pearl necklace, each bead a perfectly formed sphere with a subtle sheen of iridescence.

Her features were too unremarkable for her to be described as a beauty, except for the curiously intense expression in her emerald eyes.

"Th-the Duchess of Whitcombe," Charles stammered.

Mimi's gut twisted as she rose to her feet.

A *duchess*—come to look down her nose, perhaps instruct Mimi to leave Town, lest she taint it with her presence.

Mimi wiped her hands on her skirt, then dipped into a curtsey. "Your Grace," she said. "To what do I owe the pleasure?"

The duchess frowned. "My husband is a friend of the Duke of Sawbridge. I understand Sawbridge was a friend of your late husband? I brought this for you."

She held out a package, her hand trembling.

Surely the duchess wasn't *nervous*?

Mimi took the package and opened it. Nestled together among thin sheets of paper were a number of sweets fashioned into flowers, in delicate shades of orange and pink.

"Marzipan," Mimi whispered.

Her stomach clenched as a distant memory crawled to the surface of her mind—her nine-year-old self creeping down the stairs, drawn to the sound of voices and laughter, her parents' drawing room filled with bright colors, silken gowns, and the soft music of Bach—and a lady with gray hair and kind eyes who glided across the room to present her with a piece of marzipan, holding her finger to her lips.

She bit her lip to shatter the memory.

"Forgive me," her guest said. "Do you like marzipan?"

Mimi's mouth watered at the prospect of tasting the sweets. "It's been a long time," she said. "Would you like tea?"

"No thank you."

"Of course. I'm sorry, I should have realized."

"Realized what?"

"That you wouldn't be disposed to"—Mimi gestured about the parlor—"with me, at least. Thank you for the marzipan. Please don't feel obliged to stay. You're welcome, of course, but I understand a woman of your rank would—"

The duchess let out a sigh. "Forgive me. I find myself uncomfortable paying calls. I meant no offense earlier. I would like tea, but I'm rather particular about how I take it—with honey and cinnamon." The duchess lowered her gaze for a moment, before lifting it again, a flicker of pain in her eyes. "My husband always tells me to make clear my preferences, but it seems so uncivil to make such demands."

"I see no incivility in you, Your Grace," Mimi said. "Charles, do we have any cinnamon?"

"I don't know what that is, ma'am," the footman said. "I can ask Mrs. Brennan."

The duchess smiled at him. "Thank you, young man," she said. "It's a powdered spice—brown in color, with a warm, slightly sweet aroma. But if your cook has none, I'll be content with just honey."

The footman bowed, then disappeared. Mimi gestured to a seat, and the duchess took it, her gaze wandering about the room.

"Forgive me if I'm intruding," she said. "Your... I mean... The duke said you were newly arrived in town. I thought you might want to widen your acquaintance."

She shifted in her seat, seeming almost as uncomfortable as Mimi.

"Of course, you may have your own friends here, Lady Rex," she added.

"I have no friends," Mimi said.

"Do you want to widen your acquaintance?"

Mimi shrugged. "Doesn't everyone in Society?"

The duchess smiled, a silvery light sparkling in her eyes. "Not necessarily. I am not always fond of company."

"Yet you're here, paying me a visit," Mimi said. "Did Sawbridge send you?"

"Heavens no!" The duchess laughed. "He was most keen that I *not* come, though he tried to hide it."

"Then why did you come?"

"Perhaps because of his reluctance. And I'm not fond of mysteries."

Mimi's gut twisted in apprehension. Was this woman with the soul-searching eyes going to unearth her secret before her tenure as Lady Rex had even begun?

"I'm not a gossip," the duchess continued, "but I found myself asking why Sawbridge saw fit to find you a house in London, but disliked the notion of your having visitors. I'm happy to leave you in peace, of course, but I wasn't about to be dictated to by a profligate such as he. I… Oh! I didn't mean to impugn him, of course."

Mimi suppressed a laugh. "I didn't expect a duchess to be so frank."

"I'm not what a duchess ought to be. Many ladies will feel themselves obliged to tell you exactly that."

"Such as the Honorable Sarah Francis," Mimi said.

The duchess's eyes widened. "So you *do* have some acquaintance in London."

"Not really. I had the misfortune of meeting her this morning."

"Misfortune indeed," the duchess said. "Doubly so if she had Elizabeth De Witt with her—those two seem to be permanently joined to each other, always trying to outdo each other with their wardrobes. I swear I've never seen Miss Francis wear the same gown twice—such a waste of good silk."

"To be worn only once?"

"No—to be worn by her," the duchess said. "Tell me, where did you meet her?"

Mimi averted her gaze. "At a modiste's."

"Madame Deliet's, on St. James? Perhaps you patronize her." The duchess's gaze trailed over Mimi's gown, and she frowned. "Or perhaps not."

"Why do you think not?" Mimi asked, her voice tight.

"Because Madame Deliet is a frightful snob," came the reply. "My papa can't stand her, but he's obliged to conduct business with her. A man in trade cannot afford to be too choosy when it comes to his clients."

"Your father's in trade?"

"He's a silk merchant. Someone's bound to tell you that at some point. I'd rather you heard it from me. I trust you're not offended."

Mimi frowned. Why was this woman—this stranger—telling her such things? Weren't ladies supposed to confine the topic of conversation to the weather?

"Forgive me, I see I'm being overly frank. A fault of mine, I'm afraid. My husband, indulgent though he is, often chides me for it." She gestured toward the pianoforte. "Do you play?"

"I played a little Bach as a child," Mimi said, "but I lacked the talent. My mother…"

She shook her head, fighting the swell of sorrow that threatened to break through the armor she'd fashioned around her heart.

"It matters not. I have no sheet music with me."

At that moment, Charles returned with a tray laden with tea things. He set it on a table, then issued a stiff bow.

"Thank you, Charles," Mimi said, smiling at the young man. "Did Mrs. Brennan have any cinnamon for my guest?"

"Yes, ma'am, it's just there." He gestured to a small porcelain dish next to a bowl of glistening honey, then he bowed once more and retreated.

Mimi rose and saw to the tea, pouring the brown liquid into two cups and then, at the duchess's direction, tipping a spoonful each of cinnamon and honey into her cup, inhaling the exotic scent. She smiled to herself. The aroma reminded her of Christmas, of long nights beside a log fire, of warmth and comfort—of days long gone.

Then she handed the cup to her guest. Her hand shook, and a splash of tea spilled onto the duchess's gown.

"Oh!" Mimi cried, "I'm so sorry—what must you think of me?"

The duchess took the cup. "I think you're a very obliging hostess, willing to cater to her guest's eccentricities."

"But your gown—I've ruined it."

"Nonsense!" The duchess laughed. "The benefit of having a father who's a silk merchant is that he knows how to clean a gown better than any lady's maid—though my Harriet would be most put out if she heard me say so."

"But it's such a beautiful silk," Mimi said. "I've never seen anything so…" Her voice trailed off, and she retreated to pour her own tea. What must the duchess think of her—staring at her gown with envious eyes before pouring tea all over it?

The duchess glanced at Mimi's gown, a thoughtful expression in her eyes. "Who *is* your modiste?" she asked. "My father supplies a particular silk that would do very well for you. I could have him send her a bolt—or would that be terribly forward of me?"

Mimi averted her gaze to the window. "I have no modiste." She sipped her tea, wincing as the hot liquid burned her lips, and awaited the condescension of a superior being.

"Oh?"

"The duke instructed me to visit Madame Deliet, but she refused to serve me then evicted me from her premises."

"Under the spiteful gaze of Sarah Francis and Elizabeth De Witt?"

Mimi nodded, and her teacup clattered against the saucer as

her hand trembled.

"You make me quite ashamed," the duchess said, at length. "If you need a modiste, I can recommend mine. Madame Dupont is less…"

"Less discerning?" Mimi said bitterly.

"Less *spiteful*."

"You're very kind, but I have no wish to visit a modiste's shop again," Mimi said. "I've engaged a dressmaker who seems capable, and I'd rather patronize someone based on merit than their position in Society."

"Bravo!" the duchess said. "You must permit me to send her a bolt of silk for your gowns."

Mimi glanced at the duchess's gown—the smooth, exquisitely colored silk—fighting to conquer her longing.

"I-I'm sorry, Your Grace," she said. "I couldn't accept charity."

The duchess frowned. "It's not charity," she said, and Mimi almost detected a hint of shyness in her voice. "I'd like to think it a gift—from a friend."

"Y-you consider me a friend?"

"You have endured my company today—a guest uninvited"—she gestured to the dish of cinnamon—"acceded to my demands, and weathered my foibles. Is that not the mark of a friend?"

She leaned forward, fixing her emerald gaze on Mimi.

"I know what it's like to be an outsider—a misfit." She made a dismissive gesture. "Oh, I understand that most admire my rank. But my rank belongs to my husband. Any deference is due to him and him alone. But as to my essence—what truly defines me as *me*—I'm as much an outsider in Society as a…"

"As a doxy masquerading as the widow of a knight?"

The duchess's eyes narrowed, but to her credit, she gave no sign of disgust. She merely nodded.

"I see no doxy," she said, "just as I hope you don't merely see a duchess. I think you and I are capable of looking beneath the façade and appreciating the person inside." She rose. "Forgive me—I've a rather unfortunate habit of talking too much on some subjects, and not at all on others. I've trespassed too much on your time already, and will bid you good day. If you are not averse to it, I should like to call on you again—and you are of course welcome to visit me at any time. I've left my card in your hallway."

She offered her hand, and for a moment, Mimi stared at it. Then, trembling, she took it, and the duchess curled her long, lean fingers over Mimi's.

"Thank you, Duchess," Mimi said. "I would be delighted."

The duchess smiled, and her dark gaze filled with light, as if the sun had emerged from behind a thundercloud. Mimi understood what must have captivated the duchess's husband— she had never seen such intensity of warmth and intelligence in another creature.

"Call me Eleanor," the duchess said.

"And call me Jemima," Mimi said, before she could stop herself. Then she caught her breath. "Oh—I-I didn't mean to say… I mean—nobody calls me *Jemima*. I'm known as Mimi—*he* calls me Mimi."

Eleanor nodded, understanding in her eyes. There was no need to explain who *he* was.

"You can trust me with your name," she said. "May I, in turn, give you some advice?"

Mimi nodded.

"Guard your heart, Jemima," Eleanor said. "I know the pain of loving another with no guarantee of that love being returned. I must respect Sawbridge as my husband's friend, but—due to an unfortunate incident—his reputation is not favorable."

"I know," Mimi said.

"Then I trust you stand to gain as much as he will from your…relationship. I fear that he sees women as disposable commodities."

"Doesn't every man?"

"There are a few notable exceptions," Eleanor said, "but the greatest mistake a woman can make is to assume that a heart lies within the body of the rakehell—only to discover the truth when it's too late. I only counsel you because when the truth is revealed, it's the woman who pays the price."

"I know," Mimi said, "and it's a price I have never been willing to pay."

"Then I wish you success," Eleanor replied. She let out a soft laugh. "Perhaps now you understand why Sawbridge was reluctant for me to visit you."

"Nevertheless, I'm very glad you came."

"So am I."

Mimi escorted the duchess out. Then, on impulse, she embraced her new friend before Eleanor climbed into the waiting carriage.

CHAPTER ELEVEN

Before Alexander reached the top of the front steps, the door to number 16 Grosvenor Square opened.

"Ah, Wheeler, isn't it?" he said to the black-clad butler. "Is Lady Rex receiving visitors?"

"Naturally, sir."

The butler's expression revealed little, but Alexander could swear he caught an undercurrent of disdain. Butlers were a different breed—they considered themselves the ultimate guardians of etiquette, even greater champions of propriety than the people they served.

Even dukes.

"You'll find her in the parlor, Your Grace."

"Lead the way, then," Alexander said. "Though I'm paying for this house, this is the first time I've set foot in it."

The butler rolled his eyes, then he escorted Alexander to a door, knocked, and opened it.

"His Grace, the Duke of Sawbridge," he said, his tone almost apologetic.

Alexander heard a soft "Oh," then he entered the parlor. Mimi stood, with another woman, beside a table laden with fabric and ribbons.

His blood surged with want as his gaze slid over Mimi's delectable form. She stared back at him, apprehension in her soft brown eyes, then dipped into a curtsey.

"Your Grace, I wasn't expecting you today."

"*Weren't* you?"

She colored, then addressed her companion. "Peg, have you everything you need?"

"Yes, ma'am."

"Excellent. Perhaps you'd like to take tea with your cousin before leaving?"

"Yes, thank you, ma'am." The companion gathered the cloths and ribbons, then exited the parlor.

Alexander approached Mimi and held out his hands. After a pause, she took them, and the apprehension in her eyes disappeared, replaced by the hard smile of the doxy.

"Welcome, Your Grace," she said brightly.

She played her part well. Why, then, did he find it so infuriating? Couldn't she give him a little of the softness he'd glimpsed before? He was paying her enough to please him.

He glanced at her dress. "I see you have a new gown, though it doesn't look to be up to Madame Deliet's usual standard."

Her smile slipped.

"It's not a new gown," she said. "I had it altered to fit while my gowns are being made."

"You've been here almost a week," he replied. "Hasn't Madame Deliet finished even one gown? I'm anxious to take you out."

"Are you?" A flare of hope shimmered in her eyes.

"I want to get my money's worth."

The hope faded. "How very prudent of you."

"Prudence is overrated," he said. "Madame Deliet's intelligent enough to understand that if she works quickly, she can command a higher fee. She knows I always pay well for my...possessions."

She flinched—almost imperceptibly, but enough to confirm that his arrow had hit home.

"If a man is foolish enough to pay over the odds for the goods, then that's his loss," she said.

"Or gain," he replied, "if the gowns are delectable enough. I trust Madame won't let me down."

"I'm sorry to disappoint you," she said. "Madame Deliet isn't making my gowns. She refused to serve me."

"She *refused*?" He shook his head. "That woman would serve anyone if there's a profit to be had."

"Evidently not *anyone*."

"Well, there goes my reputation if even *she* won't deal with me," Alexander said.

She let out a snort. "*Your* reputation is intact," she said. "You're a fool if you think Society will shun you forever—your title and wealth will win them over no matter how heinous your crimes. Perhaps, when asking yourself why Madame evicted me from her shop, you should consider how Society views a *woman*, rather than a man."

"What did you say to her about me?" he asked.

"Nothing."

Defiance flashed in her eyes, and a fizz of need went straight to his groin. He pulled her close and parted his lips for a kiss, but she withdrew and approached the fireplace.

"What are you doing?" he asked.

"Ringing the bell for tea."

"I didn't come here to *take tea*."

She stiffened, then turned to face him, and cold fingers clenched at his stomach at the darkness in her eyes as she lowered her gaze to the bulge in his breeches.

"Where do you want me?" she asked.

"In the bedroom."

"Very well."

She crossed the floor, stopping to retrieve a ribbon from the floor, then stood before him, the slight tremor in her body the only evidence of emotion.

"Would you like your whore naked, my lord—or would you prefer to strip her yourself?"

A sharp intake of breath came from the doorway, and Alexander turned to see the butler, together with a footman who looked barely old enough to be out of leading strings. The footman blushed scarlet, while the butler merely arched an eyebrow.

Alexander opened his mouth to reply, but shame tightened his throat—shame at being overheard, and at having exposed her to the contempt of her servants.

"Struggling to choose, Your Grace?" she sneered. "Then let me surprise you. But next time you must tell me what you prefer. I'm anxious to earn my fee."

Her head held high as if she were the duchess and he the basest creature on earth, she swept past him. The servants parted to let her through the doorway.

"Ma'am, if there's anything you need…" the butler began.

"No thank you, Wheeler. I can see to myself. Please tend to His Grace. Give him anything he requires before he"—her voice wavered—"visits me upstairs."

She exited the parlor, leaving Alexander with the two servants.

"Fetch me a brandy," he said.

"Yes, Your Grace," the footman replied, but the butler placed a hand on the youth's shoulder.

"No, Charles," he said, meeting Alexander's gaze. "*I'll* do it."

This time there was no mistaking the butler's disdain, or to whom it was directed.

By the time Wheeler returned, Alexander's guilt no longer needled at him—it sliced through his heart with vicious strokes, like an angry duelist at dawn.

"Your brandy, Your Grace."

Alexander took the proffered glass and drained it, letting the acrid liquid tear into his senses. But it didn't numb the guilt.

"Another?" the butler asked.

"No," Alexander said. "Forgive me."

"What for?"

Alexander sighed. "I think you know what for."

"In which case, sir, might I suggest it's not *my* forgiveness you require."

"Ought a butler speak to his master thus?"

"Perhaps not, sir—but though you told Lady Rex just now that prudence is overrated, every butler knows that *propriety* is not."

Bloody hell—it was almost like being back at Eton standing in front of his housemaster, awaiting a caning for some transgression.

But perhaps a bloody good caning was needed, given the transgression he'd committed—six of the best, trousers down.

I really am an utter bastard.

By rights he should slink back to his house with his tail between his legs. But that was the choice of the coward. The least he could do was face her—match her courage and dignity.

After dismissing the butler, he made his way up the stairs, approached the nearest door, and pushed it open.

The chamber was furnished in soft shades of blue and yellow—a bed beside the window, with a two-seater sofa beside the fireplace, a table beside the window bearing a vase of flowers, and a dressing table opposite the bed. The simplicity of the interior gave it a spacious air—room to breathe. Sunlight streamed into the room from a tall sash window, illuminating the vase of flowers, rendering the petals luminescent. He approached the vase and traced the soft, cool edge of a petal with his fingers.

The dressing table was bare, save a hairbrush and a bottle of cologne—hardly the tools of a doxy's trade. Suppressing his guilt at the intrusion, he picked up the bottle and held it to his nose, inhaling the scent of rose.

This was her bedchamber—but she was nowhere to be seen.

Feeling guilty at having invaded her privacy, he slipped out and clicked the door shut.

He opened the next door along—and caught his breath.

The room was darker, furnished with thick velvet that absorbed the light and stifled the senses. The curtains were drawn, blocking out the sunlight, but two candles at either end of the mantelshelf cast an orange glow that picked out the shapes of the armchairs beside the fireplace, the vases either side of the window…

…and the naked woman on the bed.

"At last, he comes." She raised her hand and beckoned.

"What are you doing, Mimi?" he asked.

"Fulfilling my part of the bargain. After all, you're not here to *take tea.*"

He approached the bed. "Mimi, I—"

"Hush, Your Grace." She slid off the bed and placed a finger on his lips. Then she dropped to her knees and undid the buttons on his breeches. A rush of heat coursed through his veins as she slipped her hand inside and circled his already stiffening manhood.

Sweet heaven! Closing his eyes, he tipped his head back, relishing the touch of her hand as she slid it along his length.

"That's it, my lord," she whispered, her voice low and hoarse. "Your pleasure awaits."

He opened his eyes and almost spent at the sight of her ready to service him. Her eyes glittered in the candlelight, their expression soulless and cruel. She curled her lip into a smile and ran the tip of her tongue along her teeth.

Then she reached for him and parted her lips.

"No!" Struggling to conquer the lust raging through him, he pushed her back. Undeterred, she rose, took his hand, and led him to the bed, where she pushed him onto his back. Before he could sit up, she climbed on top of him.

"Mimi, I… Oh!" He let out a groan as she grasped his cock and guided him inside her. Defeated, he succumbed to desire. Tiny stars pulsed in his mind as she shifted her body back and forth, then she increased the pace, and the tide swelled, bringing him to the brink of completion. "Slow down," he rasped. "I—"

She thrust forward, her breath coming in sharp, angry puffs. Then his mind exploded, the stars bursting to life as pleasure ripped through him, until he cried out her name and fell back, his heart pounding against his chest, as if it yearned to be free.

He tried to move, but his spent body refused to obey, so he lay back, relishing the aftershocks of his climax. But as pleasure faded and he floated back to reality, he found himself overcome by shame and disgust.

Disgust at himself.

He felt like a cheap whore—which was precisely how he'd treated her.

By the time he could sit up, Mimi had moved her lithe body to one of the chairs, leaning back casually, one leg draped over the arm, her body exposed to him—as if she wished to taunt him and his cruelty.

His fingers trembling with shame, he buttoned his breeches and smoothed down the front. Then he plucked the blanket from the bed, approached the woman on the chair, and draped it around her shoulders. Her eyes widened, then she gathered the blanket around her body.

"Forgive me," he whispered.

"There's nothing to forgive," she said tonelessly.

He held out his hand. "Perhaps…" He hesitated. "Perhaps we might take tea now."

She glanced up at him, her eyes bright with moisture, and for a moment, his heart fluttered with hope.

Then she shook her head.

"Leave the money on the desk in the hallway. A sovereign should cover my expenses."

Pain stabbed his heart at her words. "Mimi, don't say that."

"Why not?" she said. "We've made a business agreement, which includes the payment of disbursements, and I must settle the account with the dressmaker. If you dealt with her yourself, it might raise questions that you wouldn't care to ask."

"At least take tea with me," he said, aware of the plea in his voice.

"Tea is what friends do," she said. "You're not paying me to be your friend. You're paying me to give you pleasure, and to parade about London on your arm to improve your reputation so that in the future you will be able to pursue better women than me. Have I missed anything?"

"Aren't *you* in need of a friend?" he asked.

"I have all the friends I need."

A spike of envy pricked at his heart. "Did the Duchess of Whitcombe visit you?"

She let out a low laugh. "Jealous, are you? Would you rather I hid myself away and paid attention to none but you?"

She stood, holding the blanket tight around her form, and he reached toward her, unable to fight the need to take her in his arms.

"Mimi, I—"

"Please," she said, her voice wavering. "Go. I need to bathe."

"Can't we take tea, at least?"

She let out a sigh. "Very well. I am at your disposal."

"No, you're not, you're…"

"We both know what I am," she said. "If you want to take tea with me, then I shall comply. Everything in this house belongs to you."

He shook his head. "I don't want to take tea with you, Mimi. I want you to *want* to take tea with me—to take pleasure from it."

Sadness gleamed in her eyes. "Then you should have stipulated that in our agreement, Your Grace. My pleasure is not for sale."

Unable to think of a reply that didn't expose himself as even more of a cad, he nodded and withdrew from the chamber. As he descended the stairs, he almost collided with the young footman.

"Charles, isn't it?" Alexander asked.

"Yes, Your Grace."

"I'm leaving now, but your mistress might appreciate a bath."

The footman nodded, flushing scarlet as he glanced at Alexander's crumpled breeches, before showing him outside. Once on the pavement, Alexander turned back toward the building, his gaze settling on the upper-floor window with its curtains still drawn.

Everything in this house belongs to you.

"No, Mimi," he whispered. "Not everything."

Hunching his shoulders against the wind, he crossed the square and returned to his townhouse. How many times had he slipped out of the home of a mistress, or a paramour, after a session of glorious rutting, having patted her on the rump and tipped a coin in a dish as payment, returning home to congratulate himself on his prowess?

What made this time so different? Why did he, for the first time, feel nothing but shame?

CHAPTER TWELVE

"OH, JEMIMA, THAT color on you is glorious!"

Mimi turned one way, then another, admiring how the colors in her skirts rippled in the light. She glanced across the parlor at her guest. "Your Grace, I—"

"*Eleanor*, please."

"Eleanor, I cannot thank you enough," Mimi said, "and you, Peg, of course."

The seamstress looked up from stitching the hem. "My pleasure, Lady Rex. I've never worked with such fine material. I hope I've been able to do right by it."

"Of course you have," Eleanor said. "I doubt even my modiste could produce something so fine—the quality of your stitching, and that bead work... I do hope you haven't strained your eyes."

"No, Your Grace, that's very kind of you to ask," Peg said, reaching for a pair of scissors. She snipped the thread, then stood back to survey her handiwork. "There! That's all done."

Mimi's wardrobe was now complete—three day dresses with matching redingotes and reticules, two evening gowns, and a fur-trimmed cloak. It was almost enough to make her believe she could be a lady again.

Would *he* like them—or would he be disappointed that they hadn't been fashioned by the modiste who catered to all his other women?

The seamstress helped Mimi out of her gown, then folded it and set it aside.

"I must settle your account, Peg," Mimi said as she pulled the bell cord by the fireplace.

"It's already done," came the reply. "Mr. Wheeler settled it yesterday."

Or rather, the Duke of Sawbridge had settled it yesterday.

"I'd best get going," Peg said. "I mustn't take up any more of your time."

"You can take tea with your cousin if you wish," Mimi suggested.

"May I?"

The door opened and the young footman appeared.

"Charles," Mimi said, "could you bring the duchess and I some tea? And tell Mrs. Hodge she can take her tea with Peg—you can join them if you wish. Ask the cook to set aside some of that delicious fruitcake—if you've not already finished it yourself, of course."

The footman blushed, then bowed and disappeared, while Peg folded the rest of the gowns.

"I can do that," Mimi said. "You go and see your cousin."

The seamstress bobbed a curtsey and followed the footman out.

Mimi sat beside Eleanor and leaned back with a sigh. "I never realized how difficult it was to stand and do nothing—though, of course, it's not as difficult as kneeling at someone's feet and embroidering a hem."

"I can't think why you don't have a lady's maid," Eleanor said.

"I can carry my own gowns upstairs," Mimi replied. "Besides, I see little point in hiring someone for only a short while."

"You'll be giving someone employment. That can only be a good thing."

"But I know how to dress myself. Why hire someone to do it for me?"

"Because it gives a young girl work when she'd otherwise starve. Besides, the right lady's maid does so much more than dress her employer in the morning and undress her at night. She's a companion, a confidante—a friend."

"I'd rather not grow reliant on another," Mimi said, "not for dressing myself, and certainly not for companionship."

"That's a bleak approach to life."

"But practical, for a woman in my position."

Eleanor lowered her gaze. "Of course. I'm sorry, Jemima. I forget that not everyone is as fortunate as I."

Nobody was as fortunate as Eleanor—a duchess both loved and respected by her husband.

Whereas I…

Mimi shuddered at the memory. Since the day Sawbridge had ordered her upstairs and taken his pleasure, he had visited her twice. But he hadn't required the use of her body. He had merely taken tea and reeled off a list of the acquaintances he was going to introduce her to, and the parties to which they'd been invited. Almost as if he were trying to impress her.

But he had already shown his true nature—in the rasp of his voice when he ordered her upstairs to *fulfil her duties*. And then the laughable way he'd tried to atone for his behavior after he finished inside her, draping the blanket over her naked form—as though he cared for her.

As if she'd fall for *that* ruse! Many a customer had acted the gallant suitor to ease his guilt. And that's what Sawbridge was— just another customer wanting to use her body. She needed to remind herself of that if she were to survive.

She jumped as a hand covered hers.

"Jemima? Are you well?"

"Yes, Eleanor, I'm quite well."

"Forgive me. I didn't mean to be so forward about employing a lady's maid."

"Perhaps you're right," Mimi said. "Rather than see it as someone indulging in a luxury merely because they can afford it, you've painted a very different picture—a means to an end, which I wish to strive for."

"Which is?"

"The empowerment of women."

Eleanor's eyebrows lifted.

"You find such a concept ridiculous?" Mimi asked.

"Astonishing, perhaps, but not ridiculous."

"I'm not so foolish as to believe I can change the whole world, but I wish to make a difference where I can."

"Is that what you're doing here—with Sawbridge?"

Mimi flinched at the undercurrent of judgment in her friend's tone.

"I know what you must think of me, Eleanor," she said.

"Do you?" The duchess leaned forward, her eyes darkening into that peculiarly intense expression that stripped a person's soul bare.

"Outwardly I'm the respectable Lady Rex, newly arrived in town and living off my late husband's annuity, but you see what I am—a rake's whore whose tenure in this house will be short-lived."

Eleanor colored and leaned back.

"You were right to warn me to guard my heart," Mimi continued, "but you had no need. I have long ago preserved my heart behind a doxy's armor. I have used my body to earn my living for the past five years. But now, at last, I can do so with a purpose. When I have fulfilled my duty here, then I shall be free to go elsewhere to fulfil my dream."

"Which is?"

"To live a life of peace and tranquility in my own little corner of the world—where I am mistress of my own fate, not a man's whims, and where I can, in my own small way, ease the suffering of others. If I can prevent even one woman from enduring the same fate as—"

She broke off as Charles entered with the tea things. After he left, she poured the tea, spooning in Eleanor's cinnamon and honey.

The duchess took a sip. "Delicious. Have you not been tempted to try it with cinnamon?"

"Cinnamon is expensive," Mimi said. "I cannot afford to accustom myself to such luxuries."

"Because once you've occupied your—what was it?—little corner of the world, you may not have the means?"

"I must take a practical approach to my livelihood, particularly if I intend to help others."

"And do you intend to help others?"

Mimi nodded. "There are some I give a little help to now—women who, through no fault of their own, are vilified and shunned. I may not have always had the financial means to help them, but I have time at my disposal—at least when I'm not required to…"

When I'm not required to service him.

Eleanor nodded. "I understand."

Doubtless she did—insightful as she was.

And yet she's willing to associate with me.

"I should like to introduce you to my sister," Eleanor said.

Mimi glanced up. "No, I-I couldn't."

"Why not?"

"She might not accept me."

"Anyone in Society should be pleased to acquaint themselves with Lady Rex."

"But I'm not Lady Rex—you noticed that at our first meeting."

"You *are* Lady Rex. But, in any case, my sister has particular reason to understand your circumstances if you see fit to tell her."

"Your sister?" Mimi asked.

"She was betrayed, and suffered because of it. But it's not my story to tell. Juliette is happy now—as happy as I'd wish *you* to be. And, if you wish to help women in unfortunate circumstances, I can think of none better to assist you in your quest."

"I cannot impose on others."

"You don't have to do everything on your own," Eleanor said, "if you can find someone in whom you can place your trust." She reached for the basket she'd brought. "Might I ask a favor?"

Mimi held her breath. Eleanor meant well, but Mimi couldn't bear the thought of receiving more visitors—ladies to turn their noses up at her, asking questions about her lineage, about the fictional Sir John Rex.

"Would you permit me to draw your likeness?" Eleanor asked.

"I-I don't understand."

Eleanor pulled out two books from her basket and flicked through one—a sketchbook, filled with sketches of trees, tree stumps, and portraits. She stopped at a page and ran her fingertips over it to trace the outline of the face depicted there—a strong face with a firm jaw, straight nose, high forehead, and full, sensual lips, framed by a mane of thick, dark hair. Despite the savage strength of his features, the subject stared out from the page with an expression tender enough to melt the hardest of hearts.

Eleanor let out a sigh.

"Is that…?"

"My husband," the duchess said. "Montague was kind enough to sit for me last week, shortly after we…" She blushed. "It's how *I* see him. He doesn't always resemble his portrait—which you'll see when you meet him. He has a rather stern countenance—I confess, I was a little afraid of him at first."

Mimi stared at the portrait. Anyone would wither under the intensity of that gaze. Doubtless, the tenderness in his eyes was something he gifted only to his wife.

It was the portrait of a man in love.

Eleanor turned to a blank page. Then she pulled a pencil out of her reticule and looked up at Mimi. "Would it be an imposition to add you to my collection?"

Mimi hesitated. Whom would Eleanor depict? Would she draw the doxy, the deceiver masquerading as someone above her station? Or would she draw the bitter, heartbroken creature that Mimi concealed within?

But she couldn't afford to hurt Eleanor's feelings, no matter how little she desired to be imprisoned by her pencil. The duchess had befriended her, gifted her with sweets and her father's silks.

Perhaps that was the mark of true friendship—doing something she didn't like, to please someone she did.

Eleanor picked up the second book. "I thought, perhaps, if I gifted you this, you might be disposed to sit for me."

Mimi glanced at the book. "*Das Wohltemperirte Clavier* by Bach."

"I know little about music, but my sister Lady Radham assured me that these pieces are within the capabilities of most. I thought you might like to play them, and I recall your saying you had no music. The book's somewhat careworn, I'm afraid."

Mimi took the book and turned it over in her hands. The pages were yellowing at the edges and there was a tear in the back cover. But its value was not in the condition of the pages—it was in the fact that someone had noted her love of Bach and sought this out as a gift for her.

It wasn't the action of a duchess. It was the action of a friend.

Mimi blinked, and moisture stung her eyes.

"Oh, forgive me!" Eleanor said. "I had no right to ask you to sit for me if you don't wish to."

Mimi set the music aside and smiled at her friend. "It would be my pleasure."

"Excellent!" Eleanor said. "I'm afraid I'm not good at knowing how to ask for favors, but my husband encourages me to just tell people what I want. But I can only ask those whom I trust not to judge me for my awkwardness."

What a strange creature the duchess was—strange enough that a woman of her station would bother with Mimi at all, but Eleanor often seemed ill at ease in her surroundings. Mimi had at first assumed she was uncomfortable because she considered a doxy beneath her. But Eleanor's frank confessions about her feelings spoke of something else—that she was in greater need of friendship than anyone.

Mimi reached for her teacup then hesitated. "Do you wish me to sit still?"

Eleanor shook her head, her pencil already moving across the page. "No need," she said. "I want to depict *you*. I despise those portraits where the subject was told to pose for the artist. You're a living, breathing woman—not a statue. Now, ignore my pencil, and tell me about your plans to help the disadvantaged women of the world."

Mimi took her teacup and relaxed into her chair. At first, she watched Eleanor's pencil, then found herself ignoring it. The duchess continued the conversation, her gaze only occasionally flicking toward the page.

At length, Eleanor paused and stretched her hands, her knuckles cracking. Then she held the sketch at arm's length.

"May I see?" Mimi asked.

Eleanor revealed the page, and Mimi caught her breath.

The woman staring back at her had delicate, elfin features and wide, expressive eyes. Her hair framed her face in gentle waves, with stray wisps softening the outline. Her mouth was unsmiling, and her face betrayed no emotion, except her eyes, which revealed a deep yearning.

It was as if she were staring at her true self, stripped bare.

"It's—" Mimi broke off.

"It's how I see you," Eleanor said. "Most subjects want me to depict them as they wish to be seen, not as I see them."

"And you didn't think to depict me as I wish to be seen?"

"You'll be doing that yourself when you enter Society," Eleanor said. "Your new gowns will depict you as a lady, to be admired by all—and you *shall* be admired. But I wanted to capture the woman I've come to know."

"You know me after so short an acquaintance?" Mimi asked.

"A brief acquaintance doesn't necessarily mean a lack of understanding of another person," Eleanor said. "I have known the

Honorable Sarah Francis for at least two years, and I confess I have no more understanding of her than I had the day I was first subjected to her company. In fact, I believe I understand her less. Whereas you…"

She set the sketchbook aside.

"In you, I saw a like mind. And no matter what happens, or where you find yourself, once your…*business* is concluded here, I hope we can remain friends."

Mimi lowered her gaze, and Eleanor let out a sigh.

"He must have betrayed you so badly, to have destroyed your faith."

"My faith in men?" Mimi asked.

Eleanor shook her head. "Your faith in the world—and in yourself."

"The Duke of Sawbridge and I have an arrangement, that's all," Mimi said. "We are, to each other, just a means to an end."

Eleanor shook her head. "I didn't mean the duke. I meant whoever betrayed you before—the man who drove you into this life."

"How did you…?"

"I see it in your eyes, Jemima—the scars of treachery," Eleanor said. "What did he do?"

Mimi let out a sigh. "He died."

"Did you love him?"

"In my own way, I did," Mimi said. "He understood that. But…"

"But, like all men, he didn't understand the plight of women in our world," Eleanor said. "He believed in his immortality rather than the necessity for practicality." She tilted her head to one side. "Do you fear recognition?"

"No," Mimi said. "I've never lived in this part of London. When I was his—" She broke off, her cheeks warming. "I-I lived in Brighton."

"And his family?"

"They wouldn't recognize me," Mimi said. "I met his heir

only a few times, and…" She swallowed the memory of the pain and loss—the grief for two lives. "I am much changed now."

Outside the parlor, a clock struck four times, and Eleanor rose. "Forgive me—I'd quite lost track of time. My husband's expecting me. We have guests for dinner."

Mimi rose and found herself pulled into an embrace.

"I meant what I said," Eleanor whispered. "I am your friend. And, for what it's worth, Sawbridge is a fool for not appreciating what he has. Our world here is the better for having you in it, and don't let anyone say otherwise. You will find someone to deserve you, Jemima."

Mimi smiled at her friend's conviction.

"It matters not if I don't," she said. "I'd rather be alone than dependent on someone who doesn't love me."

"Very good," Eleanor said, releasing Mimi and tucking a stray curl behind her ear. "Then you are safe from heartbreak. Now, take my advice—summon your housekeeper and tell her to hire a lady's maid."

After Mimi escorted her friend outside, she rang the bell for Mrs. Hodge.

She might never be able to change the entire world—but she could make a difference for one person in her little corner of it.

CHAPTER THIRTEEN

After glancing over her shoulder to ensure she was alone, and unobserved, Mimi approached the tiny house and knocked on the door.

It opened to reveal a thin woman with jet-black hair peppered with gray. Her wrinkled face creased into a gap-toothed smile.

"Oh, Mimi darlin', you don't know how wonderful it is to see you again!" She pulled Mimi into an embrace, then ushered her inside. "I was worried something had happened to you. Not that we always expect you to come—we're right grateful for anything you do for us."

"Forgive me for not coming sooner, Mrs. Briggs," Mimi said. The other woman arched an eyebrow, and Mimi bit her lip, cursing her lapse in accent. Since she'd moved into Grosvenor Square, she had accustomed herself to speaking in the accent she'd grown up with, and the accent of the slums—the harsh, flat vowels of the street whore—were all but forgotten.

"You sound different, love," Mrs. Briggs said. "What's happened?" She gestured toward Mimi's cloak. "I've not seen anything that fine on you before. Got yerself a protector? I thought you'd sworn never to depend on a man again." Then she shook her head. "I always knew you weren't what you seemed. It was the way you carried yerself. I said to myself, you're no ordinary whore."

"But I'm a whore nonetheless," Mimi said.

"Only if you let yerself be defined by how you earn a living." Mrs. Briggs pressed her hand to her chest. "It's what's inside *here* that defines what you are. I hope yer protector treats you like a lady."

"I have no protector, Mrs. Briggs," Mimi said. "But my fortunes have taken a turn for the better."

Mrs. Briggs shook her head. "Many a young woman in your position has said the same."

"But they *have*," Mimi said, taking Mrs. Briggs's hand. "I've secured a small stipend for the next six months, with a cash sum at the end. It'll be enough to set me up so that I never have to sell my body again."

Mrs. Briggs tutted. "And you've fallen for it? Girl, I thought you were smarter than that. If a man pays you a stipend, then you're his mistress."

"We've agreed to part company next summer," Mimi said. "As to the payment, he showed me a letter that his banker has signed as guarantor. Do you know what that means?"

Mrs. Briggs shook her head.

"It means I can give you more than I ever have before," Mimi said. "I can buy a house, away from London—in the country, where the air is clean. Think of that!"

"Mimi, darlin', you can't rely on this man—whoever he is."

"I don't intend to *rely* on him, Mrs. Briggs—that's the point. When our business is concluded, I'll be free. There should be enough for me to find somewhere for you—and for the girls here."

"Mimi, darlin', there's no need."

"There's every need," Mimi said. "You took me in when I had nowhere to go."

"You've paid me back a hundredfold with everything you've done for us. We're content with what we have—we're luckier than some."

"But what if I found you a home in the country?" Mimi asked. "Somewhere for you and the women here? I could set up a school—teach the girls skills so they can find employment. Maybe even a spot of land, so you can grow your own food."

"You're a kind girl, that's for certain," Mrs. Briggs said. "You indulge your dreams if they make you happy. Now, why don't we have some tea? Anna's put the pot on to boil."

She led Mimi along the narrow corridor and into the parlor at the back, where a young woman sat in the corner, leaning back, her eyes closed, while a child crawled on the floor at her feet.

As Mimi entered, the woman opened her eyes and sat upright. She picked up the child and embraced it, her eyes widening.

"Lily, darlin', this is Mimi," Mrs. Briggs said. "Remember, I told you about Mimi? She'll not hurt you."

The woman rose to her feet and turned toward the window, and Mimi's heart ached as she noticed a darkening bruise on Lily's cheek. Her body shook with fragility and the child in her arms wailed and struggled.

Mimi stepped toward her. "I'm pleased to meet you."

Lily glanced toward Mrs. Briggs, and her trembling increased.

"Shall we leave you alone, Lily darlin'?" Mrs. Briggs asked. "Or perhaps you'd like to take your rest. Your bedchamber's empty—Mary's out working."

Lily nodded, then shuffled toward the door, her gaze fixed on Mimi. Understanding her fear, Mimi retreated toward the fireplace, enabling the other woman to exit the parlor without passing too close. Lily sidled toward the doorway, then fled, clattering up the stairs.

"Forgive her," Mrs. Briggs said. "She's frightened of strangers. She wouldn't speak a word to me for a full day after she arrived."

"What happened to her?" Mimi asked.

"Her husband was killed. Fell into the river drunk—served him right, the way he'd knocked her about. She took to the streets to support her little 'un, but her landlord threw her out when she couldn't pay the rent. Mary found her on the street after one of her customers had beaten her in front of Sam."

"Sam?"

"That's her boy, poor mite. Hardly been in the world three years and he's seen more than most of us would hope to see in a lifetime. Ah—there's Anna with the tea."

A young woman entered, carrying a tray.

"Mimi!" she cried, a smile illuminating her features. "We've not seen you for a bit. We were gettin' worried, especially after what happened to Bessie."

"Bessie?" Mimi asked, recalling the flame-haired young woman from her last visit.

"She went out four days ago," Mrs. Briggs said. "Never came home."

"She might return in time," Mimi said.

Anna let out a sob, and Mrs. Briggs shook her head. "No, darlin'," she said. "Poor Bessie was found face down in the street the next night."

"Dear Lord!" Mimi said. "How can I live with myself knowing what's happening here?" She fished inside her reticule and pulled out a handful of coins. Then she shook her head and tipped out the entire contents. "Take it," she said. "Take all of it."

"No," Mrs. Briggs said. "We cannot take all your money—only what you can afford."

"What I can afford?" Mimi said. "How can I indulge in the life I have now when I know that so many others are suffering?"

"Because you've earned it, darlin'."

Mimi shook her head. "I came there by sheer luck."

"Luck—and the lack of it—is something that we must all reconcile ourselves with, darlin'," Mrs. Briggs said. "You've had your share of bad luck, like the rest of us. Don't wallow in the bottom of the ditch merely because you feel guilty for being given a chance in life. And don't feel guilty for the life you lead merely because others have less than you."

"But how can I stand it when I see the women here?"

"None of us resent you for having more than us," Mrs. Briggs said. "If anyone does, that reflects poorly on *their* character rather than yours. You do more than enough for us."

"I can never do enough for you, Mrs. Briggs," Mimi said. "But if you'll not accept my money, then I'll help in other ways."

Mrs. Briggs took her hand and patted it. "I know you will. And I'm sure Anna has plenty for you to do in the kitchen. Isn't that right, Anna?"

"Aye, that's right, Mrs. Briggs," Anna said. "Mrs. Pickersgill sent over a bit of scrag end for a stew. You can help with that if you like—and there's a pile of mending needing doin'."

"Tea first," Mrs. Briggs said. "Then perhaps a spot of cake. But you'll only get yer cake if you get to the bottom of that pile of mending. Handing over yer coins doesn't exempt you from hard work." Her eyes sparkled with affection as she poured the tea then handed a cup to Mimi. "Anna, will Ethel and Jinny be joining us, or are they out?"

"Ethel's out, but Jinny's been inside all day—she tripped over on the street and hasn't yet recovered. She's been doin' the laundry."

"Tell her to join us, Anna darlin'. She'll scrub those hands of hers raw if she's not careful."

Anna exited the parlor, then returned with a thin woman— barely older than a girl—with pale-blonde hair and a swollen lip. She limped into the parlor and smiled at Mimi before pouring a cup of tea for herself.

Tripped over on the street.

That was the doxy's phrase for having been beaten by a customer. Mimi didn't know what was worse—Jinny's injuries, or her acceptance of them.

But everyone in the room—including Mimi herself—had sustained some injury or other at the hands of a man who either refused to pay, or who took pleasure from her pain.

Which was why it was imperative that Mimi's plan worked. These women deserved a better life. In fact, *all* women deserved a better life, but if she couldn't help every woman in England, she could at least help the women who occupied this little corner of London that had once been her sanctuary after she had lost everything.

CHAPTER FOURTEEN

A T LAST—THE DAY had come.

Alexander suppressed the pulse of excitement in his body as he knocked on the door of number 16 Grosvenor Square.

Her gowns, all bought and paid for, now awaited his viewing pleasure—and London Society.

How might she look in a lady's attire?

The butler opened the door, the usual expression of disdain on his face.

"Is she at home, Wheeler?"

"Of course, Your Grace."

The butler stepped aside, and Alexander entered the hallway.

"Please wait in the parlor. The mistress will be down directly."

"Isn't she waiting in the parlor?"

Wheeler arched an eyebrow, then held out his hand. "Do you have your card, sir?"

Of course! If Mimi were to maintain the pretense that she was the respectable Lady Rex, as opposed to his doxy, then he must play a part also. A respectable widow wouldn't be sitting waiting at her window, ready to spring into life at the first sight of him.

He fished a card out of his pocket and handed it over. "Tell your mistress that I'm come to take her for a promenade."

"Very good. I shall see if she's receiving visitors."

There was no mistaking the sneer in the butler's tone.

Wheeler knew—as every servant in the house knew—that Mimi was being paid to *receive* him…in every sense of the word.

Then Alexander checked himself. He really was a complete and utter arse. He ought to at least treat her as a duke would treat the widow of an old friend—even if she were warming his bed.

His manhood stirred at the prospect of visiting her chamber later, and he entered the parlor with a cockstand that needed to be eased before he could be seen in public.

Shortly after, he heard footsteps. The parlor door opened and Alexander caught his breath.

Before him stood what could only be described as a goddess.

Her gown was the color of claret, warm and intoxicating. Her skirts concealed her form, falling from a high waistline in smooth ripples. The matching redingote was fashioned from what looked like thick velvet, trimmed in a military fashion.

Her hair was swept up into an elegant chignon that might have looked severe and uncompromising on some, but the delicate wisps of hair curling about her face softened the look.

Sweet rutting heaven—he'd never seen a sight so lovely.

The urge to claim her threatened to break his resolve. He only need dismiss the butler, then he could pull her to the hearthrug, lift those skirts, and bury himself inside her.

Then he met her gaze. Rather than the hardened doxy, her expression was that of an innocent—a young woman anticipating a promenade in the park with her suitor. She lowered her gaze, and the faint bloom on her cheeks stirred his heart as much as the thought of that delectable body stirred his manhood.

Wheeler cleared his throat, and Alexander looked away, swallowing his shame. She was the mistress of the house, and he was staring open-mouthed with a cockstand the size of a longboat in his breeches, like a pimply adolescent ready to spend at the first sight of a pretty girl.

She might be his to own—for the next few months, at least— but he owed her more than *that*.

"Your Grace," she said, her gaze flicking toward the butler.

There seemed little point in maintaining the charade, given that Wheeler understood their circumstances, but Alexander found himself compelled to step forward and hold out his hand, as if she were a sought-after debutante and he the gallant suitor.

"Lady Rex," he said, "I'm come to escort you for a promenade about the park, if you'd be so kind as to oblige me?"

Mimi took his hand, and smiled as he lifted hers to his lips.

She played her part well, with not even the slightest glimmer of irony in her eyes. He only saw pleasure and anticipation. She was either extremely accomplished at playing the part, or...

Or the life of a lady came naturally to her.

But now was not the time to ask about her birth, or her history—not when she had gifted him with that beautiful smile.

"Thank you," she said. "I should like that."

"You look beautiful," he said. "If all your new gowns are as pretty, then I consider it money well spent."

Her smile disappeared.

Shit.

She withdrew her hand and retreated into the hallway. "Shall we go?" she asked. "I'm sure you're as anxious to achieve your objective as I am to achieve mine."

He followed her outside and glanced at Wheeler in time to see him shake his head, as if disappointed.

Well, Alexander would be damned if a servant looked down on him.

"The door, if you please, Wheeler," he said.

The butler rolled his eyes, then opened the front door. Alexander held out his arm and Mimi took it, curling her gloved hand about his sleeve. Then he escorted her outside, and they set off toward Hyde Park.

Silence thickened in the air, punctuated by their footsteps and the distant clip-clop of hooves and the rattle of wheels as carriages rolled along the streets, conveying their occupants to luncheons and tea parties. Alexander cast a sidelong glance at his companion, but she maintained her gaze on the road ahead, her expression impassive.

Why did she not speak? In his experience, the most difficult challenge for a man was getting a woman to *cease* talking. Women always wanted to fill any moment of quiet with inane chatter, as if the more they said, the more interesting they became, when in reality the reverse was true. Doxies filled the void with their demands for payment and inquiries about what else they could do to please their customers—for a coin, of course. Wives were worse. Even after securing a man's hand, their demands increased, as if they sought to own him. That was why most men spent each day getting foxed at White's—to numb the pain that the incessant demands of women inflicted on their ears.

"The weather's very fine today," he said, breaking the silence. "London's often warmer than the country this time of year."

Other than arch an eyebrow, she didn't respond, keeping her gaze straight ahead.

Bugger. Where had her smile gone?

"I meant no disrespect earlier," he said, "when I said your gown was money well spent. I may only be a man"—she let out a snort—"but I can appreciate a fine gown."

Before she could respond, a voice hailed them.

"I say! I thought it was you."

A couple arm in arm approached the entrance to the park. The man—tall, with blond hair and the broad-shouldered, athletic build that appealed to women, whores, and ladies alike—raised a hand in salute.

The very same hand that had planted a shiner on Alexander's face.

The man's companion was unlike the women he usually preferred—in that she lacked the usual look of slavish adoration on her face.

"Foxton," Alexander said, "what are you doing about at this hour? I thought you'd be in White's by now on your fifth brandy."

"Whereas you're unlikely to darken the doors of White's again," came the reply.

"Why might that be, Adam?" the woman on Foxton's arm asked.

Adam? Since when had Foxton permitted his admirers to address him with such familiarity?

"Surely I've spoken of Sawbridge and his antics, Portia."

The woman frowned, then turned her gaze toward Mimi, her expression filled with what could only be described as sympathy.

"I see my reputation precedes me," Alexander said. "Gossip travels fast, even out of Season."

"Perhaps not fast enough," Foxton said, casting a curious glance toward Mimi. "Sawbridge, are you attempting to improve your standing in Society by persuading this delectable creature to be seen with you in public?" He inclined his head toward Mimi. "My dear madam, I've not seen you in London before. Are you here to persuade the rest of your sex that my friend can be trusted not to endanger the lives of his paramours?"

Rather than blush, or wither under the savagery of Foxton's gaze, Mimi tilted her head to one side, her composure unwavering.

"Forgive me, sir," she said. "I'm lately arrived in London and know not who you are."

Foxton's eyebrow twitched and his mouth set in a firm line, but his companion let out a laugh.

"Ha! Not every woman in the world awaits the day she first meets you with breathless anticipation. That must be disappointing for *you*, brother."

So *this* was Foxton's sister—rumored to have been kept under lock and key until her debut. The determined expression in her eyes spoke of bedevilment in her soul. Good—with luck, she plagued her brother daily.

"Portia—" Foxton began, but she interrupted.

"Permit me to introduce myself, seeing as my brother lacks the manners. Lady Portia Hawke, sister to this reprobate."

Foxton frowned. "Portia, you'll find that *my* crimes pale into nothingness compared to Sawbridge's. And it's not the done thing to introduce yourself—you know that."

"I'd die of old age waiting for *you* to do it," she huffed.

Mimi smiled, her eyes sparkling with mirth.

Bloody hell—why does she never smile that that for me?

"Permit me to introduce the Duke of Foxton," Alexander said, "and his sister, Lady Portia." He gestured toward Mimi. "This is Lady Rex."

"*Lady* Rex, eh?" Foxton said. "I suppose a lady's better than a mere *miss*."

"I don't catch your meaning, Your Grace," Mimi said. "I am not unmarried."

"Does your husband approve of Sawbridge accompanying you today?"

"My *late* husband," she replied, her voice steady. "I'm lately out of mourning. His Grace the Duke of Sawbridge was a family friend of my late husband's, and executor of his estate."

Alexander tempered his delight at the discomfort in Foxton's expression.

"My sympathies for your loss, Lady Rex," Lady Portia said.

"You're most kind."

"And you lived abroad before you came here?" Foxton said. "Where?"

"Italy," Mimi said, her voice tightening.

"*Really?* I know it well. Tell me, is the Trevi Fountain as beautiful as everyone says?"

"It's quite extraordinary," Mimi said.

"So you lived in Florence?"

Damn Foxton—he was trying to trap her!

She narrowed her eyes. "The Trevi Fountain is in *Rome*. I wonder how well you know Italy."

"But...you know Florence?" Foxton asked, coloring.

"My late husband and I were traveling to Florence when..." She hesitated.

"Adam, leave the poor lady alone," Lady Portia said. "I can't think what you're doing."

"I'm asking about Italy," Foxton said. "I find it astonishing that Sawbridge never mentioned Lord Rex to his friends."

"Perhaps because I don't count you as a friend," Alexander said. "Besides, while you might show an interest in a *Lord Rex*, I doubt you'd consider a mere *Sir John Rex* grand enough for you."

"Sir John, eh? A baronet or a knight?"

"That's enough!" Lady Portia said, then turned to Mimi. "Lady Rex, accept my apologies for my brother's incivility. Be assured that not everyone in London is such a boor." She arched an eyebrow and glanced at Alexander.

"Except perhaps myself, Lady Portia, given what your brother's told you about me?" he asked.

"Too many people observe the world through the lens of gossip," Lady Portia said. "I prefer to discover the truth for myself. Gossip obscures the truth."

"As do deceivers, sister."

A flicker of mischief shone in Lady Portia's eyes.

Yes, Foxton—I doubt your sister is the obedient debutante you'd have her be.

"Forgive us for not tarrying," Foxton said. "We're taking tea with Lady Jersey. Do you know her, Lady Rex?"

"No, I do not," Mimi said.

Foxton nodded, then steered his sister along the pavement. Lady Portia's harsh whisper floated through the air.

"Really, Adam! There was no need to be so insufferable."

Alexander led Mimi toward the entrance to the park.

"I like her," Mimi said.

"And Foxton himself?"

"He is as I'd expect, given his rank."

"You didn't find him attractive?" Alexander said. "Most women do—at least, that's what I'm told."

"My opinion is immaterial," she said, "but, for my part, I don't find him attractive—though I can see how most women would."

"Because?" Alexander couldn't help asking, unable to contain his jealousy.

"Because, almost without exception, everyone in Society judges others by their appearance and their rank, rather than the quality of their soul."

"*Almost* without exception?"

His heart soared with hope—did she consider him the exception?

"Duchess Whitcombe is different to anyone else I've encountered. Behind the titled women lies a good soul—which renders her unique."

"If Society judges by appearance, then you will triumph," he said, swallowing his disappointment. "Even the most insightful observer would believe your act just now. Your distress was almost convincing when the conversation turned to the nonexistent Sir John Rex. We have a fair chance at passing you off as a lady."

"A *fair chance* is all we need, given the level of intelligence of most members of the *ton*," she said, almost in a snarl.

Unable to think of a suitable response, he said nothing, and they entered the park in silence. It was already busy—couples strolled arm in arm; children held hands with prim, plain women in starched gowns. The occasional rider passed by, and in the distance, the honk of swans echoed across the landscape, against the backdrop of the chorus of songbirds that never seemed to cease.

A boy, barely out of leading strings, ran past them, toward a man and a woman. The man swooped down and lifted him up into the air.

"Come to Papa!" he cried, as the child dissolved into giggles, then they continued along the path, a nursemaid trotting after them.

Mimi followed them with her gaze, a smile on her lips. She glanced back at Alexander, and his heart soared as her smile broadened, illuminating her beautiful eyes.

Then she released his arm. "Eleanor!" she cried.

Her smile had been for another.

Alexander turned to see Whitcombe and his wife. The duchess approached Mimi, hands outstretched.

"How delightful," she said. "I'm glad you've found the opportunity to explore the park at last."

Jealousy flared as the women embraced, which intensified as Alexander caught sight of Whitcombe staring at Mimi with frank appraisal.

No you don't, Whitcombe. She's mine.

Alexander approached Mimi, and she stiffened as he placed a hand on her shoulder.

Whitcombe glanced at Alexander's hand and arched a dark brow, as if in amusement. Then the corner of his mouth creased into the precursor of a smile.

Or perhaps a sneer. With Whitcombe, one could never tell.

"Lady Rex, I presume," he said, his voice sounding deeper than usual.

Mimi nodded, and her lips parted as she tilted her head back to meet his gaze. A soft bloom colored her cheeks, and the beast within Alexander's soul let out a low growl.

Mine.

"You must be the Duke of Whitcombe," she said. "A pleasure to meet you, Your Grace."

"Oh, I doubt *that*," Whitcombe said, the crease in his mouth deepening.

"You think me insincere?" she asked.

"Not at all, Lady Rex," Whitcombe said, glancing once more at Alexander. "It was not *your* pleasure—or lack thereof—to which I referred."

Alexander removed his hand from Mimi's shoulder and placed it on the small of her back. Whitcombe recognized the gesture for what it was—a male beast laying claim to a female before his rival—and the crease in his mouth dipped into a full-blown smile. In response, he took his wife's arm and drew her close.

Whitcombe represented no threat—his devotion to his wife was legendary at White's. But no matter how much he held the duchess close, Alexander couldn't quieten the beast in his soul.

Mine.

"Did you say something, old chap?" Whitcombe asked.

"Montague," his wife admonished him, and Whitcombe chuckled.

"Forgive me, Sawbridge," he said. "You can't blame a fellow for being intrigued by your new…companion." He glanced at Mimi again and inclined his head. "I've been anxious to meet the woman who's made such an impression on my wife after such a short acquaintance. Eleanor is usually so discerning with her friendships."

Mimi's blush deepened, and Alexander curled his free hand into a fist. "Whitcombe, you've no right to—"

"Forgive my husband," the duchess interrupted, casting a frown at Whitcombe. "I may be discerning in my choice of friends, but it seems not so much in my choice of husband. Montague, you of all people should understand the difference between discernment and prejudice."

She offered her arm to Mimi. "Shall we walk, Lady Rex? I'm in need of intelligent conversation—and I'm anxious to show you some of my favorite spots in the park."

Mimi glanced toward Alexander, as if asking permission, and he nodded. Then she took the duchess's arm and the two of them strolled ahead. With a sigh, Alexander followed, Whitcombe at his side. As they approached the bend in the path, Alexander's gaze fell to the grass verge. It still bore the deep furrows— evidence of the accident that had claimed two lives. The path no longer bore the thick bloodstain, but the mark of shame still existed, carved indelibly into Alexander's soul.

"I suppose I should apologize," Whitcombe said.

What for—taking me past the scene of my disgrace to relish my shame?

"Really?"

Whitcombe nodded. "My wife would chew my ears off if I didn't."

"Where's the apology in that?" Alexander asked. "You're only doing so for fear of retribution if you didn't."

"Much like *you*, then," Whitcombe said. "Tell me, how's the leg?"

Damn you.

Alexander glanced at the furrows as the memory of that morning penetrated his mind—the coarse laughter as he urged his friend on, the crack of the whip, then the screams that froze his blood, accompanied by the splintering sound of wood and broken necks and finally the relief of oblivion.

A carriage accident, the authorities had ruled.

"It's improving," he said.

"There's no harm in walking with a stick, you know," Whitcombe said. "Some men consider a cane a fashion accessory, and I daresay you could pull it off. Though perhaps your latest paramour fulfils the same need as a cane."

"Don't talk rot," Alexander said.

"Not literally, of course—a woman that delicate would not carry your weight. But in other things—I daresay she's propping up your reputation if not your body."

"Whitcombe, I swear, if you say one more thing about her, I'll—"

Whitcombe let out a laugh, and the duchess glanced over her shoulder, frowning.

"You've got it bad, haven't you, Sawbridge?"

"Got what?"

Whitcombe shook his head. "I'm in no mood to point out that which you must discover for yourself."

"Is that what your wife tells you when you're behaving like an arse?"

Whitcombe merely smiled, then increased the pace, catching up with the ladies. He raised his hand in salute, and Alexander's heart sank as he caught sight of the couple approaching them.

Earl and Countess Walton.

Walton had assisted Foxton in throwing Alexander out of White's club. As to the countess…

That harridan had accused Alexander of being a murderer, a reprobate, and a seducer of women, and had threatened to run him through with a sword if he came within twelve inches of her or any of her friends.

Oh, for the days when a woman would merely give someone she disapproved of the cut direct! But Countess Walton would never be content with something so refined.

Alexander gritted his teeth, then joined the party.

Lady Walton's eyes sparkled with delight as she embraced the duchess. She turned her gaze to Mimi, then her smile disappeared as she caught sight of Alexander.

"Lavinia, this is Lady Rex," the duchess said. "Lately arrived in London. Mimi—this is Earl and Countess Walton."

Mimi dipped into a curtsey. "Countess."

The countess cast a sharp glance at Alexander. "Is this the same Lady Rex you've not been able to stop talking about, Eleanor?"

Mimi stiffened, and the duchess laughed. "Forgive me, Lady Rex, but I've been enthusing about you to my friends—well, the few that I have. I fear I insulted Lavinia when I was unable to take tea with her last week due to a prior engagement with you."

"You shouldn't have disappointed your friend on my account," Mimi said.

"*You're* my friend also," the duchess said. "Lavinia, we're looking forward to your ball next Tuesday, are we not, Montague?"

Whitcombe frowned. "I thought you disliked balls, my love."

The duchess gave him a sharp nudge. "Lavinia, were you not remarking on how few guests you were able to invite, given it's the winter and most families have retired to the country?"

Whitcombe visibly winced. Sometimes the duchess had a

habit of speaking most inappropriately—even though she often said what everyone else thought, but was too polite to say.

Alexander glanced at Mimi, who, given the distress lining her features, understood exactly what the duchess was doing—angling for an invitation. Eleanor meant well, but the inevitable snub from Lady Walton would distress Mimi more.

"I think it's time we left, Lady Rex," Alexander said.

Mimi's frown deepened, then understanding flickered in her gaze. "Y-yes, perhaps I should return home."

"But you haven't—" the duchess began.

"Forgive me, Eleanor," Mimi said, her voice tight. "I-I have an engagement. Lady Walton, it was a pleasure to meet you."

"Such a shame," Lady Walton said. "I was hoping to further our acquaintance, Lady Rex. Perhaps we might take tea sometime. And, of course, I shall ensure you receive an invitation to our ball. Do say you can come."

Mimi glanced toward Alexander.

"And"—Lady Walton hesitated, as if steeling herself for a plunge into a cesspool—"Sawbridge—you're invited also."

"I say, Lavinia, is that—" Lord Walton began, but was interrupted.

"I'm sure Sawbridge would forgive the informal nature of my invitation, Peregrine," she said. "Nobody expects a *written* invitation these days—not among friends."

"I hadn't realized I was a friend of yours, Lady Walton," Alexander said.

"You're invited as a courtesy to Lady Rex."

"That's good," he replied. "I'd hate to think you'd invite just anyone."

"I've long since realized that you're not *just anyone*," she retorted. "In fact, I know just what sort of man you—"

"Lavinia, my love," her husband said, placing a hand on her shoulder.

Mimi shot Alexander a frown. "You're very kind, Lady Walton," she said. "I have no fixed engagements next Tuesday, and would be delighted to attend."

"As would I," Alexander added. "Will everybody be there?"

Lady Walton wrinkled her nose. "I suppose by *everybody*, you mean every man and woman with a title. I am a little more selective with my guestlist." She paused and stared at him. "Though it may not always be apparent."

"Oh?" he asked, unable to resist the temptation to needle her.

"Viscount de Blanchard will never darken my door," she said. "As to the Duke of Dunton, well, given how badly he treated Bella—not to mention Eleanor's poor sister—you'll not be surprised if he's not on the guestlist. And as to that other repugnant excuse for a man…"

"Now, Lavinia, my love," Walton said, "I'm sure our friends have no wish to hear about him—and we mustn't give Lady Rex the impression that you're a gossip."

"Perhaps not, but I ought to at least warn her of the worst predators in town." She glanced at Alexander.

"I would consider it a great compliment if others ranked above me on your list of repugnant males," Alexander said.

"Only three others, I'm afraid."

"The third being?"

"Earl Mayhew, of course. Thankfully, he's rarely seen in London."

Mimi let out a cough and lifted her hand to her mouth. "Do forgive me," she said. "M-my throat's a little dry."

"No wonder, in this cold air," Lady Walton said. "It's not good to stand still in such cold weather. Our garden was covered in frost this morning—I fear we're in for another harsh winter."

She rattled on, about her tenants and the difficulty of ploughing hard ground—or some such—and the duchess nodded in agreement. Mimi joined the conversation, but her demeanor had changed. Her body seemed stiffer, as if she were a rabbit having sensed danger. And her cheeks—which earlier had a rosy hue— were almost completely devoid of color.

"We'll not keep you any longer," Lady Walton said. "Peregrine?"

Her husband took her arm and steered her along the path.

"Oh dear, I've done it again, haven't I?" Duchess Whitcombe said. "I never know when to say the right thing."

"I'm sure Lady Walton took no offense, my love," Whitcombe said, "and had she not wished for Sawbridge to attend her ball, she wouldn't have invited him."

"Perhaps I ought to refuse," Mimi said.

"I'll not allow *that*," the duchess said. "The ball will be all the better for your being there." She took Mimi by the shoulders and kissed her on both cheeks. "Wear the lilac silk at the ball," she whispered. "You won't be in want of dance partners if you do."

"Dance partners?" Alexander asked.

"You're not expecting to keep this delightful creature all to yourself, are you, Sawbridge?" Whitcombe said, twisting his lips into a smile. "*I* shall expect at least one dance, Lady Rex."

Before Mimi could respond, Alexander took Mimi's hand and steered her away, only slowing the pace after they'd navigated the bend in the path and the duke and duchess were out of sight. She said nothing and let him lead her across the park and through another exit. After a while, they turned into St. James Street, and he stopped before the familiar shop window with its display of orchids.

"Madame Deliet's." Mimi shook her head. "No—no, I've no wish to go inside."

"Do you fear her insults?"

She forced a laugh. "A woman such as I is accustomed to the reception I received from Madame Deliet. But perhaps you wish to take pleasure from witnessing her insult me again."

His heart twitched at the undertone of sorrow in her voice.

"Even *I'm* not that cruel," he said. "But I am anxious to settle a matter with Madame, if you'd oblige me."

She frowned, but complied as he opened the door and steered her inside.

The bell over the door tinkled. Two women in the shadows in the back of the shop looked up, then resumed their attention on a display of ribbons. A third appeared from behind a curtain, a length of measuring tape draped around her neck.

"*Le duc de Sawbridge!*" she cried, approaching Alexander, hands raised. "What a pleasure to see you again!" She glanced at Mimi. "Ah—have you brought another young lady to be attired in one of my fine gowns? Monsieur, I swear you're my most loyal customer."

Meaning the most willing to part with cash.

At the mention of Alexander's title, the two women in the rear of the shop moved closer, and Alexander recognized Lady Felicia Long and the dowager Countess Billingham—two of the worst gossips of the *ton*.

Excellent.

They eyed him with hostility.

"Ladies—well met," he said. "May I introduce Lady Rex, recently arrived in town?"

"Lady Rex?" the dowager countess asked.

"Widow of the late Sir John Rex," Alexander said. "A knight rather than a baronet, but some say that Prinny was considering granting him an earldom. Everyone who's *anyone* knows of Sir John."

"Oh—*that* Sir John Rex!" Lady Felicia said, a little too brightly. "I was most distressed to hear of his passing. Were you not, Ellen?"

The dowager countess frowned, then nodded.

"That's most kind of you," Mimi said, "though I wasn't aware the news of his passing had reached London."

"And His Grace has recommended my establishment to you?" Madame Deliet said. "*C'est correctement?*"

"I did, Madame," Alexander said, "but sadly you were too busy to help Lady Rex when she paid you a visit."

"But I 'ave never seen Lady Rex," the modiste said, her accent thickening. "I would 'ave remembered such a beauty, no?"

Alexander cringed at the sycophancy in her tone. Why had he never noticed it before?

"You were occupied with serving Miss Francis at the time, Madame Deliet," Mimi said, "though you were kind enough to notify me several times that your gowns were very expensive."

Alexander smiled to himself as the onlookers whispered to each other and the modiste cringed. And well she might—it was the height of bad form to openly discuss the price of a gown. Even *he* knew that.

"Lady Rex came here on *my* recommendation," Alexander said, "so I consider myself responsible for any slight she may have suffered here, however unintentional."

"I cannot recall saying such a thing," the modiste said.

"Can you not?" Mimi said, sweetly. "'*Chaque robe est très cher,*' I believe you said."

Heavens! Did Mimi speak French?

Alexander glanced at the modiste, who stepped back, her eyes widening.

"What was that you said, Lady Rex?" he asked.

"I spoke in Madame's mother tongue," Mimi replied. "Perhaps you'd care to translate, Madame Deliet?"

Fear shimmered in the modiste's eyes. She reached for her measuring tape and entwined it around her forefinger. "I-I did not say… I mean, I'm afraid your accent is—"

"I quite understand," Mimi said. "The Parisian accent can be a little difficult to understand."

The modiste opened her mouth to reply, then closed it again, her eyes widening. "I—I…"

"It matters not, Madame Deliet," Mimi said, a sparkle in her eyes. "I secured the services of another modiste. Twelve day dresses and eight evening gowns—she's quite the marvel."

"D-do I know her?" Madame Deliet asked.

"Possibly," Mimi replied. "She's one of your countrywomen."

"Is she?"

"Oh yes," Mimi said. "She's as French as *you* are."

The modiste shifted from one foot to another, her expression that of a schoolboy caught with his hands in the sweetmeats, and

Alexander's heart soared at the continued mirth in Mimi's eyes.

"Lady Rex's new modiste is rather exclusive," he said, "so you may not have heard of her. But her work is of exceptional quality."

"As is mine, Your Grace," Madame Deliet said. "Perhaps Lady Rex would permit me to fashion a gown for her. I have some new silks in that are just perfect."

"How very kind," Mimi said, "but I couldn't possibly."

"Consider it a gift, Lady Rex,"

"I couldn't accept it," Mimi said. "It would be akin to accepting charity, and as you made very clear when I was first here, you're not in the business of running a *charitable establishment.*"

This time there was no mistaking the modiste's discomfort. Her mouth opened and she let out a whimper.

"I think, Lady Rex, it's time to continue shopping," Alexander said, holding out his arm. Mimi took it, and he escorted her out of the shop, the bell tinkling as he closed the door behind him. He glanced over his shoulder to see the modiste staring after them, her mouth still wide open.

"Forgive me," he said after they'd walked a few paces.

"What for?"

"For not appreciating how badly she'd treated you."

She turned to face him, and his breeches tightened as she parted her lips. "Does it matter?"

"Yes," he said quietly. "It does. You've already done so much for me."

A smile played on her lips. "I have?"

"Lady Walton would never have invited me to her ball had it not been for you. The woman loathes me. I'm beginning to believe that I have a strong chance of regaining my standing in Society."

Her smile slipped. "I'm happy for you."

He took her arm and led her back to Grosvenor Square. They passed two couples on the way, and though the first looked at Alexander with disfavor, the second couple—Earl Stiles and his wife—stopped to wish him a good day, though Stiles's gaze settled on Mimi for an uncomfortably long time. The fellow was a magistrate—surely Mimi couldn't have been brought before him in her former life? But she showed no sign of recognition as she curtseyed and responded to Lady Stiles's remarks about the weather.

She played her part well—he couldn't be prouder.

Or more aroused.

By the time they'd arrived at number sixteen, his groin ached with the need to be inside her. She was his for the taking—bought and paid for—yet when he steered her through her front door under Wheeler's watchful gaze, he found himself unable to order her to the bedchamber.

Rutting beast he may be—and his body screamed at him that she would satisfy his lust ten times over if he demanded it—but he wanted more than mere physical release.

He wanted *her*. *All* of her—her body and her pleasure.

She entered the parlor, and he followed, then she removed her redingote.

"Tell me what you want, Your Grace."

She might as well have been a serving wench at an inn offering him a mug of ale.

"Will you come to the Waltons' ball?"

"Of course," she said. "You're paying me to obey your every request until our business is concluded."

He took her shoulders, and she drew in a sharp breath as he pulled her close.

"That's not what I'm asking, Mimi."

"Then what are you asking?"

"Will you come to the ball with *me*? Not because it's your duty, but because I ask it."

Understanding flickered across her gaze. For a moment he thought she might refuse. Then, at length, she nodded.

He took her hand and lifted it to his lips. "Might I be so bold as to ask to partner you for the first dance?"

She blinked, slowly, and his heart squeezed as she smiled. "You may."

"Oh, Mimi!"

He pulled her close for a kiss, but she stiffened and turned her head to the side. Her smile disappeared.

"Will you not let me kiss you?" he asked.

She closed her eyes as her chest rose and fell. Then she opened them, and the hardness had returned.

He released her and stepped back, willing his cockstand to subside. She lowered her gaze to his groin.

"Shall we retire to the bedchamber?" she asked.

He shook his head and, without speaking, retreated, pushing past the surprised butler as he strode toward the front door and let himself out.

Curse her! Why should she make *him* feel sordid when *she* was the doxy?

Perhaps it was the dignity with which she carried herself. But a small voice in his head had whispered of the hope that she was warming to him.

But no—to her, he was merely a means of earning an income.

He crossed the street and entered his house, responding to the footman's greeting with a grunt. Then he made his way to his study, where a bottle of brandy awaited. At least the bottle wouldn't stare at him with doe-like eyes to prick his conscience. It merely awaited his consumption—without judgment or admonishment.

By the time he'd worked his way halfway through the bottle, the pain in his heart had dulled—but it refused to disappear.

Perhaps Whitcombe's right—I have got it bad.

But it—whatever *it* was—was a mere passing fancy. By the time their business was done, he'd have rutted his obsession with her out of his system. With even greater luck, she would have succumbed—as all his women did—to his talents in the bedroom. Then she'd know what it was like to want something that was unattainable. All he needed to do was make her body scream with pleasure and he could enslave her as thoroughly as he was beginning to fear that she'd enslaved him.

He lifted the brandy glass to the light.

"Fuck, that's strong stuff if it's turned me into such an elo— eloquent phil…" He shook his head, struggling to voice the word. "Phillo…philosopher."

Philosopher. That was it.

"I'll have you, Mimi," he said. "All of you. It's only a matter of time."

He strolled toward the window and pulled back the curtain, and his gaze was drawn to the house across the square. He leaned against the window frame and exhaled, his breath misting on the glass. Then he lifted his finger and traced the letter *M*.

A movement caught his eye, and he saw a figure emerge from number sixteen. Though she wore a cloak, there was no mistaking her. She climbed down the steps then stopped and glanced about—as if she carried a guilty secret. For a moment she glanced toward his house, and Alexander shrank back, clutching his brandy glass, even though she'd never be able to see him.

Then, with a glance over her shoulder, she set off.

So—she turned away from him in fear when he attempted to kiss her, but she was content to spread her legs on the streets to earn an extra coin or two.

Once a whore, always a whore.

As she disappeared out of sight, he tipped up the brandy glass and drained it. Then he turned, drew his arm back, and flung the glass into the air with full force. It struck the wall and shattered into shards on impact.

CHAPTER FIFTEEN

MIMI DROVE HER needle into the hem of the gown, then pulled the thread through. She repeated the gesture and her mind drifted, no matter how hard she tried to banish *him* from her thoughts.

The Duke of Sawbridge.

Less than a month into their arrangement, she had almost succumbed to the temptation to let him kiss her.

Pleasure had been within her grasp. But pleasure was like laudanum—it soothed the ache, but with each application, the ache returned, more potent than before, until the craving became a need for survival, a dependency that would ultimately destroy her.

She had no intention to draw pleasure from their coupling, but she could no longer deny her professional pride at his groans of ecstasy while she rode him—or while he rutted her in the parlor in full view of the street outside, the danger heightening his pleasure, evident in the short, sharp puffs as he came to completion.

But despite his evident physical satisfaction, disappointment gleamed in his eyes when she turned her lips from him.

Oh, Sawbridge, if only you knew how greatly my own disappointment surpasses yours.

She was standing on a precipice—at the brink of her own destruction. The slightest transgression into pleasure and she would plunge into the abyss.

But she couldn't silence the voice in her mind that whispered of the prospect of taking her pleasure with him.

Alexander…

Her gut twisted with shame, even though she hadn't spoken his name aloud. What might it be like to cry out his name as he cried out hers?

But his name was denied her. As was her pleasure at his touch. Her release at her own hand was all she could risk—to relieve the ache in her bones.

She denied them both—his name, and her pleasure—for the safety of her soul.

But she couldn't help imagine what it might be like to have his mouth claim hers, his tongue slip between—

"Mimi!"

She startled and glanced up from her mending to see Mrs. Briggs and her companions—Anna and Mary—staring at her.

"I beg pardon?" Mimi asked.

Mrs. Briggs shook her head. "You were gone from us just then, darlin'. Anything troublin' you? You don't seem yourself today."

"N-no, I'm just struggling a little with this mending."

Mrs. Briggs narrowed her eyes as the lie hung heavy in the air. Then she nodded.

"Anna, darlin', could you see to the tea? Don't forget the cake Mimi brought—we've all earned a slice with our work this morning. Mary, look in on Lily and her little 'un to see if they'd like to join us."

"But Mrs. Briggs," Mary began, "Lily's still very—"

"Do as ye're told. I'm sure young Sam would like some cake."

The two young women set their mending aside and exited the room, then Mrs. Briggs leaned forward.

"You can be honest with me now, Mimi darlin'. Tell me about him."

There was little point asking to whom she was referring.

"There's little to tell," Mimi said. "He's paying me a stipend until next summer, then we'll part company."

The other woman let out a sharp sigh. "I didn't mean your agreement. Tell me about the man."

"He has a title," Mimi said. "And wealth."

"There's something more," Mrs. Briggs said. "Is he kind?"

Mimi paused. Outwardly Alexander was not kind—neither, from what she had seen, was he particularly liked for himself. At most times he wore the soulless expression of yet another man who believed she belonged to him because he paid for her services. Yet, on occasion, she glimpsed something more—a vulnerability he was afraid to reveal. When he claimed her body, she sensed a need greater than mere physical gratification. She saw a soul—alone and isolated—yearning to be touched, calling to her…

Mrs. Briggs sighed. "Oh, darlin', don't fall for it."

"Fall for what?" Mimi asked.

"The little lost boy act. You're experienced enough in our world to know that all men are children at heart—longing for attention, indulging in their tempers if they can't get their way, and tossing their playthings aside when they've no further use for them. Don't become his plaything, Mimi. It will destroy you. *He* will destroy you."

"You don't know him, Mrs. Briggs."

"Aye, and if you're falling under his spell I've no wish to meet him, unless it's to thicken his ear."

"I'm not falling under his spell."

Mrs. Briggs folded her arms in the manner of a governess about to lecture her stubborn pupil. "You haven't kissed him, have you?"

"No!" Mimi said. "I-I've not kissed any man since…since I first took to the streets. I understand the danger."

"Make sure you do, darlin'." Mrs. Briggs took Mimi's hand. "I only speak out of fondness for you. You never want to be dependent on a man, do you?"

"No," Mimi said, gritting her teeth as the image of another man resurfaced—and the very thought of him sent a ripple of nausea and fear through her. "I *never* want to be dependent on a man."

The door opened and Anna and Mary returned with the tea things. A third woman accompanied them, with a child clinging to her skirts.

She let out a small cry as she spotted Mimi.

"Now, Lily, what did I tell you last night?" Mrs. Briggs said. "Mimi won't hurt you. She's our friend. She's even been helping with the hem of your dress. See?" She nodded to the garment on Mimi's lap.

"I'm sorry, Lily," Mimi said, holding out the gown. "I didn't know it was your dress. Would you like it back?"

Lily turned her expressive eyes—that looked huge in her pale, thin face—toward Mimi. Then she glanced at Mrs. Briggs as if seeking permission.

"Go on, Lily darlin', she won't hurt you," Mrs. Briggs said. She turned toward Mimi. "Lily's been working on the other gown you've got there—see that lacework? The work on the bodice is all hers."

Mimi picked up the other gown. The top half of the bodice was covered in embroidery, delicate stitches forming an intricate pattern—swirls of leaves and flowers, each with a tiny knot at the center.

The work was finer than anything Mimi had ever seen—all the more for having been fashioned from plain cotton, not expensive silks, nor the shiny beads that often adorned the gowns of countesses and duchesses. The quality of the work spoke for itself, rather than letting the expense of the materials speak for it.

The child released his grip on Lily's skirts and toddled toward Mimi, arms outstretched.

"Sam!" Lily let out a cry as the child lost his balance and toppled forward, but Mimi swept him up into her arms.

"Who do we have here?" she cooed. "A fine young man,

indeed."

The child squealed with delight as Mimi bounced him on her knee.

"Are you taking care of your mama?"

"Ma-ma!" The boy pointed toward Lily.

"Yes, that's your mama," Mimi said, "and she's taking good care of you. If you promise to return the favor, you can have some cake."

Lily glanced toward the tea tray.

"Does your boy like cake?" Mimi asked.

Lily flinched.

"Do *you* like cake, Lily?"

Lily lowered her gaze to the floor.

"Answer her," Anna said, not unkindly.

"Lily's all right, Anna," Mimi said. "There's plenty of time, isn't there, Lily? No need to speak right away. Anna, would you be kind enough to pour me a cup and cut some cake for me?" She stroked the child's cheek. "You can share my cake, Sam, and tell me what you think of it—that is, if your mama doesn't object."

Mary opened her mouth to address Lily, but Mimi frowned and shook her head, and Mary closed it again, while Anna busied herself with the tea and sliced the cake.

"I-I've not..." Lily hesitated, glancing toward Mrs. Briggs, who nodded encouragement. "I've not had cake before," she said. "Neither has Sammy."

"Then I hope you'll take a slice," Mimi said. "I didn't bake it myself, I'm afraid. I was never any good at that, and nor am I accomplished at sewing. Unlike you—where did you learn such exquisite skill?"

Lily's expression shuttered again, and Mimi cursed her forwardness.

"Come sit here, Lily darlin'," Mrs. Briggs said, patting the seat next to her. Lily approached her, and as she sat, Mrs. Briggs whispered, "You're doing very well."

Lily took her cup, which rattled against the saucer. Then she took a bite of cake.

"Do you like it?" Mimi asked.

Lily nodded. "Y-yes. Thank you, Mrs....?"

"Call me Mimi. We're all friends here."

A slow smile crept across Lily's lips, and Mrs. Briggs whispered another "well done" before cutting herself a slice of cake.

Anna and Mary began to chatter—inanities about sewing and the weather, but the benign conversation served its purpose. The stiffness in Lily's body disappeared as she leaned back and finished her cake. Her gaze continually wandered across the parlor as Mimi kept Sam occupied with a piece of rag from the mending basket, showing him how to tie it into a bow.

"Perhaps next time I come, Sam, I'll bring some paper to make you a toy boat with," Mimi said. "How about that?" The boy grinned as Mimi tickled him under the chin. "We can even set sail with it," she said. "Launch it in the water, like a real ship."

"No!" Lily cried. "Not outside—please!"

"Careful, darlin'," Mrs. Briggs said, placing a hand on Lily's arm. "You don't have to go outside if you don't want to."

"We can set sail in the kitchen," Mimi said, "make a lake out of a bucket with water."

"See?" Mrs. Briggs said, taking Lily's hand.

Lily nodded, then set her teacup aside and glanced toward the door. "Perhaps I ought to…"

"Why don't you stay with us while we're mending?" Mrs. Briggs said. "You can show Mimi here how to embroider a flower. I'm sure she'd appreciate it." She glanced at Mimi, a plea in her eyes.

"Oh yes," Mimi said. "I must improve my skills. You'd be helping me a great deal."

"Would I?" Lily asked, her eyes widening further.

"Here," Anna said. "Let me take Sammy while you help Mimi. I can't think how we managed with this sewing before you came here, Lily." She plucked the boy from Mimi's arms and gave her a nod.

So much could be said without saying it! But unlike those ladies at Madame Deliet's, whose carefully worded phrases were intended to insult Mimi, the women here, in Mrs. Briggs's safe little corner of the world, sought to reassure Lily that she was valued, appreciated, and—above all—safe.

After a whispered word from Mrs. Briggs, Lily moved across to sit beside Mimi. Then she took the dress and began to embroider the bodice. At length, her body relaxed as she focused on her work, and Mimi glanced up to see Mrs. Briggs smiling, her eyes shining with moisture, as if Mimi had worked a miracle.

But it was Mrs. Briggs who had given Lily a purpose.

And, as she watched Lily's needle fly in and out and the image of a flower take form, Mimi's dream began to take shape. Imagine what exquisite creations Lily could make were she given the means—such as the beautiful silks at Eleanor's disposal! And Eleanor had expressed an interest in helping Mimi's cause— though Lily would doubtless faint at the prospect of being in the company of a duchess.

Mrs. Briggs had enabled these young women to survive. But, with the fortune from her arrangement with Sawbridge, Mimi could help them to *thrive*.

When the sun had almost disappeared beneath the horizon, Mimi stretched her limbs then tidied up her work and bade goodbye to her friends. Her back ached, but the walk to Grosvenor Square would ease the stiffness. By the time she turned into the square, the ache had all but gone.

Her heart soaring with newfound purpose, she almost skipped along the pavement toward her house. Then she glanced at the door and froze.

A huge male form stood in the doorway.

"Y-Your Grace," she said. "I wasn't expecting you today."

Alexander arched an eyebrow, then cast his gaze over her form, taking in the rough woolen cloak, the plain gown, and the thick boots with the scuff on the toes. His nostrils flared, and he set his mouth into a thin line.

"Evidently not."

"Have I done anything to offend you?"

He let out a bark of laughter. "She asks if she's done anything to offend me?" he sneered. "What kind of fool do you take me for?"

"I don't take you for a fool," she said. "I—"

"Spare me the pretense!" he snarled. "I already *know* what kind of fool I am. But no more, madam. No more. I know exactly who—and what—you are."

He stepped closer, and her senses were almost overpowered by his male scent—woodsy and spicy. But as she lifted her gaze to his eyes, her blood froze. Though they glittered in the moonlight, there was not a trace of desire in them.

Only bitterness—and disgust.

Chapter Sixteen

ALEXANDER GRITTED HIS teeth against the urge to push her against the wall and rut the fury out of his body.

Curse her! Even caught in the act of betrayal she refused to bend, instead facing him as if she were not the transgressor.

And, in his weakness, he still desired her.

"You have no need to tell me who—or what—I am, Your Grace," she said, her voice steady. "I am what you pay me to be."

"Precisely," he said. "And if a man isn't getting what he's paying for, he has every right to object."

"What precisely have you paid for that I've not provided?" she asked, tilting her head up.

"Exclusivity," he growled. "A whore may be unfamiliar with the concept, but it is, nevertheless, what you promised."

"Can you promise *me* the same?"

His heart twitched at the undercurrent of hurt in her voice. If she believed he was rutting other women then she was a fool. Other women had lost their appeal for him.

He wanted her.

Only her.

But, curse her, she didn't want him. She only wanted the money she could earn with her body.

"My only promise was to pay you at the end of our agreement," he said. "But how can you expect me to pay if you're fucking someone else?"

She flinched, then gestured toward the door. "You'd best come inside."

"No," he replied. "Not when you're inviting half the men of London to *come inside.*"

Hurt flared in her eyes. Then she blinked and it was gone. When she next spoke, her words were toneless, as if she were reciting a laundry list.

"I care not whether you come or go," she said, "but if you remain on my doorstep you risk providing your neighbors with the sort of entertainment that will jeopardize your mission to restore what little reputation you have. If you no longer want my body, then at least take my advice."

"Which is?" he asked.

"Do not disgrace yourself in front of your peers who"—she glanced about the street, at the white-fronted houses with dark, gaping windows—"who, I suspect, are watching us at this very moment in the hope of securing the latest nugget of gossip to share at Almack's or White's."

Her quiet, calm dignity—and the fact that she spoke the truth—threatened to dissipate his anger. She ascended the steps and knocked on the door. After a suspiciously short time, it opened to reveal the black-clad butler, who looked more like a beetle than ever. *Devil's coachman,* Whitcombe had once described his own butler, and Wheeler resembled that long-bodied little creature, raising his sting to defend himself—and, most likely, his mistress—against predators.

"Welcome home, Lady Rex," the butler said. "I trust you had a pleasant trip?"

"Yes, thank you, Wheeler," she replied, softening her features into a smile.

Bloody hell—was the butler an accomplice in her infidelity? Why did she gift *him* with her smile?

The butler's gaze fell on Alexander. "Lady Rex didn't tell me she was expecting a guest."

"My apologies, Wheeler," Mimi said. "Would you be so kind

as to have a fire made up in the drawing room, then perhaps a brandy for the duke?"

"Very good, ma'am. And for yourself?"

"Tea," she said. Then she turned to Alexander. "Your Grace, permit me to freshen myself up. Wheeler will tend to your needs while you wait."

"I doubt *that*," Alexander said, aware of the petulance in his voice.

"Perhaps, Wheeler, you'd better bring the entire bottle for my guest, rather than just one glass," Mimi said.

The butler's mouth twitched into a smile. "Very good, ma'am—as you wish." He gestured toward a door at the rear of the hallway. "This way, if you please, Your Grace."

Bloody hell—why did the man act toward Alexander as if *he'd* committed the transgression rather than her? And why must he be treated as a guest to be tolerated—in the house that he paid for?

But rather than voice his disgust, Alexander followed the man toward the rear of the house and into a room furnished in warm autumnal colors, rich reds and browns. Wheeler pulled a cord beside the fireplace, and shortly after the young footman appeared.

"Charles, the mistress has a guest. Be so good as to light the fire."

The young man glanced at Alexander. "Wh-while he's in the room, Mr. Wheeler?"

"That can't be helped," the butler replied. "Get on with it."

The footman approached the fireplace, where he plucked a box from the mantelshelf and struck it to release a spark. A small flame burst into life, and he held the box at the base of the fire. Shortly after, flickers of orange glowed in the fireplace, picking out the shapes of the logs.

Like witchcraft.

Alexander hadn't seen anyone light a fire before. Most servants did their best to avoid being seen by their masters, understanding that it was offensive to the eyes of those above stairs to be compelled to look upon those who resided below.

But one disadvantage of such a custom was that Alexander knew little about how to survive. His cook prepared his meals—served by footmen, lest he be offended by the sight of the kitchen staff. His valet dressed and undressed him, and the invisible housemaids and lower servants ensured that his home was kept free of dust and the fires were always crackling brightly in any room he stepped into.

As the footman replaced the box on the mantelshelf, Mimi entered the room. Gone was the shabby cloak and the plain garb of a servant. She had changed into one of her day gowns—a light-blue muslin trimmed with lace.

Did she perhaps intend to tempt him?

The footman glanced from her, to Alexander, then he retreated.

"Forgive me ma'am, for lighting the fire in front of your guest…"

"Thank you, Charles," she said. "That was most kind of you after all the effort you'd gone to lay the fire this morning." She glanced at the clock over the mantelshelf. "It's getting late. You can retire if Mr. Wheeler has nothing else for you to do."

"Thank you, ma'am." The boy bowed and retreated, almost colliding with the butler, who brandished a tray with a decanter and a single glass.

"Ah, Wheeler, thank you," she said, gesturing toward a table. "Please set it there."

"Charles will be back with your tea, ma'am," the butler said, then he poured a measure of brandy into the glass and handed it to Alexander before exiting the room, ushering the footman in front of him.

Mimi approached the fireplace, plucked a poker from a rack beside the grate, and thrust it into the fire. Then she crouched beside it and blew across the logs. The orange glow pulsed with each breath, and flames crackled over the logs. Then she set the poker aside and took a seat.

Clutching his glass, Alexander sat. Then he took a mouthful of brandy.

"You'll not join me in a brandy?" he asked.

"I prefer a clear head."

"Yes," he said, bitterly. "I suspect that's for the best, given your profession."

If he'd upset her, she gave no sign. Instead, she gave a slight smile. After Charles returned with a tray of tea things, she poured a cup and resumed her seat, stirring her tea, the rhythmic clink of the spoon against the cup in unison with the ticking of the clock.

Alexander gestured toward the fireplace. "I hadn't realized it was so easy to light a fire."

She rolled her eyes. "Lighting the fire may be straightforward. The skill is in laying it—in setting out the coal and logs such that the flame has every chance of life, without being smothered. I take it you've neither laid, nor lit, a fire, Your Grace?"

"Of course not."

"Yes, *of course not*, Your Grace."

She continued to stir her tea, the chink of metal against porcelain beginning to needle him.

"Haven't you stirred that enough?"

She set the spoon down and sipped her tea. Then he saw it— the slight shake of her hand.

He'd rattled her, though she hid it well, behind the veil of the heartless doxy.

"To what do I owe the pleasure of your visit, Your Grace?" she asked.

He gestured toward her gown. "There was no need to change on my account. That gown's pretty enough, but I've seen you in your whore's garb before."

The teacup rattled on her saucer and she clapped her hand over it.

"Do you let *him* give you pleasure?" he asked.

She set the cup on the table. It rolled off the saucer and fell onto the floor, spilling its contents on her skirts.

She let out a cry, and Alexander leaped forward.

Sweet heaven—had she hurt herself?

"Mimi, are you—"

"I'm fine," she said. "It's nothing I can't deal with. I'm capable of laundering a gown, you know."

"I-I meant, did you hurt yourself?"

He reached for her hand, and his skin tightened at the feel of her slim fingers curling around his. Oh, how he'd missed her touch! He lifted her hand to his lips, but she snatched it free.

"I'm not hurt," she said, the expression in her eyes belying her words.

"Where were you today, Mimi?"

"Or rather, whom was I with?" she replied. "There were three of them for most of the time—at one point I had five in the room with me. Is that what you wish to hear?"

"Did"—he swallowed, yearning, but also unwilling to hear the answer—"did you take pleasure today?"

She rose to her feet, her eyes bright.

"Yes," she said. "Today gave me much pleasure. What do you say to that?"

"What if I threw you out like a cheap whore?"

He flinched at his words, but she remained impassive.

"Think of your reputation, Your Grace," she said, her voice laced with ice. "How would your friends react if even a cheap whore such as myself couldn't stomach your company? If you wish me to leave, then gladly I shall—but not before I have my money."

"There we have it," he said. "Money. Is that all your care for?"

"It's easy for you to have contempt for that which you've never been without," she scoffed. "I daresay you have contempt for that young man who lit this fire—though you're incapable of lighting it yourself. But if you didn't have people to cater to your every whim—to feed and clothe you, to maintain the roof over your head, to light the fires that keep you warm—you'd not survive a single day."

Her words pricked at his conscience. She had sketched a portrait of a pathetic creature, unable to fend for himself.

Unable, even, to prevent his best friend from getting killed…

He reached for the decanter, refilled his glass, then drained it in a single swallow.

"Y-you're a liar," he said, his voice catching as the liquor burned his throat.

"No more than you," she said. "I'll admit I've played a role in the past—every woman in my profession must, if she's to survive. But I have never lied to you—neither have I broken faith, despite what you wish to believe."

"It's not what I wish to believe," he said. "It's what I *saw*. Why else were you creeping about the streets tonight? And I saw you yesterday, just after I left, in the same gown. Whatever part you were playing, it wasn't Lady Rex."

"So you thought the worst of me."

"What am I supposed to think?"

"You could always *ask*," she said, "but I suppose men of your rank prefer to condemn women like me. A whore can be trusted more than a duke—if we don't keep to our word, we'll not survive. But you…you lie to yourself each day. You convince yourself that this soulless life you lead will give you fulfilment and make you happy. But are you happy—*truly* happy?"

She stepped toward him, her eyes glowing in the firelight.

Alexander reached for the decanter.

"That won't ease your pain," she said.

He met her gaze, poured a third glass, then drained it.

She curled her lip in disgust. "Very well," she said. "If you wish to end your days drunk in a ditch, I shan't stop you."

"Don't be melodr—m-melodramatic," he stammered.

She shook her head. "Perhaps I should have left you to the mercy of those men."

He opened his mouth to ask her what men, then the memory

resurfaced—two thugs brandishing knives advancing on him, a harsh female voice, followed by a male grunt of pain—then a painted face swimming into focus as he lay in the gutter, his body aching, concern in her eyes.

"Y-you said you could use your enemy's weaknesses against him," he said. "Is that what you were doing today?"

She raised her eyebrows.

"Am *I* your enemy, Mimi?"

For a moment, she stared at him, and he held his breath, fearing her response.

Then she sighed. "No. You're not my enemy—you never could be." She turned her head toward the fire, which now blazed merrily. "I have not lain with another man since we met," she said. "Today I visited"—she drew in a deep breath—"friends. Women whose need is greater than mine. You see me as a doxy who spreads her legs for cash. It's not the cash I strive for, but the choices it gives me."

She turned to face him, and his heart almost cracked at the expression in her eyes: dignity—more dignity than any lady in Society displayed, for it came from her soul, not her rank or fortune.

And her honesty.

Shame stabbed at his hollow heart, shriveling his pathetic soul. How could he have believed her to have broken faith? He may outrank her, but she was his superior, in every sense.

"Mimi, forgive me," he said.

"There's nothing to forgive."

"But what I said—"

"Was not unexpected for a man in your position." Then she smiled. "Shall you remain here tonight?"

His manhood stirred at her invitation. The thought of taking her—of laying her down on the hearthrug and claiming her in front of the fire—was almost too much, and his hands twitched with the need to be buried in her hair as he buried himself into her willing body.

But her willingness was bought and paid for—not given freely. He wanted her consent, free from the promise of cash—and he wanted her pleasure.

"I should go," he said.

Her smile slipped.

"You'll still get your money, Mimi," he said. "All two thousand—no matter what happens. But you must answer me truthfully."

"What do you want to ask me?"

"Lady Walton's ball," he said. "Do you wish to go?"

"She has invited me."

"But do *you* want to go? Not because Lady Walton has invited you, or because I want you there—but for your own sake."

She lowered her gaze to her hands that she'd clasped together. Then she shook her head.

"No," she whispered. "But I will go, because you require me to."

"Then," he said, taking her hand, a seed of hope sprouting in his heart when she didn't withdraw it, "as my way of atoning for not trusting you, I release you from any obligation to attend. I shall go, and if you choose to come, I'll be honored to dance with you. But if you prefer not to go, then you have my full blessing. You are a free woman."

Fighting against the desire to bring her hand to his lips, he caressed her fingers.

"Mimi," he said, "Lady Rex—would you consider accompanying me to the Waltons' ball on Tuesday?"

"I…" She shook her head. "I-I don't know. B-but you may stay tonight if you wish."

He withdrew his hand, his heart shriveling with shame. She was offering her body to comfort him in the light of her rejection.

No accusation she could level at him would make him feel any more ashamed.

"I think, perhaps, you'd prefer an evening to yourself," he said. "If you have no objection, I'll call on you tomorrow, and we can explore the park again."

She nodded. "Yes, I'd like that, Your Grace."

"Might you call me Alexander?"

"If you wish."

He suppressed a sigh. "I'll see you tomorrow, Lady Rex." Then he bowed and exited the drawing room.

The butler opened the front door as Alexander approached.

"Thank you, Wheeler," he said. "Take good care of your mistress, won't you?"

"I will, Your Grace," came the reply. "As should we all."

Alexander thrust his hands into his pockets and stepped outside, then he turned back toward the house as the butler was closing the doors. Shortly after, he saw a light in a window on the upper floor—Mimi's bedchamber.

He caught his breath. Perhaps she might draw back the curtains and look out, hoping for a glimpse of him.

But she did not appear.

CHAPTER SEVENTEEN

A MYRIAD OF colors filled the ballroom—bright silks and glittering jewels shimmering in the candlelight as the ladies milled about, their bodies seeming to vibrate with anticipation of the night to come.

But none of them had any appeal—because none of them were *her*.

Alexander glanced at the longcase clock in the corner. It was almost a quarter past seven.

The doors opened and Alexander's heart swelled with hope as the footman straightened his stance, ready to make an announcement.

Lady Rex…

"Lord and Lady Radham!"

Damn.

Radham entered the ballroom, his diminutive wife on his arm—an exquisitely beautiful creature who, despite having recently emerged from her confinement, had managed to regain the figure that had once made her the toast of Society. Radham caught sight of Alexander and his expression hardened.

And well it might, given that Robert Staines—the man whose death Alexander had caused—had been Radham's elder brother.

"Sawbridge." He gave a curt nod, while Lady Radham clung to her husband's arm, as if seeking protection from the vile beast standing before her.

"Radham"—Alexander bowed—"and Lady Radham. I trust you're well."

"Quite so, thank you," she replied, after a pause, frost in her tone.

"We hadn't expected to see you at a ball so soon after your...*accident*," Radham said, his voice almost a snarl. "I trust your leg's healing?"

"It still pains me a little."

"And rightly so," Radham said.

"Andrew." Lady Radham spoke in a soft warning, and Radham turned to her. They exchanged a smile. Then he patted her hand and resumed his attention on Alexander.

"I trust you'll be restored to full health soon," he said through gritted teeth.

"Thank you," Alexander said, "I'm ashamed to say that—"

"There's Lavinia!" Lady Radham cried. "We must say how-do-you-do to our hostess. I wouldn't have her think me uncivil."

She steered her husband toward the opposite end of the room, where Lady Walton stood in conversation with one of the footmen.

No, Lady Radham—I wouldn't have you uncivil to anyone other than myself.

"Decided to show your face again, Sawbridge?" a male voice asked.

Earl Thorpe stood before him.

"Thorpe," Alexander said, offering his hand, which the man took, "your wife must have lost some of her fire if she's given you permission to speak to *me*."

"Henrietta's at home with the children," Thorpe said, "otherwise she'd insist I call you out."

"I've done nothing against her honor."

"Perhaps not, Sawbridge, but you've made quite a name for yourself." Thorpe grinned and clapped Alexander on the back. "Don't look so downhearted," he said. "Give it a few months and the world will have forgotten your little transgression."

"Hardly a *little transgression*, seeing as I got my best friend killed."

"He got *himself* killed," Thorpe said. "He chose to race a carriage while blind drunk. And you hardly escaped unscathed. I take it your dancing days are over."

"My leg's almost healed, but I don't intend to dance tonight," Alexander replied.

"Probably for the best—it'll spare you the humiliation of rejection if you asked anyone to partner you."

"There's nobody here tonight with whom I wish to dance."

"Then you'd better sit," Thorpe said. "A gentleman standing at a ball is considered fair game for an unpartnered lady."

"Even though any lady I asked would refuse?"

"The victory is in being *asked*," Thorpe said. "But I daresay there's one or two more...*forgiving* ladies inclined to accept you tonight. You might try Lady Walton, seeing as she was benevolent enough to invite you. But take care not to offend anyone. I'll wager every man in the room is poised to call you out should you misbehave tonight. You wouldn't want to find yourself at the point of a pistol at dawn."

Alexander let out a snort. "A duel? I doubt half the men in the room, save Colonel Reid, perhaps, would know one end of a pistol from the other."

"Which makes them all the more dangerous."

"How so?"

"You'd then be at risk of facing the infamous Farthing."

"The *what*?" Alexander asked.

Lady Portia Hawke approached. One friendly face, at least—Foxton's sister had been almost civil to him in Hyde Park the other day. He nodded at her and was encouraged when she returned his smile.

"The Farthing is the latest sensation," Thorpe said. "He makes a living fighting duels by proxy. If a man fears for his life due to a lack of prowess with a pistol, he hires the Farthing to do the deed instead."

"And who is *the Farthing?*"

"Nobody knows. He's called the Farthing because he's capable of hitting a farthing at fifty paces."

"Nobody possesses that level of marksmanship. A man that skilled would have no need for disguise. Unless…" Alexander glanced at Thorpe. "Where did you say your wife was tonight? Isn't she an infamous duelist?"

Thorpe's expression darkened. "Henrietta is skilled with a sword, not a pistol—and she knows better than to profit from dishonor and cowardice."

"I thought a duel was the ultimate act of honor."

"But to hire another to fight it on your behalf?" Thorpe shook his head. "Nothing could be more dishonorable. The Farthing is to be reviled, not revered. Ah, Lady Portia. How pleasant to see you."

Lady Portia scowled, her eyes dark with distaste.

"Forgive us, Lady Portia," Alexander said. "A duel is not an appropriate subject of discussion when ladies are present."

"Or, indeed, at all," she said. "If you'll excuse me."

She turned her back and disappeared into the crowd.

"Quite the pariah, aren't you?" Thorpe said. "How about we indulge in a wager? Fifty guineas says you'll not find a single woman to stand up with you."

Alexander shrugged. "Very well. I care not."

Thorpe let out a snort. "Sometimes a man can be too rich." Then his eyes widened and a broad grin stretched across his face. "How about we make it a round one hundred if you can get that lovely creature over *there* to dance?"

"Which lovely creature?"

"By the entrance. I've not seen her before, which, at least, means you've a fair shot at her if she's not heard of you. Though you'll have a fight on your hands. I wonder if the poor woman knows that the unattached males in the room will view her as fresh prey to fight over?"

Alexander craned his head to get a look, but the door was

obscured by Colonel Reid's tall form.

Then the colonel moved aside and Alexander caught his breath.

A vision of beauty stood in the entrance.

She was dressed in pale-purple silk that shimmered in the candlelight. The simplicity of her gown was not overshadowed by the fashionable creations adorning the other ladies. Rather, in its elegant lines that accentuated her form, it outshone every other gown in the room as the sun outshone a candle. Her hair was fashioned into curls, dotted with tiny violet flowers that matched the stone in the choker she wore around her neck. The jewel glimmered as her chest rose and fell, the only evidence that she was a living, breathing woman—as opposed to the statue of a goddess.

The murmur of conversation dissipated as the crowd turned toward the newcomer. For a moment, uncertainty shone in her eyes, as if she believed herself unworthy of the company.

But she was wrong. They were unworthy of *her*.

"Lady John Rex!" the footman announced.

A murmur rippled through the crowd and her eyes widened with alarm as she glanced about.

Then her gaze fell on Alexander, and his heart soared as her lips curved into a smile.

He stepped away from Thorpe and approached her, hand outstretched. But before he reached her, their hostess appeared.

"Lady Rex, how delightful!" she said. "I'd almost given up on your coming."

Mimi dipped into a curtsey. "Lady Walton—Countess—forgive me for being late."

"Only fashionably so," came the reply. "You've arrived at precisely the right time, for the first dance is about to begin, and I would very much like you to lead it—if I'm not being too forward."

Mimi glanced about, apprehension in her eyes. Then Walton appeared at his wife's side and extended his hand.

"Lady Rex, would you do me the honor of partnering me for the first dance?"

Alexander stared at their host. For what purpose was he honoring Mimi—a woman he barely knew other than by association to Alexander himself, a man whom he detested?

But rather than show surprise, or discomfort, Mimi took the earl's hand and nodded.

"Perhaps you'd care to name the first dance," he said.

Shit. Would she betray herself—her ignorance of Society parties and dances?

But, after a slight hesitation, she nodded. "Captain Cook?"

"Excellent choice," Lady Walton said, and she glided across the room toward the lead musician, who nodded and began tuning his violin. Then Lord Walton led Mimi to the top end of the dance floor and the melee of guests shifted into focus to form a line that stretched toward the opposite end.

As Lady Walton returned, Colonel Reid approached her, but she shook her head and placed a protective hand over her belly.

"My dancing days are done, I'm afraid, colonel," she said. He nodded and moved toward two ladies standing nearby. Shortly after, he escorted one onto the dance floor, joining the end of the line. Alexander caught Lady Portia Hawke watching them, arm in arm with her brother, Foxton. She whispered in his ear and Foxton shook his head. He released her arm then strode across the floor, while she frowned and sat, waving away a footman who approached with a tray of champagne glasses.

The dance began and Mimi moved, forming a figure-eight pattern with her partner as they circled the couple next in line. Then she took his hand as they glided along the line in time to the music.

How the devil had she learned how to dance?

"Perhaps you might ask Lady Portia to dance," a female voice said, and Alexander turned to see Lady Walton staring at him. "She's in want of a partner, now her brother's abandoned her. And it's the height of bad manners for a man to remain standing at a ball when there are ladies without partners."

He let out a laugh. "What—and be refused?"

"I daresay Lady Rex wouldn't refuse you," she said, as Mimi moved along the line of dancers with the fluidity and grace that was, most likely, the envy of every female in the room. "And," Lady Walton added, "given that every man is now looking at my husband with envious eyes, your association with her might render you a little more desirable among the company."

"Is that why you asked her to lead the dance? To make *me* a little more desirable among the company?"

She wrinkled her nose. "You always were the most insufferably arrogant man," she said. "I cannot think why Lady Rex associates herself with you."

"Perhaps because she, unlike the rest of Society, judges me on my current behavior, rather than past sins that I have striven—and failed—to atone for."

"For that alone, she deserves to be honored," came the reply. "She must possess a degree of compassion the rest of us lack."

"You're very kind, Lady Walton."

"Not at all." She smiled. "Lady Rex dances well. Remarkably well—I'm afraid my husband is unfamiliar with this particular dance."

"How can you tell?"

"See there?" She gestured toward the leading couple. "Peregrine took a wrong turn, but Lady Rex steered him on the right path—almost as if she anticipated his move. I wonder what other accomplishments she has. Do you know?"

"I'm afraid not."

"Does she sing, or play the pianoforte? She might entertain us at supper."

Alexander shook his head. "I've no idea."

"I thought you were a family friend."

"I-I knew the late Sir John Rex."

His cheeks warmed as she stared at him. Why did some women possess the ability to look right inside a man's soul?

"Does it matter who her family is—or was?" he asked. "I thought you were above valuing your friends only in relation to their rank."

"Oh, I am," she said. "But I find it surprising that you know so little of her background. I thought you set store by such things—background and rank."

At that moment, Mimi glided past, and Alexander's heart fluttered as she met his gaze.

Not anymore, I don't.

Lady Walton smiled. "Perhaps there's hope for you after all."

Bugger. He'd said that aloud.

The dance concluded to gloved applause, and the dancers dispersed. Alexander's gut twisted with apprehension as Walton led Mimi toward the edge of the ballroom, followed by a cluster of young men. His apprehension turned to envy as each man bowed over her hand. But as each prospective dance partner attempted to kiss her hand, she withdrew it, a benign smile on her lips. The last suitor to present himself, a gangly youth, couldn't contain his enthusiasm as he grinned broadly at her, his face flushing scarlet. She withdrew her hand with a smile, but patted his arm indulgently before retreating to the edge of the room.

She glanced about, and when she met Alexander's gaze, he felt a tug at his heart, as if an invisible thread connected them. Then she approached him, the pimply youth in tow. Alexander held out his hand to her. The youth scowled, but Alexander set his mouth in a hard line and drew himself to his full height. The youth's eyes widened as he recognized the stance of the dominant male, and he retreated with a scowl of petulance, as if he'd been denied his favorite toy.

That's it, young sir—she'll not waste her time on a boy in the presence of a man.

His heart slid into place as she slipped her gloved hand in his.

"Lady Rex," he said, "you cannot imagine what joy it brings me to see you here tonight."

"Your Grace," she said, dipping into a curtsey, a smile on her lips, and his blood warmed at the prospect of kissing them—a pleasure she had so far denied him.

"Has anyone told you how beautiful you are?"

Her smile slipped. "Frequently. I'm sure every man alive pays such a compliment to a woman when he wants to—"

"I say!" Thorpe approached and slapped Alexander on the back. "Are you not going to introduce me to this heavenly creature, Sawbridge?"

"This is Lady Rex, as well you know," Alexander said. Then he turned to Mimi. "May I introduce Giles Thorpe—earl, former schoolfellow, and reprobate."

Thorpe took her hand. "A pleasure, Lady Rex."

Her eyes widened, and Alexander caught a flicker of fear in them. Then she blinked and the fear was gone, but she stiffened and withdrew her hand.

"*Former* reprobate?" she asked.

Thorpe let out a laugh. "I suspect the former referred only to the schoolfellow. But if anyone knows about being a reprobate, it's Sawbridge here."

"Your father knew a thing or two about decadence, Thorpe," Alexander said, piqued at Mimi's interest in the man. "Famous for it, he was, leading himself, and many of his friends, into ruination."

"Perhaps, but, as I've learned, the generation that follows must pay for the profligacy of the generation before," Thorpe said. "Your heir, if he comes into being, will, I'm sure, learn that very lesson, Sawbridge."

"Lord Thorpe, I thought Sawbridge was your *friend*," Mimi said, an edge to her tone.

"In which case he'd do well to heed my warning," Thorpe replied. "I wouldn't wish any son—or daughter—to suffer destitution because their parents lacked the foresight to ensure their finances were in order."

Mimi drew in a sharp breath and stepped back.

"Forgive me, Lady Rex," Thorpe said. "I understand you're lately out of mourning. It was most remiss of me to discuss what must be a painful subject."

"Quite," she said. "Grief is afforded a set period of time, after which it must be hidden away or ignored altogether. But those dear to us whom we lose should never be forgotten, no matter how painful their memory may be."

The music struck up once more, and Thorpe bowed over Mimi's hand.

"I think Lady Rex might prefer a little air," Alexander said. "Tonight is her first social engagement in London."

"But I was going to ask you to partner me in this next dance, Lady Rex," Thorpe said.

"That's very kind," Mimi replied, "but I'm promised to His Grace."

Alexander's heart soared as she turned her wide, expressive eyes to him, and Thorpe frowned, most likely over having just lost one hundred pounds.

The music began, and Alexander steered her onto the dance floor. Mimi glanced about the ballroom as a number of couples began to twirl about the room.

"I-I'm afraid I don't know this dance," she said.

"Allow me," Alexander said, slipping an arm around her waist and pulling her close. "It's a waltz. Most scandalous, but it has three benefits over a quadrille or cotillion."

"Which are?"

"The first," he said, his blood warming at the feel of her soft body pressed against his, "is its simplicity. The steps—a repeated series of three movements—are easily learned, even for one such as I. The second is that the proximity of the couple to each other enables a more frank discussion, without the fear of being overheard."

"And the third?"

A fire raged through his blood as he felt her body softening in his embrace—a symbol of her trust.

"The third—and perhaps the *only* reason for a waltz, in my view—is that the man leads."

"Is that not what your sex does as a matter of course?" she said. "Lead, rule, dominate?"

"By law, perhaps, but on the dance floor, the woman dominates, for she has the power of refusal. And when a woman surrenders that power by submitting to a waltz, she permits her partner to lay his claim on her."

"I am at your mercy, sir, by virtue of not understanding the true nature of a waltz."

Alexander spun her round and inhaled the soft scent of rose. His cock surged with need at the sharp undertones of something else.

Female arousal.

"You may exercise the power of refusal now, if you wish, Mimi," he said.

She shook her head. "The dance has begun. Neither of us would be satisfied if it failed to reach its conclusion."

He lowered his gaze to her neckline, and his cock stiffened at the sight of her delectable form—the swell of her breasts against her gown, and the tempting valley between them that no manner of intricate embroidery could distract his hungry gaze from. And below her neckline…

Heavens! He was in danger of spending at the sight of the two little peaks poking at the fabric of her gown.

No wonder bloody Walton had such a smile on his face after he'd danced with her, if such a sight had been before him!

"Why, Your Grace, I believe you're enjoying this dance," she said, flicking her gaze down to his groin.

"Either that, or there's a prize marrow in my breeches, Lady Rex."

She let out an unladylike snort, and a nearby couple glanced toward them. The lady frowned, and Alexander recognized the Honorable Sarah Francis. He gave her a brilliant smile, then resumed his attention on his delectable partner.

How much better a prospect for pleasure she was than some brittle debutante! She had no need for the façade of genteel disapproval at anything he said, no matter how crude, and he was guaranteed entry to her bed. But more than that, her soulful eyes, which gave a glimpse of the woman behind her mask, stirred the heart that he never knew existed. When she looked at him she didn't see the duke, the title, or the wealthy suitor.

She saw *him*. Alexander.

What a pity they must part eventually! But he had months yet to enjoy her to the full.

And enjoy her he would.

The dance concluded, and he steered her toward the edge of the ballroom, almost colliding with Foxton and his sister.

"Lady Portia," Mimi said, "are you enjoying the ball?"

"Not particularly."

"Sister…" Foxton growled, and Lady Portia tilted her face to one side and gave a wide smile.

"Oh, I'm having *such* a pleasant time!" she trilled. "The company leaves a lot to be desired, but I can at least console myself that my brother will soon be exerting his dominance over the gaming room, which might afford me a little room to breathe in the ballroom."

"I won't leave until I'm satisfied that you'll not run wild as soon as my back is turned," Foxton said.

"Given that you'll never be satisfied by anything I do or say, brother, I'm afraid you must remain here for the rest of the evening rather than fritter away my dowry at the card table," she retorted. "What a disappointment that must be for *you*. I know you hate balls. And company. And dancing. In fact, is there anything you *don't* hate, brother?"

Foxton's face darkened. "Why, you—"

"Lady Portia, how remiss of me," Mimi said. "I quite forgot to tell your brother that I'd offered to chaperone you tonight. I trust that meets with your satisfaction, sir."

Foxton glanced at his sister and raised his eyebrows. At that moment, Mimi winked at Lady Portia, and Alexander suppressed a laugh.

"*There*, brother!" Lady Portia said. "You have leave to waste your fortune at the card tables, while I relish my freedom—if only for a little while."

"Don't worry, little cat," Foxton said, a sneer in his voice. "Walton refuses to permit an exchange of vowels in his home. My potential loss is therefore confined to the coins in my pocket."

"Whereas I've nothing to lose," Lady Portia said.

"Except your reputation," Foxton replied.

"Your Grace, are you impugning your sister's morality, or my integrity as chaperone?" Mimi said, her voice carrying the sternness of a matriarch.

"Lord save me from the female sex!" Foxton huffed. "Come along, Sawbridge. I daresay you have coins to wager. I'm anxious to discover if I'll have more success at the card table than I do keeping that hellion in check."

Alexander withdrew his arm from Mimi's, and she frowned.

"You're going with him?" she asked.

Foxton barked with laughter. "Ha! Grasping already, my dear? Take care, Sawbridge, if this merry little widow has set her cap at you. But I'll warn you, madam—nobody is better at the game than Sawbridge here. You have no hope of victory. Nothing is more off-putting for man than a grasping, desperate—"

"That's enough, Foxton," Alexander growled, taking Mimi's hand. "Lady Rex is an independent woman who knows her own mind."

"Ye gods, man," Foxton said. "Has she turned you into a milksop?"

"Certainly not," Mimi said. "I'm the last person who'd want anyone to forgo pleasure on my account." She glanced at Foxton, a cold smile on her lips, and Alexander caught a flicker of disdain in her eyes. "I understand how men of your rank detest the very notion of being considerate—let alone obligated—toward others. Please, enjoy the rest of your evening and permit Lady Portia and

I to enjoy ours."

Alexander's heart swelled with pride at her quiet dignity. To think—a doxy, putting two dukes in their place!

But no ordinary doxy was she.

Lady Walton's question slipped into his mind.

Do you know anything of her family?

Perhaps that was why she refused to tell him her real name, for fear he'd recognize it. Was she a lord's daughter, perhaps, who was ruined and suffered the consequences? Was that why she'd risen to Lady Portia's defense—to protect a wayward young woman as she was not protected herself?

"I fear I've been bested," Foxton said.

"Oh no, Your Grace," Mimi replied. "A man such as yourself would never permit himself to be bested—at least not knowingly."

Foxton rolled his eyes. "Come with me, Sawbridge," he said. "Save me from the tongues of harridans."

Alexander's blood warmed at the prospect of the pleasures to be had from the tongue of the particular harridan in front of him. But the urge to remain with her warred with the need to join the men in the gaming room. Tonight was his chance to reingratiate himself with his former friends and secure sponsorship for his reapplication to White's.

But as he watched Mimi glide across the ballroom, arm in arm with Lady Portia, he was struck with the realization that the prospect of a night of gaming with his friends no longer held any pleasure.

In fact, pleasure, for him, was only to be had in her company.

CHAPTER EIGHTEEN

FOR A MOMENT, Mimi thought Sawbridge might remain with her, but he clapped his friend on the back and they disappeared through a door at the opposite end of the ballroom, beyond which a cloud of blue smoke was already forming.

"Brandy and cigars!" Lady Portia huffed. "They think their propensity to consume ridiculous amounts of both places them on a pedestal. But I suppose it relieves us of their company for a while. We'd best take advantage—Lord Walton is famous for only keeping his card tables open for a short while. Lady Walton's orders."

Mimi glanced at their host, who paraded about the ballroom with his wife. "They seem very happy together," she said. "When we danced just now, he spoke of nothing but his wife. A man ready to bore his dance partner with tales of his wife's virtues must be in love."

Lady Portia let out an unladylike snort. "Happiness in marriage is as unlikely as—as a doxy marrying a duke."

Cold fingers caressed the back of Mimi's neck. "A...*what?*"

"Forgive me. Don't tell my brother—he'd be angry if I spoke of doxies. He loves me, I'm sure, but he's always so strict."

"I won't say anything," Mimi said.

"Not that I *care* what he thinks."

"You seem unusually frank, Lady Portia, compared to when we first met."

"*Portia*, please," her companion said. "You were good enough to save me from my brother's company tonight, so I consider you a friend and can therefore speak more freely. Do you have many friends in London?"

"There's Eleanor—or, I should say, Duchess Whitcombe," Mimi said, glancing about the room. "But she's not here tonight. I thought she would be."

"Eleanor rarely attends large parties," Portia said. "She dislikes the company of strangers, and when the room gets too loud, she struggles to maintain her composure. Those who don't understand her are wont to criticize her. Such as my brother. He thinks she's soft in the head. But I think he's an arse."

She glanced about the room, as if she feared being overheard, then let out a nervous giggle and gestured across the dance floor.

"Just *look* at Sarah Francis! Staring at the men as if she's anticipating a meal. I swear I saw her salivating as she watched your dancing with Sawbridge. I wonder if she'd be as desperate for male company if she knew what dreadful creatures men are."

"You dislike the company of men?"

"There's a few exceptions to the rule," Portia said, glancing toward a group of men in the center of the room. "But for every happily married couple, I'll wager there are twenty wives desperate to rid themselves of their husbands. I—Oh!" Her hand flew to her mouth. "Lady Rex, forgive me. You must think me most insensitive with you recently out of mourning."

"But I am *out* of mourning, Portia," Mimi said, "and therefore you may give your opinion of the male sex freely. I'm less likely to be offended than most."

"I'm glad to hear that. The Duke of Sawbridge has been unable to keep his eyes off you all night. I thought he was going to burst with rage when Lord Walton led you onto the dance floor."

"I doubt that," Mimi said.

"As for Miss Francis, I…" Portia's voice trailed off, and she stiffened. "Miss Francis," she said.

"What about her?" Mimi asked.

"What about me?" a sharp female voice said, and Mimi turned to see the subject of their conversation standing before them. "You seem very much in favor—*Lady Rex*," she said.

Mimi smiled. "That's too kind of you, *Miss Francis*."

"Tell me, for I've been unable to find any information," Miss Francis said, "who *was* your husband? My acquaintance is extensive, and none have heard of him."

"We did not spend our married life in England," Mimi said. "And, as a mere knight, I wouldn't expect you to know him, given your superior rank."

Miss Francis inclined her head. "Quite so," she said. "But I applaud your ambition, associating yourself with Lady Portia— not to mention Sawbridge. But then, I suppose the widow of a knight wishing to elevate her rank can be forgiven for taking such an interest in a duke."

She smiled at Mimi, her eyes glittering with spite.

"Miss Francis," Portia said, her voice tight, "I hardly think that's—"

"Oh, Lady Portia, I'm *touched* by Miss Francis's generosity," Mimi said. "But, Miss Francis, you can rest assured that my interest in the duke will present no danger to you."

"Oh?" Miss Francis tilted her head to point her sharp little nose upward.

"Yes," Mimi said. "My interest in the Duke of Sawbridge is confined to his activities in the bedchamber."

Miss Francis gasped, then her hand flew to her throat in a gesture of exaggerated indignation.

"I'm not skilled in the language of the gutter, Lady Rex," she said. "I don't understand your meaning."

Amusement danced in Portia's eyes, and her mouth twisted into a smile.

"Not only the bedchamber," Mimi said, tilting her head to one side and holding her finger to her chin as if pondering something. "Hmm…there's also the parlor—a chaise longue has its benefits. But I wouldn't recommend a hearth rug. Too scratchy on the knees—at least, on the *man's* knees."

"The...?" Miss Francis stammered, her mouth opening and closing as red patches appeared on her cheeks.

"Then there's up against the paneled walls in the hallway, and of course the dining room. Oh!" Mimi let out a cry, and Miss Francis jumped. "That reminds me, I must ask my butler to polish out the scratch on the dining table. The kitchen table is sturdier, but can you imagine the expression on my cook's face if she caught us?"

Miss Francis crumpled. Her champagne glass slipped from her grip and shattered on the floor.

"Sweet Lord—she's fainted!" a voice cried, and two gentlemen appeared. Lord Walton took her by the shoulders while Lord Thorpe fanned her face.

"Miss Francis—what's happened?" Lord Walton asked.

Mimi cursed herself. She'd only meant to humiliate Miss Francis—not shock her into a fit of the vapors.

Lady Walton appeared brandishing a phial, which she unstoppered and held to Miss Francis's nose. Miss Francis shuddered and her eyes snapped open, and Lord Walton helped her to her feet.

"Sarah—my dearest!" a high-pitched voice cried, and a woman approached in a whirlwind of silk and lace in eye-wateringly bright colors.

"Mama..." Sarah whispered. Then her eyes focused on Mimi. "You!"

"What happened, dearest girl?"

"I-it was her. Sh-she said..."

Mimi froze, awaiting the revelation that would assure her eviction.

"Lady Rex and I were discussing Miss Sarah's gown, Lady Francis," Portia said. "Then Lady Rex remarked on how pale Sarah looked, but before we could help her to a seat, she swooned. It must be the heat—or perhaps an overindulgence of champagne. That was your fourth glass, was it not, Sarah?"

"I…" Miss Francis blinked, and her gaze shifted between Portia and Mimi.

"Perhaps a turn on the terrace and some fresh air, Lady Francis?" their hostess said.

"Yes, yes," the silk-clad matriarch said. "Come, dear girl, we mustn't have you overexcited. My daughter has such a fragile constitution, you see, Lady Walton."

"Mind the glass," Lady Walton said. "Farnham—would you be so kind?"

A footman appeared and began clearing up the floor while Lady Francis led her daughter to the terrace doors.

The diversion over, the guests dispersed, while the musicians began retuning their instruments.

"Ah—the dancing is about to resume," Portia said. "Sarah will be disappointed to miss it, though I doubt the gentleman she's set her cap at would agree."

"Why did you protect me just then?" Mimi asked.

Portia grinned. "You saved me from my brother's company, therefore I owed you a debt. Though I must confess my astonishment at your turn of phrase. No doubt a result of married life on the Continent? I hear life's more…*liberal* over there."

"The life I led before coming here was a little unconventional," Mimi said.

"How wonderful! I find convention so restricting, don't you? What did you do? You must tell me about it!"

Mimi's heart sank as Portia's eyes glittered with eagerness. Deception had always been a natural part of her life—it was as natural as breathing to any woman in her profession. But she found herself liking Lady Portia, and disliking the thought of deceiving someone she was beginning to view as a friend.

"Ladies," a deep voice said, "you must permit me to ask how you managed to fell Miss Francis, thereby saving us from her company."

A small group of gentlemen had approached, eyeing Mimi with curiosity and, in the case of some, the hunger of the predatory male.

The man who'd spoken bowed and offered his hand, fixing pale-blue eyes on her. "Sir Heath Moss."

"And the rest of you are?" she asked, ignoring the proffered hand.

He frowned then gestured to the company. "Lord Thorpe—"

"We've already been introduced."

"And the rest are Lord Greyford, Sir Beverley Grant, and"—his mouth curled into a sneer as he gestured toward the young man who'd been following Mimi about earlier—"*Mister* Edward Drayton, the eldest son of the Duke of Westbury."

The youth flinched at the address, and his cheeks turned scarlet—almost bright enough to match the shade of Lady Francis's gown.

Sir Heath gave a smile of triumph, and Mimi gritted her teeth.

You bastard.

Or, rather, he'd just revealed the poor young man's status as such—how else would the eldest son of a duke be a mere *mister*?

Mimi nodded to each man in turn, then held out her hand to the youth. "Mr. Drayton, a pleasure," she said. His eyes widened and he stared at her hand. Then he took it and bowed. Rather than withdraw before he could kiss it, she let him lift it to his lips. Their eyes met and she smiled.

His color deepened, and he opened and closed his mouth.

"Mr. Drayton, did you want to say something," Mimi said, "or, perhaps, ask it?"

The young man shifted his gaze toward Sir Heath, who watched them with contempt in his eyes.

"I-I wondered if you might be engaged for the next dance, Lady Rex," he said. "But, of course, your card will already be full."

"I should be delighted, Mr. Drayton," Mimi said. "I'm not an accomplished dancer. I prefer to listen to music from the comfort of my seat. But I'm happy to make an exception for you."

His blush deepened.

"Well!" Sir Heath said. "Doubtless customs on the Continent differ to those in London. I rather think—"

"You are fond of music, Lady Rex?" Lord Thorpe interrupted, casting a frown in Sir Heath's direction.

"Very, though I have few opportunities to enjoy it," Mimi replied.

"Do you play, Lady Rex? Or perhaps sing?" Lord Greyford asked. "Our hostess would be happy to let you entertain us over supper."

"Sadly not," Mimi said. "I lack the aptitude, which is why I envy musicians so much. Not merely for their talent, but because they can take their music with them. It's always at their fingertips because they can create it for themselves."

"Very prettily put," Sir Beverley said. "Do you have any favorite pieces?"

"I've always been fond of Bach," Mimi said, allowing herself to indulge in a memory from her childhood.

"Bach, indeed?" Lord Thorpe said. "My late mother was partial to his works. She said that to master Bach, the musician needed a degree of technical prowess that surpassed all others. Though, to my untrained ear, I find it difficult to distinguish one composer from another."

"What is it about Bach that you find to admire?" Mr. Drayton asked.

Mimi smiled. "Are you fond of Bach, Mr. Drayton?"

"M-my stepmother is an accomplished pianist," he said. "B-but she's not here tonight, otherwise I'd ask her to play for you."

"You're very kind," Mimi said, smiling at the young man. "What I love about Bach is that his work is honest. It consists of a series of straightforward chords and progressions, brought together in various combinations to create a melody. Unlike the more expressive works such as those of Beethoven, for example, Bach's works must be played with accuracy."

"Surely all music must be played with accuracy?" Lord

Thorpe asked. A ripple of discomfort threaded through Mimi as his eyes darkened, focusing on her.

Did he think she spoke nonsense? Or perhaps he considered himself an authority on Bach.

"Music must, of course, be played with accuracy," she said. "But an artist can disguise their lack of technique with an excess of emotion in their playing when performing the work of artists such as Beethoven, and even Mozart. However, when a musician plays Bach, the slightest technical stumble is more easily spotted—even by the untrained ear."

Lord Thorpe tilted his head to one side, and Mimi's skin tightened with apprehension as he regarded her thoughtfully.

"Yes—that's it," he said, as if to himself. "A friend of my late mother held just such a view. Is that not extraordinary?"

"Not really," Mimi replied. "Doubtless each composer will have his own group of devotees. Bach's works are extremely popular on the Continent."

"Does your late mother's friend play, Lord Thorpe?" Lady Portia asked.

"Sadly, she is no longer with us," he replied. "I never met her, but Mother spoke of her once. She passed some years ago, when I was child—in a shipwreck, if I recall."

A shipwreck…

"What extraordinary tales you tell, Thorpe!" Sir Heath said. "Are you trying to impress the ladies?"

"Not at all," Thorpe replied. "Neither Lady Rex nor Lady Portia strike me as being susceptible to flattery or tales. And I hardly think Lady King's passing is a subject for discussion when a man is trying to impress a woman with whom he wishes to dance. If a man wishes to partner a woman, then he ought to do as young Mr. Drayton has, and simply ask her. Is that not right, Lady Rex?"

Lady King…

Cold fingers clawed at Mimi's gut, and her chest constricted.

"I…"

The world slipped sideways as she opened her mouth and gasped for breath. Then Lord Thorpe's concerned face swam into view.

"Are you well, Lady Rex?"

Mimi swayed sideways, then she felt Lady Portia's arm slip through hers.

"It must be the heat of the ballroom," Lady Portia said. "Did you see poor Miss Francis swoon earlier? I felt a little unsteady myself just then."

"Perhaps it comes from standing too long in one spot," Mr. Drayton said. "I'm sure dancing would restore your spirits, Lady Rex."

Mimi couldn't help smiling at his eagerness.

"Drayton, I hardly think it's seemly to drag a woman onto the dance floor when she's unwell," Sir Heath scoffed.

"I'm quite well," Mimi said, "and I believe a dance with Mr. Drayton is just what I need."

Lord Thorpe frowned, his gaze fixed on her, and opened his mouth to respond.

"I must say I admire the cut of our hostess's gown," Mimi said. "That color suits her complexion perfectly, do you not agree, Lord Thorpe?"

"All gowns look the same to me," he said, a note of disdain in his voice. "Though I daresay the modistes and their patronesses would disagree, so eager are they to see men such as myself part with our cash."

"Then I trust, for your wife's sake, that she has simple tastes," Mimi said.

"She has an eye for color, at least," came the reply. "Which is more than can be said for many of the ladies tonight. Take Miss Francis, for example—I'm sure her modiste has assured her of the benefits of wearing that particular shade of pink, but against it, her face has paled into nothingness."

Mimi let out a snort. "What do men care for a woman's face when there are dowries and titles to be had?"

"You speak from experience?" Sir Beverley asked.

"Naturally," Mimi said, gritting her teeth at the leer in his eyes.

"Ah, there's nothing so alluring as an attractive widow with experience," he said. "I'm beginning to regret not beating young Drayton here to the prize and securing the next dance with you."

"I think you'll find that the hungry suitors hereabouts still prefer a debutante to a widow," Mimi said, "at least when it comes to marriage prospects. After all, a debutante possesses one invaluable quality that a widow does not."

"Which is?"

"Malleability," Mimi said. "A debutante has been schooled—by her governesses, her mama, and her rivals—that she must obey a man in all things, that she must relinquish her freedom, her dowry, and her soul. Whereas a widow has experienced being owned by a man, and she is therefore less willing to walk into the lair, because she is aware of the beast that resides within."

She heard a sharp intake of breath, and glanced up to see Sawbridge had joined the party. He stared at her, his eyes filled with compassion and understanding, and she felt her cheeks smarting.

How much had he heard?

Ye gods—had he heard Thorpe mention…

Lady King.

Her heart still ached from the pain of hearing that name on Thorpe's lips. A name she had long since buried, together with her other self—the naïve creature who had died five years ago.

"You lay down a fine gauntlet, Lady Rex," Thorpe said, glancing at his companions. "I wonder which of my friends here is brave enough to accept it. Such a battle is to be relished."

"Not if you are defeated," Mimi said. "And I intend to be a victor, gentlemen."

The musicians played a brief air, and the guests once more gathered into formation. Mimi extended her hand to Mr. Drayton, and he took it.

"I wish you luck, Drayton," Thorpe said, a smile of wry amusement on his lips. "I daresay not only will you emerge defeated, but you'll be ground into mincemeat."

"Ah, but what a grinding!" Sir Beverley whispered, a lascivious glint in his eyes.

Thorpe clapped him on the back. "Not one you'd survive, old chap. We gentlemen may believe ourselves to be adept at this particular game, but I suspect Lady Rex is the true proficient. Your late husband was a fortunate man, Lady Rex—as is young Drayton here."

"Do you prefer to dance with a gauche, unsophisticated young milksop, Lady Rex?" Sir Heath said.

Mr. Drayton's eyes widened further, and Mimi hardened her voice as she met Sir Heath's gaze.

"Quite so," she said. "But you may find that women who possess free will and true discernment will always prefer Mr. Drayton's gaucheness to your particular mode of sophistication."

Confusion clouded Sir Heath's eyes, and Lord Thorpe let out a bark of laughter. "I'd concede defeat before she bites your balls off."

Mimi lowered her gaze to Sir Heath's groin. "Oh, he's quite safe from that, I assure you, Lord Thorpe—at least while I value my own personal health. And, of course, I'd have to find them first."

Lord Greyford, who was sipping his drink, gave an explosive cough, spraying champagne over Sir Heath.

"Exactly so, Lord Greyford," Mimi said, before turning her attention toward Mr. Drayton. "Shall we?"

The young man took her hand and smiled, revealing little indents in his cheeks, and led her onto the dance floor. Mimi glanced toward Sawbridge, and her gut twisted at the expression in his eyes, which was one of barely suppressed fury.

The dance began, and Mimi gave an inward sigh of relief that it was another formation dance, enabling her to observe the steps of the leading couple—this time, their host and hostess—before attempting them herself. When her turn came, she was able to steer her partner through the steps.

"Are you enjoying the dance, Mr. Drayton?" Mimi asked. "Careful!" she added, as he almost collided with Lady Walton.

He took her hands and pulled her close. "I-I feel unwell," he said, drawing in a sharp breath.

"An overindulgence of champagne?" she suggested.

He blushed, then dropped his gaze to the floor.

"Look up!" she whispered, before he collided with another gentleman.

"How else will I follow the dance?" he asked. "I must watch your steps."

"That's where you're going wrong—you should be taking the gentleman's part, not the lady's."

"Gentleman—*ha!*" a voice said, and Mimi glared at the couple next to them. Out of the corner of her eye, she caught sight of Sawbridge, who seemed to be circling the room, watching her, his expression dark. Their gazes met and he set his mouth into a firm line.

Then she turned, in time to the music, but even with her back to him, she could sense his eyes on her.

The dance progressed and she moved past the gentleman who'd insulted poor Mr. Drayton. As the steps required them to turn, she caught the man's heel with her toe, and he stumbled forward and collided with his partner. But by the time he whirled round to face the culprit, she'd taken Mr. Drayton toward the front of the line.

"Bugger," Mimi's partner muttered as he almost tripped again. "I can't keep upright. Forgive me."

"For your footwork, or your language, Mr. Drayton?" she asked, suppressing a smile at the stricken look on his face. At close quarters he looked even younger—barely more than eighteen and most likely fresh out of school. He was no match for the predators in the room.

"It's our turn to lead," she said, taking his hands as they

turned to face the line. "Follow me."

He glanced at the line of dancers stretching before him. "Oh no, I couldn't possibly—all those people. I'll disgrace you, Lady Rex."

"Nonsense!" she said, smiling at the irony of the notion that the son of a duke would disgrace a doxy. "Just look into my eyes and take my lead, and you'll not put a foot wrong."

"I-I don't know…"

She leaned close to whisper in his ear. "The trick, in dancing, and in life, is to smile and pretend that you're a proficient—that you're one of them, and not a misfit."

"*You're* not a misfit, Lady Rex."

"You may think so, Mr. Drayton, but that's because I've perfected the art of deception. You may think, based on the incivility of others, that you don't belong here—but you've more right to be here than I. Now, let us show the company that we're better than them."

His face split into the smile of an infatuated boy, and he lifted his gaze to her. Then, hand in hand, they moved along the line, stepping in time to the music. The fear in his eyes melted, replaced by confidence and pride, and finally pleasure, as they reached the end.

"There!" she said. "That wasn't too difficult, was it?"

"I missed several of the steps—what will they think?"

"What do we care what they think?" He grinned, then swayed on his feet, and she caught his sleeve. "I think you ought to sit down. Perhaps I spun you round a little too much."

He nodded.

"How much have you drunk tonight, Mr. Drayton?"

"Five glasses, no…" He shook his head. "*Seven*. Sir Heath said I wasn't a man if I couldn't hold my…" He drew in a sharp breath then closed his mouth, and Mimi led him toward a chair. "What will my papa think of me?" he asked.

"I won't tell him if you don't," Mimi said. "But I'm sure he'd say the same as I."

"Which is?"

"That you don't have to drink to excess to prove your manhood. Neither should you let yourself be influenced by others who may not be acting in your best interests. Instead, prove you're more of a man than them."

"Lady Rex, you don't know how pleased I am to hear that. I…"

He leaned toward her, parting his lips for a kiss. She turned her head aside and pushed him back, laughing.

"Mr. Drayton, the champagne's affecting your senses. You've no wish to do something you'll regret when you're sober."

"I'll not regret *this*."

He pulled her close and pressed his mouth against hers. Before Mimi could protest, a pair of hands grasped Mr. Drayton's shoulders and pulled him back.

Mimi turned to see Alexander haul Mr. Drayton across the floor and slam him against the wall. The dancers dispersed, and the music stopped as a ripple of voices threaded through the room.

The young man's eyes glistened with tears. "F-forgive me, Your Grace, I-I didn't—"

"Didn't what?" Sawbridge roared. "Didn't think? Didn't behave like a gentleman? Or didn't realize that you were taking advantage of a lady?"

Mr. Drayton's mouth wobbled and a tear slid onto his cheek. Mimi placed a hand on Alexander's arm.

"Leave him be, Your Grace," she said. "He's just a boy who's taken too much champagne."

"Do you hear that, young sir?" Alexander snarled. "You're a mere *boy*, and Lady Rex isn't the sort of woman to let herself be mauled by drunken adolescents. Perhaps you should retreat to your mama's breast and only return when you've grown into a man and learned how to treat a lady."

"*Alexander*," Mimi said quietly. He froze at the use of his name, and her skin tightened at the raw, potent desire in his eyes, and the savage possessiveness that swelled until a single word entered her mind, uttered in a low growl.

Mine.

A fire of need ignited in her blood, and she caught her breath. His nostrils flared, as if he scented her desire, and she felt his body vibrate under her hand, with the barely suppressed strength of the superior male beast who had bested a lesser rival to claim his female.

For a moment, she let herself indulge in the thrill of his possessiveness. Then Mr. Drayton broke the spell.

"I *am* a man, Your Grace. Lady Rex accepted my hand for this dance."

She caught a flare of fury in Alexander's eyes.

"*What* did you say, *boy*?"

"Sh-she was willing."

"*Willing?*" Alexander roared. "I ought to rip your throat out!" He tightened his grip on Mr. Drayton's lapels and slammed him against the wall again. The young man let out a moan of pain. "Not so much of a man now, are you?"

"Please!" Mimi cried. "The other guests are watching."

"Then let them watch while I pummel this reprobate into the ground," Alexander said. "I ought to call you out, Drayton, but I make it a rule never to duel with *babes*."

"I'd be delighted to—" the young man began, but Mimi interrupted.

"Please!" she cried. "Your Grace, let him go. I'm experienced enough to tell the difference between a drunken, infatuated boy and a predatory man."

"Yes," Alexander said. "I suspect *you* are."

Guilt flared in his eyes, but it was too late. His arrow had hit home.

"L-Lady Rex, f-forgive me," the young man said. "I-I don't know what came over me."

"An excess of champagne, that's all," Mimi said. "But I'd advise you, for your own safety"—she glanced toward Alexander—"to sit out the remainder of the dancing tonight and take a little water. Or, perhaps, go home. Your Grace, please let Mr. Drayton go."

Alexander released his grip and glanced about the ballroom, where a small crowd had formed. Mr. Drayton smoothed his collar, and his lip trembled as he spotted the onlookers.

Then Alexander let out a sigh and offered his hand. Drayton stared at it.

"I'd advise you to take it, young man." The youth nodded, then took it. Alexander pulled him close. "Leave her be," he said, his voice a low whisper. "She is not for you."

"Not until Lady Rex assures me that she'll be safe."

Mimi couldn't help admire the young man's bravery when faced with a bigger, stronger opponent.

"Very well," Alexander said. He slipped Mimi's hand into his, and before she could stop him, he lifted it to his mouth, brushing his lips against it. Even through the fabric of her gloves, the sensation sent a ripple of raw need across her skin, and she closed her eyes, willing her body to resist the flare of desire pooling in her center.

"You have my word, Mr. Drayton, that Lady Rex is safe with me—that she will *always* be safe with me."

Mimi lifted her gaze to Alexander's, and she saw a desire to match her own.

He lifted her hand to his lips once more, and his warm breath penetrated her gloves, bleeding into her soul.

"You have my word, Mr. Drayton," he whispered, "as a gentleman and a suitor."

A suitor…

Gripped by fear, she stepped back.

No—that was *not* supposed to happen. Even if it were part of their charade, he was not supposed to claim her as such, to give her even the tiniest glimpse of what life might be like were she to remain by his side.

He wasn't supposed to be gallant, or kind.

A soulless duke—that's what he was. A wastrel who'd frittered away his life and reputation by indulging in drink and debauchery—the perfect customer for a doxy wishing to earn a sizeable enough lump sum to free her from him and others just like him.

But if he gave her a glimpse of a different man—a man of honor, who wanted her for herself—then he placed her in the greatest danger of all.

The danger that she might not have the strength to leave when the time came.

Lady Walton approached, frowning. "Lady Rex, are you well?"

"Yes, thank you," Mimi said. "But I have a megrim. Would you excuse me? It's my first ball after coming out of mourning, and I fear I may have overtaxed myself."

"I can escort you…" Alexander began, but she raised her hand.

"Please, do not trouble yourself," she said, "and I believe you promised yourself to Lady Portia for the next dance. I wouldn't wish to see her disappointed."

"Let me escort you out," Lady Walton said, before Alexander could respond.

Mimi let her hostess lead her across the ballroom and through the double doors, where she glanced over her shoulder to see Alexander watching her, a mixture of confusion and disappointment in his eyes.

Oh, Alexander—you don't know how much I'd rather stay and hear, once more, your promise to keep me safe.

But if she could walk away from him now, in a ballroom full of people where he'd declared his claim on her, she could harbor the hope that, at the end of their arrangement, she could survive their parting with her heart unscathed.

CHAPTER NINETEEN

S*HE WILL ALWAYS* be safe with me.

It was as much of a declaration as he could muster—yet she had walked away from him.

No, not walked. *Run.*

But she'd called him Alexander…

His whole body had tightened on hearing his name on her lips. What might it be to hear her screaming it as he pleasured her? He took such pleasure from her—almost the slightest touch of her hand sent him into a frenzy of need. But it wasn't his pleasure he craved with every fiber of his soul. It was *hers.*

He turned to follow her, then caught sight of Lady Portia, her face flushed scarlet.

Damn.

What had possessed Mimi to declare, to the whole room, that he was promised to Lady Portia?

He held out his hand. "Lady Portia."

"I-I have no wish to dance," she said. "At least…" She glanced across the room.

"At least not with *me?*"

She lowered her gaze.

"Is there another with whom you'd prefer to dance?"

"It matters not," she said. "I'm obliged to refuse anyone who offers now you have asked me—or rather, now that Lady Rex has committed us."

"Lady Rex would not have made such a suggestion if she knew it would distress you," he replied. "I would be delighted to honor the promise made."

"Honor? Something about which you know nothing."

"Then let me at least give the *appearance* of honor by dancing with you." She frowned, and Alexander leaned closer. "If your preferred partner is here tonight, Lady Portia, the sight of your dancing with another might compel him to ask you next time. There's nothing so desirable to a man as a woman who is favored by others."

He took her hand and led her into the center of the ballroom.

"We would both rather be partnered by another," he said, "but that doesn't mean we cannot enjoy each other's company. For this dance, at least."

She arched an eyebrow. "Brutal honesty fashioned into a compliment? I find myself tempted to ask who you are, and what have you done with the Duke of Sawbridge?"

"Perhaps I'm attempting to atone for past sins."

"There's more to it than that," she said. "Perhaps there's hope for you after all, though you still have much to learn."

He smiled. "I fear I'd make a troublesome pupil."

"I'm sure Lady Rex is an adept teacher," she said. "I've not known her long, yet I see in her an intelligent, honorable, and kind woman. I wonder why she chooses to associate herself with you."

For two thousand guineas, the treacherous little voice whispered in his mind as they were separated by the dance.

Was that all Mimi valued? His cash?

The company here tonight would vilify her if they knew of their arrangement. But, in reality, the nature of their relationship said more about his character than hers.

"I see the conundrum poses as much of a challenge to you as it does to myself," Lady Portia said as they were reunited once more, and, hand in hand, they moved between their companions, forming a figure eight.

"How so?" he asked.

"Lady Rex doesn't seem the type to set her cap at a duke. She lacks the grasping avarice of other women. Women such as…"

She glanced across the ballroom and smiled. In the corner stood Miss Francis and her mother. The expression on the daughter's face—which almost matched that of the matriarch's—was enough to turn even the freshest milk sour.

"It seems as if dancing with you, while it might elicit my brother's anger, has made me the object of envy of at least one woman in the room," she said. "I ought to be grateful for that, if nothing else."

"There's no pleasure in being envied," he said. "Envy is merely a desire for the possessions of another. I would rather be envied for who I am, not what I own."

"Do you *own* Lady Rex?"

"No," he said. "I fear I never shall."

She frowned. "Was it envy that compelled you to fight that poor young man?"

"Whom?"

"Your Grace, do not take me for a simpleton. Mr. Drayton is barely more than a boy. My friend acted out of kindness when she danced with him—to spare him the barbs that Sir Heath Moss and his set were taunting him with."

"Mr. Drayton, no matter his age, should not have—"

"Mr. Drayton had taken too much champagne," she said. "An excess of liquor and an infatuation with an intelligent woman of character are a deadly combination in a naïve young man. I've no doubt that were Lady Rex in danger, she'd have dealt with it on her own terms, rather than relying on the primitive act you displayed. A desire to protect my friend was not what drove you to act in such a manner—but the desire to *own* her. Lady Rex is not Mr. Drayton's possession. Neither is she yours."

"You speak frankly for a woman in your situation," he said.

"What—the sister of a duke who's determined to keep her under lock and key until he marries her off?" She let out a bitter laugh. "I must enjoy frankness, and freedom, while I can. The time will soon come when I'm forbidden to display the former, and deprived forever of the latter."

"Your brother will act in your best interests, surely, when he finds you a husband."

"Yes," she sighed. "Women of my rank must endure the restrictions placed on us by those who *act in our own best interests.* It's no wonder that Lady Rex sought to leave the ball of her own accord."

"She left because she was angry with me," Alexander said.

"If you believe *that*, then you lack understanding of the female mind," she replied. "She didn't leave because of the words or actions of others. She left because she *could*. And for that, she deserves our admiration—and our envy."

"I thought you frowned upon envy, Lady Portia."

"I envy Lady Rex her freedom, Your Grace," she said. "Freedom is something one can envy with a clear conscience, because I have no need to take away *her* freedom to secure mine."

The dance came to an end, and Alexander led Lady Portia toward the edge of the ballroom where Foxton stood with Thorpe, his expression darkening.

"You're a brave fellow if you dance with Foxton's sister," Thorpe said. "I thought he was going to pull you off the dance floor and call you out."

"What—for offering to dance with a lady at a ball?" Alexander asked. "I thought it was the height of poor manners *not* to dance with a lady."

"That was until you almost beat that poor boy into a pulp for daring to dance with Lady Rex," Thorpe said. "A pity she had to leave—meeting a lover, perhaps?"

Alexander resisted the urge to plant a shiner in Thorpe's face.

"I daresay she'd have been willing to partner even you in that last dance," Thorpe continued.

"How so?"

"You were dancing to Bach—or are you too ignorant to know

the difference between a Bach air and a country reel? Lady Rex expressed her love of Bach very eloquently this evening. Given that she must be fond of the arts, I wonder what she's doing with a profligate ignoramus such as yourself."

"The prospect of becoming a duchess," Foxton sneered. "Grasping harpies, the female sex—every last one of them. I fail to see why we must subject ourselves to balls and parties when we know that the only reason for such events is for women to prey on us."

"I think, brother, you'd be considered more predator than prey," Lady Portia said. Then she placed a hand on Alexander's arm. "Your Grace, would you please escort me to a seat? I find the company not to my liking."

He took her arm and steered her across the ballroom, settling her into a chair.

"May I fetch you something to drink, Lady Portia?" he asked.

She shook her head. "No, but I would make a request—for your sake."

"Which is?"

"We both of us would rather be in the company of another," she said. "I'm unable to indulge my wish, but I would take consolation from knowing that you, at least, are able to indulge yours."

"You understand much, Lady Portia," he said, "for a…"

"For a woman?" She nodded. "And that is the curse of all women whose minds rise above that of the soulless mannequin. Rest assured, I shall have my freedom, even if I must wait years to achieve it." She leaned forward and lowered her voice. "Give Lady Rex my best wishes for her health and happiness."

He lifted her hand to his lips, then bowed and slipped out of the ballroom. As he entered the hall, a footman scuttled over, and Alexander gave the order to fetch his greatcoat. Then he stepped out into the night.

As Alexander entered Grosvenor Square, he heard music.

Someone was playing the pianoforte. The melodies were simple, and hesitantly played, as if the musician feared the instrument.

Then he heard a discordant note, and the melody began again, this time more slowly.

It was coming from number sixteen.

Was it Bach? He'd overheard Mimi enthusing about the composer, and Thorpe had remarked on it.

What would a doxy know about Bach?

And what doxy would know how to dance? Her accent had slipped within a day of their meeting, indicating that she was no ordinary doxy. But tonight, she'd shown that she was no ordinary woman. The natural daughter of a duke, perhaps? It would explain why she'd taken such a liking to that Drayton puppy.

It was nothing but pure savagery that had compelled Alexander to set upon young the boy—a beast challenging a rival for ownership of his mate.

But he didn't own her.

The melody stopped, then resumed, more slowly. Alexander climbed the steps and knocked on the door. Shortly after, it opened to reveal Charles.

"Oh." The footman glanced over his shoulder. "Y-your Grace, her ladyship isn't expecting you."

"May I come in, Charles?" Alexander asked.

"The mistress is in the drawing room, if you'd like to wait in the—"

"Not particularly," Alexander said, brushing past the footman. "I know the way."

He strode along the hallway, toward the music, which stopped as he opened the door at the end.

Mimi was sitting at a pianoforte. She still wore the purple

gown, but she'd removed her gloves, which lay folded on the top of the instrument. She rose, pushing back the piano stool.

"I didn't know you played," he said.

"I don't," she replied, reaching for her gloves.

"Leave those." He stepped forward and caught her hands, relishing the fizz of need at the feel of her soft skin beneath his fingers.

"You left the ball early," she said.

"After I danced with Lady Portia," he replied. "I wanted nothing more than to be with you, but had no wish to shame her."

The corner of her mouth lifted into a smile. "Perhaps there's hope for you after all."

He gestured toward the pianoforte. "You play beautifully."

She let out a snort and tried to withdraw her hand, but he held it firm.

"Let me withdraw my last remark," she said. "I prefer honesty."

"Where's the dishonesty in admiring music?" he asked. "Whether executed with proficiency or not, to me, the music I heard was beautiful. Not because you have mastered the technique, but because it was *you* playing it."

"Now you seek to flatter me," she said. "Flattery in a man does not become him—at least not when he's come to visit the whore he purchased."

"Don't say such things," he said, his gut twisting with guilt. "You're not a whore."

"Then for what purpose have you visited me?" she asked. "I doubt you came to discuss Bach."

"I came here to talk."

"You're not paying me to *talk*, Your Grace. Would you like a brandy before we retire to the bedchamber?"

Guilt needled at him at the resigned note in her voice, and he shook his head.

"Who are you, Mimi?"

"I am Lady Rex, the—"

"Very well," he said, grasping her by the shoulders. "Who *were* you?"

Fear flared in her eyes, and she looked away.

"No doxy plays Bach," he said, "and no doxy carries herself across the ballroom with the dignity you displayed tonight."

"A good whore can play any role, Your Grace," she said. "You should be pleased I'm giving you value for your coin."

"Mimi, I—"

"Or perhaps you wish to take your pleasure in here, Your Grace?"

"Damn it, woman, will you desist?" he demanded. "I'd be the worst sort of fool if I didn't see that you have the breeding and demeanor of one born into privilege. There's no shame in it—your history is shared by countless women fallen on hard times. I cannot bear the thought of your having to—"

"Please!" she cried, her eyes glistening with moisture. "Speak no more of it. I am what you pay me to be, nothing more. There is no history for you to concern yourself with. There's only the future—your future, with your reputation restored so that you might continue to enjoy the pleasures afforded by a man of your rank."

He pulled her close, and she drew in a sharp breath as she tilted her head up to meet his gaze.

"Do you not understand?" he asked. "I cannot bear the notion of your having suffered a downfall. Too many women are born into privilege then forced to endure a life of destitution."

"So you care nothing for women born into destitution?" she said. "Nothing for those who did not have the start in life that you take for granted—that I once..." She bit her lip and closed her eyes.

"I find that I *do* care, Mimi," he said. "I first came to care when I saw the marks on your body—the scars of hardship. I came to care when I saw the marks on your hands—your beautiful hands."

He lifted her hands to his mouth and brushed his lips against her calloused knuckles, his body tightening with want.

"But I will never care as much for those women—unfortunate though they may be—as I have grown to care for you."

Her eyes snapped open, and his chest tightened at the raw need he saw in them, the desire that darkened their color until they were almost black—black with tiny sparks of silver in their depths, as if her soul cried out to him.

Then he lowered his mouth to hers. For a heartbeat her body softened and his soul soared with hope as she parted her lips with a whimper. Then the whimper turned into a cry and she pushed him back.

But she had revealed something of herself—the tiny part that wanted him as much as he craved her. He lifted her into his arms, and she relaxed, wrapping her arms about his neck as he carried her out into the hallway and climbed the stairs. His heart ached at how she feared the intimacy of a kiss, yet willingly yielded her body for his pleasure.

He strode along the upstairs landing toward the first door, which he pushed open.

"Not in there," she said.

The bedchamber was as he remembered it—welcoming shades of blue and yellow, softened by the dancing firelight. He paused, inhaling the scent of rose, and his body surged with desire.

"*Please*, no," she whispered, the pain in her voice filling the air.

He caught his breath to fight the deep yearning. She was his—bought and paid for—yet the joy of having her willing surpassed any gratification in having her at his mercy. Gritting his teeth, he turned and carried her to the chamber across the hallway, the one where she took him each time he visited.

But tonight, the deep reds and dark wood gave the chamber an air of debauchery that lessened the pleasure to that of mere physical gratification. He might gain release from it, but the thirst in his soul would remain unquenched.

He set her down, and, at once, she reached behind her gown and began untying her sash, while he undid his cravat. She pushed him toward a chair, where he sat and watched her peel each garment off, her face an impassive mask, as if she were performing a dull household task—first her gown, which she draped over a chair by the dressing table, then her petticoats and chemise, until, at last, she stood beside him, naked save her stockings.

He had always taken pleasure in removing a woman's stockings—the feel of the skin of her thigh against his hands as he caressed the tops of her legs, and the soft silk as he hooked his fingers beneath the top, then the slow reveal of her flesh as he peeled each stocking down. The way her skin tightened as he brushed his fingers along her leg, tracing a path toward her ankle—the little creases in the silk as the stocking bunched around her ankles, then the rush of pleasure as he held each stocking up, suspending it in the air, before letting it fall to the floor. That pleasure, since he'd taken Mimi into his life, had swelled into the most potent ecstasy, such that he was in danger of spending each time he touched her stockings.

But that pleasure was yet to come. Wordlessly, she approached him, and he feasted his eyes on her body—the slender neck, those sweet breasts that grew heavy in his hands when he caressed them, her delicate waist, and the flare of her hips, with the triangle of curls above the tops of her stockings. Then she reached for him, the movement lifting those delicious teats, and removed his jacket. Her nimble fingers untied his shirt laces, and she peeled away each layer until, no longer the Duke of Sawbridge, he had become what he yearned to be in her eyes...

A simple man in love.

He placed his hands on her shoulders, running the tips of his thumbs across her collarbone, then he dipped his head for a kiss, but she turned away. She took his hands and stepped toward the bed, where she lay back. He reached for her stockings and peeled them off, unable to resist placing a kiss on each ankle. She stiffened, but did not push him away. Encouraged, he placed his hands on her thighs and parted them, inhaling the sweet, sharp scent of her need. He dipped his head and brushed his lips against the inside of one thigh, and she caught her breath. He glanced up to see her eyes closed, hands at her sides, fisting the bedsheet, and the scent intensified.

She was not playing a role. Her body wanted him—*she* wanted him.

He placed another kiss on her thigh, and she let out a low mewl. Then he traced a path toward the tops of her thighs with his lips, until he reached the curls at her center. He drew in a deep breath, relishing her scent.

What might she taste like?

Closing his eyes, he flicked his tongue out, tasting the salt on her skin. She jerked and then grasped his wrists.

"No!"

He opened his eyes to see her staring at him, her eyes glistening with moisture. "Mimi, I—"

"Let me give *you* pleasure," she said, pulling him over her body with a strength born of resolve that belied her frame. Then she wrapped her legs around his and drew him closer, until he could feel her damp heat against his manhood.

Sweet heaven—she was ready for him!

Unable to conquer his body's need, he thrust inside her, shuddering with pleasure at her slickness. Her scent intensified, smothering the woodsy, spicy cologne that clung to the air in the chamber like a thick fog.

Perhaps that was why she refused to pleasure him in her own chamber—the scent of female desire would overpower the delicate aroma of rose. But how pleasurable it would be to have her chamber marked by her scent, to have her acknowledge her desires each time she went to sleep at night—desires that only he could fulfil.

He withdrew and plunged inside her again, and she lifted her hips to meet each thrust. Pleasure grew, swelling like a tide, and he fought against the instinct to succumb.

No…

She squeezed her thighs together, and he gritted his teeth at the familiar surge in his groin at the delicious friction.

Not until she takes her pleasure…

He gripped her arms, pinning her to the bead, and lowered his face to claim her mouth.

"No!" she cried, twisting her head to the side.

"Let me kiss you, Mimi," he growled. "Would you not take pleasure from my kiss, from my body?"

He withdrew and slipped inside her once more, slowly, and her nostrils flared as a whimper escaped her lips.

"I can feel your pleasure," he said. "I can smell it."

"No…" she whispered. "It's a lie."

"Your body—and your eyes—belie your words, Mimi," he whispered. "Why deny yourself the pleasure I can give you in return for that which you have given me?"

"Alexander, I—"

She broke off, tears swelling in her eyes.

"Does it pain you to speak my name?" he asked. "Can you not take pleasure from it? You deserve to be happy, Mimi, to indulge in pleasure, as I do, as so many do. Why suffer for a sake of a principle—a whim?"

She grasped his arms, pushing him back. "You think I'm indulging in a *whim*? You have no right to take that which I do not wish to yield."

"I don't want to take from you, Mimi," he said. "I only wish to *give*—my heart, and your pleasure."

"No!" she cried. "You know nothing of hearts—and you have no right to my pleasure. You're paying for my body, nothing more."

"Then I'll pay you more," he said. "Name your price. I'll give you everything I own if you would give me your pleasure."

"Some things are not for sale."

"Everything is for sale," he said, lowering his mouth to hers. "Let me kiss you, and I'll—"

He yelped as a sharp pain tore into his arms where she raked her nails over the flesh.

"Devil's bones, woman!" he cried, sitting up. "What the bloody hell did you do *that* for?"

He glanced at his upper arms, which were now smeared with blood—blood to match that under her fingernails.

Fuck—that hurt!

She stared back at him, eyes wide, a feral fear glimmering in their depths.

"You're despicable!" she cried. "Can't you honor our arrangement, if nothing else? You can take my body—use it as you wish. Why must you demand more?" She shook her head. "Perhaps I should have realized. You're all the same. You feel entitled to take what you want if you throw coin at it, and us lesser beings will be grateful for the scraps you condescend to give us."

"Scraps?" he said. "If I recall, you negotiated a hard bargain for your body. Two thousand guineas is a pretty price for a doxy."

"And it's nothing to a selfish reprobate who wastes the life and advantages he was born with," she snarled. "You spend all day indulging in debauchery, when you could be so much more!"

"What would you have me do when the world *expects* me to indulge in the pleasures to be enjoyed by a man in my position?"

"So you live a wastrel lifestyle because Society expects it?" she said, bitter laughter in her voice. "You know nothing of the true nature of nobility if you believe your title gives you free rein to act as you do. A man of your rank does not live in isolation, does he?"

"I am my own man, Mimi."

"And what of those whose lives depend on you?" she asked. "The tenants at your estate—the servants who cook your meals, clean your house, and even dress you because you're incapable of buttoning a waistcoat yourself?"

"My steward sees to them."

"So you absolve yourself of your responsibility to care for them? What if they fall ill, are unable to work, or are preyed upon by the unscrupulous? What if they're left destitute by circumstances within your control but without theirs. Must they suffer?"

A tear swelled in her eyes, and he brushed it away with his thumb, then lifted it to his lips, tasting the salt.

"Mimi, I understand—"

"You understand nothing, Your Grace."

"Then show me," he said. "My ignorance may be due to my station in life, but I can change if you'll teach me. You're already teaching me what it means to be honorable."

She frowned and opened her mouth to respond.

"I am aware that I'm an appallingly bad pupil," he said. "Willful, unintelligent... But I'm eager to learn—to change—if you'd let me. Is that not why we made our arrangement? So I could be a better man?"

"I thought it was so you could give the *appearance* of goodness, to enable you to resume your life of debauchery unhindered by the disapproval of others."

Her words cut through his heart.

"You make me quite ashamed, Mimi," he said. "But you can teach me to be better. Perhaps I can teach you in return."

"What can you teach me about?"

"Trust," he said. "I can teach you that there are some in the world in whom you can place your trust."

"I've survived five years trusting no one," she said. "I see no reason to change now."

"Pleasure, then," he said, shifting his body, still inside her.

Her eyes widened, as if he'd caught her unawares, and her jaw bulged as she gritted her teeth.

"Wait," she said.

"Until what?" he asked. "Until you can let your mind slip sideways once more, so you can deny the pleasure that you crave?"

"I will not become a slave to pleasure," she said. "Not even for a moment."

"Why not?"

She looked away, and he grew still, letting the silence fill the room—waiting for her to break it. At length, she sighed.

"Because once you've tasted pleasure—genuine pleasure—you want nothing else. And so you taste it again, and again, until, each waking moment, you *crave* it."

"Is that so wrong?" he asked. "I find myself craving you each waking moment."

"But you're a *man*."

"Do we not suffer as your sex does?"

"In one aspect, you'll never suffer as we do. Some consequences a man will never have to face. There are—" She broke off, her voice cracking, and he placed his hand on her face, caressing her cheek with his thumb.

"I am no fool, Mimi," he said. "If you are referring to a child, I assure you that I would accept my responsibility if you were to—"

"Stop!" she cried. "*Please*—do not speak of it. If you care about me as you claim to do, then you'll desist."

His heart cracked at the grief in her tone. What had she lost to make her fashion such a thick shell around her heart to hide her despair?

"What do you want of me, Mimi?" he asked.

For a moment, she stared at him, a flicker of understanding in her eyes. Then she blinked and her expression shuttered once more.

"I want to give you pleasure."

Would it have been too much for her to say that she wanted to trust him? That she wanted him to love her?

He shifted inside her once more, and she curved her lips into a smile.

"Thank you," she whispered.

A smile was perhaps the best he could hope for. Closing his

eyes, he let the image of her smile fill his senses while he withdrew from her, then slipped inside again. He continued to move, letting the pleasure build solely so that he could savor it, until it sparkled and shimmered in his mind, enveloping his soul.

"Oh, Mimi…" he murmured as the pleasure rose, a tide swelling in his mind. "How you unman me."

She lay back, her breathing growing more uneven, and he felt her body begin to ripple around him.

Sweet Lord—would she come to pleasure at his touch?

Hope swelling within him, he increased the pace as the wave swelled and soared, then it crested, and his body shattered.

"Oh, Mimi—my love!" He cried her name as, with one final thrust, he fell forward, claiming her body, clinging to her as if his life depended on it. He continued to thrust, his movement growing weaker as he drew out every last drop of pleasure. Then, at last, with a sigh, he pulled her close, placing his head on her chest.

She remained still, her heartbeat racing against his ear. He lifted his head to see her lying beneath him, her head tilted back until the tendons in her neck stretched, jaw clenched, brow furrowed in pain.

"Did you…?" His words hung in the air as she opened her eyes.

She shook her head. Her hands, which she'd formed into tight fists, now unfurled, to reveal tiny red marks in her palms where she'd dug her nails into the flesh.

He took her hand and brushed his thumb over the marks, and she winced as a thick red droplet swelled on her skin—evidence of the pain she endured, rather than surrender to pleasure at his touch.

"May I stay here tonight?" he asked. "With you?"

Fear flared in her eyes once more.

"I only want to hold you," he said, aware of the pitiful tone in his voice. "I-I want to be more than just…"

"We have a business arrangement, Your Grace. But you're

entitled to stay here. After all, you are paying for this house."

The temptation to stay was almost more than he could bear. But he wanted her to be willing—no, *happy*—to receive him.

"I should leave you be."

He withdrew and climbed off the bed, glancing about the chamber for his discarded clothes. With a sigh, she followed and picked up his breeches.

"Here, let me."

He stood, meekly, while she dressed him, buttoning his breeches and shirt, slipping on his waistcoat, and tying his cravat before, finally, she slipped on his jacket and smoothed down the lapels.

His cheeks warmed with shame. She had spoken the truth. He knew nothing about how to take care of himself, let alone those whose lives depended on him. But, from today, he would strive to do better.

"Excellent," he said, glancing at himself in the dressing mirror. "My valet wouldn't be able to tell the difference."

"It's what you're paying for, is it not? I must give you good value for your two thousand."

She flinched as he turned toward her.

"I meant what I said earlier, Mimi," he said. "I want you to show me how those less fortunate live—the women you help. Not to toss a few coins at them, but to *understand*."

"They are not to be toyed with," she said. "You can do what you wish with me. But *they*—"

"I understand," he said, placing his hand on her cheek.

For a heartbeat, she leaned into his hand and closed her eyes, as if drawing comfort from his touch. Then she withdrew.

"I shan't make any demands of you, Mimi," he said. "And I'll not take that which you aren't willing to give. You can trust me on that, if you cannot bring yourself to trust me on anything else."

He reached for the bedsheet and draped it around her shoulders. Then he took her hand and lifted it to his lips. She stiffened, but did not withdraw. Then he bowed and exited the chamber. As he closed the door, he heard the rustle of the sheets and a soft sob. Fighting the urge to burst back inside and take her in his arms, he descended the stairs.

The footman was waiting in the hallway.

"Charles, be so good as to take some hot chocolate to your mistress's chamber," Alexander said, "and a little brandy."

"Yes, Your Grace."

"And take care of her, won't you?"

"Sh-she has a lady's maid."

"Then you must *both* take care of her."

"Are you not staying, Your Grace?"

Alexander shook his head. "Much as I wish it, that would be a violation, Charles."

"I don't understand, Your Grace."

"You will one day, young man," Alexander said. "When you have fallen in love, you'll understand."

He approached the door, which the footman opened, then stepped out into the night, no longer able to deny his heart.

What he felt wasn't mere desire, or the need for gratification. His own pleasure was secondary to hers. And if she did not trust him enough to give her physical pleasure when they made love, then he must find other ways to make her happy.

He would have to woo her.

CHAPTER TWENTY

MIMI STARED AT the mirror, watching her maid's reflection as she styled her hair into ringlets and weaved in an array of pearls. Then she shifted her gaze to her own reflection.

The woman who stared back at her bore an expression of regret, and hope. She steeled herself and shifted her expression until the woman in the mirror was, once more, the elegant Lady Rex.

"Is your hair not to your satisfaction, your ladyship?"

"It's beautiful as usual, Gracie."

"The duke will be even more in love when he sees you tonight," the maid said.

"Don't talk nonsense, Gracie," Mimi replied, as her cheeks flushed pink in her reflection.

"But ma'am…"

Mimi reached up and took her maid's hand. "Gracie, your words are kindly meant, but I cannot afford to think of love."

The maid resumed working on her hair.

When pleasure risked her downfall, what might love do to her soul, other than destroy it?

Mimi forced a smile and nodded encouragement to her maid to continue.

She had come close to pleasure when he'd last visited—the feel of him inside her, filling her completely, and the expression in his eyes as he came to pure bliss. And when he cried her name, his voice deep and soulful…she had almost succumbed. It had taken every last drop of resolve to stem the swell of pleasure that had ignited deep inside her body, flaring with each touch of his hands and mouth.

That had been almost a sennight ago, and he hadn't visited her since. But perhaps that was for the best. His absence had given her leave to visit Mrs. Briggs and console herself in honest, hard work. And she had summoned the courage to take a walk in the park alone, holding her head high, as befitted the respectable widow of a knight. The excursion had not been without its pleasures, as she encountered Eleanor taking the air with her sister and brother-in-law, Lord and Lady Radham. But when Lord Radham had let slip that he was a vicar, Mimi was reminded of just how far beneath these people she existed.

She closed her eyes, recalling the last vicar she'd encountered in her former life: a man caught up in his own piety, who referenced his sermons when casting judgment on her while demanding she service his body—a man who believed himself above the messages he preached, including the basic principle of kindness to others. Would Lord Radham, civil as he was when he believed her to be a knight's widow, treat her with contempt and cruelty if he knew she was a whore?

No—Society would spit on her if they knew the truth. She may have belonged in this world years ago, but that was another life.

A life she had forgotten, until *he* had blundered into her world, setting her pulse racing and her heart aching. He had made her feel again, when feelings were a luxury she couldn't afford, not even for two thousand guineas.

Alexander…

Her maid's eyes widened, and Mimi cursed herself for voicing his name. Did Gracie know that Mimi whispered his name as she brought herself to pleasure in her cold, empty bed? But the craving that had grown in her soul was no longer satisfied by her own hand, the release all too brief, leaving her hollow.

And now, she was on the brink of seeing him again. Tonight would call upon her resolve.

She caught a flash out of the corner of her eye as her maid held up the necklace that had arrived yesterday, along with a brief note telling her to be ready to receive him tonight at six. As Gracie placed it about her throat and secured the clasp, Mimi ran her fingertips over the stones—five diamonds of increasing size, either side of a single amethyst.

"I've never seen anything so beautiful, ma'am," the maid said. "It's perfect for you. The color matches the embroidery on your gown and emphasizes the color of your eyes. The duke is to be admired for his taste."

"Doubtless there was little thought put into the gift, Gracie," Mimi said. "A man of his means can pay others to acquire gifts on his behalf."

"If you say so, ma'am."

A clock struck six in the distance, and Mimi's heart leaped with anticipation.

No—I must not descend into such girlish nonsense!

Mimi rose and let her maid place her cloak about her shoulders. Her heart fluttered at the memory of a similar act, when Alexander had placed the bedsheet about her naked form with a tender reverence that threatened to breach her defenses.

She heard a knock on the main doors and made her way to the top of the stairs, where she saw Charles cross the hallway floor below.

"If I may be so bold, ma'am," the maid said, "may I make a request?"

"Anything, Gracie."

"Enjoy your evening. And take friendship where it's offered."

Mimi patted her maid's hand. "I will."

Then she descended the stairs.

Alexander stood by the front door talking to Charles, his broad back to her. Then he turned to face her.

His eyes, the color of sapphires, darkened as she approached, and he stepped forward and held out his hand. Before she could stop herself, she drifted to his side, slipping her hand through his—a falcon returning to her master.

"You look…" he said, then shook his head. "Forgive me, I know you're not fond of flattery." He nodded to the necklace. "Do you like it?"

His voice wavered and she saw uncertainty in his eyes, as if he were a male bird having brought an offering to his mate and now awaited her verdict.

"It's beautiful, thank you."

"I saw several necklaces, but none were the right color—I wanted it to complement your eyes."

"My eyes are *brown*, Your Grace."

"Y-yes," he said, "but I recalled at the ball how the color of your gown seemed to emphasize your eyes, and I wanted a necklace to suit."

"Then I thank you for your consideration, Your Grace."

"Might you call me by my given name while we're alone?"

She glanced across the hallway to the footman, who stared straight ahead, making a pretense, with little success, of nonchalance.

"Thank you…Alexander."

He smiled and his eyes sparkled with pleasure, the color intensifying to that of a deep ocean into which she yearned to dive. Then she broke their gaze and gestured toward the door.

"Perhaps we should go," she said. "It's past six, and you've yet to say where you're taking me."

He steered her outside, where his carriage stood waiting. Then he helped her inside, climbed after her, and rapped on the side. They set off with a lurch and she almost lost her seat, but he caught her and she was beset by the aroma of wood and soft spices—the scent of a man.

She sat back, fixing her gaze on the window while he spoke about his day, as if they were a courting couple venturing out for the evening. But despite the urge to look at him again, she refrained, for fear that she would see, once again, the expression in his eyes when she'd spoken his name—the spark of joy, and of love.

At length, the carriage passed between a pair of iron gates, entering a drive that led to an enormous building emblazoned with light. A row of torches flanked a wide set of steps that led to a doorway guarded by two liveried footmen.

The carriage rolled to a halt at the foot of the steps, amid a number of other carriages, and excited chatter filled the air as the occupants climbed out and ascended the steps—mostly couples, but the occasional lone gentleman, and Mimi spotted a family of six, a husband and wife and four young women, their feathered headdresses nodding as they chatted animatedly to each other.

Mimi had never seen so many people in one gathering. A private ball she could weather, but a large public event such as this…

She was bound to be discovered—if not due to the nonexistence of Sir John Rex, then as herself. What if a former customer were among the party?

Or worse…

Her gut twisted with fear, and she drew in a sharp breath to temper the nausea.

Then a large hand took hers, and she turned to see a pair of blue eyes focused on her.

"You've nothing to fear tonight, Mimi," he said. "I'm certain you'll have an enjoyable evening. But I promise that if you wish to go at any time, I'll take you home. I merely ask that you come inside, if only for a moment."

"What is this?" she asked, nodding toward the building.

"It's a surprise," he said. "One I hope you'll like. I won't ask you to trust me—I've no right—but I ask that you give me a chance."

The plea in his voice spoke of sincerity.

"Very well," she said.

He smiled and gave a little growl of pleasure, then he pushed open the carriage door and climbed out, helping her after him. He steered her toward the steps and led her inside.

The hallway was enormous—a marble cavern, all pale floors and walls, and a chandelier ablaze with light. Mimi's feet echoed on the stone floor as her companion led her toward a set of double doors, beyond which a small crowd milled about. Strains of music competed with excited voices.

Perhaps it was a ball—but with considerably more guests than Lady Walton's.

"Let me introduce you to our hosts," Alexander said, steering her toward a couple who stood beside the doors, next to a young man she recognized. "The Duke and Duchess of Westbury."

The duke, a tall man with black hair and clear blue eyes, fixed his gaze on Mimi. He towered over the duchess, who regarded Mimi with interest.

"So this is the famous Lady Rex," she said. Mimi glanced toward Alexander, who gave her hand a reassuring squeeze.

"I'm afraid Lady Rex is not fond of compliments, Your Grace," he said. "She is unused to them."

"A travesty that must be rectified if my stepson's account of you is true, Lady Rex," the duchess said. "Is that not so, Edward?"

The young man offered his hand. Mimi took it, and he lifted her hand to his lips.

"Lady Rex," he said, casting a glance toward her companion. "A-and Sawbridge, Your Grace."

"Mr. Drayton, a pleasure to see you again," Alexander said before Mimi could reply. "I fear I was most uncivil when we last we met, for which I apologize."

The young man blushed, and the duchess gave him an indulgent smile before resuming her attention on Mimi. "Lady Rex, I hear you're fond of Bach."

"Bach?" Mimi said.

"Is that not why Sawbridge asked that we extend our invitation to you? Of course, your kindness toward Edward ensures you a welcome in our home at any time."

"Jeanette, my love," the duke said, "we mustn't keep our guests waiting."

The duchess rolled her eyes, though she exchanged a look of adoration with her husband. "I consider myself admonished, Henry," she said. "Lady Rex, I trust you'll enjoy the concert. Please—do go in."

She gestured toward the doors, and Alexander led Mimi through them, into an enormous ballroom, paneled with mirrors along one side, filled with chairs set out in rows. At the far end, a quartet of musicians sat, tuning their instruments, beside a grand pianoforte.

"You've brought me to a concert?" Mimi asked.

He smiled and drew her arm through his. "The duchess opens her concerts up to everyone in Society. For a price, of course—to support her various philanthropic ventures. In fact, when she heard of your charitable efforts, she promised to pass a share of the proceeds to you. She's particularly interested in easing the plight of disadvantaged women."

"You shouldn't have asked," Mimi said.

"But if a man doesn't ask, he's in danger of never having his wish fulfilled."

Desire flared in his eyes, and she turned away, casting her gaze over the crowd.

"Ah! There we are," he said, picking through the crowd toward a pair of empty seats. Mimi's apprehension lessened as she recognized Eleanor and her sister Lady Radham, together with Eleanor's husband. Of Lord Radham there was no sign.

"Ah, Lady Rex, *there* you are," Lady Radham said. "I was beginning to fear Sawbridge had frightened you off."

Alexander stiffened at the sneer in her voice, but he steered Mimi toward the seats. "Lady Radham, Duchess—a pleasure, as always," he said.

"Oh, I doubt that," Lady Radham said. "I—"

"Juliette, remind us what you are to sing tonight," Eleanor said.

Lady Radham let out a sigh. *"Jesus Bleibet Meine Freude."*

"How fitting," Mimi said, "given that Advent is almost upon us."

Lady Radham smiled, her clear blue eyes twinkling in the candlelight. She really was the most exquisitely beautiful creature, but she lacked the vanity that generally came hand in hand with such beauty. She leaned across and took Mimi's hand.

"How gratifying to find someone with a true appreciation of Bach," she said. "I only trust I'll not disappoint you with my lack of prowess. Perhaps you should play for the company tonight. Tell me—have you tried any of the pieces from *The Well-Tempered Clavier* yet?"

"Not to any degree of proficiency," Mimi said.

"Few people in this room, save our hostess, would be able to distinguish between a beautifully played Bach piece and my daughter's screams when she's demanding her supper," Lady Radham said.

"That's very true," Eleanor said. "I have no ear at all."

"Ah, but *your* talent lies in your pencil," her husband said.

"Montague, my love, I've told you before not to flatter me."

"But your husband is right to do so in this instance," Lady Radham said. "I saw your latest portrait of Lady Rex. It's exquisite."

"Portrait?" Alexander asked. "What portrait?"

"It was drawn in your absence, Your Grace," Lady Radham said. "Believe it or not, some women can function perfectly well without any gentlemen present."

"Juliette," Eleanor said, her voice a harsh whisper, and Mimi suppressed a smile at the stricken expression in Alexander's eyes.

The guests quieted as their host and hostess entered the room. Westbury and his son took their places on the front row, while the duchess stood beside the musicians to welcome the company, before she sat at the pianoforte and the music began.

The guests stilled as the gentle melody of Bach's aria filled the air, elegant in its simplicity. Then the duchess began to play the variations, toying with the melody, adding richness and flavor to the music.

"She's a true proficient, is she not?" Eleanor whispered. "An excellent choice to change the program for tonight."

"The duchess did not intend to play the Bach?" Mimi asked.

"Her favored piece is a Mozart sonata. But I understand her husband asked her to make a change, on the insistence of a friend." She gestured toward Alexander.

Mimi glanced at the man next to her, whose eyes sparkled with delight.

"*You?*" she asked.

He nodded, and a slight hint of pink colored his cheeks. Surely he wasn't blushing?

"I promised you'd enjoy tonight," he whispered, "and I've no wish to break any promise I make to you."

"Alexander, I—"

"Hush," he said, his voice a low rasp. "Much as I enjoy hearing my name on your lips, I wouldn't want you to miss the music." He reached for her hand and laced his fingers through hers.

Mimi relaxed into her seat as the music filled her senses, letting her gaze wander about the room. Almost every guest was rapt in concentration, except one couple where the husband seemed to be struggling to keep awake. He'd stare toward the front, wide-eyed, then his eyelids would droop until they closed, and his head would nod forward onto his chest. Then the woman next to him would poke his ribs, issue a sharp word in his ear, and the process would repeat.

Clearly not everyone was a lover of music.

Smiling to herself, Mimi glanced about the rest of the guests, until her gaze fell upon a man who looked familiar.

The woman at his side, whom Mimi recognized as Lady Elizabeth De Witt, stared straight ahead, a bored expression on her face. Then she curled her lip in a sneer and leaned toward him to speak. He turned to respond, and Mimi's gut twisted in revulsion.

It was Ralph—Earl Mayhew.

She suppressed a cry as his pale-gray eyes met her gaze. The music faded into nothingness, replaced by that familiar hated voice, declaring her a whore and issuing the order to toss her out onto the street. Cold fingers clawed at her insides.

"Lady Rex?"

She startled at the voice, and looked up to see Lady Radham standing before her.

"Forgive me, do you mind?" The woman held a sheet of music to her breast.

Mimi glanced about. Most of the guests were staring at her—what had she done?

"Mimi?" Alexander said. "Are you well? Is something amiss?"

She shook her head.

He squeezed her hand. "It's Lady Radham's turn to sing. Here, allow me."

Taking her elbow, he helped Mimi to stand. Lady Radham nodded her thanks and slipped along the row of guests, who each stood to make room, until she reached the end, then she made her way toward the pianoforte.

Only after Lady Radham had started to sing did Mimi summon the courage to glance across the room once more. But Earl Mayhew was absorbed in a discussion with his companion, and he did not look in her direction again.

I must be much changed.

Yes—she *had* changed. The naïve young girl who'd believed in honor had been destroyed five years ago, her joy replaced by sorrow, her faith by cynicism, and her capacity to love…

Mimi glanced down at Alexander's hand, which held hers. Though he was absorbed in the music and Lady Radham's exquisite voice, he caressed her hand with his fingertips absent-mindedly, as if it came naturally to him. She had long since learned that grand gestures and professions of love were more to satisfy the proclaimer's vanity than a true expression of feeling.

But the small gestures—asking the hostess to change the recital to include Mimi's favorite composer, a delicate touch of the hand…

They were the true declarations of love.

Stop being such a fool!

He didn't love her. He *couldn't*.

A man in his position could never feel anything more for a doxy than physical attraction. But while she sat next to him at a Society concert, almost as if she belonged there, she could indulge in the dream for a little while.

When Lady Radham's song concluded, the room erupted with applause. Their hostess announced the interval and directed the guests to a buffet in the adjoining room, and footmen appeared with trays of champagne.

"Shall I fetch you something to eat?" Alexander asked. Mimi nodded. "Come, Whitcombe," he said. "Duty calls."

"It's a pleasure, not a duty, to serve my wife," Whitcombe said. He exchanged a glance with Eleanor, and Mimi's heart ached at the love in their eyes. "Eleanor, my love, you stay here with Lady Rex."

Eleanor nodded, and the men left, picking their way through the crowd. The noise and chatter increased, and laughter filled the air. Eleanor seemed to shrink under the weight of the clamor of voices, and she closed her eyes and began to pick at her sleeve and toy with the bracelet about her wrist.

"Eleanor, are you well?" Mimi asked.

The duchess opened her eyes and shook her head. "I-I cannot hear you. The noise…"

"You're not fond of crowds, are you?" Mimi said.

"I'll be all right."

A group of young men walked past, roaring with laughter, and Eleanor flinched. She hid her distress well, but the advantage of Mimi's profession was that she had learned to understand people. Eleanor's distress was evident with careful observation— the slight shake of her hand as she continued to twirl her bracelet, the measured rhythm of her breathing, which suggested a deliberate attempt to control her apprehension, and the spark of longing in her eyes as she glanced toward the doors.

Mimi rose, fanning herself.

"Oh dear," she said, "I've come over a little hot. Duchess, would you mind helping me outside? I'm in need of fresh air."

Eleanor blinked and lifted her gaze to Mimi, who offered her elbow.

"Forgive me for making such an imposition, but I'd be most grateful."

Eleanor stared at Mimi's arm for a moment, then she stood and took it. Mimi steered them along the row and toward the doors at the rear of the room, while Eleanor clung to her.

"I dislike crowds myself," she said brightly as they passed the young men. "I'm of the opinion that if one has nothing sensible to say, then it's best to remain silent—in which case, most of the guests here would be required to say nothing for the rest of the evening."

Eleanor giggled, then let out a cry as they collided with a young woman, and Mimi suppressed a curse. Of all the women to encounter, it had to be Sarah Francis.

"Oh! Forgive me, Miss Francis," Eleanor said.

Sarah arched an eyebrow and stared at Eleanor.

"Duchess," she said, in a tone clearly intended to convey the least amount of respect possible. Then she creased her upper lip as if encountering a particularly bad smell. "Lady Rex," she said. "You *are* moving up in the world. I applaud your tenacity."

"You're too kind," Mimi replied.

"I should warn you, as a friend, to take care with whom you associate," Miss Francis said. "A title always carries more value when it is inherited, rather than married into—wouldn't you agree, *Duchess* Whitcombe?"

Eleanor stiffened.

Mimi suppressed the urge to slam her fist into Miss Francis's sneering face. Instead, she returned the smile.

"You're always *so* considerate, Miss Francis," she said. "And generous with your advice. Is she not generous, Duchess?"

Eleanor nodded.

"Such consideration cannot go unrewarded," Mimi continued. "Permit me, Miss Francis, to express my gratitude for your generosity by sharing a little advice of my own."

Miss Francis nodded, in the manner of a monarch receiving her subject. Mimi leaned toward her and lowered her voice.

"Why don't you fuck yourself with a broom handle, Miss Francis?"

Wearing the sweetest of smiles, Mimi stepped back.

Miss Francis paled, opened her mouth to respond, then closed it again.

"I-I beg your pardon?" she said.

"It's not something I'd recommend on a constant basis," Mimi continued, "but it does wonders for the complexion if undertaken at least twice a day before meals."

Eleanor suppressed a snort, and Miss Francis stared at her, her eyes glittering with hatred.

"I've heard such a practice is employed frequently by young women who find it difficult to secure a suitor," Mimi continued. "And, of course, there's the benefit of being able to sweep the floor afterward."

Miss Francis let out a squeak, and Eleanor burst into laughter, shaking with mirth, which culminated in a volley of coughs.

"Quite right, Duchess," Mimi said. "The air is a little stifling in here. Let us take a turn outside." She led Eleanor into the hallway. "Would you like to walk outside, Eleanor? I could ask someone to fetch your cloak."

"No, I'll be all right here," Eleanor replied. "Forgive me, I-I'm not fond of crowds. And Miss Francis always unnerves me. I'm a little afraid of her—at least when Montague's not with me."

"Why, because she thinks herself superior?"

"She always seems to know what to do, and say, at parties and social gatherings. Whereas I..."

"Whereas you understand the value of only speaking when

you have something of value to say and when you are with someone with whom you can have an intelligent conversation," Mimi said. "I doubt the *Honorable* Miss Francis has ever experienced an intelligent conversation—at least one she's capable of understanding."

"Oh, I assure you, she understood your meaning," Eleanor said, blushing. "I-I can't quite believe you suggested that she—that she…"

"Sweep the floor?" Mimi said. "Yes—an outrageous idea that a woman of her disposition would ever sweep a floor."

"Eleanor what are you doing?"

Mimi turned to see Whitcombe approaching, Alexander at his side.

"It's all right, Montague," Eleanor said. "I was—"

"I saw Lady Rex almost drag you out of the ballroom," he said. "I've left your food at your seat. Lady Rex, what are you about?"

Mimi cringed at the thinly veiled anger in Whitcombe's tone.

"I say, Whitcombe, there's no need—" Alexander began.

"There's every need when my wife's welfare is at stake, Sawbridge," Whitcombe said.

"What are you accusing Lady Rex of?" Alexander asked. "I daresay your wife's in better hands with Lady Rex than anyone else in the room, including yourself."

"Eleanor was kind enough to escort me outside when I grew a little faint," Mimi said.

Alexander took her hand. "Are you unwell?" he asked. "Do you wish to leave?"

Whitcombe let out a huff, and Eleanor raised her hand.

"Montague, don't be tiresome," she said. "I know you have good intentions, but Lady Rex is the kind one, not me."

"How come?" Alexander asked.

Eleanor averted her gaze. "I-I'm not fond of crowds," she said. "Or an excess of noise."

"And Lady Rex noticed when others did not," Alexander said.

Eleanor nodded.

"I saw you speaking to that odious Francis woman," Whitcombe said.

"Not by design," Eleanor said. "And Lady Rex told her to—"

"Eleanor!" Mimi cried, suppressing laughter.

"With a broom handle," Eleanor added.

Whitcombe raised his eyebrows, confusion in his eyes, but Alexander let out a snort.

"Let us hope she doesn't," he said, winking at Mimi. "For the sake of the poor broom."

"But she suggested Miss Francis sweep the floor afterward," Eleanor continued, her eyes sparkling like emeralds, "which would at least put the broom to its proper use."

Whitcombe glanced from Mimi to Eleanor, then threw back his head, roaring with laughter. A nearby crowd of guests stopped talking and turned to stare at them.

The duke extended his hand to Mimi. "Let me shake your hand, Lady Rex," he said. "I believe we have been furnished with a treasure. Sawbridge, I envy you and would advise you to do one thing."

Mimi tilted her head to one side. "Does it involve a broom handle, Your Grace?"

"I trust not," Whitcombe said. "Cherish this woman, Sawbridge. You'll never encounter another like her."

Alexander's smile disappeared, and Mimi held her breath, awaiting the declaration that he had no time for women. Instead, he took her hand and lifted it to his lips.

"I fear you're right, my friend," he said. "It's something I've believed for some time now, and with each passing day, that belief has grown into the strongest of convictions."

He drew Mimi close, and she leaned into his touch.

Then she glanced over at the group watching them and froze.

Earl Mayhew stood beside Earl Thorpe. The two seemed deep in conversation, then Thorpe gestured toward Mimi, and Mayhew lifted his pale-gray gaze to her. His eyes glittered like cold, hard diamonds in the candlelight, and a sneer curled the corner of his mouth. Elizabeth de Witt joined them, together with Miss Francis, and icy fingers clawed at Mimi's insides as all four of them turned toward her.

"Mimi, my love, are you well?" Alexander whispered.

My love…

She closed her eyes, letting the brief flare of hope wash over her. Then she opened them again and nodded.

"Yes, I-I'm well," she said, glancing toward the group by the door. But they had returned into the ballroom.

"Perhaps you need something to eat. I've a plate waiting at your seat—that is, if Lady Radham hasn't accidentally sat on it."

"Thank you," she said quietly.

"Or perhaps Miss Francis may have sat on it, thinking it a broom handle."

Mimi smiled, and he returned her to her seat, where he presented her with a plate of chicken and a glass of wine. For the rest of the evening, she endeavored to enjoy the music, though her instincts screamed in protest at the predator in the room. But each time she glanced across the room, Mayhew was engrossed in the woman next to him, the music, or the glass in his hand.

He had no reason to recognize her. But she couldn't suppress her fear at the memory of those pale eyes staring at her unblinkingly, like an adder poised to strike.

CHAPTER TWENTY-ONE

WHAT HAD DISTRESSED her so much during the interval?

One moment Mimi was trying not to laugh at the suggestion that the unpleasant Miss Francis pleasure herself with a broom, then the next, she was trembling and darting her gaze about like a fox that had spotted a pack of hounds. During the second half of the evening, she occasionally glanced across the crowd of guests, but Alexander saw nobody with whom she was acquainted. Unless…

Unless she recognized a former customer. In which case, *they* had more to be ashamed of than her.

The urge to ask her swelled in his heart, but he couldn't bring himself to betray her trust by posing such a question. She did not deserve to be treated like a doxy. He had long since ceased to think of her as such.

As the guests filed into the hallway uttering the usual pleasantries and superlatives about the evening, Alexander and Whitcombe left the ladies in the ballroom while they went in search of their cloaks. Then he spotted Thorpe in conversation with the odious Earl Mayhew.

"Ah, Sawbridge, Whitcombe," Thorpe said. "An excellent evening, was it not?"

"Very," Alexander said. "We don't often see *you* in London, Mayhew."

"One must make an appearance for the sake of giving charity

to the lower classes," Mayhew replied.

"Are you in Town long?" Alexander asked.

"I return to the country for Christmas." Mayhew tilted his head to one side. "I was hoping to see Radham tonight," he said. "To console him on the loss of his brother. Such a bitter blow, for the sake of a drunken whim, do you not think, Sawbridge?"

Alexander fisted his hands to suppress the rage boiling in his gut. How long must he be punished for what happened to Robert Staines?

"I say, Mayhew, I hardly think that's called for," Thorpe said.

"Sawbridge doesn't mind, do you, old chap?" Mayhew said, fixing his soulless gray gaze on Alexander. "The events of the past, particularly sins, should always be acknowledged."

"Which they have been, Mayhew," Alexander said. "Have you acknowledged all *your* sins? I'll wager they're plentiful."

Mayhew let out a mirthless laugh. "You always were a rum fellow, Sawbridge. Tell me—who is that delectable creature you brought with you tonight?"

"Nobody who'd care to know *you*."

"I'm sorry to hear that," Mayhew said. "A woman robust enough to hazard an acquaintance with you is to be admired— unless she's unaware of the fate of Robert Staines."

"She's aware of it," Alexander said.

"Thorpe tells me she's lately arrived in England," Mayhew said. "What's her opinion of London Society?"

"Favorable so far," Alexander said. "So you can, therefore, understand why I have no wish to introduce you. And if—as you're trying to say without having the courage to speak outright—I pose a danger to those within my vicinity, you'd be advised to quit it forthwith."

Mayhew let out a laugh, but his eyes remained cold. Then he inclined his head, wished Thorpe and Whitcombe a pleasant evening, and disappeared into the crowd.

"That was almost an insult," Thorpe said.

"Only *almost?*" Alexander replied. "I must be losing my

touch."

"Did Lady Rex enjoy the concert?" Thorpe asked.

"I believe so."

"I understand the duchess chose to play Bach at your request. That strikes me as the act of a man in love."

"I made a request because Lady Rex likes Bach, that's all. A small gesture."

"It's the small gestures that give us away, my friend," Thorpe said. "Few men are so considerate. More to the point, when have *you* ever shown such consideration?" Then he grinned. "But it's not your extraordinary consideration for another person that I wanted to mention," he said. "As I listened to the music, I found myself once more recalling Baron and Lady King."

"And they are...?"

"*Were*, my friend," Thorpe said. "Do you not recall my mentioning them at Lady Walton's ball? It was Lady King who was particularly proficient when it came to Bach."

"And she's no longer alive," Alexander said.

"A tragic story," Thorpe said. "Baron and Lady King died in a shipwreck, together with their son."

"Tragic indeed, but I fail to see why you'd take a particular interest in them tonight."

"They also had a daughter—Jemima."

"I've never heard of her," Alexander said. "How about you, Whitcombe?"

The duke shook his head.

"Baron King and his family rarely visited London," Thorpe said. "They traveled abroad, and managed only a small estate in the country."

"Do *you* know her, Thorpe?" Whitcombe asked.

"I never met her, but my mother did," Thorpe replied. "Mother was a guest at a house party at their estate, some fifteen years ago, and she encountered a child—a girl—in the drawing room."

"And the child was Jemima?"

Thorpe nodded. "Mother said she never forgot her—a precocious little thing who knew a great deal about Bach, and had a fondness for marzipan. She'd hidden in the drawing room to listen to the after-dinner recitals. Mother spotted her, and the child swore her to secrecy."

"So a precocious girl took advantage of your mother's kindness," Alexander said.

"I think Mother felt sorry for her. The girl was a late child—when she was born, her brother was already well into his twenties. There was a rumor at the time that she might have been the result of an illicit liaison. And we both know the impact rumors can have on a person." Thorpe let out a sigh. "I wonder what became of her?"

"Didn't she inherit?"

Thorpe shook his head. "The title passed to a cousin, but no provision was made for the girl—I doubt Baron King expected his heir to die with him."

Alexander folded his arms. "Why are you telling us this?"

"I just wondered…" Thorpe made a random gesture in the air. "It seemed particularly interesting that Lady Rex had such a fondness for Bach, and had spent much of her life overseas. I wondered if she might be a relative. After all, Rex is Latin for—"

He broke off as footsteps approached, and Alexander turned to see Mimi flanked by Duchess Whitcombe and Lady Radham. She stared at Thorpe, open-mouthed. Then she glanced toward Alexander, her eyes glistening with fear.

"Ladies, forgive me for detaining the gentlemen," Thorpe said. "I fear there's something of a crush for coats, and unless you enjoy a melee, I'd advise waiting. Now, I must thank our hostess."

He bowed and disappeared. Shortly after, Westbury's son appeared, brandishing a number of cloaks.

"Ladies, I hope it's not too forward of me, but I took the liberty of bringing your cloaks. There's something of a battle taking place in the hallway."

Mr. Drayton handed the cloaks to Alexander—all except Mimi's, which he placed around her shoulders.

"A pleasure to see you, Lady Rex," he said. "I'm so glad Mama Jeanette extended the invitation to you."

"As am I," Mimi said. Mr. Drayton took her hand and kissed it, and she smiled—but the light had gone from her eyes.

"That's enough of that, young man," Alexander said, pulling Mimi close and placing a possessive hand on the small of her back. "Shall I take you home?" he asked.

She cast a quick glance in the direction in which Thorpe had gone, and nodded. Then, after they took their leave, Alexander escorted her outside and into his carriage.

The ride back to Grosvenor Square took place in silence. Mimi sat opposite Alexander, focusing her gaze on the window, her eyes wide as if she expected a demon to leap through the glass at any moment. When the carriage rolled to a halt outside number sixteen, they climbed out and he escorted her up the steps. The butler opened the door.

"Welcome home, ma'am. I trust you had a pleasant evening."

"Very much so, Wheeler, thank you," she said.

Alexander followed her inside, helped her with her cloak, and handed it to the butler.

"Some tea for me, please, Wheeler," she said. "And a brandy for His Grace."

The butler bowed and disappeared into the back of the house, while Mimi strode across the hallway and into the parlor, where a fire was already blazing.

"There was no need to ask your butler to bring me a brandy," Alexander said.

"I assumed you'd want one before retiring." She approached the fireplace, plucked a poker from the rack, and began jabbing at the base. The flames flared, illuminating her face with an orange glow, and Alexander's heart ached at the sorrow in her eyes.

"Did you enjoy the evening?" he asked.

"I enjoyed the music. Duchess Westbury and Lady Radham

are very accomplished."

"There's no need to exchange pleasantries with me, Mimi. You can trust me with the truth."

She poked the fire again. "I asked Charles to make sure that the fire in the bedchamber was lit tonight."

"In *your* bedchamber?" he asked.

"No—the other one. We can retire there as soon as you've had your brandy."

Guilt gnawed at him at the matter-of-fact way she spoke—as if she'd resigned herself to having to service his physical needs.

But he no longer wanted her to perform a physical service. He wanted her to *want* him, to take pleasure from being in his bed…

…and to love him.

"Perhaps I should go," he said.

She turned. "Do you no longer enjoy what you've paid for?"

"Mimi, tonight has shown me that I want to spend time with you in places other than the bedroom."

"Such as over the table? Or…over this?" She gestured toward the chaise longue on which he'd taken her with such vigor that he thought it might collapse under the weight of his frenzied thrusting. His cheeks warmed with shame at the pleasure he'd taken from the act. "Or perhaps up against the wall?" she continued, her voice tightening. "There's always the garden. For some, the pleasure of rutting outdoors can be most—"

"Stop!" he cried. "You misunderstand me. Can't you see I want more than just sexual gratification?"

As he spoke, the young footman appeared, and he almost dropped the tray he carried. Alexander rushed toward him and grasped the tray, but a teacup rolled off and shattered on the floor.

"Beg pardon, ma'am!" the footman cried, his face going as red as fire.

"It matters not, Charles," Alexander said. "I'll clear it up. After all, it's a mess of my making."

The footman fled, closing the door behind him. Alexander set the tray on a table and picked up the shards of porcelain. Then he met Mimi's gaze, and his heart ached at the pain in her eyes. But he knew not how to ease it. Something had shattered her peace tonight—but he had no right to ask her what, if she couldn't bring herself to trust him.

"Mimi, didn't tonight show you that there's more to what we have than…"

"Sex?"

"There's more to life—to *us*—than sexual gratification," he said. "You know it. I see it in your eyes."

"What do you want?" she asked.

"To know you," he said quietly. "*Really* know you. Who you are—what you care for. Whom you love…"

She blinked, and a tear splashed onto her cheek. He approached her and placed his hand on her face, and she leaned into his touch as he brushed the tear away.

"Teach me to be something other than I am," he said. "Teach me to be better so that I might be worthy of you."

"How?" she whispered.

"Show me the world as you see it."

She closed her eyes as her chest rose and fell in a sigh. He waited, a sinner anticipating his fate—condemnation, or redemption.

At length, she opened her eyes.

"Very well," she said. "If you truly wish to see the world through my eyes, I'll show you. Spend a day in my shoes, and we'll see if you want more. Come on Tuesday."

"Thank you." He drew her close for a kiss, but, as usual, she turned her head aside and his lips brushed against her forehead.

His manhood strained in his breeches as he fought the urge to sweep her into his arms, carry her upstairs, and claim her, and his cheeks warmed with guilt as she lowered her gaze to the bulge in breeches. But if he were to woo her, he must forget the desires of the rake, and act in accordance with the principles of the gallant suitor. He took her hand and bowed over it.

"Until Tuesday," he said.

"Six in the morning."

He winced, and her lips quirked into a smile, but he nodded.

"Six it is."

Then he exited the parlor, leaving the woman he desired more than anything else—the woman he'd bought and paid for, though he was ashamed for having done so—and stepped out into the night.

CHAPTER TWENTY-TWO

"H E'S ARRIVED, LADY REX."

Mimi glanced at her maid, who stood at the parlor window.

"Really, Gracie? I didn't think he had the tenacity."

"We're at our most tenacious when we're in love, ma'am. Shall I ask Charles to admit him?"

Mimi nodded, and Gracie exited the parlor as the clock over the fireplace struck six times.

Shortly after, the parlor door opened.

Mimi's heart tightened as her gaze fell on the man standing beside Charles in the doorway, wiping the drowsiness from his eyes. He stifled a yawn, then covered his mouth with his hand and a faint blush colored his cheeks.

"Forgive me, Mimi," Alexander said. "I've not seen the world at this hour before."

She returned his smile. "You astonish me, Your Grace," she said. "I'd have thought you familiar with this hour, given your propensity to indulge in parties throughout the night."

His smile disappeared, and Mimi caught a flash of sorrow in his gaze—sorrow that tore at her heart. She approached him and offered her hand, and he took it.

"Forgive me, Alexander. I forgot about your friend, Robert Staines. I'm sorry."

His eyes widened at her use of his name. Then his smile returned.

"I am ready to be of service today," he said.

Mimi cast her gaze over his clothes. "Your Grace, you can hardly expect me to take you to Mrs. Briggs dressed like *that*."

"What's wrong with my attire?" he asked. "My valet had to rise even earlier than I this morning."

"He dressed you like a duke."

"I *am* a duke."

"You'll not last five minutes near the docks. You'll be a duke-shaped beacon announcing to the world, 'Rob me, please, and there'll be pickings for all.'"

"I'll be wearing my coat."

"Trust me, ruffians on the street can smell a duke at a hundred paces," Mimi said. "Don't you recall the night we met?"

"Oh yes," he said, his voice growing hoarse. "I recall every delicious minute of *that* night."

"You'll have to change," Mimi said. "Charles, would you see if we have anything? A jacket and boots—breeches if you can find any. And a coat. Nothing too…elegant."

The footman nodded and disappeared, returning shortly after with a pile of clothes in his arms.

Mimi suppressed a laugh at the expression on Alexander's face.

"You expect me to wear *those*?" he said.

"I'm giving you a choice," she replied. "Stand out in your gentleman's garb, or blend into the background and preserve the safety of your person." She approached the door. "Charles and I will give you privacy."

Charles held up the garments—a ragged undershirt together with a plain cotton overshirt, a necktie, and a pair of breeches fraying at the knees with a matching jacket and overcoat.

"These are all I could find that might fit the duke, Lady Rex," he said.

Alexander stared at the garments. "I-I'm afraid I don't…" He hesitated, his forehead creasing into a frown.

"Don't what?" Mimi asked. "Don't like them? Don't think

they're good enough for you?"

"I-I don't know how to put them on."

"You don't know how to—" Mimi broke off, suppressing laughter. "Shall I send Charles across the road to fetch your valet?"

His eyes filled with humiliation. Ashamed at her gentle teasing, Mimi gestured to the footman.

"Charles, place the garments on the table, then you may take your breakfast."

The footman bowed and disappeared.

Alexander removed his jacket and waistcoat, then reached for his cravat.

"Damnation!" he muttered, tugging at the ends.

"Let me," Mimi said. "You're tightening the knot." Her hand brushed against his as she reached for the cravat, and she drew in a sharp breath at the fizz of need that rippled across her skin. She glanced up to see him staring at her, his eyes dark with desire. He curled his fingers around hers, then released her hand and stood, meekly, while she loosened the knot, removed his cravat, and placed it on the table.

He fell silent, his gaze focused on her while she removed the rest of his garments. The only sound inside the parlor was the steady tick of the mantel clock, punctuated by the occasional hitch in his breath as her hands came into contact with his body while she tugged at his laces and undid his buttons. When she reached for his breeches, she glanced up to see him staring at her, his eyes wide with anticipation. Then she undid his breeches and pulled them down, letting them bunch on the floor while he stepped forward.

Silently, she dressed him, letting her hands follow the contours of his body while she smoothed each garment before picking up the next. As she buttoned his shirt, she succumbed to the temptation to feel his heartbeat beneath her fingers and placed her hand on his chest, relishing his warmth on her skin. When she picked up the necktie, he dipped his head and closed his eyes, and his breath caressed the skin of her hands while she reached around his neck and knotted the tie. Unable to resist, she ran a light fingertip along the back of his neck, and a low growl escaped his lips.

"Mimi…"

How could such an act—the simple service of dressing a man—be so *intimate*?

After securing the knot, she tucked the ends of the necktie into his shirt, then stood back to admire her handiwork.

"Thank you, Mimi," he whispered, his voice heavy with desire.

"You're welcome…Alexander."

She reached toward his chest, unable to suppress the desire to feel his heartbeat beneath her fingers once more. Then he drew her to him and lowered his mouth to hers.

Desire flared within her, and she melted into his embrace, letting his lips slide over hers. His tongue probed, gently at first, then more insistent at the seam of her lips. When she parted them, he slipped inside, teasing, stroking. He tasted of spice, smoke, and raw, primal need—an intoxicating liquor that promised to satisfy every unmet need that she had denied herself…

Pleasure—and love.

With a whimper, she surrendered and responded to the kiss, inviting him to claim her. His body vibrated with a growl of raw, primal desire, and he pulled her against him, his body hard and ready. The heady scent of male potency and female desire filled her senses as he deepened the kiss, as if one taste of her could never be enough—as if he wanted to consume her, *devour* her…

What the devil am I doing?

Mimi broke the kiss and drew back, shaking.

By letting him kiss her, she had taken herself to the edge of the abyss. And in responding, she had almost plunged over the precipice.

Her heart racing, Mimi lifted her gaze to his, anticipating his disappointment—anger, even.

But all she saw was resignation, as if he understood he'd breached her trust. Then he lifted his hand and, with a light fingertip, traced the outline of her face.

"Shall we go?" he whispered. "I'm eager to meet your friend—Mrs. Briggs, is it?"

She nodded and placed her hand over his, and he smiled. Then he reached for the overcoat and put it on.

"At least I'm capable of donning a coat, if little else."

"You could achieve much more if you employed your mind appropriately, Alexander."

"I'm in your hands, Mimi."

They exited the parlor to find the footman waiting by the door.

"Take care, Lady Rex," he said.

"You can leave your mistress's care to me, Charles," Alexander said, taking Mimi's arm and linking it through his.

"Make sure that you do."

Charles's eyes widened, as if he regretted the words as soon as he'd uttered them. By right, Alexander's rank could demand the footman's dismissal at such impertinence, but instead he laughed.

"Your loyalty to your mistress does you credit, young man," he said. "I'll take your warning with the seriousness it commands, and assure you that there are none so committed as I when it comes to Lady Rex's welfare."

Charles nodded, then the two of them exited the building.

The journey to Mrs. Briggs's establishment was uneventful. They picked up a hackney carriage almost as soon as they left Grosvenor Square, and the driver, other than a cursory look, paid them little attention. Perhaps he thought they were a footman and maid running an early morning errand. Or maybe an eloping couple, given how Alexander refused to let go of Mimi's hand for the whole journey.

After they climbed out, the driver tipped his cap, then, with a crack of his whip, set off and disappeared. The first strains of dawn light were bleeding into the sky—cold, gray threading through the inky blackness. Voices echoed along the street, cursing and yelling, accompanied by the splash of water as residents emptied their chamber pots into the street. Carts rattled as coalmen made their deliveries.

London—or this insalubrious little part of it, at least—was waking up.

Before Mimi could knock on Mrs. Briggs's door, it opened to reveal the woman herself.

"Mimi darlin', I didn't expect you so early."

"It's my usual time," Mimi said.

"But you've brought your young man this time." Mrs. Briggs cocked her head to one side and cast her sharp glance up and down Alexander's body. "And who might *you* be?"

"I'm…Mr. Sawbridge."

"*Mr.* Sawbridge?" Mrs. Briggs folded her arms. "I suppose it's as good a name as any."

"It is my name."

"It's all the same to me, Mr. Sawbridge, but I'll not take kindly to deception in my establishment. Trust is a privilege—and it's not given lightly here."

"Then I shall consider myself privileged if you're kind enough to admit me."

Mrs. Briggs gave a wry smile. "He makes a pretty speech, Mimi darlin', I'll give 'im that. So what are you then, sir? For I doubt you're a plain mister, for all that you're dressed like one of us. You a lord or something?"

"I'm a duke. But I've not come here today as a duke. I've come here as Mimi's…" He hesitated.

"Mimi's *what?*" Mrs. Briggs asked. "Admirer? Benefactor?" She let out a laugh. "*Protector?*"

"Mrs. Briggs, you promised to be kind," Mimi said.

"Just so long as he's kind to *you*, darlin'." Mrs. Briggs unfolded her arms and poked Alexander in the chest. "It was one of your sort who destroyed our Mimi's life and tossed her out on the street. Mind you"—she took Mimi's hand and gave it an affectionate squeeze—"she couldn't find better friends round here than the likes of us. We love her."

She released Mimi's hand and gestured back into the hallway.

"Well? What's with the dawdling? Are you comin' in or not? There's much to do today, what with the coal delivery, that I can't be spending time gossipin' on my doorstep. We work for a living here, Mr. Sawbridge."

Alexander grimaced at her sharp tone, and Mimi suppressed a smile. Then he nodded. "I'm here to work, Mrs. Briggs. That's why Mimi brought me."

Mrs. Briggs grunted. "I doubt you've seen a day's work in your life—not with those baby-smooth hands of yours. Mind you, we can do somethin' about that. There's four bags of coal needing shiftin', and I can't do it all myself. A good, strong man is what I need, though I'm loath to say it."

"In the absence of a good, strong man, will *I* suffice?" Alexander asked.

Mrs. Briggs let out a low chuckle. "I suppose when there's nothin' better, I could settle for you. Well? Stop your dawdling and come inside—I've not got all day. There's a pile of mendin', and the chamber pots to clean, and I've only got one pair of hands."

She ushered them into the dark, windowless hallway.

"Ouch!" Alexander cried.

"Are you all right?" Mimi asked.

"I caught my toe on something—a table, I think."

Mrs. Briggs's snort cut through the darkness. "I'm not made of money—I can't afford candles in every room. A good dose of work will take your mind off a sore toe. There's folk in here who've endured far worse. Follow me."

Mrs. Briggs led them to the back of the house and down the stairs to the kitchen.

"Tea, I think," she said. "There's a pot on the boil."

"I'll make it," Mimi said. She crossed the floor to the store cupboard and set out the tea things while Mrs. Briggs busied herself with scrubbing a pile of carrots at the sink.

"I've got a nice bit of pork if you're stopping for supper later," she said.

Alexander stood in the center of the kitchen, discomfort in his eyes. Perhaps he'd never entered a kitchen before—or any room below stairs.

"What can I do?" he asked.

Mrs. Briggs let out a huff. "Can't you *find* something to do? I can't be spending my time looking around for something to keep the idle occupied. Men! You're useless, the lot of you. And gentlemen are the worst. Didn't you hear me say there's them bags of coal needin' shifting? You can carry them to the store first, then fill the scuttles and take them to the bedchambers. But don't go in the bedchambers, mind. The last thing my girls want to see when they wake is *your* face gawping at them."

"Why, because I'm a duke?"

"No, because you're a *man*. Some of the women here service men just like you to make a living, but they're not always kind— often give a girl a blackened eye, they do."

His forehead creased into a frown. "It's a cruel world that does that to a woman."

Mrs. Briggs snorted. "It's a *man's* world, that's what it is. But our Mimi here is doing all she can to help us—though I can't think what she was doing bringing you here if you're not going to do what I tell you."

He opened his mouth, and Mimi braced herself for an angry retort. Then he sighed and nodded.

"Very well."

"That's better," Mrs. Briggs said. She gestured toward the back door. "The coal's out there. Scullery's round the back. You'll need to tip the coal out of the sacks and into the store. There's a shovel by the door if you need it—if you don't want to dirty those soft baby hands of yours. Can you manage *that*, at least?"

"Of course I can," he retorted. "What do you take me for, Mrs. Briggs?"

"I doubt you'd appreciate my answer," she replied, gesturing toward the door. "Now, get on with it—or the day will be over and you'll still be standing there having not done a lick of work. Mimi, darlin' when you've put the tea to brew, take it to the parlor, then we can set to the mending."

Alexander met Mimi's gaze. She smiled encouragement, and he gave a slight shrug of his shoulders and exited through the back door. Soon afterward, he returned, dragging a sack, straining with the weight.

"Mind my floor!" Mrs. Briggs barked.

"Yes, ma'am," he replied, his voice tight.

Mrs. Briggs chuckled. "Good to see you know your place—in here, at least. Hurry up—you're letting the cold in with that door."

He rolled his eyes, but continued to drag the sack into the scullery. Then Mimi heard the sounds of shoveling and grunting, followed by a curse.

"The tea should be ready now," Mrs. Briggs said. "There's the remains of a fruitcake in the cupboard if you want to set it on a plate." She wiped her hands on her apron. "It's time Anna and Lily were up. I'll go and wake them, and they can have tea with us."

"What about our guest?" Mimi asked, gesturing toward the scullery as another curse rang out.

"He must earn his tea."

"I meant, he might need help. After all, he's not done a day's work in his life."

"Then it's time he learned, Mimi darlin'. A bleedin' good dose of hard work never harmed no man. Now, run along to the parlor with that tray, or the tea will get cold."

Mimi took the tray and climbed the staircase just as another curse echoed from the scullery.

"Dam-bloody-nation!"

Then the scrape of the shovel against the stone floor contin-ued and Mimi exited the kitchen, followed by Mrs. Briggs, who climbed the stairs to the top floor.

By the time Mimi had poured the tea, some of the occupants of the house had entered the parlor. Dawn had long since broken, and sunlight filled the room. The women had set to mending a pile of bedsheets that a benefactor had dropped by, and the air was filled with the chatter of women at work. When the door opened to reveal Lily and her son, Mimi's heart lifted to see the young woman's face break into a smile.

"Mimi! I'm glad you're here. Look who's come to see us, Sam."

The little boy toddled across the floor, arms outstretched, and Mimi lifted him onto her lap.

"What's that you have there, Lily?" she asked, gesturing to the pile of clothing in Lily's arms.

"It's a gown I'm finishing for Mrs. Painter." She smiled at Mimi expectantly.

"Mrs. Painter?"

"Her cousin's your housekeeper."

"You mean Peg?" Mimi asked.

"That's right. She said her cousin told her how I could do lacework, and she offered to give me work. This is the third dress I've made up for her—it's for a merchant's wife in the City. Imagine that!"

"That's kind of her," Mimi said.

"I've *you* to thank," Lily replied. "Sammy and I are ever so grateful, aren't we, Sammy love?"

Mimi bounced the child on her lap, and he reached for a lock of her hair, curling his little pink fist over it.

"Is Mary joining us?" Mimi asked.

"Mary's out with a…customer," Mrs. Briggs said. "She'll be home soon. He's giving her an extra sovereign for staying until dawn. Imagine that, girls! We can have a goose this Christmas."

"Is Mary safe?" Mimi asked.

"Of course she is, darlin'. It's that old widower who wanted to marry her. He's kind enough, and pays her well for her time."

"Come sit beside me, Sam," Lily said as she took the seat beside the window. "You can sort out these ribbons if you like."

"Ribbons!" the boy cried, and he slid off Mimi's lap and toddled toward his mother.

Mimi returned to her work, and the gentle buzz of conversation filled the room.

Then heavy footsteps approached and the room fell silent. Lily looked up, her eyes widening, then set her work down and drew her son close.

The door opened and Lily let out a scream.

Standing in the doorway, his body filling the space, was a man.

Or what *looked* like a man.

His jacket and shirt were smeared with dust. One leg of his breeches was adorned with a black handprint, and the other sported a tear just below the knee. His hair was tousled, framing his face. His cheeks and forehead were blackened with coal dust, against which his eyes shone whitely.

With his wide-eyed expression of bewilderment, he looked like a chimney sweep on his first day.

He stepped into the room, leaving a trail of footprints. Then he brushed his jacket and a cloud of coal dust filled the air before settling on the rug.

Mrs. Briggs rose to her feet then lowered her gaze to the dust on the rug. Then she folded her arms, and cocked her head, and glared at him in the manner of an enraged nanny.

Mimi fought the urge to laugh at his stricken expression.

Sam wriggled out of his mother's embrace and approached Alexander, tilting his head to look up at him.

"You're all dirty!" he squealed with delight. "Mama—he's so *dirty!*"

Lily rose to her feet, fear in her eyes. "S-Sammy…"

Alexander met Mimi's gaze before he looked down at the

little boy.

"Why are you so dirty?" Sam asked. "Are you here to sweep the chimney?"

Mimi held her breath as Alexander stared at the child. Then he swooped down and lifted the boy into the air, before lowering him.

"Again!" Sam cried.

Alexander lifted the boy higher and spun him around.

"Sammy!" Lily screamed.

Alexander lowered the boy and held him in his arms. "Forgive me, madam—is this your son?" he asked. "Here, take him."

Lily took a step back, trembling. "I-I…" She glanced about the room, as if searching for an escape, but Alexander stood in front of the doorway. He glanced behind, then gave a slight nod and crossed the room to the chair furthest from Lily, then he set Sam down.

"Go to your mama, sir," he said.

"I want to sit with *you*."

"Sammy darlin', your ma needs you," Mrs. Briggs said. "Didn't you promise to look after your ma after what happened to her?"

Alexander glanced at Mimi and raised his eyebrows in question. She shook her head, and understanding filled his expression. Then he fished into his breeches pocket, pulled out a coin, and handed it to the boy.

"There you go, sir," he said. "Share that with your mother, mind."

The boy curled his fingers around the coin, then ran toward Lily, who lifted him onto her lap.

Alexander gestured to the chair. "May I take tea, Mrs. Briggs?"

"Have you finished with the coal?"

"Of course."

"There's the chamber pots next," Mrs. Briggs said, "but I suppose you could take your tea now, provided none of the girls have any objection. Lily, what do you say?"

Lily colored but didn't respond.

"Let him stay, Ma!" Sam cried, and Lily sighed.

"Very well." She picked up her work and resumed stitching the gown, but she was tense and cast the occasional glance toward Alexander.

Anna rose and approached the tea tray. "How do you take your tea, sir?"

Alexander glanced at the tea things, then his gaze flicked to Lily before it settled on Mimi. He shook his head.

"Perhaps I should see to those chamber pots first. Mrs. Briggs, I take it the chambers are unoccupied? I wouldn't want to frighten anyone."

His gaze settled on Lily, who continued stitching. She glanced up, and their gazes met for a moment before she resumed her work.

"Yes, the chambers are clear," Mrs. Briggs replied.

"I could clean the fireplaces," he said. "But I can't lay a fire, I'm afraid."

"That's disappointing," Mrs. Briggs said, the sparkle in her eyes belying her harsh tone. "But it'll have to do. Scrub those pots properly, mind. They stink somethin' dreadful if they're not rinsed out fully. They should always be scrubbed by hand. There's a brush in the scullery you can use. With the brown handle. You can't mistake it—it stinks worse than my grandma's drawers."

His eyes widened with horror.

"Empty the pots into the ditch first before you rinse them," Mrs. Briggs said. "When you've finished that, you can have your tea, provided you wash your hands. If you do it properly, we'll save you a slice of cake. What do you think, girls? Shall we save him a slice?"

"Yes."

The room's occupants all looked at Lily, who'd spoken. Then she blushed and resumed her attention on her work.

Alexander inclined his head in a bow, then exited the parlor.

Mrs. Briggs's face creased as if she fought to maintain her composure. Then she threw back her head and laughed.

"Mrs. Briggs!" Mimi said. "You mustn't tease him—he's unused to it."

"Then it's time he grew used to it, darlin'. Oh, the look on his face when I told him to scrub the chamber pots by hand! I never thought I'd see a duke getting his hands dirty."

"A *duke*?" one of the women asked.

"That's Mimi's young man, Biddy," Anna said. "Isn't that right, Mimi?"

"Is he your suitor?"

Mimi shook her head. "No, Biddy. He's…a friend."

"I wouldn't say no to a friend like that," Anna said. "Right handsome, he was. I think—"

"Anna, why don't you get on with your work rather than rattling on? You don't want to be called a gossip."

"No, Mrs. Briggs."

By the time they'd finished their tea, there was no sign of Alexander. Mimi rose to clear the tea things and then took the tray to the kitchen. She heard a noise in the scullery and came upon Alexander, swilling out four porcelain pots, his face a greenish hue.

"Are you all right?"

He glanced up. "I'm better for seeing *you*," he said. "I saved the worst pot for last, and thought I was going to lose my breakfast."

"You don't have to do this," Mimi said.

"Ah, but I *do*," he replied. "I said I wanted to learn about your life. Unless you've never had to rinse out a chamber pot."

"I've cleaned plenty in my time," she said. "Those very pots, in fact."

"Then I cannot refuse to do it."

"Why, because you wish to prove that a man can do anything a woman can?"

"No," he said, moving close until she could feel his hot breath on her lips. "It's because I wish to prove how much I—"

"Mimi!" Mrs. Briggs called out from the kitchen. "Them potatoes need scrubbing."

Alexander pulled away and resumed his attention on the chamber pots. Mimi returned to the kitchen, her cheeks warming.

"*There* you are, darlin'."

Shortly after, Alexander emerged carrying four chamber pots.

"Let me see them," Mrs. Briggs said. He held them out and she leaned over, peering inside. "A passable attempt," she said. "Next time you should scrub them for longer."

His eyes flared, and Mimi suppressed a laugh at the expression of horror in them. Then he nodded and exited the kitchen.

"Don't forget to clean the fireplaces!" Mrs. Briggs called after him.

"He's trying, Mrs. Briggs," Mimi said after he'd gone.

"Aye, he's a trial, all right. But I'll tell you something for nothing. If I were twenty years younger, I'd..."

She winked and licked her lips.

"Mrs. Briggs!" Mimi laughed. "You've treated him abominably today."

"Nothing his servants don't have to put up with, I'm sure. Now, why don't I scrub the potatoes and you slice them for me?" She tipped a bag of potatoes into the sink. "I'll give him his due," she said. "He's taken it like a soldier and marched on. I didn't think he had it in him."

"Is that why you've been so hard on him today?"

"I wanted to discover what he was made of," Mrs. Briggs said.

"And what have you discovered?"

"That he's made of finer stuff than he let on," Mrs. Briggs said, placing a cleaned potato on the table. "There's iron on the outside, but inside..." She let out a sigh, and her expression softened. "He keeps it well hidden, but there's a tender heart in there—though I'm sure it's not something he holds for just anyone."

Mimi reached for the potato and began to slice it.

"It takes a certain kind of man to weather the insults of those he deems beneath them," Mrs. Briggs said. "But I suppose that's the great leveler—more so than liquor."

"What is?" Mimi asked.

"Love," came the reply. "The greatest leveler of all. He must love you a great deal."

CHAPTER TWENTY-THREE

BY THE TIME they returned to Grosvenor Square, the sun had already dipped below the horizon and streaks of red stretched across the sky.

Mimi leaned against Alexander, relishing the solidity of his body, despite the odor of coal dust that clung to him. He hadn't complained once during the day—not even when Mrs. Briggs ordered him to clear up after supper.

In fact, he'd been the epitome of charm. Not the gallantry that a suitor employed to court an unsuspecting debutante, nor the false declarations of chivalry that a rake adopted to debauch an innocent—but genuine kindness, born of a desire to improve the lives of others.

Even Lily had warmed to Alexander, venturing to exchange a few words with him while she handed the potatoes around. As for Sam, by the end of the evening, the little boy's expression of admiration as he looked at Alexander had turned into one of adoration.

Today, Mimi had seen a different man—someone who weathered Mrs. Briggs's orders, entertained a small boy, and even had the insight to notice Lily's wariness and treat her with gentleness and compassion.

That man presented a very real danger of capturing her soul—and she was in danger of willingly giving it to him.

Clinging to his arm, Mimi ascended the steps. The butler

waited at the top, his forehead creased into a frown.

"Ma'am, we were wondering when you'd be home." He glanced at Alexander and arched a dark brow.

"I think, Wheeler, a bath is in order," Mimi said after they'd entered the hallway. "In my dressing room, please."

"Will His Grace be staying?"

A plea shone in Alexander's eyes—not a demand to stay, nor a bid to claim her body…

But a plea, from his heart, not to be hurt.

"Yes," she whispered. "He'll be staying."

"Very good, ma'am." The butler bowed then strode across the hallway, calling for Charles and Mrs. Hodge.

Alexander placed a hand on Mimi's cheek. "*May* I stay?" he whispered. "I will, but only if you wish it."

"Of course," she replied, smiling. "We must get you clean, at least. Your poor valet thinks badly enough of me as it is—he'd have a fit of apoplexy if I sent you home covered in coal dust and—"

"Don't speak of it!" He laughed. "I've never done anything so disgusting as clean out those chamber pots. I'll look at chambermaids differently from now on. Women with stomachs as strong as oxen. I salute them."

"And the women at Mrs. Briggs's house?"

"I admire them also, but none more than you."

She held out her hand. Smiling, he took it, and she led him upstairs. He approached the door leading to the bedchamber they usually shared and turned the handle.

"No," she said.

He turned to face her, sorrow clouding his expression. "You want me to go?"

She shook her head. "I don't want to sleep there tonight." She gestured to her bedchamber—the chamber she had vowed never to share.

Hope ignited in his eyes.

"But first," she said, "methinks the duke needs a bath."

She opened the door to her dressing room, where her maid was already pouring water into the bathtub.

"Water's all good and hot, ma'am," Gracie said, opening a drawer to pull out a dish of soap. "It's—Oh!" She let out a yelp as she noticed Alexander, dropping the soap. "Y-Your Grace. I didn't expect to see you in here." She turned to Mimi. "Ma'am, are you sure you want to…"

"It's all right, Gracie," Mimi said. "You may retire now."

"But won't you need me to—"

"I have all I need for tonight, Gracie."

The maid glanced at Alexander again and blushed. Then she curtseyed and exited the chamber.

Mimi gestured to the tub. "Your bath awaits, Your Grace."

Smiling, he removed his jacket. Then he unbuttoned his shirt and peeled it off. She approached him, but he raised his hand.

"No," he said, his voice hoarse. "Let me remove my own clothes, while you watch."

He continued to remove his garments until he stood before her, naked, the candlelight casting shadows across the planes of his muscles. She lowered her gaze and saw the evidence of his desire jutting proudly from the thatch of wiry curls.

"Does my lady like what she sees?"

"Very much." She took his hand and led him to the bath. He stepped into the water and sank back, submerging his body, then gave a low growl of pleasure and closed his eyes.

"Oh, that feels so good."

"Your Grace, we've not even begun."

"My body aches all over after a day's hard toil. What shall you do to ease it?"

Mimi reached for the soap and held it to her nose, inhaling the scent of lavender and herbs. She dipped it in the water and rubbed it against her hands until bubbles formed. Then she began to lather his body, running her hands along his neck and shoulders, until the tension in his muscles began to ease.

"Mmm," he murmured, a lazy smile on his lips. "If only I

could remain here forever."

"You'd catch cold as the water cooled, Your Grace, and your skin would shrivel."

Mimi continued to lather his chest and moved her fingers across his body in circles, spiraling inward toward his nipples, which stood, firm and erect, glistening in the candlelight.

"Oh, Mimi, to feel your hands on my body… I—Oh!"

He let out a low cry as she flicked his nipple with her fingertip.

"Witch," he growled, and reached for her, curling his fingers around her upper arms. "Would you abuse the power you have over me? We must restore the balance."

"Alexander, I'm fully dressed. I cannot—"

"Oh yes you can," he said, and pulled her into the bath. She let out a squeal as water splashed over the edge of the bathtub and he held her against his chest.

"My gown!" she cried. "It's—"

"An inconvenience, I know," he said. "I must do something about that."

He reached behind her and began to untie her sash. Then he tugged at her gown, but the sodden fabric clung to her body.

"Oh, damn it!" he cursed at the sound of material tearing. "I'll buy you another."

Then he gripped her gown and ripped it apart.

"Alexander," she said, "at least let me—"

"No!" he said. "This is my pleasure and I shall indulge in it."

Her body throbbed with desire at the raw, primal need in his voice, and she grew still while he tore off her garments until she lay on top of him in the bath, clad only in her stockings.

He grasped her thighs and parted them until she could feel his manhood, hard and hot against her center. She parted her legs further and moved to impale herself on him, but he held her still.

"Not yet," he rasped. "The pleasure will be all the sweeter for the wait."

Then he took her face in his hands and pulled her toward him to claim her mouth.

Pleasure flared in her center and a low mewl escaped her lips as she fought against the swell of pleasure, rising like a giant wave against which she had little defense.

He plunged his tongue inside her mouth, and she surrendered to the invasion, melting in his arms as the soft, velvety weapon sought to claim every inch of her. She curled her own tongue around his, and his whole body vibrated with a long, low growl of the primal beast claiming his mate.

To surrender was to step onto the path of destruction—but what sweet destruction! The urge to succumb to desire threatened to overwhelm her as their tongues circled each other in a slow, sensual dance, until he began to devour her, guttural sounds of pleasure vibrating throughout his body, sending a fizz of need through her blood—a pure, primal need to be thoroughly pleasured.

He was a drug and she the victim, unable to survive without tasting it.

She surrendered and, with her own tongue, began to devour him in turn, relishing the taste of spice, desire, and pure masculinity. One taste was not enough—it would never be enough—but if one taste were all that she could have, then she'd take her fill and relive the memory in the years to come.

She let out a cry of surrender, and he broke the kiss, cradling her face in his hands as if he cherished her more than his own life. His eyes, the color of dark sapphires, glowed with desire—and love, as if his soul called out to hers across a chasm, seeking to entwine with hers forever. Understanding shimmered in his eyes as if he recognized her cry for what it was. Wordlessly, he pulled her to him, then he rose to his feet, cradling her in his arms. Water ran off his body in rivulets as he stepped out onto the carpet. Then he took her hand and led her toward the door adjoining her bedchamber. He paused and lifted his eyebrows in a gentle plea, then waited, on the brink of the abyss of her total surrender.

One word and she would be his.

But he remained still. No persuasion, nor coercion—he simply waited for a sign, for permission, his gentle patience piercing her heart.

At length, she nodded. Then he pushed the door open and stepped inside her chamber. She stiffened as the door slammed shut, as if she had sealed her fate. Then he placed a kiss on her lips and stood still, as if waiting for her to relax once more.

He carried her across the chamber and placed her on the bed. He caressed her body with his gaze, and a delicious warmth spread through her blood at the desire in his eyes—not the desire of a man wanting pleasure, but the raw need of a man who wanted nobody but her, a man who wanted her so badly that he would destroy the world around him to claim her as his.

It's a dream—a folly…

Mimi curled her hands into fists, digging her fingernails into her palms to silence the voice inside her head.

The voice might speak the truth, but she would gladly silence it for one night of pleasure—the pleasure that he promised with a single, smoldering glance.

He reached for her stockings and peeled them off, peppering the bare skin of her legs with gentle kisses, tracing a line to her feet, where he kissed each toe with gentle reverence.

"Such soft skin," he whispered. "And I shall worship every inch of it tonight."

"Alexander, I—"

"Hush," he said. "Let me give you that which you desire. Let me satisfy the need that I have seen in your eyes—the need that governs your every waking moment."

"The need to be pleasured?" she asked.

Hurt flickered in his eyes, and he shook his head. "No, Mimi," he said. "The need to be safe."

He crawled onto the bed and placed a kiss on her belly, and want surged as his tongue flicked against her skin.

"The need to surrender and to trust…"

He followed a trail with his lips until he reached her breast, and her nipples hardened to painful points.

"And," he whispered, his breath hot against the skin of her breast, "the need to be loved."

He flicked his tongue over her nipple, and a fizz of need ignited in her center. She arched her back, offering her breast, chasing the pleasure.

"That's it, my love," he said, and she let out a mewl of frustration as he lifted his head from her breast. She drew in a sharp breath as an inferno filled her mind until all she could focus on was her body and its raw, base need to be satisfied.

"Alexander, I…" she said as she arched her back once more in offering. "I—Oh!"

She let out a cry as his hot, wet mouth clamped over her breast. He suckled hard, drawing her nipple into his mouth, then a spike of pain morphed into pleasure as he grazed his teeth over the tip. He continued to feast on her, then he lifted his head and smiled, his eyes almost black with desire, before he gave her other nipple the same loving attention.

When he withdrew and sat up, the skin of her breasts tightened at the rush of cold air. She tried to sit, but he pushed her back, a smile of satisfaction on his lips.

"Oh no, my sweet one," he whispered, "I've not finished with you yet. Lie back."

Her body obeyed, sinking into the bed, and she parted her thighs.

"That's my good girl."

A pulse of pleasure throbbed in her center at his gentle praise, and he placed his hands on her thighs and nudged them further apart.

"Much as I enjoyed supper at Mrs. Briggs's, I find I'm hungry again," he said. "Perhaps it's time for dessert—something a little sweeter."

He dropped his gaze to her thighs, and shyness engulfed her as he looked upon such an intimate part of her.

Then he lowered his head, his nostrils flaring as he inhaled. Beset by panic, she stiffened.

"Alexander, I…"

He lifted his gaze. "What is it, my sweet?"

"You… I mean, I…" She swallowed her shame. "I've never…"

"You mean you've never had a man pleasure you with his tongue…?"

She blinked back tears and shook her head. He grew still, and she braced herself for ridicule.

But none came.

"Will you trust me?" he asked.

She nodded. She had already given him her trust the moment she accepted him into her bedchamber.

"Then lie back and let me give you that which you have denied yourself for too long," he said. "Your body is beautiful and deserves to experience pleasure. *You* deserve pleasure, and I'll not let anyone—even you—deny it."

He placed a kiss on the inside of her thigh, then inhaled.

"Ah," he whispered. "Your body is ready for pleasure—the most perfect scent known to man. And I shall treasure it, for I know it's for me"—he placed a kiss on her curls—"*all* for me."

He flicked his tongue against her skin, and she drew in a sharp breath as the sensation of pleasure began to build.

"Let it happen, my love," he whispered. "You're safe with me."

He dipped his tongue into her curls, and she swallowed a cry as he ran the tip along her flesh. He grew still, as if he waited, and she parted her thighs wider, chasing the pleasure. He let out a growl of approval, and she tilted her hips while he dipped his tongue in and out. A surge of pleasure flooded her center and a shudder vibrated through her bones, rippling across her body until, after a few heartbeats, it subsided.

Sweet heaven! How could so much pleasure be taken from his ministrations? Not even at her own hand had she elicited such sensations. It was as if her body were an instrument and she a mere novice—but he was its master, a true proficient in the art of pleasure.

He lifted his head and smiled. Then he crawled on top of her, molding his body over hers, as if they were two halves of the same whole.

"My beautiful Mimi," he said. "Do you know how much I've longed to see the pleasure in your eyes? Are you ready for pleasure at my touch?"

"There's more?"

His eyes flared. "Oh, my love, what has life denied you?

He shifted position until she could feel him, hard and hot, moving slickly against her flesh. A deep pulse throbbed in her center, like the glow of a flame, moving in and out as each breath ignited it further. Then he eased himself inside her, inch by inch, as if he savored each moment until he was fully sheathed. He closed his eyes, his lips curving with pleasure while he withdrew and entered her again.

The flame swelled in her mind as he increased the pace, until each movement grew harder. His breath came out in hoarse rasps, in time with each thrust as he increased the pace. Mimi arched her back and lifted her hips, meeting each thrust.

"That's it, my love, you're close," he murmured, "so close..."

"H-how can you—Oh!" she gasped, her breath catching in her throat as he slammed inside her body. He plunged in again, his movements growing more frenzied, and a nugget of pleasure began to ripple and throb, deep inside, with a powerful sensation, radiating outward from her center until her whole body shook with it.

"Oh, Mimi!" he cried. "I can feel it—you're so...so... Sweet saints alive!"

He let out a hoarse cry as her body clenched and rippled around him. Then he threw back his head, his mouth open as if he strained for breath, while he continued to pound inside her.

Then her body tightened for a heartbeat before it ignited.

"Alexander!" She let out a scream as the sensations tore her body to pieces, shattering then re-forming to disintegrate all over again as wave after wave of ecstasy ripped through her, until, finally, she lay boneless beneath him. At length, he grew still then reached for her hand, curling his fingers through hers and tightening his grip as if his life depended on her.

Then, with a deep sigh, he settled, his heartbeat pulsing against her chest in unison with hers, as if they were a single creature, forged from pleasure, passion…

…and love.

She closed her eyes and relaxed into the bed, relishing the delicious sensation of his weight on top of her. Then he brushed his mouth against hers and she tasted salt on his lips.

"Alexander…" she breathed, and he clung to her, molding his body against hers as he moved onto his side, taking her with him. He curled his arms around her and held her close.

"I promised you'd be safe with me," he whispered, "and you always shall."

He kissed her again, and his breathing grew steady as he drifted into sleep, his final words barely discernible.

"I love you Mimi—and I'll never let you go."

CHAPTER TWENTY-FOUR

WHEN ALEXANDER WOKE, the room was already light. He yawned and stretched, relishing the warmth on his skin, and rubbed the drowse from his eyes. The room sharpened into focus to reveal furnishings in soft-pastel shades of blue and yellow, and he inhaled the soft aroma of rose and lavender.

Where the devil am I?

He reached out, and his hand met the warm, soft body of a woman.

It was her.

Sweet heaven, she had never been more beautiful—all the more so because…

His heart soared with delight and desire.

Because last night they hadn't merely rutted. They had made love.

She had trusted him enough to take her pleasure.

He placed his hand on her cheek and caressed her skin with his thumb. Her lips curved into a smile. She tilted her head, leaning toward him as if, even in her sleep, she craved his touch.

Doxy she may be, but in many ways she was an innocent. Her wide-eyed wonder as he brought her to pleasure with his tongue had almost undone him. He had longed to see her in the throes of passion, but to be the first man to awaken her to such pleasure…

"Oh, Mimi!"

Her eyelids fluttered open, and his heart gave a jolt as her gaze focused on him. Illuminated by the morning sunlight, her eyes were the color of honey—sweet and warm.

He placed a kiss on her lips.

"I love you, Mimi."

She sat up, clinging to the bedsheet, and glanced about the bedchamber, as if she feared punishment from having committed a transgression.

"It's late," she said. "I can't recall the last time I slept this late."

"We must indulge in many such times to come," he said.

"N-no, this isn't something a woman in my position should grow used to."

She climbed off the bed, still clutching the corner of the bedsheet. Then she let go and, as if ashamed of her nudity, darted across the room to a chest of drawers, pulled out a chemise, and slipped it on.

"There's no need for coyness," Alexander said, "not after what we shared last night."

"L-last night was…"

"Wonderful," he said. "Beautiful, magnificent. I finally realized the depth of my feelings for you—and what I want."

She turned toward him, her eyes glistening. "Wh-what do you want?"

"You," he said, rising from the bed. "I want *you*."

"You have me, Alexander."

"Only until the end of our arrangement," he said. "But I want more. I want you to be *mine*."

She flinched. "Y-yours?"

He nodded. "I'll honor our original agreement and settle two thousand guineas on you today."

"A-and then?"

"Then our arrangement can be made more…*permanent*."

She blinked, slowly, and silence thickened the air, save for his heartbeat thudding against his chest.

Then she shook her head.

"No."

His gut twisted with disbelief.

"*No?*"

Her expression hardened. "Must I repeat myself?" she said. "Is a woman always to be disbelieved—her wishes ignored—when she says no?"

"At least tell me why," he said.

She lifted her hand and brushed it across her eyes. When she lowered it again, they were wet with tears.

"Because I swore I would never endure that life again."

"You mean—you had a protector before?" he asked.

"Yes."

Jealousy stabbed at his heart. "What happened?"

She flinched as he took her wrist.

"Tell me, Mimi," he said. "If I am to be rejected with such coldness, then you owe me a reason. Who was he? Did you love him? Do you *still?*"

She closed her eyes, and he tightened his grip.

"Tell me!" he said. "Is it all just a game to you?"

"No, it's not a game!" she cried. "Yes, I loved him—as one loves a dear friend. He was kind and gentle—almost like…an uncle. H-he looked after me when I had nowhere to go. And then he…"

She shuddered and let out a sob.

"He what?" Alexander said, swallowing his nausea. "He took advantage of you? An older man taking in a young girl then using her as—as his…"

"It wasn't like that!"

"He's a cad, Mimi—he deserves to be shot."

She shook her head. "He was the kindest man I'd ever known. He gave more than he ever took."

"What, money, jewels, silk gowns?" Alexander winced at the bitterness in his voice. "*I* can give you that."

"*He* gave me consideration, and respect," she said. "Many

men will throw trinkets at a whore so she'll part her thighs, but few will give her kindness. Do you know why?"

"Pray, tell me."

"Kindness is the one gift that's given without condition, because it is a gift of the heart."

"Then why aren't you with him now?"

"Because he died."

She crossed the floor and climbed onto a chair, tucking her legs beneath her. Then she rocked back and forth. Alexander's heart ached to see the vulnerability in her eyes.

"What happened?" he whispered.

"I waited for him one morning, but he never came. Instead, his son…h-his son strode into my home, told me his father was dead, and threw me out—but not before he tried to force himself on me." She dipped her head. "My one consolation is that…that kind, gentle soul never knew the depths of his son's depravity."

"Dear Lord, Mimi," Alexander said. "Who is he? Do I know him?"

"It matters not who he is," she said. "What matters is that I swore, from that day, never to be beholden to a man again, no matter how much he may profess to love me."

"But surely you don't think *I'd* treat you so abominably?"

He placed a hand on her shoulder, and she stiffened.

"I don't care that you sold your body for a living before we met," he said. "Do you think I care that you were some man's mistress?"

She looked away.

"I was pregnant."

Alexander let out a curse. His gut twisted in revulsion, and he withdrew his hand. She lifted her gaze, her eyes glazed with pain.

"That's the one sin a man in your position can never forgive—isn't it, Your Grace?"

"No, you misunderstand me!" he said. "You were wronged. You think I'd blame *you*—or the child you bore—for the sins of the man who took advantage of you? Where is the child?"

"I lost it," she said. "So you're spared the indignity of *that*, at least."

He drew her into his arms. At first, she resisted, then the fight drained from her body and she lay limply against him.

"My love, I'd *never* throw you out," he said. "I can gift you a house—*this* house, if the landlord is amenable to selling. Or I'll buy you another. All I ask is that you let me visit you from time to time."

He took her hands and kneeled before her.

"What do you say, my love?" he asked. "A house of your own, plus the two thousand guineas, of course. You'd be set for life. Then you needn't fear what might happen if..." He gestured to himself. "And, of course, if you were caught, I'd ensure any child was taken care of."

She closed her eyes and grew still.

"Mimi, what do you say?"

He held his breath, awaiting her reply.

Then she opened her eyes, and his hope faded at the resignation in them.

"Thank you," she said. "It's a generous offer for one such as I."

"Then you'll take it?"

She shook her head. "Forgive me, Alexander. The price is too high. I-I cannot risk it."

"Mimi, if you're angling for something more..."

She withdrew her hands. Alexander caught a blur of movement before she struck him on the cheek, delivering a stinging slap.

"I'm angling for nothing!" she said. "But if I accept your offer, then I'm in far greater danger than I ever was with Wal...with *him*."

"Why?" he asked.

"Because my feelings for you far surpass any feelings I had for him!" she cried. "Because he didn't occupy my every waking moment, and fill my hopes and dreams—and because I didn't love him with every fiber of my being!"

He recoiled at the force of her passion—finally unleashed, as if, at last, she revealed her soul.

He opened his mouth to reply, but she raised her hand.

"I believe we've both said enough on the matter," she said. "Please, go."

The pain in her eyes pulsed like an open wound. Guilt gnawed at him at the knowledge that he was the cause of it. He held up his hands in appeasement and retreated toward the dressing room.

"I'll send for Charles to help you dress," she said. "I shall, of course, continue to honor our agreement, but I'd be obliged if you give me a little respite from my—my *duties* today.

"I've no wish to cause you pain, Mimi," he said. "I'll meet with my banker today to settle the money owing to you."

"There's no need."

"There's *every* need," he said. "If you cannot accept my love, then at least accept my honor. Perhaps then you might come to believe that there are some men in this world who keep to their word—and that there's one man in the world who loves you."

She nodded, but did not reply.

Leaving her alone in the bedchamber, he entered the dressing room and closed the door behind him. Moments later he heard a soft knock on Mimi's door followed by female voices. Then Charles entered the dressing room, carrying Alexander's own clothes, and helped him to dress.

After he'd dismissed the footman, Alexander approached the adjoining door to Mimi's chamber, but the female voices indicated that her maid was still with her. Then he heard a soft sob, followed by the maid's voice in low, soothing tones.

He didn't know what broke his heart more—Mimi's anguish, or the fact that, in her moment of despair, she turned to someone other than him.

CHAPTER TWENTY-FIVE

"WELCOME HOME, MA'AM. I trust you had a pleasant walk. There's a gentleman to see you."

"Is it the Duke of Sawbridge, Charles?" Mimi asked, her heart fluttering with anticipation as she approached the front door.

The footman shook his head, and the flare of hope died. Alexander hadn't visited since declaring his love and tempting her with a life of comfort and dependence as his mistress. But, true to his word, he had deposited two thousand guineas into an account on her behalf.

He had given Mimi her freedom.

It was second best to his love, but freedom would, at least, save her from heartbreak and destruction.

"Who is it, Charles?" Mimi asked, removing her redingote and handing it to him.

"He didn't give a card, but he said you were old friends. He's in the parlor. Shall I bring tea?"

"You didn't think to ask his name?"

"Forgive me, ma'am, I'm always forgetting things. Mr. Wheeler will be ever so angry."

"It matters not," Mimi said, touching his arm. "What Mr. Wheeler doesn't know won't harm him."

"Thank you ma'am. We're going to miss you when you leave."

"I'm sure whoever takes over this house will be a fair mistress—or master," Mimi said.

"There's none so fair as you."

"You flatter me, Charles."

"It's not just me who says so. You should've heard what Auntie…I mean, Mrs. Hodge said last night over supper. 'Charles, it's a shame Lady Rex will be leaving us after such a short time, for she's been the kindest mistress.' And even Mr. Wheeler said—"

"Charles, we mustn't keep my guest waiting," Mimi said.

"Very good, ma'am."

The footman bowed and disappeared along the hallway. Then Mimi pushed open the parlor door.

Her guest stood at the window, his back to her, a cane in his right hand.

"Do I know you, sir?" Mimi said.

"I saw you from the window."

Her gut twisted with horror at the familiar voice—with its sharp, nasal tones that had swelled her fears and plagued her nightmares. It was a voice she'd hoped never to hear again, but that hope faded the moment she'd looked into his eyes at the concert.

He turned slowly to face her.

"Earl Mayhew," she whispered.

He approached, tapping his cane on the floor, his pale-gray eyes filled with contempt.

"Lady Rex," he said, his tone mocking. "My, how you've risen in the world—*Miss Jemima King.*"

She stepped back, her stomach churning at the stench of his cologne.

"My name is—"

"Spare me your falsehoods," he sneered. "You may have convinced everyone else that you're a respectable widow, but I'm not so easily fooled. Lady *Rex*, indeed! You think I don't know Latin, Miss King? No knight—not even one liberal enough to live on the Continent—would take a whore for a wife." He gestured about the parlor with his cane. "I take it Sawbridge pays for this," he said. "Does he know you're a common whore?"

"Lord Mayhew, please, I—"

"Please what? Do you wish me to keep your sordid secret? Are you fishing for a marriage proposal from Sawbridge? Ha! A whore could never snare a duke—especially *that* one. You're just the latest in a long list of tarts he's fucked."

"I care not what you say," she said. "I'm leaving Town."

"Come to his senses and tossed you out, has he?"

He stepped closer, and Mimi moved to dodge him, but he blocked her with his cane.

"Not so fast, my lovely Jemima," he said, thrusting his face close. "I can take over the lease of this house. I'm prepared to be generous—you're a friend of the family, after all. The pater always did say you were a bloody good fuck."

"How can you say such things?" Mimi said. "Your father would never have said—"

"Oh, but he *did*, my dear. He and I used to laugh about it— about how he couldn't bear to look at your whining, cajoling face, so he'd prefer to rut you from behind, like the bitch you are."

She recoiled with revulsion. "You're vile!" she cried. "You never deserved to have Walter as a father. He was a good, kind man. I'm only glad that he never knew—"

"Knew what? What a filthy slut you've turned out to be? Spreading your legs for every man in Town? Well, it's time I took *my* turn. I'm prepared to pay, or"—his face twisted with lust— "perhaps I should just take what I'm owed."

"I owe you nothing!"

"I disagree, my dear."

He moved closer. She retreated until she felt the parlor wall against her back.

"You bled my father dry when you whored yourself out," he said. "All those pretty trinkets he gave you, bought with my inheritance. So you *owe* me, woman. Now's the time to collect."

He grasped her arms and pulled her against him. His hardness poked against her stomach, and she let out a cry and tried to break free.

"That's it, my filly," he rasped. "I relish a struggle—it makes the conquest all the sweeter."

"Ralph, let me go!"

"Oh, *Ralph*, is it?" he said. "Such intimacy stirs my blood. Soon you'll be screaming my name as I rut you."

She struggled, but he tightened his grip and forced his mouth over hers. She tried to twist her head free, but he fisted a hand in her hair, then yanked her head back.

The world shifted out of focus as Mimi fought for breath against his thick, savage tongue. Then she bit down, hard, and rammed her knee into his groin.

"Bitch!" he cried, stumbling back, then he backhanded her across the face.

Pain exploded in her cheek and she staggered back with the force of the blow. With the metallic taste of blood on her lips, she crumpled to the floor, turning her ankle as she fell.

"Filthy whore!" he snarled. "You'll pay for that."

He stood over her and began to unbutton his breeches. She kicked out, but he dodged the blow.

"Think carefully, madam, before you deny me," he said, brandishing his cane. She tried to stand, but her ankle gave way. She reached out to defend herself as he advanced on her, and she braced herself for the blow.

The door burst open and a primal roar, the bellow of a savage beast, filled the air. Mimi's assailant was pulled back and propelled across the room. She winced at the sound of splintering wood, and lifted her head to see him lying on top of what was once a side table, which now lay in pieces.

"Leave her alone, Mayhew, you blackguard!"

Alexander stood over the earl, his face scarlet with fury. He picked up the cane, and Mimi flinched as he raised it. Then he brought it down on his knee, where it snapped in two, then tossed the pieces at the man he'd vanquished.

"S-Sawbridge!" Mayhew panted. "I say, old chap, there's been a misunderstanding. I was only taking what was on offer."

Alexander grasped Mayhew's lapels and pulled him upright as if he weighed no more than a child.

"You were *what*?"

"Be reasonable, man!" Mayhew said, laughing, though fear glistened in his eyes. "A whore will spread her legs for any man if the price is high enough. Perhaps you're not paying her as much as my father did."

Mimi suppressed a cry of shame as Alexander glanced toward her, raising his eyebrows. Then he resumed his attention on Mayhew and bared his teeth.

"Lay one finger on her, Mayhew, and I'll end you!" he snarled. Then he released the earl and pushed him back, wiping his hands on his jacket.

"I'd like to see you try, Sawbridge," Mayhew said.

"Don't play games and don't make promises you cannot keep," Alexander said.

"Are you calling me a coward?"

"You've earned that title through your actions," Alexander said. "Only a coward would try to take a woman unwilling."

"No whore is unwilling." Mayhew cast a look of contempt at Mimi. "I trust you got your money's worth, Sawbridge. My father certainly did."

Alexander turned to Mimi, and she lowered her gaze, unable to witness his condemnation.

"I'll never blame Mimi for what she had to do to survive, Mayhew," he said.

"She didn't merely survive, Sawbridge—she *thrived*," Mayhew said. "After fellating my father, she would beg for my cock if it earned her a little extra cash."

"Why, you *filth*!" Alexander raised his fist and smashed it into Mayhew's face. The earl staggered back, his nose twisted at an unnatural angle, his face smeared red.

"Bastard! You've broken my nose!"

"I'll break a damn sight more than that," Alexander said, advancing on him again.

"Stop!" Mimi cried. "Please!"

He paused, fists raised, and turned toward her. "Surely you're not wanting to protect this…*creature?*"

"No, but I would protect you. Alexander, you're the better man. You—"

"*Alexander*, is it?" Mayhew sneered, his voice muffled as he held his hands to his nose. "Such an intimate address. She called me *Ralph* earlier, you know—just before she parted her thighs."

Alexander grasped his lapels again.

"Don't you care that your whore is being shared about London?" Mayhew said, his voice tight with fear.

Alexander shook his head. "I care nothing for what you say, Mayhew—a sniveling creature preying on those he deems weaker than him. Men like you are ten a penny."

"As are women like *her*."

Mimi flinched at the hatred in Mayhew's voice.

"That's where you're wrong," Alexander said. "But you're too foolish to understand."

"And you're—" Mayhew began, but he broke off as Alexander shook him.

"I have no wish to listen to you anymore."

Alexander marched Mayhew out of the parlor, ignoring the other man's protests, and their raised voices and footsteps echoed in the hallway outside. Then the main doors opened and shut with a crash, followed by silence, save for Mimi's own ragged breathing.

She struggled to her feet, her face throbbing, then limped over to the window, where she caught sight of Mayhew disappearing round a corner at the end of the street.

She heard Charles's voice followed by a sharp command, then footsteps approached.

"Mimi?"

She turned to see Alexander standing in the doorway, staring at her.

She awaited his condemnation, but saw only compassion in his eyes. He moved toward her and enveloped her in his arms. She stiffened, but he held her tenderly until she relaxed against him. Then he lifted his hand to guide her head onto his shoulder and caressed her hair.

"My poor love," he said. "I'm so sorry."

"Wh-what he said, I…"

"Hush," he whispered, his voice a soft caress. "I care not what he says. All that matters is you."

"But I… His father…"

He kissed her hair. "There's no need to tell me anything, Mimi. I care not for your past—I care for *you*. Here and now."

He took her head in his hands and tilted her face up. Pain flickered in his eyes when she winced.

"I-I need to tend to…" she began, gesturing to her throbbing cheek.

"Let me take care of you."

He took her hand and led her to the chaise longue beside the window. Shortly after, Charles entered carrying a tray.

"Lady Rex!" he cried. "What's happened? Are you hurt?"

"Just bring the tray like I asked, and stop fooling about," Alexander growled.

"I'll be all right, Charles," Mimi said. "I was…" She hesitated at the memory of Mayhew's snarling face and the fear of his overpowering her. "I-I was…"

"You were *magnificent*," Alexander said, brushing a stray tendril of her hair behind her ear. "Charles, set the tray here and fetch a brandy for your mistress."

The footman obeyed then exited the parlor.

Mimi closed her eyes, beset with shame and nausea. She heard a movement and caught the soft scent of herbs. Then a cool cloth was pressed against her cheek. She opened her eyes to see Alexander staring at her.

"Be still," he whispered. "This will help with the bruising."

Then he smiled, his eyes shimmering in the afternoon light. "I learned from the best, did I not? Ah—the brandy." He turned as Charles entered with a glass. "Thank you, young man," he said, taking the glass. "Forgive me for speaking harshly earlier. I was concerned for your mistress."

The footman bowed and exited the parlor.

Alexander held the glass to Mimi's lips.

"I can take care of myself," she said.

"I know, my love," he said. "But, just this once, I would beg you accept the care of another—he who loves you."

She reached for the glass, and her hand trembled. He took her hand and guided the glass to his lips, kissing each finger.

"There's no shame in being tended to after the ordeal you've just endured," he said. "Here, drink the brandy—it'll help."

Her heart threatened to yield at his earnestness, and she nodded. Silently, he tilted the glass until the liquid trickled into her mouth. She caught her breath as the fiery liquor warmed her throat.

"There!" he said, in the manner of a nursemaid coaxing a sick child. Then he continued to dab her face with the cloth. "Better?" he asked.

"A little."

He pushed her gently back, and she resisted.

"You're still shaking," he said. "Take some rest. I'll be here—unless you wish me to leave?"

The hope in his eyes melted her heart, and she held out her hand, suppressing her shame at how violently it trembled.

"Stay," she whispered.

He kissed her hand again, then nodded. "As long as you need me."

He reached for her shawl from the back of a chair and draped it over her. Then he kneeled beside her and caressed her forehead with a light, gentle touch that belied his huge hands—hands that had, not ten minutes before, pummeled her assailant to the floor then thrown him out onto the street. Gentle hands capable of protecting her—of loving her.

She relaxed under his touch and sank back.

"That's it, my love," he whispered. "I'm here to take care of you. Trust me."

With his gentle fingers coaxing her into submission, she closed her eyes and let her mind drift into sleep.

WHEN MIMI WOKE, the parlor was empty. She sat up, a thick ache throbbing in her head. The shawl was still draped over her body. She lifted her head and caught sight of the half-empty glass of brandy silhouetted against the window, the last rays of the setting sun illuminating the deep amber liquid from behind. Dying embers glowed in the fireplace—someone must have lit the fire while she slept.

How long had she been asleep?

Footsteps approached, and Mimi smiled to herself.

Alexander had been true to his word. He said he'd stay while she needed him.

But when the door opened, it wasn't Alexander. It was Charles.

"Good evening, your ladyship." The footman moved about the parlor, lighting the candles and drawing the curtains. "Will you be wanting supper at the usual time, ma'am?" he asked.

"Is my…guest still here?"

"Sorry, ma'am, he had to leave."

Mimi looked away, ashamed at the hope in her voice.

"Yes, of course, Charles, I understand. You may serve supper as soon as it's ready. Then I'll retire."

"Begging your pardon for being so forward, ma'am," Charles said, "but the duke will return. He had an errand to run—one that I believe will be to your benefit."

"To my benefit?"

"Forgive me, ma'am—he told me not to say anything."

Her gut twisted with apprehension. "Is anything wrong, Charles? Where did he go?"

"To the park, I believe."

"To do what?"

"I don't rightly know, but he said it was for your sake."

She shook her head. "I don't understand, Charles. What could there possibly be in the park that's of relevance to me?"

"He didn't *exactly* say for your sake, ma'am. He said something about your honor."

"My…?"

"Honor. Yes, that was it," Charles said. "I thought it strange at the time. He said he was going to restore your honor. But he didn't want me telling you." His eyes widened. "You won't tell him, will you? I'm already in trouble with Mr. Wheeler for dropping a plate in the kitchen. Said it was to come out of my wages, he did. I…"

He rattled on, while a cold hand of dread squeezed Mimi's heart.

"Charles, did the duke say when he was going to the park?"

The footman hesitated.

"You have my word you're not in any trouble, but it's vital that you tell me."

He nodded. "Dusk."

Mimi's throat constricted and the air rushed out of her chest. She glanced out of the window to see the sun disappearing below the horizon and let out a cry.

"Oh, ma'am!" the footman said. "I knew I shouldn't have said anything. Forgive me!"

"You did the right thing by telling me," Mimi said. "But the duke…"

An image forced itself into her consciousness—Alexander standing before Mayhew, weapon in hand…a crack in the air and a puff of smoke…

…and Alexander's broken body prone on the ground, his

sapphire eyes wide and lifeless.

"Charles, fetch my cloak," she said, leaping to her feet.

"You're hurt, ma'am. The duke told me to ensure you stayed at home tonight."

"Charles, please do as I ask."

"But ma'am—"

"Charles!" she cried. "Damn you—*just do as I say!*"

The footman recoiled, then he mumbled his assent and retreated into the hallway. Mimi followed, and as she approached the main doors, he reappeared with her cloak.

"Let me come with you," he said.

"No, Charles, I'll not put you in danger."

"What danger?"

"The duke has gone to fight a duel," Mimi said.

And, if she couldn't prevent it, Alexander might be killed.

CHAPTER TWENTY-SIX

A ROW OF trees towered over the path, their bare branches like thin, taloned fingers stretching upward to claw at the sky.

Alexander's foot caught on a stone and he stumbled sideways, colliding into his companion and second.

"Shit."

A flock of birds rose from a treetop, cawing angrily at each other while they circled the air, then settled once more into their roosts.

"Careful there, Sawbridge—you'll not defeat your opponent if you're too inebriated to shoot straight."

"I may be a fool, Foxton…" Alexander began.

"Of that, at least, we're in agreement."

"…but I'm not so much of a simpleton as to lengthen my odds of success by getting foxed."

Foxton let out a chuckle. "From what I hear, Mayhew's hardly a crack shot. You'll be the more experienced of the two."

"I've not fought a duel before," Alexander said.

"Really? Given the number of women you've compromised, I find that astonishing."

"I've never been moved enough to want to kill a man for the sake of a woman."

"Until today," Foxton said. "You've fallen hard for our little widow, haven't you? I should have realized it when I first saw you with her."

"Then you can bask in the superiority of knowing that you were right," Alexander retorted.

Foxton snorted. "I can't understand a man who makes an arse of himself over a mere *woman*. Bed her, then shed her—that's my rule. There's far too many women to be enjoyed to want to restrict yourself to just one."

"If you're going to insult me, then I'll do this on my own," Alexander said.

"Don't be so stuffy!" Foxton laughed. "Heavens—if this is what love does to a man, I must take care never to lose my heart."

"No great challenge, given that you're not in possession of one."

They rounded a corner, and Alexander's chest constricted.

His opponent stood in the center of the lawn, next to another man carrying a slim wooden box. Behind them, a hackney carriage formed a dark shape against the backdrop of the Serpentine, which glistened malevolently in the rising moonlight.

Alexander stepped toward his opponent.

"Pleasant night for it, Mayhew." He glanced at the earl's second. "Sir Heath Moss—I should have guessed. I said to myself I was sure Mayhew had a friend somewhere in the world. Reason dictated otherwise, but the world is large enough to make it a mathematical possibility that two such creatures as you existed in it."

"I think that's the pleasantries done with, don't you?" Mayhew said, his breath misting in the air. He nodded to Sir Heath, who opened the box to reveal a pair of pistols nestling together on a bed of velvet. "Choose your weapon."

"Wait!" Foxton cried. "Permit me to inspect them."

"For what purpose?" Mayhew asked.

"To ensure a fair fight."

"I give you my word as a gentleman."

"Gentleman—ha!" Alexander roared. "Is that the same gentleman who tried to violate Lady Rex?"

A muffled cry came from the hackney carriage.

"Get on with it, then, Foxton," Mayhew said. "I've not got all night."

Foxton lifted the weapons and inspected each one. Then he nodded.

"They're sound," he said. "Both loaded. But just in case, Sawbridge should make first choice."

"Why not?" Mayhew said, smiling. "I can be generous—it's all the same to me."

Why did the blackguard look so damned sure of himself?

Alexander plucked a pistol from the case and felt the weight in his hand. Mayhew stared at the box and smiled, triumph glittering in his eyes.

"What's the matter with you, Mayhew?" Foxton asked. "Get on with it! I, for one, have no wish to get caught by the authorities."

Mayhew turned toward the carriage. "You can come out now!"

A slim form climbed out—a masked man dressed in dark breeches and jacket, with a tricorn hat. His eyes gleamed behind the mask, then widened as his gaze settled on Alexander and Foxton.

Alexander's gut knotted with horror.

"Are you…"

"Gentlemen," Mayhew said, "may I present my proxy—the Farthing."

A second form climbed out, equally clad in dark clothes and mask. He gestured to Mayhew. "My master requires payment before we begin."

"Very well," Mayhew said. "Twenty guineas, wasn't it?"

"Fifty, and well you know it."

"I'm of a mind to spend a little less. How about thirty? What does your master say to that?"

Wordlessly, the Farthing retreated toward the carriage.

"Stop!" Mayhew cried, but the Farthing ignored him.

Alexander let out a chuckle. "Why don't you stamp your foot?"

Mayhew rounded on him, teeth bared. "Fine words for a dead man," he snarled. "All right! Fifty it is."

He drew a sheaf of notes from his pocket and handed them to the manservant, who made a show of counting them. He nodded, and the Farthing returned and picked up the remaining weapon. He held it as if it were an extension of his arm, then, with his free hand, caressed the barrel before aiming it toward the trees.

Alexander's blood froze. The man's arm barely moved—not a tremor nor a shake.

"A farthing at fifty paces," he breathed. "Sweet Lord!"

"That's just a rumor," Foxton said.

"Rumors are founded on truth," Alexander said. "Look at him! With a grip that steady, he cannot fail to miss. I'll only be twenty paces from him, and my heart's a considerably larger target than a farthing."

"Then you must shoot him first."

"That's the point," Alexander replied. "I don't want to shoot *him.*"

The Farthing lowered his arm and glanced over at Alexander.

"Might I know my opponent's identity?" Alexander asked.

"You may not," the servant said.

How young was he? Both the Farthing and his manservant seemed like boys. The latter had the thin, reedy voice of an adolescent.

A little like Mimi's footman…

No, surely it wasn't Charles—not when he'd pledged to remain at the house and take care of Mimi.

But I made that same pledge this very evening.

"Come along!" Sir Heath snapped. "Like you said, there's no time to lose. Stand back against each other. Walk forward one pace as I count and, on the count of ten, you're at liberty to fire."

"I know how it's done," Alexander growled.

He approached the Farthing and issued a mock bow. The two stood back to back for a heartbeat, then Sir Heath began to count.

"One, two, three…"

Alexander's palms grew slick, and he tightened his grip on the pistol, holding the barrel with his free hand to quell the tremors in his arm, focused on placing one foot before the other.

Perhaps he might fire at Mayhew. But no—if he did that, the Farthing would shoot him dead.

"Nine…ten!"

Alexander paused, his ears ringing.

Ten…

Shit!

He whirled around and lifted his arm.

His opponent stood still, the barrel of his pistol gleaming in the moonlight, his aim steady and true.

He couldn't fail to miss.

Alexander cocked his pistol, curled his finger around the trigger, then hesitated.

Could he shoot another man—a stranger with whom he had no argument?

Was he a coward—or a killer?

Coward…

He drew in a deep breath, his heartbeat thudding in his ears.

Why did his opponent not shoot?

"Well?" Mayhew cried. "What the bloody hell am I paying you for, man? Get on with it!"

Alexander's arm trembled more violently as he tightened his grip—but he couldn't bring himself to shoot a man with whom he had no quarrel.

I'm going to die.

His heart ached with despair. Not at the pain, or the thought of meeting his maker…

…but at the thought of never looking into her eyes again.

"Forgive me, Mimi."

A crack shattered the air, and a puff of blue smoke burst from the muzzle of his opponent's pistol. Moments later, Alexander heard a soft whistle in the air, then a sharp, hot pain tore through his ear and he jerked backward and dropped his pistol. He reached up and touched his ear, which was slick with a hot, sticky liquid, then he inspected his hand.

His fingers were smeared with blood.

Bloody hell—that hurt!

Foxton sprinted toward him. "Are you all right?"

Alexander nodded.

Foxton retrieved Alexander's pistol and uncocked it. "You're one lucky bastard," he said.

"I'll say so," Mayhew yelled, his voice shaking with fury as he turned toward the Farthing, who stood, erect, his arm lowered, the pistol at his side. "What the devil do you think you were doing?"

"My master did what you paid him to do, your lordship," the manservant said, while the Farthing placed his weapon back in the box. Foxton approached with the other pistol and the Farthing darted back—almost as if he feared him.

"Do you not speak?" Foxton asked. The Farthing shook his head and retreated.

"*I* speak for my master," the manservant said. "The terms of the contract have been fulfilled."

"No, they haven't!" Mayhew snarled. "I wanted him dead!"

"Then you should have stipulated that in the contract," the manservant said. "My master agreed to win the duel as your proxy, and he has done precisely that. Honor has been satisfied with relatively little blood spilled."

"Honor be damned." Mayhew grasped the loaded pistol and strode toward Alexander. "Say goodbye, Sawbridge."

"No!" a female voice screamed, and hurried footsteps approached. "Stop—please!"

Alexander froze as Mimi appeared, sprinting along the path.

The Farthing let out a low cry.

"Hush!" the manservant said, pulling the Farthing toward the carriage. "It's time we left."

"But—"

"It's too dangerous," the servant said. "You can't help her."

Mayhew watched the exchange with amusement, then aimed the pistol at Mimi.

Alexander darted toward her and shielded her with his body.

"Shoot if you wish, Mayhew," he said. "But you shan't harm the woman I love."

Mayhew laughed. "Very well, seeing as you've given me permission."

He squeezed the trigger, and Mimi let out a scream, pulling Alexander to one side and stepping into the line of fire.

The pistol clicked, but did not fire.

"You need to cock it again, you fool," Sir Heath said, but before Mayhew reacted, Foxton snatched the pistol from his grip, cocked it, then fired into the air. The shot echoed across the park, and a volley of quacks of protest carried across the air from the Serpentine. The hackney carriage jerked forward as the horse startled, and the driver tugged at the reins, coaxing the animal into submission.

"Enough!" Foxton said. "You've had your satisfaction, Mayhew. Get your sorry arse out of my sight before I kick you into the next country."

Mayhew hesitated, but Foxton stepped toward him, his powerful body dwarfing Mayhew's form.

"Try it," he said. "Cross me and there will be no proxy to save you."

Mayhew shriveled under Foxton's gaze, then scuttled off, Sir Heath in his wake.

Foxton turned to the Farthing. "You should be ashamed of yourself, sir, trading on the misery of others. Leave now, and pray to the Almighty that I never discover your identity."

The Farthing hesitated, then slipped into the hackney carriage, his manservant following. Shortly after, the driver cracked his whip and steered it out of the park.

"Sawbridge, get yourself home and get that wound seen to," Foxton said.

"You're hurt?" Mimi asked. "Oh, Alexander—why did you do it?"

"For you, my love."

She lifted a trembling hand to his face, and he winced as she brushed her fingertips across his ear.

"He missed," she said.

"I don't think so," Foxton replied. "The Farthing's too good a marksman. A death is always difficult to explain. This way he earns his fee neatly and quietly. Much like a whore, his motivation is money, not honor."

Mimi stiffened, and Alexander drew her close.

"That's enough, Foxton," he said. "Leave me be."

Foxton's eyes widened, then he gave a sharp sigh and shook his head. He bowed to Mimi. "Ma'am, I trust you're recovered from your ordeal at Mayhew's hands."

"A little, thank you," she said, her voice wavering.

Foxton glanced toward Alexander, his eyebrows raised in expectation. Then he gave a mock bow.

"Oh, you're *welcome*, Sawbridge," he said. "There's nothing I like better than to wander about Hyde Park in the dark for an ungrateful, lovesick fool." He nodded to Mimi. "Your servant, ma'am." Then he strode away, his footsteps crunching on the gravel.

Alexander began to shake. Mimi slipped her arm through his and steered him onto the path and toward the park gates.

"What were you *thinking*?" she asked.

"I only thought of you," he said. "I-I wanted to do something, to—to…"

"To what? Put your life in danger for the sake of honor?" She shook her head. "Honor is not worth dying for—at least *your* definition of honor."

"My definition?"

"A gentleman's," she said. "Your idea of honor isn't what's

good or what's right. It's merely an excuse to seek retribution on your enemies, or to punish others for not following the social rules you impose on them. Or"—her breath hitched as she clung to him—"it's a stick with which to beat a woman who sells her body to earn enough to live on."

"I don't think less of you for being a…" He hesitated, unable to voice it.

"A whore," she said. "It's what I am. As a woman, I'll forever be defined by what I did to survive, even if I intend never to do that again."

"Foxton didn't mean *you* when he referred to whores and money," Alexander said.

"Nevertheless, it's Society's view of women like me."

They turned a corner, and the buildings of Grosvenor Square came into view.

She gestured toward number sixteen. "No matter how fine a house you place me in, or the gowns or jewels you gift me, it makes no difference to what I am on the inside."

"What you are is the woman I love," he said. "Don't you see that?" He stopped and pulled her to him, his heart aching at the bruise on her cheek. "I care not who you were, or what you have done. I love you regardless."

She blinked, and her eyes glistened with moisture, then she shivered.

"Let's get you inside," he said. "Damnation!" he cried as pain throbbed in his ear. "I almost wish the Farthing had shot me in the heart—it couldn't hurt more than *this*."

She steered him up the steps, and the door opened to reveal a red-faced Charles.

"I want a word with *you*," Alexander said. "How the devil did Lady Rex find out—"

"That's enough, Alexander," Mimi said. "He isn't at fault." She turned toward the boy and gave him a sweet smile. "Charles, I'll be wanting clean cloths and some of that tincture we used on Mrs. Brennan when she cut her hand the other week."

"Yes, ma'am." The footman scuttled off, and Mimi led Alexander into the parlor and toward the chaise longue. She sat him in the very spot where he'd tended to her earlier that evening—where he'd watched her fall asleep before abandoning her to shoot the bastard who had laid his filthy hands on her.

After Charles brought in the cloths and tincture, she dabbed it on his ear, and Alexander winced, letting out a groan of pain.

"Forgive me," he said.

"What for?" she asked crisply. "There are many transgressions to choose from."

"For not being as brave as you," he replied. "You uttered barely a whisper when I tended to your cheek earlier."

Her lips curved into a smile. He took her hand and kissed it, but she withdrew it and resumed cleaning his ear.

"I never knew so small a wound could bleed so profusely," he said.

"It's slowing," she said. "Once I've cleaned it up, you'll hardly know the wound was there. The bullet must have just grazed the skin."

"Enough to draw blood and secure victory, but not enough to cause great injury," he said. "The Farthing is to be commended."

"How can you speak so?" she said. "You could have been killed!"

"How else could I defend you, Mimi? Do you know how much it pained me to see that man, what he was doing to you, when I should have been there to protect you?"

"He didn't violate me, Alexander," she said. "I defended myself."

"But he hurt you," he said, placing his hand on her cheek. "My poor darling—he hurt you and I wasn't there to stop him. But from now on, I'll *always* be there. I love you, Mimi."

She looked away.

"I *love* you," he said. "It's because of that love that I challenged Mayhew to a duel."

"Lord Mayhew is but one man," she said.

"And I can protect you from him—I want to. It's my honor and pleasure."

"Honor," she said, shaking her head. "Why must it always be about honor? What about the others, Alexander?"

"Others?" He recoiled. "Were you another man's mistress as well as Mayhew's father's?"

Hurt rippled across her eyes. "No—I mean all the other men who, as soon as they know what I am, will consider me fair game."

"I'll fight them also."

"Each and every one?" She shook her head. "You can't fight them all. You entered into our arrangement to restore your reputation, so that your association with a respectable widow might make your company more palatable in the eyes of your friends—and other women."

His conscience stabbed at his heart. What a cad he'd been—seeking to use her for his own ends.

"Mayhew will tell the world who, and what, I am," she said.

"You think I care?"

"Maybe not at first," she said, "but you've been used to the adoration and admiration of all. A word of contempt, a sly look—you may brush them off at first. But when access to the best clubs and parties is denied you because of the woman at your side..." She shook her head. "We can never give each other what we truly need to be happy."

"Can't we try, at least?"

"The price would be too great."

He swallowed his frustration. "Must you always mention the price? Can't you take a leap of faith and trust in my love?"

"I wish I could, with all my heart, Alexander," she replied, "but I couldn't bear to see your love for me wither and die."

"You think I don't love you enough?" he said. "You think so little of me that my love is a mere fancy that will fade over time? Would I have risked my life had my love been a mere inclination?"

"I didn't ask you to risk your life!" she cried. "And I cannot bear the thought that you may be compelled to do such a thing in the future."

"Then I swear that I'll never do such a thing again."

"Just as you swore earlier tonight that you'd remain inside while I had need of you?"

The door knocked and Charles appeared.

"Beggin' your pardon, ma'am, but Mrs. Brennan's asking if she should start supper."

Mimi withdrew from Alexander's embrace and approached the footman. "Yes, thank you, Charles. And I think a sherry each before supper, if you could…" She leaned toward the footman and lowered her voice. He glanced at Alexander, then nodded.

"What did you ask him?" Alexander said when Charles had left.

"I asked if he could pour you a large glass, on account of your injury."

He offered his hand, and for a moment she stared at it. Then she took it and he pulled her onto his lap.

"Let me stay tonight," he said.

She placed a kiss on his cheek. "Of course."

When Charles returned with two glasses of sherry, Mimi handed the larger to Alexander. Then she raised her glass.

"To tomorrow," she said, smiling, though resignation shone in her eyes.

He clinked his glass against hers. Then she tipped her head back and drained hers.

"It's good for the pain," she said. "Wheeler procured it from a man called Trelawney."

"Trelawney's an excellent man," Alexander said. "He supplies the very best. Perhaps I ought to savor it."

"I've asked Charles to bring you another," she said.

He drained his glass, his breath catching as the liquor warmed his throat. "A rather unusual sherry," he said, licking his lips. "There's a bitter aftertaste."

"Oh?" She raised her eyebrows. "I have another bottle. You could try that instead."

"Yes, that would be…" He blinked as the world shifted out of focus, then he shook his head. That injury must have affected him more than he thought.

But then, it wasn't every day that a man got himself shot.

He relaxed back into the chaise longue, and she nestled into his embrace. The warmth of the fire caressed his senses and a delicious languor flowed through him. The woman in his arms took his hand and kissed it, and he curled his fingers around hers.

"Oh, Mimi, I love you so much…" he murmured.

"And I you," she whispered. "Whatever happens, please believe that I love you more than I have ever loved another—or ever will."

What did she mean, *whatever happens*?

But it mattered not when her soft fingers caressed his face—when her warm, sweet lips kissed him.

With her whispered words of love in his mind, Alexander closed his eyes and welcomed the darkness.

CHAPTER TWENTY-SEVEN

WHEN ALEXANDER WOKE, the air had cooled. The soft orange glow of the embers of the fire had been replaced by the cold, harsh light of the dawn.

He sat up and winced as a sharp pain sliced through his head. His mouth felt dry, and a bitter taste lingered at the back of his throat.

Rubbing his chin, the beginnings of stubble abrading against his fingertips, he looked around. The room was empty, save for the furniture and the clock on the mantelshelf. The pile of books beside the door was gone, and there was nothing on the tables except…

Except the two sherry glasses, empty save for a sticky residue at the bottom. He picked up the larger glass and sniffed the contents. Sherry—and another odor.

What was it?

He drew in a deep breath, inhaling the aroma—the faint, bitter afternote to match the bitterness in his throat.

Laudanum.

He leaped to his feet and stumbled toward the mantelshelf, willing his eyes to focus as he approached the clock.

It was almost half past six in the morning.

He stumbled out of the parlor.

"Charles!" he cried. "Wheeler—anyone!"

His voice echoed across the hall as he glanced about.

Then he saw it—a folded note in the dish by the door. He picked it up and read the inscription.

Alexander.

His hands trembling, he unfolded it and read the words.

Forgive me, my love. We both want what the other cannot give, and if we remained as we are, the wanting would drive us both to destruction. I pray with all my heart that you, at least, will be happy, and I trust that, in my actions, I am doing all I can to make that possible.

Mimi

Footsteps approached, and Alexander snapped his head up, buoyed by hope. But it was the butler. His heart ached at the sadness and resignation in the man's eyes.

"Where…?" he asked, but Wheeler shook his head.

"Even if I knew, Your Grace, I wouldn't…"

"I understand," Alexander said, as the knot of pain swelled in his heart.

Mimi had gone.

"She sent for your clothes last night," the butler said, his gaze wandering over Alexander's crumpled shirt and breeches. "A fire has been lit in the guest bedchamber for you, and I took the liberty of sending Charles in with a washbowl and razor. Shall I assist you, or would you rather I send for your valet?"

Alexander shook his head. "There's no need to disturb him. Perhaps some tea before I shave?"

"Charles is already making it."

"I see you're fully prepared, Wheeler."

"Her ladyship's orders were quite specific."

"What were her orders?"

"To see to your every need so that you might enter the world with pride, in the knowledge that you have nothing but a bright future ahead."

"Is that what she *really* said?"

The butler frowned. Then he averted his gaze, but not before Alexander caught a sheen of moisture in his eyes.

Evidently Alexander wasn't the only one who would miss her. The stoic butler had a heart after all, even if he concealed it.

"Thank you, Wheeler," Alexander said.

The butler raised his eyebrows in response. There was no surer sign of a breach of etiquette than a man of Alexander's rank actually *thanking* the staff. But it seemed the appropriate thing to do—not just appropriate, but kind.

Since when had he, a selfish profligate, considered kindness toward others?

Since she *came into my life.*

He strode upstairs, then paused outside Mimi's bedchamber—or what had been her bedchamber until this morning—before entering the guest bedroom, where Charles was already setting a tea tray on a table. A fire blazed merrily in the hearth, almost as if it had no idea of what the house, and Alexander, had lost, and a long cheval mirror had been placed in a corner beside a washstand, which bore a bowl of steaming water with a washcloth, towel, cutthroat razor, and leather strap.

Charles poured the tea—just how Alexander liked it, with a splash of milk and one spoonful of sugar—then set to work on the razor, sharpening it against the strap while Alexander drank his tea, then splashed hot water over his skin.

"Will you require assistance to shave, sir?" the footman asked, holding up the razor. The blade shimmered in the firelight, while the young servant's hand shook.

The butler stepped forward and plucked the blade out of the footman's hand.

"I think, Charles, His Grace would prefer to survive the morning with his throat intact. Why don't you see to his boots?"

The butler steered Alexander to a chair beside the mirror. "Did you shave yourself when you stayed here, sir?"

Alexander shook his head.

She had shaved him, her touch lighter even than his valet's, though he'd never admit that, at least not when Larry held the blade to his throat.

How he'd relished her touch—the soft drip of water when she rinsed the razor, then the gentle caress of the blade on his skin. The knack, she'd said, was to ensure that the blade was really sharp, so that hardly any pressure was required to remove the stubble.

And she had not cut his skin once.

No, the wound she'd inflicted was far deeper—a knife lodged in the core of his soul.

He remained still while the butler ran the razor across his skin, then inhaled sharply as the blade nicked his throat.

The butler muttered an apology, and Alexander caught the familiar odor of tincture before a cloth was dabbed against his throat. He winced at the bite of soreness.

"Forgive me, Your Grace. It'll heal quickly."

"No matter, Wheeler," Alexander said. "It's a good day when my valet nicks the skin less than three times."

"And Lady Rex?"

Alexander stood and gestured toward the pile of clothes on the bed.

"Of course, Your Grace," the butler said, an undertone of compassion in his voice, as if he understood that when it came to shaving a man—and many other such tasks—Mimi surpassed them all.

"Charles?" the butler said, and the footman approached Alexander and begun to undress him. "No—not like that!" Wheeler snapped as the footman tugged at Alexander's cravat. "Let me show you."

The butler deftly undid the knot and placed the cravat on the chair Alexander had vacated. Then, with Wheeler issuing orders, the two men undressed Alexander until he stood before them as naked as the day he was born.

The last time he'd stood naked in this room, Mimi had

kneeled before him and…

Stop it!

He closed his eyes and drew in sharp breath to dispel the surge in his groin at the memory.

Memories—bloody memories. That was all he had of her, now, a memory to fist his length to at night.

"Ahem."

Alexander opened his eyes to see the butler eyeing him with disapproval.

"Proceed," he said, not daring to lower his gaze.

The butler arched an eyebrow, then reached for his breeches.

"On the other hand, perhaps I'll dress myself."

"Your Grace, are you sure?"

Alexander nodded. "I know what goes where."

"And your cravat? Your style is somewhat intricate."

"I…learned how to tie it myself."

"Or perhaps you were taught by another."

"Yes, Lady—" Alexander broke off, his throat tightening.

"Charles, clear away the tea things," Wheeler said. "I'll see to His Grace from now on."

"Yes, Mr. Wheeler."

After the footman had gone, the butler handed Alexander the rest of his clothes, and watched in silence while he dressed himself in front of the mirror, finishing with his cravat.

"A passable effort, if I may say so, Your Grace." Wheeler stepped forward to smooth the knot and tuck the cravat into Alexander's waistcoat. "She taught you well."

"She taught me much."

Alexander met the butler's gaze in the mirror, and for a moment, the two men stared at each other.

"Forgive me for speaking out of turn, but there's no sin in missing her," the butler said.

"You *do* speak out of turn, Wheeler," Alexander said, swallowing the stab of pain in his heart. "If my valet spoke in such a manner, I'd dismiss him."

"Then it's as well that I'm not *your* valet, for I can speak the truth with no fear of reprisal. That is the benefit of not being employed by a single family."

"What will you do now, Wheeler?"

"What I always do when a tenant vacates the premises. I'll arrange for the outgoing tenant's belongings to be conveyed to their solicitor, then will oversee the preparations for the house."

"Preparations?"

"When an occupant vacates a house, it must be cleaned, dusted, and the furniture covered, to preserve it for the next occupant."

"And the outgoing occupant?"

"I know not where she has gone."

"But her solicitor—"

"A solicitor is bound by honor to respect client confidentiality, Your Grace. You should be bound enough by honor not to expect him to breach such confidentiality. A woman such as Lady Rex will, I'll wager, value confidentiality and privacy more than others, given her history."

Was it his imagination, or had the butler's voice carried a note of accusation?

"I care not about her history, Wheeler—you must know that," Alexander said.

"Of course, Your Grace. But nevertheless, her history has led her to this point, has given rise to events that have limited her choices in life. I'm certain that she'll be well—or as well as she can be."

The hard edge to the butler's voice reeked of disapproval—and disappointment.

"What could I have done, Wheeler?" Alexander asked. "She chose her path."

"Perhaps, sir, she believed her choice to be the best one given her circumstances—at least, the best choice out of those presented to her."

"What the devil do you mean?"

"Your Grace, few of us are given freedom to tread on the path that we *wish* to take. I daresay Lady Rex took the path that she knew she *must* take."

Cursed man—what the devil was he talking about?

"You speak in riddles, Wheeler," Alexander said.

A clock struck seven in the hallway, followed by echoes from its companions around the house.

"Will you be wanting breakfast before you leave, Your Grace?" the butler asked.

"I see little point in lingering here now that she has gone."

"Very good. In which case, there are just a few items you need to retrieve, then I can set about preparing the house."

"Items?"

"If you'd follow me?"

Wheeler led Alexander into the hallway and Mimi's bedchamber.

Dust sheets covered the furniture, and the vase in the window, which had always contained fresh flowers, was now empty, a forlorn silhouette in the center of the table.

The butler picked up a flat, square box from the dressing table.

"What's that?" Alexander asked as Wheeler handed it to him.

Then he opened it and caught his breath. Nestled on a bed of thick, dark velvet was a necklace—a delicate chain bearing five diamonds, in graduating sizes, either side of a central stone. The stone seemed to shimmer with life, each facet a different shade of purple—from the rich burgundy of port wine, to the soft, cool lavender of the delicate flowers that nodded in the summer breeze and filled the air with their healing aroma. He reached out to caress it, tracing the shape with his fingertips, and flecks of light twinkled from within, as if the stone were alive.

"She left this?" Alexander whispered.

"Her instructions were to return it to you."

"But it was a gift."

"Perhaps it came with too high a price."

Yes—it had come with a price. And Mimi had left knowing that she could not bear the cost.

"What have I done?"

You've driven away the woman who completes your soul.

Alexander held out the box. "Take it."

The butler's eyes widened, then he shook his head. "Sir, I cannot."

"Consider it payment for your services," Alexander said. "You're a man of business, aren't you? What man of business would refuse payment?"

"A man who understands that there are far more precious things in the world than jewels, Your Grace."

Alexander caressed the amethyst, and it pulsed with life. Perhaps it had captured a piece of her soul while it nestled against her throat.

"It's hardly my style," Wheeler said, a trace of humor in his tone. "Besides, a piece so beautiful, so unique, deserves to adorn the loveliest neck in England. Wouldn't you agree, Your Grace?"

His voice caught in his throat, all Alexander could do was nod. The butler pushed the box toward him.

"Keep it, Your Grace," he said. "Keep it as a symbol of hope."

"Hope?"

The butler nodded. "Hope that, perhaps, one day, you may find it in your heart to seek true happiness—not merely that which you believe will make you happy."

Then he bowed and exited the chamber, leaving Alexander alone, clinging to the necklace.

A poor substitute it might be, but he had nothing else.

CHAPTER TWENTY-EIGHT

Oakhurst House, Surrey, five months later

MIMI POURED THE tea and handed it to her guests—Eleanor and Lady Radham—before settling into her chair. She glanced about the parlor—*her* parlor—while children's laughter could be heard in the garden outside: Lily's son Sam, and Gabriel, Lady Radham's eldest.

Since Mimi had taken possession of her house on the outskirts of Radham Village, bringing Lily and Sam with her, Lady Radham had visited almost every day. Mimi relished her privacy, but found herself welcoming her new neighbor's company—particularly today, when she'd brought Eleanor with her.

"Your school's almost ready, Miss King," Lady Radham said. "I rode past yesterday. The work on the roof is complete."

Mimi blushed at the reference to her real name. But if she were to make a new life, she needed to do it with honesty. Lady Rex, the respectable widow, no longer existed—neither did Mimi, the painted whore. The time had come for Jemima King to take her place in the world.

"When will the school open?" Lady Radham asked.

"I hope we can admit our first pupils in September," Mimi said. "I've received several inquiries—thanks, I suspect, to you."

"There are many girls in the county in need of education," Lady Radham said. "Is Lily to teach there?"

"She'll be giving lessons in embroidery," Mimi said. "I've said she can live with me as long as she wishes, and I've set aside a parlor for her dressmaking work. But she insists on moving to the school once Mrs. Briggs has settled there. I'm not certain Lily's ready—she's still wary of strangers—but I commend her courage."

"As do I," Eleanor said. "Are Lily and her son enjoying life in the country?"

Mimi nodded. "She's quite transformed, and little Sam has blossomed. He spends all day helping Mr. Wade in the kitchen garden. He was so proud that he'd picked the beans for supper last night, the dear child."

Someone tapped on the window, and Mimi turned to see Sam and Gabriel holding a basket aloft.

"Look what we've got, Miss King!" Gabriel said. Then they disappeared with a clatter of footsteps and laughter.

Eleanor leaned forward, fixing her intense gaze on Mimi. "How does it feel to hear your real name?"

A somewhat forward question, but Mimi had accustomed herself to her friend's frankness.

"Eleanor!" Lady Radham chided.

"It's all right, Lady Radham," Mimi said.

"*Juliette*, please."

"Juliette." Mimi smiled. "Your sister has every right to ask. I deceived everyone into thinking I was a widow. I cannot imagine what you must think of me."

The sisters exchanged a glance and smiled, as if sharing a private joke, and Mimi felt her cheeks warm.

"F-forgive me, I…"

Eleanor let out a snort, and Juliette stifled a giggle.

"There's nothing to forgive," Juliette said. "Posing as a widow is a family tradition of ours."

At that moment, the door burst open and two whirlwinds entered—Sam and Gabriel, followed by Lily.

"Boys!" Lily cried. "Sammy—look at your hands!"

The smaller of the whirlwinds stopped and inspected his hands. Then he wiped them on his breeches and clasped them behind his back.

"Gabriel and I have been picking peas, Miss King. We've got a whole basketful! And we've cut some roses for you. Mr. Wade helped so we wouldn't cut ourselves."

The larger boy approached Juliette and moved to put his thumb in his mouth, but she caught his wrist.

"Wash your hands first, sweetheart."

"Yes, Mama. Mr. Wade cut a rose for you and Aunt Eleanor as well."

"And he cut one for *you*, Ma," Sam said to Lily. "Mr. Wade likes you."

"What nonsense you speak!" Lily said, blushing, and Mimi smiled to herself. Mr. Wade, the soft-spoken manservant, seemed to have appointed himself as Lily's personal guardian. The timid young woman had responded to his gentle kindness in a manner that warmed Mimi's heart. Lily had little reason to trust the male sex, but Mr. Wade was evidence that there was at least one man in the world who could be trusted.

Or, perhaps, there was another...

"Come along, boys," Lily said. "Shall we see if your tea's ready? It's such a fine day, I asked Cook if we could have a picnic in the garden. What do you say to that?"

"I say hurrah!" Gabriel cried, abandoning his mother's side for the prospect of a picnic.

"Wash your..." Juliette began, but before she finished, the boys had gone, Lily in their wake. "Boys are such a handful," she said, leaning back with a sigh. "I can never get Gabriel to sit still. And he just *eats*!"

"He's growing, that's all," Eleanor said. "He's tall for his age."

"If he grows to be as tall as his father, he'll *need* to eat," Mimi said, laughing.

Juliette drew a sharp breath and exchanged a glance with Eleanor.

"Forgive me," Mimi said. "I meant no offense."

"None taken," Juliette said. "We are of a kind. I have lived as you."

Mimi turned to face her. "Were you a—a…" She gestured to herself, unwilling to voice the word.

"In a manner of speaking." Juliette turned toward the window, from which the boys' laughter could once more be heard. "Gabriel is not Andrew's son."

"So you *were* a widow?" Mimi asked.

"I let myself be seduced by another, then found myself with child, and friendless."

Eleanor took her sister's hand. "Not entirely friendless."

"You're too kind, sister, given how I behaved toward you." Juliette turned to Mimi. "The world frowned upon me nonetheless. Any woman who doesn't conform is branded unworthy. So, I fled to the country and passed myself off as a widow."

"And Lord Radham?" Mimi asked.

"He was the vicar of the parish I settled in," Juliette said. "The villagers were somewhat judgmental, save a few exceptions—most notably Andrew himself. So you see, Mimi, it's quite possible for those on the opposite ends of Society's idea of respectability to find happiness—and love." She gave a smile of contentment. "Andrew loves Gabriel as if he were his own. And while a…*natural child* may be subject to the cruelty of a judgmental world, I'm assured that our little corner of it is free from such prejudice. The villagers hereabouts were very welcoming when Andrew brought me here after our marriage, and they adore Gabriel. And there's great excitement about your school, Mimi. It will be a haven for your young women. I'm certain it will be a success."

"There's still much to do," Mimi said. "And the success of the enterprise can only be measured by its financial self-sufficiency. We cannot rely on your donations forever."

Eleanor let out a laugh. "*Financial self-sufficiency*—you sound like the Duchess of Westbury! She has a head for such things, and is rumored to have single-handedly restored the fortunes of her husband's estate within a year of their marriage. I'm certain she could be persuaded to patronize the school."

"But—" Mimi began, and Eleanor raised her hand.

"Permit your friends to assist you in your endeavors, Mimi. The duchess thinks very highly of you, given your kindness to her stepson. You settled half your fortune on the school—those of us who love you wish to contribute also."

"It wasn't my fortune to give," Mimi said. "It was—"

"It was money earned in good faith," Juliette interrupted, "under the terms of your agreement with…with another. There's no shame in earning an honest wage—nor the manner by which you earn it."

"Even if I earned it by whoring?" Mimi asked.

The door opened as she was mid-sentence. A man entered, followed by Betsy, the young girl she employed from the village to keep house.

It was Lord Radham.

He stopped in mid-stride and focused his clear gaze on Mimi. Her cheeks burned as she cast her gaze over his form—from the perfectly fitting dark-green jacket, his top hat tucked under one arm, the cream-silk embroidered waistcoat and matching cravat, to the formfitting breeches and polished calfskin boots. He pulled off his gloves and placed them in his hat, then inclined his head.

His expression, though not showing disapproval, held a gentle quietness that disconcerted her more. He blinked, and his expression remained the same.

He was a man who shuttered his emotions behind a calm demeanor.

"Andrew!" Juliette said, rising. "I wasn't expecting you home today. I thought you were still in London."

"I arrived not ten minutes ago."

"And you came here directly? Is something amiss?"

"I'm come to inquire whether my wife will be returning home, given that Mrs. Smith told me you were expected an hour ago. Georgiana is missing her mother."

"You exaggerate, as usual," Juliette said. "Our daughter is most likely asleep at this hour. Besides, she has Frances to take care of her."

Lord Radham drew Juliette into his arms. "I can never be angry with *you*, my love—you know that."

Mimi flinched as he glanced at her over the top of his wife's head.

"To whom is your anger directed, brother?" Eleanor asked.

"It matters not," Mimi said. "Lord Radham, do you have news of London?"

His expression darkened. "Number 16 Grosvenor Square is let again."

Mimi's heart stuttered.

Had Alexander established her replacement there already?

"Andrew, I hardly think—" Juliette began.

"Juliette," Mimi said, "it's all right."

"No, it's *not*," Eleanor said.

"I agree," Lord Radham said. "It's *not* all right—and it never will be." He turned to Mimi. "I'd hoped to see *you* settled there, Lady Rex—" He shook his head. "Forgive me—*Miss King*."

"Has she"—Mimi hesitated—"has the new occupant kept on the staff?"

"I believe so," came the reply. "My housekeeper mentioned it. She said your housekeeper—apologies, your *former* housekeeper—was seen coming out of the back door. Even your maid has been kept on."

"Mrs. Dryburgh is turning into something of a gossip, Andrew," Juliette said. "Shame on you for encouraging it."

"H-have you met the new occupant?" Mimi asked.

"No," he said. "I have no occasion, nor any wish, to visit Grosvenor Square."

This time she caught the flash of anger in his eyes.

"Andrew," Juliette said, her voice sharp, "we've already discussed this. It's not your place to speak of it."

"Speak of what?" Mimi asked. "If my presence here offends you, Lord Radham, I'm sure I can find somewhere else to—"

"It's not your presence here that offends me, Miss King," he said, "but the necessity of it."

"I don't understand."

"Andrew, that's *enough!*" Juliette said. "My friend has no wish to hear your opinion of...of her circumstance. She's here by her own choice, are you not, Mimi?"

Mimi nodded. "But I have no wish to remain where I'm not welcome."

"You *are* welcome, Miss King," he said, extending his hand to her. She stared at it, unmoving. "Will you accept my apologies? I meant no offense to *you.*"

"Then whom did you intend to offend, sir?"

He colored, and his hand shook. Then she took it. "Him," he said.

Alexander...

Mimi caught her breath, and Juliette rolled her eyes. "I *told* you not to speak of Sawbridge in front of my friend. It's distressing enough for Mimi to leave London, let alone be reminded of her circumstance."

"Am I not permitted to disapprove of the manner by which Sawbridge treated your friend, Juliette? She deserves better."

"*She* is in the room, Lord Radham," Mimi said. "And she knows enough of Society's rules not to place undue expectations on men of your rank."

"I was content to break such rules for the woman I love," Lord Radham said, taking Juliette's hand once more.

Mimi swallowed the knot of pain, and Juliette let out a huff.

"You mean well, Andrew, but you're exacerbating the matter for my poor friend. Your sex is too ready to criticize mine for overly loose tongues, but sometimes it's best for the *man* to remain silent."

He clicked his heels together and bowed in Mimi's direction. "Forgive my lack of insight," he said. "But I still condemn him. We have a shared history, you see, due to what happened to my brother, Robert."

"I know," Mimi said. "I am sorry for your loss, but I beg you don't think too badly of Alexander."

His eyes widened at her familiar address.

"He suffered greatly over your brother's death," she continued. "It plagues him at night when he sleeps… I-it lies heavily on his conscience. It's not my place to expect you to forgive him, or to ignore the loss you suffered. All I ask is that you consider the possibility that at some point in the future, you might come to understand him, even if you can never bring yourself to think kindly of him."

"And his abandonment of you, Miss King? Can you think kindly of him for that?"

"He did no such thing, Lord Radham," Mimi said. "We had a temporary arrangement that has now ended. Besides"—she gestured about the parlor—"if it weren't for him, I wouldn't be here, and nor would my school. You may view our arrangement as distasteful, and I assure you that you're not alone in that view. It was, nevertheless, one of few choices open to me for survival. And having taken it, I've gained my independence, and a handful of women will be given an opportunity in life that they could never have afforded before."

"I know, and I salute you for it."

Mimi shook her head. "It's *him* you should salute, Lord Radham. He brought it about."

"You make me quite ashamed, Miss King," he said. "But you've confirmed my opinion that Sawbridge was a damned fool for letting you go."

"A mistake that I'm sure he'll cease to regret in due course."

Now that he has a new mistress in Grosvenor Square.

"Andrew, I think you've said enough," Juliette said. "If you're eager to take me home to our daughter, we should take our leave."

"Gabriel's having his supper with Sam," Mimi said. "He is welcome to stay the night if you've no objection."

"None at all," Lord Radham said. "You honor us with your invitation to our son." He bowed over Mimi's hand and kissed it.

Juliette rolled her eyes. "One moment they're making fools of themselves by demonstrating a complete lack of understanding, and the next, they're falling over themselves in an act of gallantry to make up for their shortcomings. *Men!* I'll never understand them."

"My Montague is the same," Eleanor said. "I've given up trying to understand him."

"Yet they're such simple creatures," Juliette added. "It's an enigma, to be sure."

Mimi suppressed a laugh at Lord Radham's bemused expression, and Juliette slipped her arm through his.

"Be not afraid, my love," she said. "There's hope for you yet, provided you accept my instruction with good grace."

She winked at Mimi, then steered her husband toward the door. Shortly after, Betsy arrived with Juliette's cloak and ushered the couple out, leaving Mimi alone with Eleanor.

"Would you like me to leave also?" Eleanor asked. "Forgive me—I'm no good at understanding when it's time to go."

"You may stay as long as you wish," Mimi replied, taking her friend's hand. "For dinner, if you like. Gabriel and Sam would be delighted to hear your opinion of the beans they harvested this afternoon."

"We've guests for dinner tonight at Rosecombe," Eleanor said with a sigh. "I dislike social occasions, but they're a necessity. Of course, *you'd* be welcome at Rosecombe—come and stay for a few days when you can spare the time."

"Won't there be danger of my meeting...?" Mimi gestured in the air in front of her.

"No danger, I assure you," Eleanor said. "I understand little of social convention, but even I know that it's not the done thing to invite my friend to stay at the same time as the man who broke her heart."

"Thank you," Mimi said. "More tea?"

Eleanor nodded, Mimi refilled their cups, and they sat, sipping their tea in silence. At length, Eleanor set her cup aside and leaned forward.

"He still loves you. I'm sure of it."

"Eleanor, please."

"I know I mustn't speak of it, and I wouldn't say anything in front of anyone else—not even my sister. But I noticed a transformation in him when he was with you. I confess I never could abide him. But when he was with you, I surprised myself by beginning to contemplate the possibility of liking him a little."

"And now?"

"I've seen him in London a few times since…"

Mimi held her breath as her heart rate increased. "Was he well?"

"He seemed in good health."

"And…happy?"

Eleanor shrugged. "He wasn't smiling, but few people smile unless they know they're under observation."

"No, I mean"—Mimi hesitated, hope and fear warring with each other—"was he with company?"

"Oh!" Eleanor cried. "You mean was he with a woman—a lover?"

Mimi winced at Eleanor's bluntness. But she couldn't berate her friend. Eleanor didn't adopt the niceties of Polite Society. She asked direct questions and gave direct responses.

"He was alone," she said at last. "Except when I saw him at Lord and Lady Walton's soirée. In fact, Lady Walton inquired after you. I'm sure I could persuade her to send a donation to the school—she's another who applauds the independence of women."

"Hardly independent if I'm reliant on the charity of others," Mimi said.

"May I ask you a personal question?" Eleanor said. "I'm afraid you may think it forward of me, but I'm curious."

"Then ask."

"Are you lonely?"

"What an odd question!"

"Forgive me, I meant no offense."

"I know," Mimi said. "No, I'm not lonely. I have friends—you and your sister. There's Lily and Sam, and I'll soon have the school to occupy myself with. I'll be too busy to be lonely."

"No, I meant…" Eleanor shook her head. "Forgive me, Mimi, but I thought you were also in love. You don't deserve to spend your days alone. Montague has friends who—"

"Eleanor, I dream of freedom, not a husband."

"The two aren't always mutually exclusive."

"But in most cases they are," Mimi said. "Besides, I could no longer look at another man without seeing…"

Without seeing Alexander: the way his lips quirked into a smile each time he saw her, the soft sighs he'd made as she brought him to pleasure—and the intensity in his eyes when she had let him kiss her…

She shook her head. "You heard Lord Radham. Alexander has moved on to the next woman without a backward glance. I did the right thing by leaving before it was too late."

"Unless it *is* already too late," Eleanor said. "You still love him, don't you?"

Mimi blinked back the moisture in her eyes.

"He still loves *you*," Eleanor added. "I'm certain of it."

A person always claimed certainty when they sought to convince others of that which they knew to be false.

But Eleanor only wanted Mimi to be happy, and Mimi loved her for that. She kissed her friend on the cheek, then the duchess bade her farewell, calling for Betsy to fetch her cloak. Moments later, Mimi heard the crunch of wheels on gravel as Mr. Wade summoned the Whitcombe carriage to take Eleanor home to the husband who loved her to the exclusion of all else.

"He may have loved me," Mimi whispered, placing her palm on the cold pane of the window while she watched the carriage drive away. "But not enough."

CHAPTER TWENTY-NINE

London

"CHEER UP, OLD chap. It might never happen."

Alexander glanced at Thorpe as they approached the entrance to White's.

It already has.

The footman at the door arched an eyebrow at Alexander, then bowed.

"Welcome back, Lord Thorpe, and…Your Grace."

"The Duke of Sawbridge is my guest, Grantchester," Thorpe said. "I'm sponsoring the renewal of his membership application."

"Of course, sir, very good." The footman gave an obsequious little bow. "Welcome back to White's, Your Grace."

"There's no guarantee that the secretary will approve my application, Grantchester," Alexander said. "It would therefore be wise to restrain yourself from an excess of civility toward me until you're in a better position to determine where your loyalty lies."

The footman's smile slipped and Thorpe ushered Alexander inside.

"There's no benefit in abusing the staff here," he said, "or they'll spit in your brandy."

"Might improve the taste," Alexander said. "The stuff they serve here is barely fit to polish the silver."

"If you're going to be churlish, I'll take you elsewhere," Thorpe said. "My wife would never forgive me if I lost my membership on your account."

"Lady Thorpe doesn't strike me as the kind of woman who's

concerned whether White's admits you or not," Alexander said.

"No, but she's concerned about my association with *you*," Thorpe said. "Perhaps she fears your debauchery is contagious."

Alexander eyed the clubroom where the occupants were visible through a haze of blue smoke, and footmen paraded about holding trays laden with brandy glasses.

Perhaps if he imbibed a bottle of the stuff he might be able to forget...*her*.

But no—he'd tried that the night before, and all it had earned him was a dry throat, the expulsion of his supper, and a megrim the next morning reminiscent of a stampede of racehorses in his head.

Thorpe steered Alexander toward a group of empty button-backed leather chairs and waved over a footman.

"My usual, please," he said. "And the same for my guest."

The footman bowed and scuttled off.

"I say, I *thought* it was you!" a familiar voice said. "May we join you?"

The Duke of Westbury appeared, brandy glass in hand, with his eldest son.

"Of course," Alexander said, rising and offering his hand. "And Mr. Drayton. A pleasure."

"So," Westbury said, settling into a seat, "you've been read-mitted to White's."

"Only as a guest," Alexander said. "Thorpe's sponsoring my reapplication."

"Are you in need of a second?" Westbury asked. "I'm happy to oblige."

"I never considered us to be friends," Alexander said. "Why would you honor me in such a manner?"

"Perhaps because I'm honoring another."

Mr. Drayton leaned forward, his youthful face displaying his eagerness. "Is Lady Rex well?" he asked. "I've not seen her lately."

Alexander sighed. Couldn't he be permitted to enjoy one drink without being plagued by the memory of what he'd lost?

"Drayton, I don't think that's any of your—" he began, then broke off as the footman arrived with two glasses of brandy.

Westbury watched him, his sharp gaze filled with understanding.

"My son was inquiring out of kindness, Sawbridge," he said after the footman left. "He considers Lady Rex to be the paragon of kindness, do you not, Edward?"

The young man nodded.

"Lady Rex was well the last time I saw her," Alexander said. "But she's left London for the country. I know not where."

"Didn't she—" Drayton began, but Westbury interrupted.

"Edward, perhaps you'd care to tell our friends how you're progressing with your studies." He nodded to Alexander. "My son goes up to Oxford later this year."

"Christchurch College, I presume," Thorpe said.

Westbury nodded. "Naturally. The dean has promised him my old room."

"Mine was better—the windows overlooked the River Cherwell," Thorpe replied. "Your room was on the wrong side of the building—and too close to the tower. You always complained about the clock keeping you awake at night when it struck."

As his friends reminisced about their Oxford days, Alexander glanced about the clubroom. Then he froze.

Sitting among a group of the least savory men of Society—Viscount de Blanchard, and the utterly vile Mr. MacDiarmid—was Earl Mayhew. A fat cigar in one hand and a brandy in the other, he seemed to be regaling them with some no-doubt-sordid tale. Every so often, one of them would throw his head back in an exaggerated gesture and roar for more brandy, much to the tutting of the members sitting nearby.

Then Alexander caught a name, and a ball of anger coiled like a spring in his heart.

"*Lady* Rex, indeed!" Mayhew chortled. "In my experience, no lady screams like a bitch in heat when I…"

Laughter drowned out his voice.

The spring snapped. Alexander leaped out of his chair and strode toward Mayhew, whose laughter died as he approached, the relish in his eyes turning into terror. He glanced toward his friends, but like all bullies, they shriveled when faced with a stronger opponent, and fell silent, their portly figures wobbling with fear as Alexander's three companions followed him over.

"S-Sawbridge," Mayhew stammered, looking to his friends for support.

"What are you doing here?" De Blanchard asked.

"Be quiet, you worm," Westbury said. "Or shall I send for my wife to deal with you as she sees fit?"

De Blanchard paled, and his hands involuntarily covered his groin.

So—the rumors were true that Westbury's wife had once come close to castrating De Blanchard with a single blow after he'd tried to force himself on her.

"As for you, MacDiarmid, I'm surprised to see you showing your face here. Don't you prefer to spread rumors about those whom you seek to demonize, rather than face them like a man? You always were a sniveling wretch, though you're among your kind here."

De Blanchard rose to his feet. "I'm not willing to remain here and be insulted," he said, his voice wavering. "Come along, chaps."

MacDiarmid stood, but Mayhew remained sitting.

"I'm staying," he said. "I've my brandy to finish, and I want to get my money's worth—just as I did with that slut."

De Blanchard and MacDiarmid exchanged a glance, then exited the clubroom.

Thorpe placed a hand on Alexander's shoulder.

"Come away, friend," he said quietly. "Mayhew isn't worth risking your standing in the club."

"I couldn't give a farrier's fuck about my standing in the club," Alexander said.

"That much is apparent," Mayhew sneered, "given that you

were content to associate yourself with that whore whom you tried to pass off as a lady."

"She's more of a lady than you are a gentleman," Alexander said. He raised his hand, and Mayhew flinched. "What is it?" Alexander said, gesturing toward the bruise on Mayhew's face. "Afraid I'll finish the job now you've not got a paid subordinate to fight your duels for you?"

Mayhew touched his bruised face. "Do you see what sort of savage you're sponsoring, Thorpe? And you, Westbury—given the circumstance of your son's birth, I'd have thought you the last man who'd want to associate himself with this savage."

"Savage?" Alexander snarled. "Tell me, Mayhew, what kind of gentleman would toss an innocent woman out onto the street—the woman his father loved?"

"She was his whore," Mayhew said. "I'm sure you've tossed out many a whore onto the streets when you've grown tired of rutting her."

"She was pregnant, you bastard!" Alexander cried, and a volley of tuts rippled through the clubroom. "She lost the child because of you."

"I say, old chap," Thorpe said, "there's no need to—"

"There's every need!" Alexander replied. "She was carrying Sir Walter Mayhew's child. Don't you see, Mayhew? Your own flesh and blood—your sibling. In throwing her out, you murdered that child."

"You've no right to lecture *me* on murder, Sawbridge," Mayhew said. "You killed Radham's brother."

"What happened to Radham's brother was an accident," Alexander said. "And I've regretted it every day since. What *you* did to her was motivated by greed and envy."

"I was only claiming what was rightfully mine," Mayhew said. "I've no cause to regret that. And if she lost the brat, so much the better. One less bastard to litter the world with."

Drayton gave a little cry, and Westbury stepped forward, his eyes darkening with fury.

"I *beg* your pardon?"

"W-Westbury, I-I didn't mean—"

Westbury blinked slowly, then reached toward his son and patted his arm, twisting his body around. Then, with a blur of movement, he swung his free arm forward and slammed his fist into Mayhew's face. Mayhew let out a sigh, then crumpled to the floor.

Two footmen rushed over.

"Your Grace, I hardly think it proper—"

"It was a matter of honor, gentlemen," Westbury said. "Besides, I barely touched him."

He poked the prone form with his foot, and Mayhew stirred with a groan. Thorpe stooped, hooked his arms under Mayhew's shoulders, and helped him into a seat.

"You tripped and fell, didn't you, Mayhew?" he said. "Just as you were apologizing for insulting Mr. Drayton here and offering to make amends."

Mayhew glanced from Westbury to Thorpe, his eyes shimmering with fear. At length, he nodded.

"Say it," Westbury said, his voice quiet and even. "Say that you intend to make amends."

Mayhew nodded. "I-I intend to make amends."

"In any manner that my friend here chooses," Westbury said, gesturing toward Alexander.

"That *I* choose?" Alexander asked.

"Naturally," Westbury said. "My son and I no longer care for the taunts of the likes of Mayhew here, but I suspect he may have caused you greater injury. Mayhew, say it."

Mayhew nodded again. "In any manner that Sawbridge chooses."

"Very good," Westbury said. "Gentlemen?" He turned toward the footmen. "Be assured we'll be on our best behavior from henceforth. And, in a gesture of goodwill, please bring Mayhew a drink of his choice, on my ledger. Mayhew, do join us."

The footmen bowed and disappeared while Westbury and Thorpe took the seats either side of Mayhew. Alexander sat opposite, beside Westbury's son.

"I must apologize, Sawbridge," Westbury said, gesturing toward Mayhew, who flinched. "I trust you'll forgive me."

"You gave him what he deserved," Alexander said.

"But it was, perhaps, more *your* right to give than mine."

A footman reappeared with a glass of brandy, but before Mayhew took it, Westbury plucked it from the tray.

"Not yet, Mayhew—you must earn your reward and await my friend's instructions."

"Instructions?"

"Sawbridge, if you please."

Alexander glanced at his friend, then nodded. "I want nothing for myself, Mayhew—but I demand that you atone for what you did to Lady Rex."

"*Lady Rex!*" Mayhew scoffed. "You don't know who she really is, do you?"

Thorpe leaned forward, a cold smile on his lips. "Of course we do," he said. "She's Jemima King, is she not?"

Mayhew's eyes widened. "Who told you?"

Thorpe let out a cold laugh. "I believe *you* just did, but even a simpleton could work it out. I've suspected it for some time. Her alias gave her away. Rex is the Latin for king, though not having an Oxford education, one cannot expect *you* to know that."

"I went to Cambridge," Mayhew said.

"Exactly," Thorpe said. "Your poor father wasted his funds on your education."

"Better than wasting his funds on that whore."

"Desist!" Alexander cried. "Do you mean to tell me that you knowingly threw Baron King's daughter out onto the street, to fend for herself—to subject herself to selling her body to survive?"

"She whored herself to bleed my father dry," Mayhew said. "I did her a favor, sending her out onto the streets where she could spread her legs for the whole of England."

"Take care, Mayhew," Westbury said. "You still have the use of all four of your limbs. I take it you wish for that state to continue?"

Mayhew nodded.

"Perhaps you ought to enlighten us as to how your late father was—as you say—*wasting* his funds."

"He was spending my inheritance on jewels and trinkets for that"—Mayhew hesitated and glanced at Alexander's curled fists—"for Miss King. He even gifted her my late mother's ring."

"For what purpose?" Alexander asked.

Mayhew wrinkled his nose as if he'd encountered a foul odor.

Alexander leaned forward. "Did he intend to marry her?"

Mayhew stared at him, defiance in his eyes. Then he nodded.

"She coerced him into offering," he said. "I discovered it when his solicitor asked me to witness the signing of the contract—as if I'd sign away my rightful property to that slut!"

"Mayhew," Alexander growled. Thorpe placed a hand on his arm.

"Continue."

"I confronted the pater about it, and he admitted it—quite shamelessly. We quarreled, and he collapsed. And then…"

"He died, giving you free rein to renege on the contract and act against his wishes," Westbury said.

"I acted within the authority of the law," Mayhew said.

"What about the higher authority?" Alexander asked.

"I acted within the law of the Church also," came the reply. "Even if the contract would have been signed, I doubt any man with morals would approve of my father gifting his property to a slut."

"Why you…" Alexander rose, but Thorpe grasped his wrist.

"Sawbridge, what good would it do to engage in a brawl?"

"It'd make me feel a damn sight better."

"What about Miss King?" Thorpe said. "Surely you can think of a better punishment that also atones for the wrong done to her?"

Alexander glanced at Mayhew, then the idea slid into his mind.

Of course…

"Mayhew," he said, "I promise that I, and my friend, shall never lay a finger on you again if you grant me one thing—which will absolve you of all your sins toward…toward Miss King."

"Which is?"

"Your late mother's ring you may keep, as a trinket for the unfortunate woman who becomes your wife. But as to your father's other gift, I ask that you honor it."

Mayhew shook his head. "I-I don't understand."

"I ask—no, demand—that you settle the property on Miss King that your father originally intended. That is, if you've not frittered it away to settle your gaming debts."

"Of course not!" Mayhew scoffed. "Whatever you think I am, I'm no gamester."

"That's not what I heard," Thorpe said. "I heard you've been searching for a rich wife to fund your habit, but nobody is forthcoming. In fact, not even the infamous Mrs. Dove-Lyon, who facilitates matches between desperate titled men and wealthy women of doubtful virtue, wishes to inflict *you* on her clientele."

Mayhew's cheeks reddened and he lowered his gaze.

"Then that's settled," Westbury said. "I suggest we visit your solicitor forthwith."

Mayhew's eyes widened. "N-no, I have another appointment."

"Come, come, Mayhew," Alexander said. "As a gesture of faith, you must come with us now. You wouldn't want us to think that you intend to renege on your promise and bolt as soon as we leave the building?"

"Oh, Sawbridge, how unjust," Westbury said, amusement in his voice. "I'm sure the thought didn't even *begin* to enter Mayhew's mind."

"I'll wager his mind has limited capacity for thought," Drayton added, grinning.

Westbury patted his son on the back. "Quite right, my boy. Who is your solicitor, Mayhew?"

"John Allardice."

"Of Allardice, Allardice, and Stockton?" Alexander said. "Mr. Stockton looks after my affairs. We can have the contract drawn up and witnessed this afternoon—is that not fortunate, Mayhew?"

The look on Mayhew's face conveyed that it was anything but.

Westbury held out the brandy. "I think our friend has now earned his reward."

Mayhew grasped the glass, tipped it back, and drained the contents.

"Good, very good," Thorpe said, taking one of Mayhew's arms, while Westbury took the other. "We can return here once our business is concluded, and I'll stand you a bottle of champagne. What say you to that?"

"What say you to the prospect of my not agreeing to this?" Mayhew sneered.

"Only that I'll make it known that you were responsible for the murder of your sibling and the ruination of Baron King's daughter," Westbury said. "You confessed it yourself—took pride in it, even. Can you be certain that, given the damage Sawbridge did to his own reputation over a drunken accident, your reputation will emerge unscathed if the world knows of your cruelty? A man—not even a titled one—cannot afford to damage his reputation while he's seeking a rich wife."

"Now," Thorpe said, "I think the time has come to shake Sawbridge's hand like a gentleman, then we'll conclude our business."

Alexander held out his hand, biting back his revulsion as Mayhew took it.

"The devil take you, Sawbridge," Mayhew hissed, his eyes filled with venom.

"Perhaps he already has," Alexander replied. "But before I

enter the gates of hell, I can say that I've done all I can—for *her*."

He could at least take some consolation in *that* in the years to come, even if he never saw Mimi again.

CHAPTER THIRTY

"THERE'S A GENTLEMAN to see you, Miss King."

Mimi glanced up from her ledger to see her manservant in the doorway, cap in hand.

"A gentleman, Mr. Wade? From the village?"

"He's come from London. Shall I take him to the parlor?"

"Where is he now?"

"At the front door."

"You've not kept him waiting at the *door*, Mr. Wade?"

The burly man blushed and curled his fingers around his cap. He resembled a boy awaiting admonishment from his nursemaid, and Mimi suppressed a smile.

"Mr. Wade?"

"I-I thought it best," he said, shuffling from one foot to another, "on account of Lily. She's a little unwell today, and I don't want her upset."

Mimi nodded. She'd heard Lily's cries last night—pleas for mercy as her nightmares visited her again.

"I suggested she remain indoors," Mr. Wade continued, "while Sammy helped me in the garden. But I didn't want to bring a stranger inside while she…" He made a random gesture in the air.

Mimi nodded. "I'm glad she has you to take care of her, Mr. Wade."

He gave a shy smile. "I-I was wonderin'…about Lily and

Sam…"

"My visitor, Mr. Wade?" Mimi said. "We mustn't keep him waiting."

His blush deepened. "Sorry, ma'am."

Mimi placed a hand on his arm. "You're a good man," she said. "Is Lily in her chamber?"

He nodded.

"Then she must remain there. Bring my visitor to the parlor, then perhaps you could ask Betsy to make tea?"

He nodded and exited the study. Mimi closed her ledger and made her way to the parlor. Almost as soon as she sat, the door opened and a red-faced Mr. Wade appeared.

"Mr. George Stockton to see you, ma'am," he said, stepping aside to reveal Mimi's solicitor.

"Mr. Stockton," she said, rising. "I wasn't expecting you."

"Evidently," the solicitor said, glancing toward Mr. Wade.

"Forgive my manservant, Mr. Stockton—he's a little cautious."

Stockton nodded. "A sentiment that does him credit. It's a sensible man who proceeds with caution, and I always advise caution over the alternative. Besides"—he turned toward Mr. Wade and smiled—"a man is to be admired when he wishes to protect the woman he serves." He stepped inside, his cane tap-tapping on the floor, then took Mimi's outstretched hand and bowed over it. "Or is it old-fashioned of me to say such a thing to an enterprising young woman like yourself?"

"Not at all," Mimi said. "Would you like tea, Mr. Stockton? Or something a little more…warming? I have no brandy, but there's a very passable port—a gift from Lady Radham."

"My days of indulging in port are over, I'm afraid, my dear," Stockton said. "My doctor advises against anything I might find pleasurable. But I wouldn't refuse tea."

"I'll send Betsy along, ma'am," Mr. Wade said, then he bowed and closed the door.

"To what do I owe the pleasure, Mr. Stockton?" Mimi asked.

"I have some news for you."

"Couldn't you have written? I hate to think of your enduring the journey here."

"It's barely ten miles, my dear. Besides, my doctor advocates country air and exercise. And I particularly wanted to convey this news in person. It's somewhat…extraordinary."

Mimi's stomach fluttered in apprehension. "Is there something wrong with the finances for the school?"

"Quite the contrary. You see, you've been gifted a property."

"A property?"

"A townhouse, to be exact. In Brighton."

"Brighton?"

"The contract was signed last week." He drew out a sheaf of papers from his pocket and handed it over.

Her hand trembling, Mimi took it, but her vision blurred as she tried to read the first page.

"It's the deed to number 10 Royal Crescent," Mr. Stockton said.

Mimi caught her breath.

My former home. Where I lived with…

She blinked, and a tear spilled onto the parchment.

"I'm holding the original deed for safekeeping," the solicitor said, "but I wanted to bring you this copy in person, so that you might accept it as the truth."

"Why?"

"Because it's rightfully yours and has been for some years."

"But you said the contract was signed last week," Mimi said.

"It's legally been yours only for a few days, but it was yours by right when the original benefactor bequeathed it to you."

"The original…"

"Earl Mayhew," he said. "The seventh earl, that is, not the present one."

Mimi's cheeks warmed with shame. She glanced up to see him staring at her, kindness and compassion in his eyes.

"What is this?" she asked.

"Justice being served, at last," came the reply. "My partner Mr. Allardice, who drew up the contract, informed me that he was asked to draft a similar contract several years ago, but it was never signed."

"I don't understand."

"It seems, my dear, as if the son has finally chosen to honor his late father's wishes." He gave a wry smile. "I'll wager there was a little persuasion involved, but the outcome remains the same. Number 10 Royal Crescent is now yours. And, if you'll forgive me an act of self-indulgence, I'd like to confirm the matter by giving you this."

He fished something out of his pocket and handed it to her.

It was a large iron key. She took it and ran her fingertips along its form, then she held it in her palm, feeling the weight of it, before she curled her fingers around it.

"Walter…"

She drew in a shuddering breath and a tear splashed onto her hand. A warm hand covered hers.

"My dear, the late earl wouldn't have wanted you to be sad."

"But I don't deserve it," she said. "I only loved him as a friend. I was his—"

"Do not underestimate the value of a true friendship," the solicitor said. "What matters is that he loved you, and his wishes have now been honored—perhaps at the direction of one who loves you as much, if not more."

Before she could ask his meaning, he continued.

"Do tell me how your school is faring."

"We're making progress," she said. "We hope to admit at least a dozen young women. But with *this*…" She held up the key.

"Royal Crescent's an excellent part of town," he said. "I've spent some time in Brighton myself. There's a direct view of the sea from the street."

"I couldn't live there," she said. "The memories…"

He nodded. "I understand. I can make inquiries if you wish to sell—discreetly, of course."

"I wouldn't wish to dishonor Walter's memory," she said. "I owe him that."

She glanced about the parlor, and her gaze landed on the pile of sewing on the table by the window—a gown that Lily was finishing for Lady Radham.

Of course!

"Mr. Stockton, is Brighton as fashionable as it was seven years ago?" she asked.

"Even more so. Ask my wife and daughters—they're constantly begging me to take a house there so they can attend the assembly rooms."

"Then perhaps I can put the house to good use. The young woman living with me is a talented dressmaker. All she needs is an establishment in a fashionable area, and I'm convinced she'd be a success as a modiste."

"You are a most extraordinary young woman," he said. "Most women in your position would have either taken the house for themselves, or sold it to fund a dowry to find a husband. But then, most women would have kept a fortune of two thousand guineas for themselves rather than spend half of it to benefit others."

"I am not most women, Mr. Stockton."

"That you're not, my dear, and I'm heartily glad of it. If I can assist you in any way with your endeavors—you only need ask."

"Naturally," she said. "You're my solicitor."

"I meant as a *friend*, my dear. And if your young woman is as talented as you claim, then I shan't hesitate in ensuring that my wife recommends her to all her friends when they visit Brighton."

"That is most kind," Mimi said.

"Not at all," he replied. "I only ask you to do one thing in return."

"Which is?"

"You must take time to look after yourself. You spend your days thinking of others—who is there to take care of *you*?"

At that moment, the door opened, and Betsy entered with the tea tray. After she'd set the tray down and exited the parlor, Mimi rose and poured the tea. She half filled one cup, then topped it up with milk and handed it to her guest.

"Just how I like it," he said after taking a sip. "It's extraordinary how you always remember, Miss King. You should be proud of the woman you've become."

She blushed and resumed her seat. "You're most kind, Mr. Stockton, and I thank you for not judging me for having been a who—"

"My dear," he interrupted, "your past matters not. And I'm not alone in my sentiment. There are others who admire you for yourself. One in particular."

Whom did he mean? Perhaps, if she asked, he might speak of *him*. But could she bear to hear that he was indulging in the pleasures of London Society without her?

No—I must stay strong and look to the future, not dwell on what could never have been.

"Now," Stockton said, interrupting her thoughts, "tell me about your school. I happened to see it from the carriage window and saw a young man perched rather precariously on the roof."

The danger averted, Mimi described her plans for the school, and tea passed without any mention of that which she would rather forget.

After the solicitor took his leave, Mimi cleared the tea things and took them to the kitchen, then she returned to the parlor to read the contract.

There it was—written in stark black letters against the white parchment.

Number 10 Royal Crescent, Brighton, belonged to her.

Her gaze wandered to the foot of the page, and she swallowed the knot of nausea as she saw the name of the signatory.

Ralph Derek John Mayhew, eighth Earl Mayhew.

Then her gaze fell upon the signatories of the two witnesses—the first, Earl Thorpe, and the second…

She traced the name with her fingertips, to reassure herself that the words were not the fruits of her imagination. But they were written in a clear, cursive hand.

Alexander James Ffortescue, fifth Duke of Sawbridge.

CHAPTER THIRTY-ONE

Rosecombe Park, Hertfordshire

"ARE YOU ENJOYING your breakfast, Your Grace?"

Alexander glanced up at his hostess and swallowed the mouthful of bacon. "Very much so, Duchess."

"I'm so glad," she said. "I have a particular excursion planned for you today, which I trust you'll find a rewarding experience."

A rewarding experience? What in the name of heaven did she mean by that? Usually, when someone spoke of a *rewarding experience*, they referred to some sort of sufferance deemed to be good for a man's moral wellbeing—if not quite so good for his person, or his purse.

But Whitcombe's wife had always been something of an oddity with her particular likes and dislikes—one of her chief dislikes being Alexander himself.

So why the devil had he been invited to spend a week at Rosecombe on her insistence?

What torment was she about to inflict on him?

Alexander glanced toward his friend, but Whitcombe merely winked at him then exchanged a smile with the duchess. Whitcombe was a fool, in thrall to his wife. He even flouted the tradition that dictated a husband and wife sit at opposite ends of the table to spare them from the necessity of actually talking to each other. Instead, he cozied up to her at the breakfast table, as if they were adolescent lovers.

Whitcombe waved across a footman. "Our guest is in need of more bacon."

The footman nodded and brought over the silver dish piled high with pink slices of deliciousness that filled the air with an aroma intense enough to make a stone statue salivate.

"I couldn't possibly," Alexander said. "I've eaten five rashers already."

"Eight, by my count," the duchess said.

"Eleanor, my love, Sawbridge is our guest," Whitcombe said. "He can eat as much as he wants."

"Did I say he couldn't?" she replied.

"Not everyone is as observant as you, my love."

And not everyone had the ability to unsettle even the stoutest of men with a single emerald stare, but the duchess managed to achieve it. Doubtless she could fell an army just by glaring at them.

"Did you have a pleasant journey from London yesterday?" she asked.

"I did," Alexander said, "as I believe I told you last night."

Whitcombe let out a chuckle and leaned back, as if awaiting the entertainment of watching his wife verbally eviscerate his friend for daring to answer back.

"No doubt there are many ladies mourning your departure," she said, an edge to her voice.

"My love," Whitcombe whispered, and she let out a sharp sigh.

"Where are we going today, Duchess?" Alexander asked.

"To visit my sister. We're to stay there for a few days."

"Perhaps I should remain here, then."

"I particularly want *you* to join us."

Alexander looked to his friend for support, but Whitcombe averted his gaze.

"Why the need for my company, Duchess?" Alexander asked. "Forgive me, but I'm aware you don't like me."

Whitcombe made a noise that sounded like suppressed laughter—or perhaps a prayer for mercy on Alexander's behalf.

"My sister's overseeing the opening of a new school this

afternoon and wishes you to be among the party," she replied.

"Lady Radham likes me even less than you," Alexander said. "With good reason, I'll admit. As to Lord Radham, he despises me."

"You could always consider the invitation an opportunity to change their opinion."

"Opinions rarely change," he said, "particularly unfavorable opinions—as I know from experience."

"Then you may be surprised to know that I was beginning to like you," she said.

Alexander let out a snort. "To what do I owe *that* particular honor?"

She tilted her head to one side. "Well, I *was*, at least."

Then she stood, almost knocking her teacup aside. Whitcombe rose and Alexander followed suit, glancing at the remaining rasher of bacon on his plate.

"Shall we make ready?" she said. "We should leave directly if we're to arrive in time for the opening. I don't want to push the horses too hard. They're the last creatures in the world who deserve to suffer."

She fixed her gaze on Alexander, and his heart withered at the prospect of being stuck in a carriage with her. Then she glanced at the remaining rasher on his plate.

"Do finish that," she said. "I wouldn't want my guests to think me inhospitable."

"Perish the thought," Alexander said.

Her mouth quirked into a smile and she exited the breakfast room, Whitcombe in tow.

Alexander glanced at the footmen, who were all staring directly ahead. Then he snatched the bacon and swallowed it before following his hosts outside.

Less than half an hour later, he stepped onto the drive to see Whitcombe and his wife bidding farewell to their children, pink-faced, giggling toddlers in the arms of their nursemaids, before they climbed into the carriage and set off.

What the bloody hell am I doing here?

What could be worse than being confined in a carriage with Whitcombe and his intense, judgmental duchess? Alexander had only accepted Whitcombe's invitation to stay because it took him away from London—away from the park, where doting couples promenaded, away from parties where lovesick young men danced with the women they desired…

…and away from his house in Grosvenor Square that overlooked number sixteen, where he had finally understood what it was to make love—and to fall in love.

A family lived there now, a man with a wife and two daughters. Pleasant enough except for one thing.

They weren't *her.*

Which was why London gave him no pleasure—it was filled with people who were *not her.*

After they stopped for luncheon at an unremarkable inn, the journey continued, and Alexander fixed his gaze out of the window, watching the countryside pass by. When he heard a snore, he turned to see Whitcombe fast asleep, a smile of contentment on his lips. Beside him sat the duchess, holding his hand, her fingers intertwined with his. She lifted her husband's hand and kissed it, her eyes filled with love.

What might it be like, to be loved with such ferocity?

And you were—*only you were too blind to see it.*

He blinked, and moisture stung his eyes. When he wiped them, he saw the duchess was staring directly at him.

"Are you well?" she whispered.

The armor he'd fashioned around his heart was no defense against the compassion in her voice.

"I did love her, Duchess," he said.

"Did?"

He turned toward the window and sighed, his breath misting on the glass. "I still do. But what good will come from confessing it?"

"To the exclusion of all others?"

"God's teeth, woman—must you be so belligerent?" he snapped.

"Hush!" she said, glancing toward her sleeping husband. Whitcombe stirred, and she caressed the back of his hand. "Montague is always accusing me of belligerence, though I prefer to call it *tenacity*, which has less of an air of malevolence."

"Nobody could accuse *you* of being malevolent, Duchess."

She frowned. "Are you teasing me?"

He shook his head. "I wouldn't dare. I value my balls."

Her eyes sparkled with mirth. "Your balls are safe with me."

He returned her smile. "I'm glad to hear that. I did wonder, on receiving your invitation, whether I'd return home a pound or two lighter."

She gave a soft laugh. "You can be quite disarming when you're not in your cups."

"And you can be brutally frank," he said, "when your lips are moving."

Whitcombe stirred and opened his eyes. Then he yawned and stretched.

"Have I missed anything, my love?" he asked.

"Only a slight improvement in my opinion of your friend here."

Whitcombe chuckled. "I trust you've not been too hard on him."

"No more than I deserve," Alexander said.

The journey continued in silence, but Alexander sensed a shift in the atmosphere, as if the duchess warmed to him. When the carriage rolled to a halt at the entrance to Radham Hall, she even deigned to smile at him as he climbed out.

Lord Radham and his wife waited by the front steps. Lady Radham greeted her sister with a warm embrace and effusions of love, and though she was cooler in her reception of Alexander, at least her greeting lacked open hostility. Even Radham himself managed a word of welcome before he clapped Whitcombe on the back and led them inside.

"I hope we're not too late, sister," the duchess said.

"Not at all. We're due at the school in a little under an hour, so you've time to freshen up first. I thought we might walk to the village—it's such a pleasant afternoon. They're waiting for us there."

Both ladies glanced toward Alexander, then they linked arms and went inside.

Something was afoot.

Did that explain the duchess's civility during the journey? Perhaps she was engaging in some form of deception to lull him into trusting her.

Then he shook his head. The duchess was the least devious woman he knew, save…

Do not think of her.

⟫⟪

A SMALL CROWD set off for the village—the entire household of Radham Hall, by the look of it. Lady Radham led the party, hand in hand with a young boy, while Whitcombe and Radham followed, deep in conversation.

Which left Alexander with Whitcombe's wife.

"The school opening looks to be something of an occasion," he said.

"It marks the culmination of much effort and hard work," she replied. "Many hands were involved, though none more than the person who directed the enterprise."

"Lady Radham, I suppose."

She remained silent, but gave him a smile.

He glanced over his shoulder at the small crowd following then, then recognized a young woman among the party, hand in hand with a small boy.

"Is anything amiss?" the duchess asked.

"I thought I recognized that woman with the boy."

She glanced over her shoulder. "Lily and Sam? Yes, I heard

you'd met them."

"Who's the man with her?" Alexander asked, glancing toward the tall, thick-set man who held Lily's arm with a proprietary air. "That's not the man who hurt her, surely?"

"Heavens, no!" she said. "That's Mr. Wade. He's Jem—" She hesitated. "He's from the village, and has quite taken Lily and Sam to his heart. There are *some* good men in the world."

"But not many."

She turned her gaze to him. "Perhaps there's one more than I first thought."

"Careful, Duchess," he said, "or I'll begin to believe you intend to pass me a compliment."

"I would never insult you with flattery."

"No," he said, laughing, "only with brutal honesty."

He glanced over his shoulder again and met Lily's gaze. She smiled and nodded, then resumed her attention on the man at her side.

When they reached the school—an enormous red-bricked building in the center of the village—Lady Radham led them inside to a hall filled with rows of chairs, already half occupied, with a central aisle and a raised platform at the far end.

"Take your seats, everyone," Lady Radham said. "Eleanor, there's room for your party on the back row."

"What the devil's going on?" Alexander asked as the duchess led him to a seat. "Why have you brought me here?"

"To witness what you helped bring about."

"Me?" he replied. "Forgive me, but I don't—"

"Hush!" the duchess whispered. "Lady Radham's about to speak."

The chattering among the party lessened as everyone settled into their seats. Then Lady Radham stepped onto the platform.

"Thank you for attending, on this special occasion," she said, "the opening of our first school for young women. Many of you remember this building as it once was—barely four walls, and hardly any roof, not even fit for Mr. Finch's sheep to reside in, though that never stopped their enthusiasm for spending many a night in this establishment."

A ripple of amusement threaded through the onlookers.

"But while I'm sure that sheep would benefit from a good education, many of you know that the cause most dear to my heart is that of young women—to give them the independence that only a good education can provide. And it's for this reason that I championed this venture—something that I trust we're all proud of."

Someone said, "Hear, hear!" and Lady Radham raised her hand.

"Of course, I cannot go without praising the efforts of those who worked with such dedication to make today happen—the men who repaired the roof..."

A ripple of applause and male mutterings of agreement broke out.

"...and the women," she added. "Those who helped to furnish the building, and the many wives who were content to release their men into our employ. For it's a poorly kept secret who's *really* in charge in a household."

She paused to titters of female laughter.

"But I'm sure that you'll not fail to agree that there's one individual among us more deserving of praise than any other." She gestured toward the front row. "One unique woman who, through hardship and adversity, has never wavered in her desire to see others flourish. A woman whose first thought is for others rather than herself, who gave her fortune so that others might have a better life. A woman who understands that while she cannot make a difference for everyone, she can change the world for those fortunate enough to know her."

She placed her hand on her heart, then smiled.

"And we *are* most fortunate. Ladies and gentlemen, I present to you Miss Jemima King!"

Alexander's stomach clenched, and the breath left his lungs as the crowd stood. Applause thundered through the hall while he struggled to his feet. He teetered to one side, and a steadying hand caught his arm.

"Mimi?" he whispered. "*My* Mimi—she did all this?"

The duchess nodded, and his heart swelled with pride. He blinked back the tears as the cheering subsided. Then the crowd resumed their seats to reveal a single woman climbing onto the platform next to Lady Radham. Then Lady Radham retreated, applauding, leaving Mimi standing alone, a delicate bloom on her cheeks.

"I…" She hesitated, and her blush deepened. "I don't know what to say. I did nothing, really. It wasn't my fortune to give, but I thank you all, especially dear Lady Radham, for your generosity." She gestured toward the front row. "And Miss Petford—soon, I'm delighted to say, to be Mrs. Wade. Dearest Lily, you have been at my side throughout."

She lowered her gaze, and Alexander caught the faint tremor in the hem of her gown.

How different she was—this shy, unassuming young woman, unable to accept praise for her generosity—to the brash doxy with the fake accent from the docks. She had shed her armor entirely, to reveal the true woman beneath—the best of women.

He had never been more in love with her than at that moment.

She continued, her voice growing steadier.

"This school is a long-held dream of mine," she said. "There are too many women in the world unable to live to their full potential—intelligent women, bright and compassionate women, who only need a little help to live the lives their deserve. Women who can do so independently if given the chance."

Alexander blinked, and a tear splashed onto his sleeve. He wiped it away, and a soft hand took his.

"Why didn't she tell me she was here, Duchess?" he whispered.

"You need to look into your heart to find the answer."

Mimi continued. "Orphans, natural children, young girls

unexpectedly thrust into a world with no resources other than their wits. This school will be the means by which they can stride out into the world and find employment, so that they might never know what it means to be alone, and unloved." Her voice had grown hoarse, and she clasped her hands together. "Alone— as I have been…"

Alexander leaped to his feet.

"No!" he cried.

A ripple traveled through the crowd as they turned to see who'd interrupted her speech. Mimi lifted her gaze and froze.

Wide brown eyes stared at him, and she clasped her hands together as Alexander strode along the aisle.

"A-Alexander…"

"You stand not alone, Mimi," he said.

She glanced toward Lady Radham as if in panic—as if she sought to flee.

But he would never let her take flight again.

He extended his hand toward her.

"My love for you says that you are not alone, Mimi," he said. "You need never be alone again."

Then he lowered himself onto one knee. Whispers and in-takes of breath ran through the hall but were quickly silenced while he remained still, his gaze fixed on the woman he could not live without.

"Alexander…" She shook her head then glanced to one side. "Wh-what's happening? Lady Radham, did you plan this?"

Lady Radham shook her head. "I planned nothing, my dear. I merely invited the duke so that he might witness your success."

"He's a *duke?*" someone said, followed by an outbreak of whispering as the onlookers jostled against each other to get a better view.

Take a good look, all of you, while I offer myself to the woman I love.

Mimi stepped off the platform and approached him, her eyes glistening with moisture.

He shuffled forward and grasped her hands. "Mimi, my love, please," he said. "I'm in torment, and have suffered since the day we parted. I beg you to ease my pain and consent to become my wife."

The crowd seemed to emit a collective sigh, followed by shushing as they—and he—awaited her response.

"You have shown that you can change the world, Mimi my love," he said.

"I cannot change it for everyone."

"Then change it for those fortunate enough to know you," he said. "Change it for the man who loves you—the man who was, at first, too much of a fool, too bound to the niceties of Society, to look beyond his nose and into his heart."

He drew her hands to his lips, relishing the soft scent of her— the aroma of rose that he'd kept with him in the lonely nights when he had cried out for her in his dreams.

"Change the world for *me*," he whispered.

A flicker of desire flared in her eyes, as if her soul called to him. Then her expression shuttered.

"Will you answer one question?" she asked.

He nodded.

"Truthfully?"

"Of course," he said. "My heart—and my soul—are yours, laid bare."

"Who currently resides at number 16 Grosvenor Square?"

The hard edge to her voice couldn't disguise her pain.

"A copper merchant called Mr. Chinwell and his family," he said. "Pleasant enough, but I preferred the previous tenant." Then he caught her meaning. "Mimi, surely you didn't think that I would establish another..."

Her color deepened, and her lips began to tremble.

"Do you not know, Mimi, that from the moment I first laid eyes on you, that first morning"—he pulled her closer—"that first morning in my bed, when you were at peace, asleep, free from the façade of the...of the..."

"The doxy?" she whispered.

"That was the moment you first revealed yourself to me. For when a person is asleep, their true self emerges. I saw you then, Mimi, and I have loved you from that moment. With every minute we've shared since then I have grown to love you more, even if I was too foolish to see it. There exists only one glimmer of hope for this sad soul kneeling before you today, my love—and that is the hope that you will take care of me as you have always done for those fortunate to know you—as my duchess."

"And your friends?" she asked. "Your reputation?"

"What would I care of reputation when I'd have you?" he said. "Besides, there are few whose opinion I care for. I would fight to the ends of the earth to ensure you are given what is due to you—respect, admiration…"

His voice trailed off, and she tilted her head to one side.

"So it *was* you," she said. "The property in Brighton."

"I needed a little help, but Westbury and his son were willing to oblige."

"Edward Drayton?" she asked.

"Do I have cause to be jealous?" he said. "That young puppy is smitten with you."

"I don't love *him*."

His heart soared with hope at her words. "Then might I begin to hope that success is within my grasp? Can you bring yourself to love this tormented soul before you—to make him worthy?"

She paused, and Alexander's heartbeat pulsed in his ears. Then, at length, a slow smile curved her lips.

"To make you worthy?" Her eyes sparkled with mischief. "I daresay, after establishing this school, I am ready for a much greater challenge."

"Then…" He held his breath in anticipation.

"Yes," she said. "My answer is yes."

The crowd erupted into applause. Alexander rose to his feet and lifted her into his arms. He claimed her mouth, and she parted her lips for him. What surer gesture could she make to affirm her love? She had been willing to sell her body—to sell everything, except the one thing she was unprepared to give.

A kiss—the most intimate of gestures, and in gifting it, she gave him her heart.

EPILOGUE

Sawbridge Church, one month later

"I NOW PRONOUNCE you man and wife."

Mimi's heart fluttered as the vicar spoke the words that bound her forever to the man beside her.

She turned to face the groom, and, slowly, as if he wished to savor the anticipation, he lifted her veil. A spark of desire glimmered in his eyes, and her body pulsed with pleasure at the memory of his ministrations last night when he'd slid into her bedchamber and lifted her night rail with the same delicate touch.

But last night, he had kissed her somewhere far more scandalous than her mouth, his skilled tongue making her cry his name into the night. Then he'd slipped out of her bedchamber, leaving her wanting, with a promise of a resumption of his attentions on their wedding night.

He brushed his lips against hers and gave a self-satisfied smile.

She suppressed a laugh.

Arrogant man! Thinking she'd melt into a puddle of desire at the merest touch.

But her body knew different, and she squeezed her thighs together to temper the flare of need.

"Tonight, my love," he whispered.

"I might deny you, husband," she said.

"Say that again."

"I might deny you."

"No," he said, lowering his voice to a growl. "Say *husband*. I like hearing it on your lips."

"Husband."

"Mmm." He kissed her again, this time shamelessly thrusting his tongue into her mouth. She grasped his arms and pulled him close, curling her tongue around his.

The vicar cleared his throat.

Alexander broke the kiss, then mumbled an apology.

The vicar's mouth twitched into a smile, then he winked—he actually *winked*!

Mimi's husband took her arm, and they turned to face the congregation, who rose to their feet as organ music filled the church. Then he led her along the aisle and outside to the waiting carriage, amid the cheers of the well-wishers who gathered behind them.

Mimi turned and tossed her bouquet into the air, and it landed near Lady Portia's feet. Lady Portia picked it up, her cheeks coloring, and her brother, Foxton, rolled his eyes and thrust his hands into his pockets.

Then Alexander bundled Mimi into the carriage and it set off.

"Alexander!" she cried. "I wanted to say goodbye to everyone."

"I was too eager for you to stand on ceremony."

"Too eager, eh?" she said. "When you brought me to the brink of pleasure last night then left me wanting? I'm minded to wait until we reach the inn."

"That's over two hours away!"

"It would be a good lesson in restraint," she said. "A lesson a man is in need of."

"Do they teach restraint at your school?" he asked.

"The pupils have no such need," she said. "Which reminds me—have I thanked you today for agreeing to establish another school here?"

"You've voiced your gratitude several times already," he said. "Though I can think of another way to express it."

He reached for her gown, and she slapped his hand away.

"Careful!" she cried. "I won't have Lily's beautiful gown

destroyed by a savage."

"I thought you relished being claimed by a savage," he said with a grin.

"Not in this gown."

"The gown is only beautiful because you are wearing it."

"Very gallant," she retorted. "But if you wish to enjoy your wedding present, you must unwrap it carefully and without a single tear."

His hands shook as he took her shoulders. "I can wait no longer. I've denied myself the pleasure of your body for too long."

"But husband," she said with mock surprise as she unpinned her hair, "didn't you know that the longer the wait, the greater the pleasure?"

He reached behind her gown, and his fingers fumbled against it as he struggled to undo the buttons.

"Allow me, my lord," she said.

"Oh *yes*," he growled. "You may call me *my lord* when I'm buried inside you."

Mimi reached behind, they worked the buttons free together, and, after several maneuvers, she lay before him, naked except for her stockings. She squeezed her thighs together to temper the rush of heat, and the scent of their joint desire filled the carriage.

"I find I prefer you like this," he said, his nostrils flaring. "Perhaps I'll insist that you remain in our bedchamber in nothing but your stockings for the duration of our honeymoon."

As he unbuttoned his breeches, the carriage lurched sideways. He lost his balance and fell to the floor, and Mimi let out a giggle.

"Laughing at your husband, are you?" he said. "I must think of a fitting reprimand."

He reached for the window blind and drew it down.

"What are you doing?" she asked.

"You, my dear, are *mine*," he said, clambering on top of her. "Nobody is permitted to enjoy this lovely body of yours but me. Given that the merest glimpse of you is enough to send a man wild with desire, I have no wish to cause fits of apoplexy among any travelers we pass on the road."

"The merest glimpse, you say?" she said, parting her thighs. "I thought—Oh!" She let out a cry as he entered her swiftly. "Alexander!" she cried.

"That's it, my love," he said. "Now lie back while I enjoy my wedding gift, for we have two hours with which to occupy ourselves."

"*Your* wedding gift?"

"Yes," he said, placing a kiss on her lips. "Your pleasure, my love. I want nothing more than to give you pleasure."

She closed her eyes and lay back, relishing her husband's touches and trusting her soul—at last—in the hands of the man who loved her.

About the Author

Emily Royal grew up in Sussex, England, and has devoured romantic novels for as long as she can remember. A mathematician at heart, Emily has worked in financial services for over twenty years. She indulged in her love of writing after she moved to Scotland, where she lives with her husband, teenage daughters, and menagerie of rescue pets—including Twinkle, an attention-seeking boa constrictor.

She has a passion for both reading and writing romance with a weakness for Regency rakes, Highland heroes, and Medieval knights. *Persuasion* is one of her all-time favorite novels, which she reads several times each year, and she is fortunate enough to live within sight of a Medieval palace.

When not writing, Emily enjoys playing the piano, baking, and painting landscapes, particularly of the Highlands. One of her ambitions is to paint, as well as climb, every mountain in Scotland.

Follow Emily Royal
Newsletter Signup: subscribepage.io / RKBvRE
Facebook: facebook.com / eroyalauthor
Bookbub: bookbub.com / authors / emily-royal
Instagram: instagram.com / eroyalauthor
Amazon: amazon.com / stores / Emily-
Royal / author / B07NCBKJZ4
Website: www.emroyal.com
Goodreads:
goodreads.com / author / show / 14834886.Emily_Royal
Twitter: @eroyalauthor